**Nicholas Monsarrat** wa[...] a distinguished surgeo[...] at Winchester, then at Trinity College, Cambridge, where he studied law. He gave up law to earn a meagre living as a freelance journalist while he began writing novels. His first novel to receive significant attention was *This is the Schoolroom* (1939). It is a largely autobiographical 'coming of age' novel dealing with the end of college life, the 'Hungry Thirties', and the Spanish Civil War.

During World War Two he served in the Royal Navy in corvettes in the North Atlantic. These experiences were used in his best-known novel, *The Cruel Sea* (1951) and made into a film starring Jack Hawkins.

In 1946, he became a director of the UK Information Service, first in Johannesburg, then in Ottawa. Other well-known novels include *The Kapillan of Malta*, *The Tribe That Lost Its Head*, and its sequel, *Richer Than All His Tribe*, and *The Story of Esther Costello*.

He died in August 1979 as he was writing the second part of his intended three-volume novel on seafaring life from Napoleonic times to the present, *The Master Mariner*.

BY THE SAME AUTHOR
ALL PUBLISHED BY HOUSE OF STRATUS

A FAIR DAY'S WORK
HMS MARLBOROUGH WILL ENTER HARBOUR
LIFE IS A FOUR-LETTER WORD
THE MASTER MARINER
THE NYLON PIRATES
THE PILLOW FIGHT
RICHER THAN ALL HIS TRIBE
SMITH AND JONES
SOMETHING TO HIDE
THE STORY OF ESTHER COSTELLO
THIS IS THE SCHOOLROOM
THE TIME BEFORE THIS
THE TRIBE THAT LOST ITS HEAD

Nicholas
# Monsarrat
❖

# THE
# WHITE RAJAH

HOUSE OF
STRATUS

This edition published in 2000 by House of Stratus, an imprint of Stratus Books Ltd., 21 Beeching Park, Kelly Bray, Cornwall, PL17 8QS, UK.

www.houseofstratus.com

Typeset, printed and bound by House of Stratus.

A catalogue record for this book is available from the British Library.

ISBN 1-84232-161-7

Cover design: Jason Cox
Cover image: AKG London

# The Island of Makassang

## (CIRCA 1850)

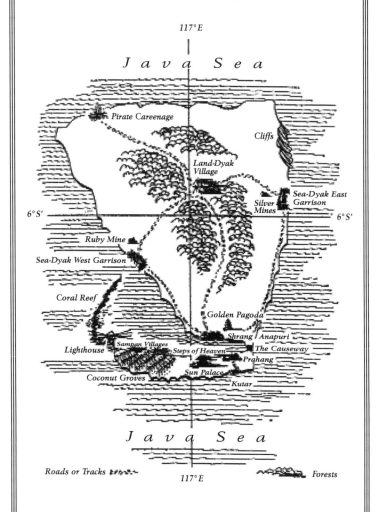

117° E

*J a v a   S e a*

Pirate Careenage

Cliffs

Land-Dyak
Village

Silver
Mines

Sea-Dyak East
Garrison

6° S'

6° S'

Ruby Mine

Sea-Dyak West Garrison

Coral Reef

Golden Pagoda

Shrang  Anapuri

Lighthouse

Sampan Villages   Steps of Heaven

The Causeway

Prahang

Coconut Groves   Sun Palace

Kutar

*J a v a   S e a*

Roads or Tracks

Forests

117° E

BOOK ONE

The Heir: 1850

The great house of Marriott was shuttered against death: its noble façade, of palest Cotswold stone, stared blindly across parkland towards the long silver serpent of the River Wye, and the distant Welsh Marches beyond. Under a lowering West Country sky, the returning funeral carriage – its horses blanketed in jet black, their mournful plumes ruffled by blustering winds – wound slowly between the avenue of oaks, as if reluctant to return to this house of sorrow. A patter of raindrops served for tears, as if nature herself would bear witness that in the Year of Our Lord, 1850, Sir James Marriott, Baronet, of Marriott in the County of Gloucester, had gone to his last reward.

Within the house, also, there was blustering; indeed, the carriage had scarcely been dismissed before his two sons fell headlong into quarrelling. It was an unbecoming turn: indeed, it was shameful; but a single glance at the two men, so different, so long divided, could have supplied reason enough.

The elder, Miles Marriott, resplendent in the frock coat, ceremonial sword, and gold-tasseled epaulettes of a post-Captain of Her Majesty's Navy, was a small man, meticulous and opinionated in the way of many small men; he looked about him constantly, as though on guard for some insult or fancied slight. A few weeks short of twenty-one, he seemed already set in the ways of self-importance;

1

high rank – and his rank, for his years, was certainly distinguished – had brought him, not ease and confidence, but the watchfulness of a man who, earning swift advancement either by merit or manoeuvre, insists upon its recognition from the very first moment. I am a post-Captain of the Royal Navy, his darting glance seemed to say; treat me as anything less, and it will be the worse for you.

The younger brother, Richard Marriott, was of a different mould altogether. He was tall, and broad-shouldered, with a look of wildness about him very different from his brother's neat formality. He was dressed correctly enough, in a morning coat, and the funereal black stock dictated by the occasion; but he seemed often to be bursting from the confines of these drab trappings, as if he were life itself, rebelling against death and death's dark dominion. His fierce, handsome face had a careless pride – a pride not of rank but of the fact of masculinity. His expression had been set and bleak when he entered the house, for he had loved his father dearly; but presently, under the goading of their quarrel, it took on a mutinous petulance which betrayed the ever-present division between them.

The occasion of their falling-out had been innocent enough. In the oak-panelled hall, with its array of grave Marriott faces looking down, an old servant took their topcoats, and Miles's gold-trimmed cocked hat, and Richard's crêpe-bound headgear. Then he asked, bowing: 'Will that be all, Mr Miles?'

'Sir Miles,' Miles Marriott corrected him coldly.

Richard Marriott, overhearing, muttered: 'Good God!' and turned away abruptly. When the servant had left, and they were alone, Miles Marriott looked at his brother under lowered eyebrows. It was the sort of occasion which he could never have let pass, nor overlooked. He was not that quality of man, and he never would be. He said: 'What do you mean by that, pray?'

'By what?'

'You know perfectly well to what I am referring, Richard,' said Miles Marriott, with lofty condescension. 'You thought fit to exclaim "Good God!" while I was giving some instructions to Jeffreys. Why so?'

'Sir Miles?' queried Richard, with perceptible mimicry. 'I must confess it seemed to me an odd moment to insist upon the use of a new title.'

'I am Sir Miles Marriott,' said Miles, coldly.

'Beyond a doubt,' agreed Richard. 'But' – he indicated the drawn curtains, the sad and heavy twilight of the room – 'surely these are early days. Old Jeffreys is confused. Allow him some latitude, for heaven's sake! He has his own grief, you know.'

'Then he must learn to control it.'

Richard laughed shortly. 'Brother Miles, brother Miles, I swear there is no one in the world to match you ... We come straight from our father's grave, and you are instantly the fourth baronet, as soon as we set foot inside the house. Perhaps you have been studying?'

'Enough of that!' snapped Miles Marriott. His heavy epaulettes seemed to bristle, and his look was sharp. 'I was Sir Miles Marriott from the moment my father died. The sooner that is realized, the better for all concerned. The better for you ... There are certain courtesies due to rank, and I will exact them at all times.'

'From me?' inquired Richard coolly.

'Especially from you,' said Miles Marriott.

He turned, as if dismissing some junior suppliant from his quarter-deck, and went to the great mahogany sideboard, with its cut glass decanters of Waterford and Bohemia, its array of sherries and cordials, its locked tantalus of whisky and brandy. He busied himself ostentatiously, pouring a glass of Madeira, his back towards his younger brother, while Richard controlled himself with a mighty effort. This new Miles was no different from the old one, save that there was an added consequence, an increase of pomposity and pride, to complete a picture which he had loathed for as long as he could remember. But he controlled himself because of the day, and the moment; raw from his father's death, still aware of that creeping graveside chill, he knew that he was especially vulnerable, and that he must guard against it. He and Miles, progressing from quarrelsome children to ever-fighting boys, from boys to the sullen rivalry of young men, had never found common ground at all. Perhaps this was the only possible moment for such a reconciliation to take place.

But Miles appeared to have no such thoughts – or if he did so, he managed to conceal them without effort. He left the sideboard with a brimming glass, and took his stand in front of the wide log fire, warming his coat-tails, sipping his wine. After a moment, Richard said: 'I think I will take a glass myself; it was chilly outside,' and crossed to the sideboard. A voice behind him, cold, correct, said: 'Pray help yourself.'

The tone, and the invitation, made him turn and stare. Miles – his legs apart, very much the master of his house – was regarding him as if he were a stranger who had overlooked some common courtesy.

'Help myself?' repeated Richard Marriott crisply. 'Of course I shall help myself! What nonsense is this?'

Miles continued to stare at him. 'It is my fashion of reminding you,' he answered at length, with heavy emphasis, 'that you now enjoy the hospitality of my house.'

'Your house?'

'Even so.'

Richard Marriott checked himself, on an angry, irrevocable word. However offensively it was phrased, Miles was speaking the literal truth; with their father's baronetcy, he had inherited Marriott itself – the great house, with its thousand acres of farmland and deer park and rough shooting, was entailed to the eldest son, and Miles was now master of it. But there were methods of taking possession which need not grate upon the souls of those dispossessed … He made a resolve that he would not be put down in this cavalier fashion; he might be the younger son, but he was a son none the less, and sons were not to be turned out at a snap of the fingers, like a trespassing beggar, or a dog ordered to the stables.

He gulped his Madeira heartily, and poured a second glass, careless of the look of disapproval on Miles's face. Then he said, as though the subject had no connection with what had passed between them before: 'I invited Lucinda and her aunt to dine with us this evening.'

'Indeed?'

'Indeed.'

They were both staring fixedly at each other now, as if some challenge had been thrown down; the tall clock in the corner ticked away the seconds, while anger on one side, and pride on the other, ebbed and flowed between them. It was Miles Marriott who broke the silence.

'Apart from the propriety of such an invitation –' he began, portentously.

'Oh, stuff!' interrupted Richard rudely. 'Propriety? Devil take it, man, you talk like some village gossip! Lucinda is our own cousin – they are both our own kin! What has propriety to do with it?'

' – the propriety of such an invitation,' Miles went on, as if he had heard not a word, 'proffered on the very day of Father's funeral, I must remind you again that this is my house, and that I, and no one else, will play host in it.'

There was another silence now, longer, more ominous still. The logs settled in the grate, the wind moaned in the chimney, while Richard glared at his elder brother, and Miles stared back, holding his gaze. There were rights on his side, and they both knew it; but they were grudging rights, lawyers' rights – there should have been room for generous family rights as well, and Miles clearly had shut his mind against these, as if he had been waiting for this moment, for a long time ... It was this which drove Richard past restraint into anger.

'Now by God!' he burst out, 'this is too much! You may play host if you wish, but do not play Almighty God!' And as Miles, shocked at the blasphemy, sought to interrupt: 'No, I will not be put down!' Richard shouted. 'Are things so changed, suddenly, that I cannot invite our own cousin, a cousin whom one day I hope –' he came to a stop, nearly choking on his anger and deep feeling; and Miles, with the advantage of control, stepped in, coldly precise.

'Things are so changed,' he answered. 'And suddenly, as you say.'

'I have enough rights still,' insisted Richard roughly. 'You are not the only son, though you act as if you were. I have a share in all this.'

After a moment, Miles, smiling thinly, answered: 'I would judge it a mistake to place your hopes too high.'

There was a spiteful certainty in his voice which brought Richard up short. Miles was no card player – he was far too proper a young man for such rank dissipation – but he spoke as a gambler who, outfacing an opponent, relies on a hand of cards which he knows cannot be beaten. This show of confidence was no bluff – once again, Miles was not a man who dealt in bluffing, he advanced step by delicate step, with every plan laid, and the ground ahead tested. He must therefore know something, something to his advantage; some astonishment was at hand, and he had chosen this way of bringing it out into the open.

Richard, impulsive, bull-headed, had no patience with such devious methods. He drove his way in, spurred by anger, despising subterfuge.

'Hopes?' he said. 'What hopes? Speak plainly, man! Is it the will you are talking about?'

Miles, taken aback by such directness, raised his hand. 'You forget yourself, Richard. We cannot discuss the will now. At the appointed time – '

'Appointed time! If it is the appointed time to hint that I have been left less than my share, or no share at all, then it is the appointed time for me to learn the truth.' He darted an accusing, direct finger at Miles. 'Speak out! Say what you have to say. What did you mean, that I should not place my hopes too high?'

Miles hesitated. Clearly, matters had moved more swiftly than he had planned; he had intended a different sort of progress, even a cat-and-mouse enterprise with himself establishing a clear superiority before he condescended to reveal the truth. But there was something of menace in Richard's bearing which warned him not to delay his dénouement too long. He took a leisurely sip of his wine, and said: 'Well, if you must be so precipitate … All the property, both real and personal, is now mine.'

'All?' Richard, astounded, obeyed his first impulse, which was angry disbelief. 'I'll not credit that! This is some trick or other. How did you learn this? Is it in the will? Where is the will?'

'In a safe place, in the library.'

'You have seen it?'

'Naturally.'

The single, disdainful word infuriated Richard almost past endurance. He himself could cool his heels, waiting to be shown the will; yet his elder brother, 'naturally', had seen it already, and would take his time about imparting its contents. Once again, he resolved not to be treated in this fashion. He set down his glass, and advanced towards his brother, still warming himself at the fire.

'I will see it myself, now,' he said gruffly.

Miles Marriott stood his ground. 'That you will not,' he answered, with finality. 'It is in his strong-box. The box is double-locked, and the lawyers have the key. They will open it, and read the will, when I give them the word.'

'But you have seen it?'

'I have seen it, and I have a copy.'

Richard, checked, shifted his ground. 'Where is the copy, then?'

Miles smiled his thin smile. 'You are so eager to know your fate? I would be the last one to stand in your way, Richard …' He pointed, negligently, carelessly, at the desk which stood in one corner of the hall. 'It is in the upper drawer, on the left-hand side.'

Richard, without a word, strode across to the desk and pulled at the drawer. It held fast – indeed, it was locked, as he immediately discovered. Baulked, he looked across at Miles with hatred in his eyes.

'You have the key?'

'I have all the keys.'

'Then I wish to see the copy.'

'I will read it to you.'

He walked across to the desk with small, precise steps, his back stiff, his bearing formal; he might have been on parade. Richard, giving ground so that Miles could open the desk drawer, found himself trembling with fresh rage. As on countless occasions in the past, he was being made to look a fool, at this and every other point; and there must be worse to come, or Miles, the post-Captain so confident of his future, would not behave with this loathsome self-assurance ... Miles opened the drawer as if he were performing some office far beneath him, and drew out a document of crisp parchment, closely over-written in the sloping style affected by lawyers' clerks. Then, holding it, he turned on his heel, crossed to the fireplace, and took up his stand in front of the mantelpiece once more.

It was clear that he was going to milk the occasion of every jot of self-gratification; and Richard, fuming, felt his patience about to break.

'Miles,' he said, between clenched teeth, 'I swear to God, if you continue in this fashion I will pick you up and shake you until your skull rattles!'

Miles, from his vantage point, surveyed his brother as though he were some distant landscape, indistinctly seen, indifferently appreciated. Then he looked down at the paper, the copy of their father's will.

'Much of this,' he said, coldly, 'can be of little interest to you. It repeats the terms of the entail – that is, that the house and the land devolves upon the eldest son, myself. Then there are various bequests – to old friends, and servants, and the like. There is a sum of one thousand pounds left to the Cottage Hospital at St Briavels ...' He looked across at Richard. 'Generous, I think you will agree? Of course, he had been the principal patron for many years. Then – ' he ran his finger down the page, affecting to search for some particular passage, ' – ah yes, this is the paragraph which concerns yourself.' He settled his neck snugly into his collar, enormously content with what was about to come. 'It is by no means a long one. You would like to hear it verbatim?'

'Yes,' said Richard.

'You shall do so ... "I give and bequeath absolutely to my younger son Richard",' he read, sonorously, pompously, ' "my pair of matched pistols, with the chased silver stocks and the cannon barrels, by Griffin, Gunsmiths of London, together with the great terrestrial globe customarily kept in my library." '

He fell silent, though he continued to look at the copy of the will, a slight smile on his face. Richard waited; he knew that Miles had planned that he should wait, but he felt none the less impotent to vary his role. This was the way he had long been doomed to listen to his father's last testament ... But presently, when the silence had stretched intolerably, he made a huge effort of will, and broke it. He broke it with a question to which, already, he knew the fatal answer.

'That is all?'

Miles nodded, abstractedly. 'Yes. That is all.'

'But why? Why should he do such a thing?'

Miles raised his eyebrows. 'They are handsome pistols.'

It was as much as Richard could do, to hold himself from starting forward, and doing swift violence to that smug face. 'Do not play the fool with me!' he said passionately. 'I am not in the humour for it ...' He stared at Miles. 'You must have known of this already.'

'Yes.'

'Did he talk of it?'

'He did me the honour,' answered Miles smoothly, 'of discussing the terms of his will before it was drawn up.'

'Then this was your plan?'

Miles shook his head. 'Not so. He had it in mind for a long time that the whole estate should devolve upon myself. I could only agree, when it was put to me, that it was a more – suitable arrangement.'

'I don't believe you.'

Miles tapped the parchment with a precise forefinger. 'Whether you believe me or not, is no great matter. The outcome is here, in black and white.'

It was his moment of triumph, and Richard, sick with the knowledge of his defeat, could do nothing to rob him of it. Though Miles's interest was patent enough – and Richard could imagine the adroit argument which had gone to further it – yet he could not fathom what had been in his father's mind. Of course, Miles had been the elder son, the natural heir; yet he himself, and his father, had always been close enough, and friendly enough – there had been no hint of such a breach – no serious cloud had ever marred the tie between them. It was this which he could not interpret. It was this which he must probe.

'I don't believe you,' he said again, his voice harder, his anger returning. 'You must have worked on him, you must have dropped some poison. I know how you can twist the truth itself, when you wish … What did you mean when you said it was more suitable that you should be the sole heir?'

Miles was affecting to be busy, folding the copy of the will, placing it on the mantelpiece behind him. Over his shoulder he said: 'Come, Richard, we need not fence with each other. There are some people fitted for the inheritance of great estates, and others who are best off without them.'

Richard bit his lip, controlling his fury. 'And why am I thus unfitted for any share of his fortune?'

Miles turned, his eyebrows raised in mortifying disdain. 'Shall we say,' he answered, 'that there is a certain unbecoming wildness in you, which impressed our father more than any claim you might have had on his generosity.'

'Wildness? What wildness?'

'My dear Richard, let us spare each other a catalogue of your transgressions. You know very well what stories and scandals have been put about. The whole county knows them.' He sniffed, delicately. 'Of course, you are a grown man. If you choose to drink immoderately, and involve yourself in questionable contacts with women, that is your affair. But such things do not qualify you for consideration, when the time comes to decide who is to inherit an estate and who is to be passed over. I have no doubt that this was what was in Father's mind.'

'But he never spoke a word of it.'

Miles settled back comfortably on his heels. 'Perhaps he thought that it did not greatly matter. Perhaps he thought that this small legacy was the best he could do for you – with propriety.'

Richard stared at him, genuinely puzzled. 'What do you mean, propriety? You seem to have a sudden liking for the word. What riddle is this?'

Miles shrugged. 'If you do not know, and cannot guess, it is not my task to enlighten you.'

He made as if to leave his place in front of the fire, ending the conversation at his own will, and this was more than Richard could endure. He stepped forward, and put both his hands firmly on Miles's shoulders. The heavy gold epaulettes mocked him with their richness and splendour.

'Not so fast,' he said threateningly, 'and not so high and mightily. I am not one of your wretched sailors, to be dismissed when you have finished talking.'

'By God, you are not!' exclaimed Miles. He shook off the detaining hands. 'If you were aboard any ship of mine, you would soon learn your place!'

'What place is that?' Furious, Richard was ready to goad his brother to anything – to quarrel, to a blow. 'Tell me my place, brother Miles,' he said contemptuously. 'So that I do not transgress any further.'

Miles looked up at him, his eyes snapping. He was conscious, as never before, of being a small man confronted with someone so much taller and stronger that he could not be challenged. But a moment earlier he had been in full command of the situation, and he was determined to keep it so. Brushing past Richard, almost stooping under his arm, he walked to the door with what dignity he could muster. There, with a safe distance between them, he turned and spoke: 'Your place is elsewhere. Have I made that clear? I'll have no beggars in my house, and no libertines either. You can take your toys, and go, as soon as may be.'

Then, with no undue delay, he was gone himself, and Richard was left alone.

II

Richard moved heavily upwards through the great house, room by room, staircase by staircase, landing by landing; it was as if he were already saying his farewells. When Miles had left him, he had crossed to the sideboard, and drunk deep, and drunk again; anger and sorrow combined to give him a great need for comfort, and, at that low moment, wine had seemed the only comfort to hand. But now, when astonishment had given way to a dull acceptance of the facts, he knew that he must have comfort of another kind – he must talk of his troubles to a friend. Thus, as on so many other occasions, from boyhood onwards, when he had stood in this same sort of need, he climbed up to the topmost storey of the house, and the modest room under the eaves where lived and worked his old tutor, Sebastian Wickham.

But the journey upwards had its own aspects of unhappiness and disquiet; shrouded by curtains and heavy hangings, the house seemed shrouded also by fate. He passed the many portraits of his ancestors, who now appeared to have disowned him; he passed the upper landing, with its suits of armour and its creaking linen presses, whence, peeping through the balustrade and down the wide staircase, he had long ago watched the adult world of his parents assembling for some hospitality, or setting out on some great and elegant occasion. He passed his old nursery, where he and Miles had played and fought and sulked, where the terrors of childhood had melted before the warm and tender presence which was all he remembered of his mother.

Rich carpeting gave way to half-worn, coarse drugget, and then to the bare deal boards of the upper quarters. Was this to be the future pattern of his life, this progress from easy of sixty-five, they were still astonishingly compatible; latterly, indeed, Wickham had become something of a father-confessor. But his position at Marriott had now grown tenuous: though he had done some secretarial work for the head of the household, and had enjoyed the run of the library, yet his continued employment was no more than an old servant's pension; and at this moment of change, perhaps, his time was running out.

His former master was dead, and his new one, Miles Marriott, saw all men, young or old, through a spyglass of appraisal made small by a small spirit.

It was this thought, above all others, which prompted Richard Marriott, in spite of his preoccupations, to greet the old man with especial gentleness. There was something about the frail Sebastian Wickham, reading so painstakingly in his shabby attic, oblivious of the cruel world, content with the rags of learning, which moved him strongly. But Richard was young, and he had his own troubles which pressed in on him harder still, more than could those of any other man. Thus, he had scarcely added to his greeting a cautionary word: 'You must take care of those eyes, Sebastian – they are precious,' before he fell silent, frowning. As he leant against the window frame, looking out across the parklands of Marriott, he was the very picture of a young man with all the cares of the world sitting on his shoulders.

Sebastian Wickham, glancing up at him, slipped a tasselled leather bookmark into his book, and closed it. There would be no more reading for a space … Then he himself stood up, and put his hand on Richard's shoulder, looking out where he was looking, at the broad Marriott acres fading into the evening mists.

'What's the trouble, Richard?' he asked. 'Something displeases you. It cannot be the view.'

'It is the view,' answered Richard, morosely. 'The view of what I shall never enjoy.'

'How so?'

Richard turned, and looked at the old man's lined face – the old man who had nothing also, whose prospects had been meagre from his very birth. But his own wound was too hurtful for such delicate comparisons.

'I have seen my father's will,' he said abruptly. 'Miles has all the estate.'

Sebastian Wickham nodded, not yet surprised. 'But it was entailed to him.'

'Only the house and the lands. But he has been given everything! Every penny! I have two pistols. And a map-maker's globe.'

Wickham, taken aback, reached out a hand towards the desk, and lowered himself into his chair again. From there, he looked at Richard with swift concern.

'Is that really so?' he asked. 'Miles has all the money? You will see none of it?'

'I will see the door tomorrow,' said Richard bitterly. 'Brother Miles has made that much clear.'

'I cannot believe that,' said Wickham, shaking his head. 'Miles would not be so hard.'

'He would be so hard, and you do believe it!' Richard looked at the old man, so generous, so far from the world, so innocent of its deceits and betrayals. 'Come, Sebastian – you need not practise the art of tact with me. There was never any love lost between Miles and myself. He is delighted at this turn. More than money, it gives him a chance to put me in my place at last. He must have worked on my father to bring it about. I know he did! By God, I hate him!'

'He is your brother, Richard.'

'He is a dog … He said' – Richard mimicked Miles's precise tones – ' "There is a certain unbecoming wildness in you, Richard, which must have impressed our father more than we knew." … I'll wager he was the one who first pointed it out. He was always a tale-bearer!'

Sebastian Wickham smoothed the lapels of his rusty black frock coat, a slight smile on his lips. 'He had some tales to bear, did he not?'

Richard frowned. 'What do you mean by that?'

Wickham sat back in his chair. He wished to soften the moment, to make it less dramatic, less harsh, and he could only do it in his own gentle fashion.

'You have told me I need not practise the art of tact with you, Richard. I will take you at your word … You are wild. I have often told you so. There is no vice in you, but there is plenty of boldness and – and appetite.' His voice robbed the words of any sting; this was a mood of reminiscence, not of chiding. 'I have been your close escort for many hundreds of miles, over much of Europe. Do you wish me to forget that? Do you wish to forget it yourself? Do you not remember the beer cellars at Heidelberg? – the inn-keeper's wife at Zurich? – the contessa and her sleeping gondolier in Venice? – the Chief of Police at Dijon? And later, when you came home to Marriott – ' he sighed, not sadly, but as if in contemplation of something which he could not share, ' – the tales which Miles told were very likely true, were they not? There have been drinking bouts, and gambling. There was the coach, overturned and smashed in the race on the Cheltenham road. There have been girls … If you are seeking a reason – '

'But why should it cost me my whole patrimony?' interrupted Richard. He felt that he must fight back; the old man was right in what he said and what he hinted, but they were not strong enough arguments, they were childish. 'Of course I have done all these things! I am a man, not an old woman, not a post-Captain who plans to be an Admiral.' Agitated, he was striding up and down the narrow room, while Sebastian Wickham watched him gravely. 'But is that reason enough to cut me off without a penny? To leave me two pistols and a damned globe!'

Wickham smiled, as though at some private joke. 'Tennis balls, my liege!' he quoted, almost to himself.

'What was that?'

'A stray thought …' Wickham gathered his wits. 'I don't know what was in your father's mind, Richard, nor why he did it. It may be true, as Miles said, that he was shocked or displeased by your behaviour.'

'He was no saint himself!'

A wary look came into Sebastian Wickham's eye. 'That is not a proper observation, Richard,' he said, almost coldly. 'On this day of all days.'

'But it is true!' answered Richard stoutly. 'He was fond of a glass, he liked pretty women … Who does not, for God's sake, in this day and age – except for a cold fish like Miles, with his career where his manhood ought to be! … Nay, I am sorry, Sebastian,' he said instantly, noting the old man's deep embarrassment. 'I would not shock you for all the world. You are too close to me.' He checked his pacing, and put his hand on Wickham's shoulder. 'Forgive me. I am in a vile mood … It has been a day of sadness, and surprises, and then to be shown the door tomorrow … And Miles talking in riddles about "propriety".' He came to the alert suddenly. 'Now I had forgotten that. What did he mean by it?'

'By what?'

'He said' – Richard knitted his dark brows in the effort of remembrance – 'that a small legacy was all that my father could leave me, with propriety.'

He remained looking down at the floor for some moments, in deep thought; when he glanced up, he was astonished to see that the old man had risen, in obvious agitation, and was staring at him almost with consternation in his eyes. At first he thought that Wickham was still taken aback by his coarseness, or had only just fully comprehended it; but this was dispelled when Wickham said, on a note of great distress: 'Miles had no business to say anything of the sort!'

'Why, what's this?' asked Richard, astonished. 'What do I care what he says? I hear too much of his babbling to give it any attention. It puzzled me, that was all. But something in Wickham's continued discomfort caught and held his interest. 'I see that it does not puzzle you. What did he mean, Sebastian?'

'It is no great matter,' answered Wickham. Clearly, however, it was a great matter – to his thinking, at least; he was pale, and close to trembling with the effort to preserve his calm. 'Let us forget about it.'

'I'll not forget about it,' said Richard, suddenly stern. He was aware that he had stumbled upon something, and that Sebastian Wickham knew what it was. It was some matter important enough to have cut the ground from under him, distorting his whole future, and he must get to the bottom of it. He caught the old man's arm, in a grip not too gentle. 'I'll not leave you,' he warned, 'until you have answered the riddle. What did Miles mean? What does he know? What do you know?'

'I know nothing,' answered Wickham. 'I beseech you to let it rest.'

'Sebastian …'

'You are hurting my arm, Richard. Leave me be.'

Richard released his hold on the meagre, stick-like forearm. 'I would never hurt you, but I will not leave you either.' He changed his tone, softening, wheedling as he had often done in the past. 'Tell me, Sebastian. You are my friend. Tell me. I must know, now.'

The old man shook his head, waveringly. 'It is far better that you do not know.'

'You have said too much, or too little. Tell me.'

Wickham looked at him, searching his face, which was set and determined. He could not resist the appeal in it, the vulnerable hunger to know the best and the worst; and they had been too close to each other, during too many blossoming years, for lies or evasions. 'Very well,' he said at last. 'I will tell you … When Miles said – ' he hesitated, and fell silent for some moments. 'I do not want to wound you, Richard. I would not do so for the world.'

'I have had wounds already today,' answered Richard hardly. 'One more will not be the death of me.'

Wickham sat down, and lowered his head into his bony hands, as if he had to collect his courage before he could speak. From outside, the clock in the stable tower chimed a half-hour, and was echoed by other chimes, far away, across meadow and parish, as if all men's time were the same, and none had more pain than any other. Fatal, terrible illusion ... Presently, not looking at Richard, Sebastian Wickham asked in a low voice: 'How much older do you suppose your brother is?'

Richard Marriott stared. 'Older than I? A year, I suppose. A year at most.'

'Richard, he is scarcely three months older than you.'

'Three months?' repeated Richard, uncomprehending. 'How can that be? We are brothers. Our mother – '

He broke off, as if struck across the face; the appalling truth reached him in a single instant. A hundred questions and puzzlements of the past were suddenly resolved; stray words overheard, side glances that had seemed strange, silences, long forgotten, which now sounded louder than the loudest voice. So this was the truth, the truth of all things ... He turned away, his composure utterly shattered, and walked blindly to the window. From there he spoke in a questioning, self-torturing tone which was as hurtful to hear as to utter.

'Who knew of this?'

'Miles. Some servants who were dismissed. The vicar of the parish where you were baptized.'

'And you?'

'Your father had sometimes hinted of it, when – he was in a careless mood. And then I came upon his journal in the library.' Wickham's voice was suddenly pleading. 'I meant no harm, Richard. I believe he intended me to read it.'

'It is no matter ... Then there was another woman, at the same time as – as his wife?'

'Yes.'

'Who was she?'

'She was – in the household.'

'Who was she?'

'A kitchen maid.'

Richard laughed harshly, violently; an ugly sound to mark the ugliest moment of his life. A bastard – a bastard, by a kitchen maid. No wonder brother Miles gave himself all the airs of nobility ... A kitchen maid, seduced and brought to bed almost in the same season as the lawful wife, the mother who was not his mother. There could be no speedier nor more certain way to have two sons ... And this was his own father, who had disinherited him because of his 'wildness'... The thought made him turn round suddenly.

'But he loved me,' he declared loudly. 'He always loved me. Why should he disown me now?'

Sebastian Wickham, the bearer of the terrible news, looked at him with shame and compassion. 'He did love you, Richard. That was certain, and you must never think otherwise, even now. He would not disown you. But he had a sense of the fitness of things, also.'

'Somewhat tardily,' said Richard, on a savage note of sarcasm.

'Do not speak like that,' said Wickham. 'Of course he sinned – he sinned greatly. Perhaps this was his way of making some amends.'

'Amends?'

Wickham nodded slowly. 'He must have felt guilty because he had wronged his wife, Miles's mother.'

'He wronged my mother, far more!'

Wickham nodded again. 'That is so. And it was a hard choice. But with your father's sense of family – '

'Sense of family!' Richard burst out. Anger was returning now, in full flood; he felt as if he could scarcely breathe; the formal clothes – the clothes of mourning for his father – felt like a cage from which he must escape, or else suffocate. 'Where is the sense of family, in a man who gets himself a bastard and then leaves him a pair of pistols to live on? No wonder Miles is ready to show me the door. He can hardly endure to breathe the same air. A post-Captain with a bastard brother! It might cost him the Queen's commission!'

He turned away, unable to say more, unable to remain in the room where he had heard the news. His face was drawn, and his heart pounding enough to shake the broad shoulders.

'Forgive me,' said Sebastian Wickham, humbly. 'It has been a hard secret to bear.'

'Well, it is a secret no longer.' His anger boiled over at last, uncontrollably. 'A kitchen maid, you say? Such refinement! Such rare taste for a baronet ... I must take my leave Sebastian,' he said, with cruel formality. 'I must go to dress for dinner. Indeed, perhaps I should be cooking it.'

III

John Keston stood sentinel by the high-backed zinc hip bath, a brass pitcher of cold water in his hand, waiting for his master to give the word. It was a service he had performed a thousand times before, just as he had performed countless other services for Richard Marriott, during the four years he had been his servant. He was a small, compact young man, ruddy and strong as a countryman should be; he was habitually silent, almost taciturn, and when he spoke his West Country burr came slowly, as if each word were measured out.

On the Grand Tour he had been invaluable, doing battle stubbornly for railway seats and ships' cabins and clean bed linen and log fires, looking after baggage, warding off beggars, treating the strange and glittering life of Europe as if it were some quaint morality play in which he must act the part of Common Sense. Back home at Marriott, he served Richard alone, keeping his clothes, shining his boots, holding his horses, cleaning his guns; and, as now, waiting to douse him with cold water after his bath was complete – the bath for which he had already carried eight successive buckets of hot water up three flights of stairs.

A faithful servant with a still tongue and a strong right arm, John Keston would never have questioned his place in life. He only questioned anyone, or anything, which seemed likely to disadvantage the man he served.

Now he watched, as Richard completed the soaping and sponging of his muscular body. Keston was aware that the man in the bath was angry and preoccupied, and he knew, from servants' gossip below stairs, why this was so. If there should come a moment when he could help, he would be ready.

Richard rinsed away the soap, paused, and then growled over his shoulder: 'Now!'

He gasped and spluttered as the stream of ice cold water cascaded over his head and back. Then he shook himself, like a dog surprised by a sudden wave pounding up the seashore, and rose quickly to his feet. John Keston, dropping the pitcher, advanced with a huge rough-grained towel which had been warming by the bedroom fire, and wrapped it round him.

Richard Marriott nodded his thanks, and stepped out on to the lead flooring which lined one half of the dressing-room. Rubbing his head with his free hand, he was aware that the head was not entirely clear; five full glasses of Madeira had gone some way towards dulling his wits. In the vile circumstances of the present moment, there was only one thing to be done about that.

'Go and open the champagne,' he commanded.

John Keston, without a word, walked from the dressing-room to the bedroom, where the champagne stood in its moulded silver cooler by the fireside; while Richard, towelling himself to restore his blood after the cold shower, returned to his thoughts. If there were one night on which to get drunk, this was the night ... He had been supremely angry when he had left Sebastian Wickham's room – angry with the whole world, angry even with Wickham, who had been the bearer of fearful news. He could well understand why the tyrants of ancient times always put to death any messenger who brought evil tidings. Now his savage spirit was easier, but the anger remained, mixed with sorrow, mixed with shame. The stigma of bastardy, undreamed of, unimaginable, had touched him fatally; it was like some black bird of ill omen, sitting on his shoulders, announcing to all the world that the man below was impure.

He was not so made as to feel that he would never hold up his head again; but certainly he could scarcely bear the thought of facing the polite world with this hideous secret ready to be betrayed by a chance word.

The sharp pop! of a champagne cork sounded clearly from his bedroom, a messenger with tidings of another sort. That was the answer, for tonight, and perhaps for many nights … He walked through, his slippered feet slurring on the thick carpet, to find John Keston stationed by the wine cooler, bottle in one hand, crystal stem glass in the other. Admirable man, faithful servant … He took the filled glass, and drank it off at a draught. Then he held it out.

'Again,' he said.

Let brother Miles count the glasses, if he would. He himself, tonight, would count by the bottle.

John Keston, holding out the freshly filled glass, said: 'Sir, it is past seven o'clock.'

Richard, sipping his champagne, nodded abstractedly; then he set the glass down on the dressing-table, and began to put on his clean linen. At Marriott, by custom, they dined late, at half past seven; in his present mood, he would have loitered, and made his appearance later still, if it had not meant keeping Lucinda Drysdale waiting. She was too dear to him, tonight and any other night, for such boorish ill-manners … He drew on his starched white shirt, while the firelight flickered on the ceiling, and drew golden spears of light from the bubbles within his glass. It was a comfortable room, much loved, much enjoyed as a repository for his private treasures; it had been his own since he was five years old, when the canopied four-poster had seemed bigger than the tallest ship, and the fire shadows round the walls had first frightened him and then lulled him to delicious sleep.

Now it was lived-in, crowded, masculine. There was a long rack of guns, their polished stocks gleaming; fly rods standing in one corner; silver-backed brushes on the dressing-table; rows of boots, all with their ebony boot-trees; racing cups and goblets, dumb-bells and Indian clubs; sporting prints of grouse moor and steeplechase; and a great wardrobe of veneered walnut to hold his coats, and a Dutch press for his linen. Its view was to the south, across a rose garden, and down to one of the home farms; but the brocade curtains were already drawn against the autumn twilight, making of the room a warm enclosed haven. It was this that he had to leave.

He said, suddenly: 'I will wear the burgundy jacket.'

John Keston, surprised, turned from the wardrobe. 'Sir?'

'The burgundy jacket.'

Keston, thinking that he had become forgetful with the wine, ventured: 'Sir, there are ladies dining.'

'I know it.' He took a fresh gulp of his champagne, and savoured its sharpness. It was his father's funeral day, and there were ladies dining, and he would wear his red velvet smoking jacket, just to see Miles raise his prim eyebrows as soon as he noticed it. 'I will wear it, none the less.'

'Yes, sir.' Keston put away the black tail coat, and drew out the dark red jacket in its place.

Richard, standing before the mirror, knotted a white four-in-hand tie round his high stiff collar. Then, without turning round, he said: 'I shall likely be going on my travels again, Keston.'

'Aye, sir,' said John Keston, unsurprised.

'I shall want you with me, if you have a mind for it. But we shall be long away.'

'Aye, sir,' said Keaton again.

'You do not want to stay at Marriott?'

After a moment of silence, John Keston, struggling to find the right words for what was in his mind, said: 'No, sir. We'll do no good here, I reckon.'

Now it was Richard who was surprised. 'Why do you say that? What do you mean?'

Keston came forward, holding the velvet coat, the sleeves spread. 'It's the talk downstairs, sir.'

23

Richard looked closely at him, alert for the thing he feared. 'What talk is that?'

Keston's broad smooth face was expressionless. 'Just that there's changes on the way.'

'Changes?'

'Aye, sir.' He summed it up in a rough country proverb. 'New dunghill, new cockerel to crow.'

'What other talk is there?'

'None that I know, sir.'

There was no guile in his expression; he seemed to be speaking the truth. Richard drew on his coat, and Keston, standing behind him, smoothed and brushed it across the shoulders. Then there was a sound of wheels in the carriage sweep below, and horses' hooves slowing to a halt.

'That's the ladies now, sir,' said John Keston.

'Pour me another glass.'

Once more he finished it at a gulp; then he set the glass down, steadily enough, and shot his cuffs. The light gleamed on the heavy gold cuff links, which had been his father's last birthday gift. He might be selling them to the Jews before the week was out … John Keston opened the door, and Richard walked out on to the landing, into the brighter light from the great chandelier which hung down two full flights into the hall. There were voices from below, and a girl's gentle laugh which he recognized, and loved.

He began to go down slowly, carefully, holding on to the curved mahogany banisters. There must be troubles ahead of him, great changes to be made and to be endured. But at least there was Lucinda.

IV

Dinner, starting under perceptible constraint, had never improved; as course succeeded course, the conversation grew more stilted and the silences more pronounced, until even Mrs Merriman, the deaf aunt who was Lucinda Drysdale's companion and chaperone, grew uneasy and ceased her durable smile. Miles Marriott had reacted to the burgundy jacket with foreseeable distaste, and was in a mood of icy politeness; he had not wanted to entertain tonight, in any case, and he felt that he had been doubly put upon. Lucinda herself seemed out of humour: she had frowned at Richard when he made his entrance, knowing him well enough to be sure that he had been drinking; and his conduct as the evening progressed did nothing to retrieve the unfortunate impression. Mrs Merriman, a hesitant woman entombed in her deafness, was not of such quality as to enliven the gathering.

They sat round the long, mirror-polished Chippendale dining table; the candlelight glittered on the magnificent silver, the table ornaments, the delicately branched epergne which was the centrepiece, and then spread outwards to put its warm glow on their sombre faces. Behind them, in the darkness of the heavily-curtained room, Jeffreys, the butler, and the two footmen, in pale blue Marriott livery with mourning bands, moved silently to and fro, serving a dinner of uniform excellence. But it was clear that it would take more than beef broth, grilled trout, lamb cutlets, breast of pheasant, and crème caramel (as a compliment to the ladies) to make an enjoyable evening; more, even, than golden Chablis, red Bordeaux, and chilled champagne to lift their spirits above a dull formality. Tonight, the Marriott table, famous over three counties, the solace and delight (in its time) of kings, seemed to have met its match.

Miles sat at the head, stiff and unbending in his blue mess dress with the bright crested buttons; he gave great attention to his food, and made the minimum of conversation with his guests. He ignored, completely, Richard, who sat, almost lounging, opposite him – eating negligently, drinking deep, and motioning from time to time, with crude insistence, to have his wineglass refilled. By now, his head was buzzing with more than anger, and he scarcely essayed to speak unless he were addressed. When he laughed, which was seldom, it had a savage sound, as if the butt of the joke were himself.

Between them sat Mrs Merriman, thin and dried up, severely coiffed and corseted, pecking like a bird – but with a bird's persistence and skill; and Lucinda Drysdale, who would have graced any gathering, however elegant or sparkling, and who positively illumined this one.

She was a distant Marriott cousin, a glowing beauty, and a toast as famous in far-off London as she was here in the West Country; but when one had said that (thought Richard, looking at her through a pleasurable haze of wine), one must pause, and begin the catalogue again … Tonight she seemed to him entirely ravishing; under the auburn hair her full face was lovely, and her bosom, candidly revealed in the fashion of the day, rose in creamy opulence from the severe black gown which marked her mourning.

She and Richard had been play-fellows from his boyhood days, then open-hearted companions; latterly there had been something stronger, a promise of love, well understood between them, which he had hoped to bring to flower. She seemed to admire him, even when she admonished him for what she called his 'masculine pursuits'; and he was very ready to love her … Both her parents were dead and she had little money; but it was a good match none the less, and he would not doubt his luck if she consented to marry him. The wildness, with which she sometimes taxed him, would disappear if he had such a wife … And they could continue to make fun of Miles – a shared joke which had persisted from the earliest nursery years.

Part of his stray thought returned to him, casting a fringe of shadow on this happy prospect, and he frowned as he emptied his wineglass and motioned to a footman to refill it. She had little money … But now he himself had none at all. What would happen to his hopes, when she came to know this? What would happen, when she came to know the other news which had so shocked him today? Would she have to know it? Could it be hidden? He frowned again, and noticed suddenly that Lucinda was staring at him, her large brown eyes fixed intently on his face.

Miles was speaking of local matters to Mrs Merriman, and his voice, perforce, was raised. Under cover of it, Lucinda remarked softly: 'You are dull tonight, Richard.'

He stirred himself, and sat up, and took a mouthful of the pheasant. It tasted dry on his tongue, and he washed it down with half a glass of wine.

'Yes, I am dull,' he agreed. 'But you are very beautiful, Lucinda. And very accomplished. You can be entertaining enough for both of us.'

Now it was her turn to frown. She had never liked a public display of their affection, even within the family circle, and this was certainly not the moment nor the mode which she would have chosen.

'The wine speaks for you,' she said briefly. 'I see you have forgotten your promises of last week.'

'No promise could survive a day like today,' he countered. 'I have had a glass or two, I admit. In the circumstances, it was necessary.'

'It is always necessary.' But she could never be angry with him for long, and swiftly her glance melted to its accustomed softness. 'I know how sad a day this has been for you, Richard. I did not mean to read you a lecture.'

Richard blinked at her; the warm candlelight, falling on the curve of her bosom, seemed to reflect a whole world of love and sweetness. Here was one person who would understand, who would not fail to comfort him … He leant forward.

'It has been a sad day in more ways that you can know.' He became aware that Miles, his laboured conversation finished, was listening to what he was saying; across the candlelight, between the curved branches of the silver epergne, his sharp eyes were fixed on Richard, with cold concentration. Such overseeing would not halt him; rather the reverse. 'I have had some bad news,' said Richard boldly. 'My brother was kind enough to communicate it to me.'

'Richard,' said Miles warningly.

Richard looked at him over the rim of his wineglass, hating him, mocking him. 'What is it, Sir Miles?'

'We will not speak of it now.'

'Do not be shy on my account, Sir Miles. You should be proud of your new estate.'

Miles gave a side-glance at the servants who, having removed the plates of the last course, were handing round the dish of crème caramel. His voice was authoritative, coldly correct. 'At the proper time,' he said, 'you may impart your news, if you wish. This is not the proper time.'

Richard, quickly angered, brought his fist down on the polished table top, so that the glasses jangled. 'I want no instruction from you,' he said roughly. 'If I have something to say, I will say it when I choose!'

Lucinda, perturbed by his violence, intervened quickly. 'Come, Richard,' she said, coaxingly. 'It cannot be of such importance. Tell us later.'

Richard waved away the dish which was offered him; and there was an awkward silence as the servants, their work completed, withdrew from the room. Richard wondered, with an inward flash of contempt, how long it would be before John Keston learned of his outburst. He might be hearing the tale, which would lose nothing in the telling, at this very moment ... Miles was still staring at him across the table; the surveillance further angered him, and he responded to his anger with a determination to have his way. He was touchy with damaged pride, ready to see an insult anywhere, in a word or a look; and Miles's cool insistence that he alone should decide what subjects would, and would not, be talked of at table, was the worst insult of all.

As soon as they were alone: 'It is of great importance,' insisted Richard belligerently. In his excitement, he slurred the words, and Miles's disdainful expression irked him more potently still. He gathered himself, and mastered his tongue. 'It is my father's will,' he said, with careful distinctness, so that they all might hear. 'I learned of it, for the first time, a few hours ago ...' He waved his hand towards Miles, knocking over his empty wineglass. 'Behold the new baronet!' he said loudly. Then his hand fell on his own chest, with a sharp slapping sound. 'And the new pauper!'

'You forget yourself, Richard,' said Miles Marriott, in the astonished silence which followed. His baleful glance, with which he was wont to freeze his junior officers to the quarter-deck, bore down on his brother. 'There are certain subjects which one does not discuss openly, even' – his eyes narrowed – 'even when one is in liquor.'

Richard laughed, a harsh and savage sound. 'I am in liquor, my dear Miles, to celebrate your good fortune. Surely you are not ashamed of it?'

'What have I to be ashamed of?'

'That is between God and your conscience.' Richard turned to Lucinda Drysdale, his face exhibiting an artificial calm which did not mask his deep feeling. 'What would you say of an heir who takes, not only his own portion, but his brother's as well? Would you congratulate him? – or ask him to reveal the secrets of success? Would you say, "Tut, tut! That was a somewhat greedy stroke"? Or would you say, "Well done, thou good and faithful post-Captain"?'

'You go too far, Richard,' said Lucinda reprovingly. But there was little or no embarrassment in her expression; rather was it inquisitive, sharper than he had ever seen it before. She looked from one brother to the other, from Miles's furious face to Richard's careless scorn. Convention dictated that she should take no part in the quarrel, that she should pass over it and make small talk with her aunt until the squall blew by; but there was something here which overrode convention, a naked conflict which it would be almost as inconceivable to ignore as to notice. She stole a second glance at Miles, and decided to risk her curiosity. 'In any case, your riddles are too deep for my poor brain. What is this about being a pauper?'

Miles Marriott glanced at her with extreme disapproval, and her aunt, who had that uncomfortable capacity of many deaf persons for hearing well enough when it was least convenient, leant across and said: 'Really, Lucinda – this is not your concern at all!' But Lucinda's attention, like her question, was for Richard alone, and her audacity was rewarded when he answered, with the same assumed lightness of tone: 'I can assure you, my dear Lucinda, that I did not choose the word by accident. It describes my new situation exactly. Since this afternoon I have been living in this house only on sufferance. Marriott, and all that goes with it, now belongs to my brother alone.'

'Of course Marriott belongs to Miles,' began Lucinda, puzzled. 'There was the entail – who else could it belong to? But as for being a pauper – '

'With Marriott,' interrupted Richard, 'goes the whole of my father's fortune. The whole of it.'

Her eyes widened. 'You are joking, surely?'

He shook his head; in the silence of the room, the creaking of his chair as he leant forward was very loud. 'No, I am not joking. I have not the least cause to joke. In my father's will, I have fared less well than the Cottage Hospital at St Briavels. I have nothing.'

On an impulse, he rose, and crossed to the sideboard, and poured himself a fresh glass of wine; the breach of etiquette seemed all one with the shock and surprise of what he had said. Lucinda was looking at him with an expression he had never seen in her face before; as if, with the words, 'I have nothing', he had become a different sort of man altogether, a stranger she had never met. Miles was staring impassively down at the table; he was choosing to ignore the entire incident – he would not pay it the compliment of disapproval, much less of embarrassment. It was left to Mrs Merriman to bridge the chasm of social dislocation which had been opened up.

She turned to Miles Marriott. 'I have never understood,' she said, seizing on the first topic that came to mind, 'what is meant by the term post-Captain.'

Miles collected himself. 'I beg your pardon?'

'Post-Captain,' repeated Mrs Merriman. 'What exactly does it signify?'

'It means,' answered Miles, well content to play this game, 'a captain in a sea-going post – that is, in command of a ship of twenty guns or more.'

Richard, walking unsteadily, slopping his full wineglass, returned to the table and sat down. From there he stared fixedly at Mrs Merriman. 'You should have asked me,' he said. 'I can tell you what a post-Captain is.'

Miles, stung out of his false calm, tried to head him off. 'Hold your tongue!' he snapped. 'You have caused us enough discomfort already.'

'A post-Captain, my dear Aunt Merriman,' said Richard, ignoring him entirely, 'is a baronet with twenty different ways of securing his fortune. He has a brave ship with twenty guns, and every gun is trained on his brother, ready to blow him to perdition.' He was drunk, and he knew it, and he was past caring; even Lucinda's eye, bent on him with such inquiring sharpness, could not stop him. 'A post-Captain, Aunt Merriman, has taken the place of Mustela Nivalis, the common weasel, as the lowest form of animal life. It preys on much larger animals, using cunning instead of strength. It preys on me ...' He was in full flood now, not to be stopped; one of the young footmen, returning to serve the last of the wine, paused open-mouthed in the doorway, until a violent gesture from Miles at the head of the table made him turn in his tracks and bolt from the room. 'All post-Captains are wealthy men,' said Richard, in an inane sing-song voice. 'They are their father's favourites, their mother's only darlings ... Shall I reveal to you the secret of my birth? I was born under Taurus, the stupid patient bull. Post-Captains are born under Sagittarius, the archer who shoots you between the shoulder-blades while you are looking elsewhere ...' He raised his glass, blinking wildly. 'Ladies, I give you the toast! To post-Captain Sir Miles Marriott, Baronet! The richest baronet in the West Country. The smartest baronet that ever put to sea. And the smallest baronet that ever ruled a great house!'

He swallowed the wine at a gulp; then he raised his hand and hurled the glass with all his strength at the open fireplace. It splintered against the mantel, and the dregs of the wine fell hissing on to the burning embers.

In the heavy silence that followed, Mrs Merriman was, once again, the first to recollect the demands and usages of polite society. She rose to her feet.

'Come, Lucinda,' she said brightly. 'We will leave the gentlemen to their port.'

Miles and Richard both rose; Richard unsteadily, holding on to the table edge, Miles with a controlled impassivity which masked a furious anger. As soon as the ladies had passed silently from the room, Richard sat down again heavily; but Miles remained where he was, standing at the head of his table, staring at his brother with an expression of implacable hatred. Blinking up at him, Richard said: 'Sit down, brother Miles ... We have a full half-hour yet, before we need join them ... I have it in mind to drink a bottle of port.'

'You have drunk enough,' said Miles icily. 'More than enough.'

'Nonsense! We have scarcely begun. A glass of port! It is my last evening.'

'It is certainly your last evening,' said Miles, 'and I am glad of it.' He walked round the table until he was standing by Richard's chair, looking down at him. 'You are a drunken animal,' he said, very distinctly. 'You have made a vulgar fool of yourself, in the presence of ladies, before the servants, and I would not take wine with you if we were the last two men left on earth ...' And as Richard, startled, sought to rise to his feet: 'Stay where you are!' commanded Miles. His face was stern, with the desperate courage of a small man who has been pushed and provoked too far. 'Stay until the morning, if you choose ... I can assure you, the ladies will excuse your withdrawal.'

V

He had vomited, and doused his head in a basin of cold water; later, sobered, but still angry and raw-skinned, he had come downstairs again after an hour of seclusion. He had had some second thoughts during this time of solitude, but not many, and none that could really change his mood. Of course, it had been a mistake to get drunk, whatever the provocation – that was boy's behaviour, an act of immaturity which Miles, the cold strategist, had been quick to seize on. Richard could even feel a twinge of admiration for Miles, who had turned brave in the face of intolerable insult. Who would have thought that the little post-Captain had such stuff in him? ... But the unwilling tribute did not alter the hard facts which beset him; he was still poor, he was dispossessed, he must leave Marriott, like a servant dismissed, within a short time. These were still things which had to he reckoned with, when it came to casting up the accounts. He had insulted Miles because of what Miles had come to mean to him; not simply on this day of defeat, but over the years, the years of being a younger brother ... It was only this evening, seeing Miles, the new baronet with the new fortune, lording it at the head of his dining table, that Richard had been brought face to face with the fact of his repulse, and had exploded into fury.

Now, reaching the bottom of the broad staircase, he stood in the great hall, listening. The only sound in all the house was the playing of a piano, gentle, harmonious, in the drawing-room. The jewelled notes, strung like pearls, mocked him with their assurance of a world of civilized delights. Lucinda was playing – but not for him.

On an impulse, Richard crossed to the double doors which led to the garden, and passed out on to the terrace. It was a fine night, starlit, clear; the moon shadow of the great house fell sharply on the stone flags, the smell of the night was of flowers, cooling lawns, rose gardens drenched with their own scent. He walked a few paces, till he came level with the windows of the drawing-room. Through one of them, uncurtained, he could see the lamplit room within.

Lucinda was playing, as he had known she must be. She sat at the rosewood piano, her face studious, her beautiful body bent forward, her arms – as white as ivory – moving gently over the keyboard. Miles was in an armchair beside her, watching her, listening intently to the music. Across the room, Mrs Merriman, at ease on a low-cushioned couch, was intent on her needlework, a fire screen of gros-point which had been her leisuretime engagement for at least three years. To Richard, outside in the darkness of the terrace, the music sounded faintly. But the rest of the scene was as clear and as foreboding as the bell which, this afternoon, had tolled for his father.

He watched Lucinda, as she let her hands drop from the keyboard, and then smiled at Miles Marriott. He watched Miles, a figure of imposing correctness, bow towards her and then bring his hands together in intimate applause. He watched Mrs Merriman, the aunt, the chaperone, so engrossed in her task that she did not feel called upon to raise her head even when the music ceased. The message of their harmony could not have been clearer if the three actors had jointly turned towards him and said: 'Stay where you are. Keep your distance.'

Possessed by jealous rage, he could not bear to watch further. He felt as if he were a hurt animal, lurking in the shadowy dark, surveying with hatred the warmth and lightness of the habitations of men. Today he had been excluded from Marriott, excluded from his father's fortune, excluded from the world of lawful wedlock; now he seemed excluded from the world of Lucinda Drysdale, whose smiles, whose glowing presence, were so pointedly offered to another. He moved away from the lighted window, and entered the house again, by another door.

The room in which he found himself was his father's library, which also gave on to the drawing-room across a small vestibule. It had been terra incognita during the small years; his father was a great reader, as the massive rows of leather-bound volumes testified, and great readers were not to be interrupted, particularly by rumbustious little boys whose pleasures ran to sunshine and trout tickling and wild cross-country pony rides. But latterly, Richard had seen more of it; it contained, besides books in abundance, other things which he had grown absorbed in – ancient maps, old prints of far-off places, sailing ship models with their rigging minutely strung, and the 'great terrestrial globe' which was now, incontestably, his own.

Crossing the room past the leather-topped mahogany desk, he put his hand on the curved surface of the globe. His father, a world traveller in his youth, had had it specially made for his entertainment; it was more than four feet in diameter, and it revolved as ponderously upon its axis as if it were the great world itself ... In his adolescence Richard had been wont to play a game, turning the globe on its free-running spindle, shutting his eyes, stabbing with his forefinger at the surface of this manikin earth, opening his eyes again to see where fortune would take him, sometime in the distant future. He was destined, he learned, to voyage to Fukien Province in far-off China, to Peru, to the Ivory Coast of Africa, to a spot in mid-Pacific labelled 'Three Thousand Fathoms Here' ... Now it was almost all he possessed. He could play with it to his heart's content – his terrestrial globe, and his two pistols.

The music, which had started again, came to its appointed end. Moving a few steps within the library, lit by a single lamp, he could see through the open door into the drawing-room. Lucinda had risen from the piano, and was talking to Miles, smiling at him again; but presently, as Richard watched, Miles bowed slightly, excusing himself, and turned away. It must be some estate matter; or perhaps, as he sometimes did, he was going to visit the stables, to give orders for the morning. Left alone, Lucinda remained standing by the piano, her graceful figure in the black gown outlined against tall gold curtains. From where Richard stood, Mrs Merriman was out of sight.

He called softly: 'Lucinda!'

She heard him, and looked, startled, in his direction. But she made no move until he called again: 'Lucinda – in the library.' Then, with a side-glance at her aunt, she walked through, and stood in the doorway, staring at him. In the half-light, her face was withdrawn, even cold.

She said: 'I can scarcely see you, Richard.' Her tone also was remote and without warmth. 'Why are you here? – I thought you had retired.'

He took a step towards her. She seemed intensely desirable at that moment; he wanted to take her in his arms, without a word spoken. It would be for the first time, but his discontent and unhappiness were so great that it seemed only her close presence could cure them. He took another step, and reached out his hand. 'My dearest Lucinda,' he said.

She drew back as if he had offered her some astonishing insult. 'You forget yourself,' she said. There was a freezing tone in her voice which he had never heard before. 'You have done so all evening … It would be far better if you did retire.'

She turned, making as if to leave him again. Her remoteness was more than he could accept; love and anger warred with each other, and anger overtopped all other emotion. He put his arm across the threshold, barring her way. 'I am not drunk,' he said.

She was immobile again, disdaining to touch him. 'I do not care if you are drunk or not.' Then she suddenly melted – but she melted into scorn, not into tenderness. 'Richard, why did you do it? You have behaved disgracefully!'

'Why did I do what?'

She gestured, impatiently. 'You know very well what I mean! You insulted Miles – you behaved like a boor – you were not even sober when I arrived!'

'It has been a hard day, Lucinda.'

'No harder than you deserve.' She looked at him with cold eyes. 'And to wear that ridiculous red coat! It is unforgivable, at a time of mourning. What are you thinking of? You should be ashamed of yourself.'

'I can mourn my father as well in red as in black,' he answered her curtly. 'Or perhaps you would prefer me to parade in naval uniform?'

'What do you mean by that?'

'I was watching you together. You were smiling at him. You have never smiled at Miles in your life! Why this sudden change? Because I am poor?'

'There is no sudden change. Being poor has nothing to do with what I feel.' But she was embarrassed by his questioning; she looked away from him, towards the drawing-room, and her breathing was faster. 'I must go back,' she said briefly. 'Let me by, please.'

'Hear me out, Lucinda.' He had not been in the humour for pleading; but her lovely face, and her magnificent body so close to his, were deeply distracting, 'Don't be cold – not tonight! It's more than I can bear.' He swallowed, overcoming his nervousness; he had not meant to speak, but at that moment there was nothing in the world he could do except avow his love. 'You must have known for a long time.'

'Known what?'

'That I would ask you to marry me.'

Now there was silence between them; it seemed to stretch to infinity, while slowly his hopes turned cold, and despair, waiting to capture him, drew nearer. For her face was averted, and though she was clearly moved, yet there was no answering softness in her expression, no element of love or tenderness. After a moment she said: 'I cannot marry you, Richard.'

Despair flooded in; her voice was so final, and her expression now so firm, that he knew she would never change her mind. He dropped his arm, and moved back a pace.

'Because I am poor?'

'I cannot marry you, Richard,' she repeated. Perhaps it was all she intended to say; but, raising her eyes, she saw such an odd look in his face, so strange a compound of sadness, anger, and scorn, that she could not ignore it. 'How can we marry?' she asked, almost violently. 'You are poor. You know my own position … It is true that I had hoped – '

'That I would inherit half the estate?'

Suddenly she was angry herself. 'Yes – if you must know the truth! I have lived in poverty ever since I can remember! It has been scrimp and save, scrimp and save, since the day my father died. I could not even stay a whole season in London! Do you know what that means?

Do you think I plan to spend the rest of my life in the same situation?
I would rather die!'

'You mean, you would rather marry Miles.'

'You are insulting!'

She moved swiftly to leave him – imperious, not to be trifled with
any longer – but this time he grasped her by the shoulders and held
her close. It was a moment he had often dreamt of; but now, when
at last it happened, it was as if he were embracing a figure of stone.
Even her superb bosom, so frankly displayed for his delight, might
have been cold marble. He pressed her more closely to him, in
intimate contact, seeking to melt the ice into the warm passion he
knew was waiting within. But her body, as tense as a coiled spring,
did not relax its rigor by a single heartbeat.

'Let go of me,' she said contemptuously, as if she were speaking
to some beggar who was pestering her. 'I am not one of your village
conquests.' When he failed to obey, she raised her hand and dealt
him a stinging slap on the side of his face. 'Now do you
understand?'

It was a moment of such vile shock that he could scarcely
comprehend what had happened. This avenging stranger could not
be Lucinda … Yet it was, and she was looking at him with eyes from
which all trace even of friendly feeling had vanished.

'For the first time,' he muttered, momentarily stunned by the
pain. Then he dropped his arms, releasing her. 'Yes, I understand,
Lucinda.'

'Then see that you remember it tomorrow,' she said, with cutting
emphasis. She eyed him once more, searching his face as if on the
watch for any hint of defiance. Then she was gone, leaving him
bereft and alone, and slowly awakening to the full measure of his
desolation.

VI

'But sleep on it!' pleaded Sebastian Wickham, in agitation. He was sitting up in bed, the covers drawn up to his chin against the colds and draughts of the attic room; atop his head, an absurd old nightcap, of threadbare red flannel, was perched like a weathercock on a church steeple. He had been dozing over a book when Richard had found him; now he was fully awake, and intent on dissuading Richard from his plan. 'There cannot be such need for haste. To leave like this, in the middle of the night! What do you intend? Where are you going?'

'I will go anywhere,' answered Richard violently. He was already geared for the road; his heavy boots fell solidly on the bare floor, and the shoulders of his frogged top coat cast giant shadows on the ceiling. 'Anywhere to escape this cursed place. I will join Garibaldi's redshirts in Italy! I will go to the California gold fields!'

'California!' echoed the old man, in dismay. 'It is half across the world. What will you do there?'

'Make my fortune, I hope. Certainly I have none here.'

'Only wait till the morning,' pleaded Wickham again. 'Things will seem different when you have weighed the good and the bad. You cannot leave like this, in a sudden rage. Sleep on your decision, I beg you.'

'I cannot,' said Richard. 'My mind is made up.'

And indeed, it was. Since the terrible scene with Lucinda, he had moved swiftly, spurred by a desperate, all-embracing rage such as he had never known before. His servant, John Keston, roused from his bed over the stables, had already packed a single trunk for him – he would not burden himself with the clutter of the past, he would shake as much dust as he could off his boots … He had two hundred sovereigns in gold, the residue of a fortunate win at cards which had come his way a few days previously; a light carriage, already ordered, would take him to Chepstow, and thence he would board the morning stage for Gloucester and Bristol. There was nothing to stop him, and everything to impel him onwards. He had climbed up to Sebastian Wickham's room, not to discuss his plans or to seek advice, but simply to say farewell. Save for two or three of the older servants, it would be his only farewell in all Marriott.

'But there cannot be such need for haste,' said the old man again. 'You were angry this afternoon, and shocked by what I told you, but you did not plan to leave within a few hours, did you? At least, you did not tell me so. What has brought things to such a desperate pitch?'

'I have been thinking,' answered Richard. Then the need for honesty, the compulsion to speak the truth to Sebastian Wickham, the one man in the world who now commanded his respect and his love, took possession of him. 'Nay, Sebastian, I would not lie to you. I have been drinking, not thinking. I had a final quarrel with Miles. Indeed, I forced it on him. He came near to telling me to leave the house, then and there.' He raised his arm in a hopeless gesture. 'What is the use of staying, anyway? I have no money, I have no place here. There will be no secret about my birth, after a few months have gone by. Miles will see to that. I must go!'

'You had a quarrel with Miles? When was this?'

'At dinner, in public ... Oh, I am not proud of it, but I would do it again, with pleasure!'

The old man looked at him, more closely. 'Was Lucinda present when this happened?'

'Yes. And her aunt as well. And some of the servants. We had a most attentive audience.'

'What does Lucinda say?'

Richard's expression was bitter. 'She says the same as Miles, in the way that a woman can say it best.'

'I do not understand.'

'She will not marry me, because I am poor.'

'I cannot believe that.'

'Nor did I, until I heard it.' His bitter expression returned, and his hand went up to his cheek. 'And felt it ... One way in which I could quickly restore my fortunes would be to wager ten thousand pounds that she will be marrying brother Miles, within the year.'

But the old man hardly heard the taunting phrase; he was sunk in thought again. He felt already that his protests were doomed to be unavailing; he had known Richard Marriott, from a boy to a man, for fifteen years, and he recognized – none better – when Richard's stubborn spirit was intent on something from which he could not be turned. Perhaps it was better, if there must be a farewell, that it should come thus, swiftly and decisively; Richard had been mortally hurt, but he might be hurt even more if he lingered on, in a situation which contained all the seeds of strife and insult. The girl – the pretty girl whom he had been ready to love – must have seemed to be dealing him a final stroke of treachery ... Wickham himself could not, in all honesty, counsel patience and forbearance, when Richard might well break his heart before he improved his condition by a hair's breadth.

Now he said, resignedly: 'So you feel you must go ... Well, in that case I'll say no more, Richard, But what about money for this journey of yours, wherever it takes you? Have you any funds available?'

'I have enough,' answered Richard. He smiled wryly. 'And I will take half of my legacy with me.'

'Half?'

'Aye. I'll leave the globe, and take the pistols.'

The old man nodded, abstractedly. 'Perhaps there was a message for you, there.'

'Message?'

'Yes.' He looked up at Richard's tall figure; he was becoming reconciled to many things, reconciled even to saying farewell. 'Your father loved you, Richard. You cannot know the true reason why he left all his money to Miles. No other person can. It might be that he thought Miles would need it more – to keep up the title and the estates. Or perhaps he thought that you would not need it at all – that you were the sort of young man who would make his way in the world, whatever happened, without a fortune ready to hand.'

Wickham leant forward, and his old man's voice strengthened and gained in encouragement. 'Aye, that was it! That was what the legacy meant. He left you the world, and he left you the weapons to conquer it! Don't you see what was in his mind? He trusted you, Richard, and he believed in you, and this was his method of telling you so.'

'I had rather he had told me so with fifty thousand pounds,' answered Richard, sarcastically. Later, he might dwell on this thought of Sebastian Wickham's, and even draw comfort from it; but at this moment, it would take more than the doubtful symbolism of a legacy to ease his spirit. 'There is one thing you can tell me, Sebastian,' he continued. 'My mother. Do you know if she is still alive?'

The old man shook his head. 'I do not know, Richard. I have never known – it was not spoken of. Perhaps it is better if you gave it no more thought.'

'Why so?'

Wickham hesitated. 'We cannot tell what became of her,' he said finally, 'nor what misfortunes may have followed. It is a cruel world for women in such a situation.'

'But do you know anything?'

'No.' He felt he must reassure the young man, so clearly troubled. 'I swear that is true, Richard. I know simply that she was sent away.'

'Like myself,' said Richard hardly. 'It seems to be a family custom.'

'You must not judge harshly.'

'I do not judge at all. I accept what has happened. But certainly I will make my own terms in the future.' He came to a stop at the foot of the bed, and looked down at the old man, so frail, so defenceless himself. 'I doubt we shall meet again, Sebastian. You will have your own troubles, I know. I wish I could help you.'

'Oh, I shall manage well enough.'

'I hope so, with all my heart.' Suddenly Richard was deeply moved: they were both beggars, he and Sebastian, but the old man was the worse off, because he had the fatal score of five-and-sixty years chalked against his name. It was, in truth, Sebastian who was likely to be betrayed, and he himself who had hope and strength for the future ... He walked to the edge of the bed, and took Sebastian's hand in his. It was paper-thin; it would be no match for the traps and spites of the world. 'If I cannot have a father's blessing,' he said, with difficulty, 'or a brother's either, may I have a tutor's?'

The old man looked up, startled. He had thought that Richard might be jesting, but a single glance at the other's face was sufficient to tell him that he was in earnest, and that he felt this moment of parting more than any other.

'Why, Richard!' he said, much moved in his turn. 'Of course you have all my good wishes! And my prayers too, for what they are worth. I will think of you constantly, and with great affection. You know that.'

'I will remember it.'

'Remember something else, then.' Wickham pressed his hand, and then released it. 'You are bitter and angry now, and perhaps you have some right to be. But do not bear it as a grudge forever. Bitterness will be wasteful, destructive, and can profit you nothing at all. Five years from now, ten years from now, it will not matter a jot that you were baulked of your inheritance. You will be laughing at it. You will make your own inheritance – your own kingdom! Your father knew this, and I know it. Believe in it yourself!'

'I will try.' Richard rose from the bed, and drew his coat across his chest with a gesture of finality. At this last moment, he was near to tears, and he sought to dissemble it. 'I go to seek my own kingdom,' he said lightly, 'with the whole world to choose from.'

'When you find that kingdom,' said Sebastian Wickham, 'make sure you use it well.'

He said no more goodbyes; Lucinda and her aunt had long departed, and Miles, if he were still awake, would scarcely thank him for the courtesy. Coming downstairs from his bedroom, treading the broad staircase easily, he felt a swift return of his confidence; this need be no tragedy after all, it was the threshold of the real world. In his father's library, he sought and found the box of pistols which were lawfully his. They were beautiful weapons, which he had long admired; a matched pair, silver-crested, on the butts of which were inlaid curious masks, of smiling lions' faces. He put the polished teak case under his arm, and strode out into the hall.

John Keston was standing ready, soberly clad in a long coat of dark grey. Beyond him, the great front door was open, and the yellow carriage lights were flickering.

'Ready?' asked Richard curtly.

'Aye, sir,' answered John Keston. 'The luggage is corded up and loaded.'

Richard looked at him. There was no particular expression in his servant's face, simply an acceptance that this sudden midnight departure was necessary. A stolid young man whose devotion was grounded in a hundred forgotten incidents of the past, he was taking all these strange events in his stride. Richard remembered his earlier words: 'We'll do no good here.' They had been, it seemed, enough to dispose of the whole matter. But there was still room for the doubtings of conscience.

'I would not wish to press you,' said Richard suddenly. 'My own mind is made up, to leave now. I have reasons enough. But if you would rather stay –'

'Sir, my place is with you,' answered John Keston formally. Then he added, in a rare display of feeling: 'But I will be happy enough to go. I have as little to take leave of here as you yourself.'

Richard clapped his tall hat on his head, and laughed cheerfully. 'I have nothing,' he declared, 'and so nothing delays us. Let us make a start.'

Then, without a backward glance, he walked out towards the carriage, and towards all else that lay in wait for him – Bristol, the sea, and the wide world.

BOOK TWO

The Pirate: 1860

The brigantine Lucinda D, two hundred and twenty tons, becalmed on a moonless night after eight hard-pressed days of storm, was hopelessly lost. It was not the first time that this had happened, in these Far Eastern waters, where a burning sun could be dowsed by fog within the hour, where a typhoon could come up like a bolt of lightning, where a south-westerly monsoon might veer, at the change of seasons, until it blew from the opposite point of the compass; where trustworthy charts were as precious and as secret as the state papers of the Dutch Government itself. But it had never before happened in such harsh circumstances.

They had lost a top-mast, in that eight-day turmoil; they had lost two Kanaka seamen, swept overboard as if they had been plucked out of life by a giant hand; they had lost a foresail, torn from its bolt ropes in a single violent second. Above all, they had lost their way; and now they were wandering, fingering their progress in the uncertain dark across a sea suddenly calm, suddenly blank.

They might be anywhere, thought Richard Marriott, standing feet apart in his accustomed place beside the helmsman – the helmsman transformed by the night into two disembodied hands clasping and unclasping on the wheel spokes, and a face made spectral by the yellow glare of the binnacle lamp. When darkness had fallen, great thunder-headed clouds had obscured the sky; later, when the heavens had cleared, Sirius the Dog Star – beloved friend of all mariners – had faded too early for his sextant to be any use. Now it was the blackest hour of the night, the hour before the dawn; and the Lucinda D, battered and bruised from her fearsome struggle, wallowed under storm canvas which could not be replaced until daylight showed them the extent of their damage. All that Richard Marriott knew was what any common ruffian on board knew; they were still afloat, on a pitch-black night, on a pitch-black sea.

A week earlier, they had been idling down the outer coast of Sumatra, seeing what they might see, stealing what they might find. The fury of the typhoon had blown them north-eastwards through the Sunda Strait, the great sally port to the Indian Ocean, and up into the Java Sea. Then there had followed days of violence and fury, with a pounding easterly drift which could not be checked. Now they were somewhere between Borneo and New Guinea – anywhere, that was, within an enormous featureless box a thousand miles long and five hundred wide.

There was a stirring and a stumbling on the ladders as the watch changed; shadowy forms could be glimpsed against the fo'c'sle lantern, rolling figures loomed nearer, bare feet padded on the smooth planking of the deck, matching the flap-flap of canvas as the idle sails slatted. There were voices he recognized, oaths and greetings he had heard a hundred times before. The helmsman at his side – that was Peal, the ex-tinker turned skilful seaman – growled at his relief: 'North by east – there's barely steerage way,' and the man taking over the wheel – Peter Ramsay, the lower deck Queen's Bencher, the real sea lawyer – growled back: 'North by east it is!' as if he were turning away a rebuke or dismissing an argument.

Richard Marriott stood fast; the change was not for him; captains did not change with the watch, they endured forever, sustaining themselves, and their whole command, until the ship was out of danger. He had been wakeful for many days now, nursing the Lucinda D through her ordeal, trying to fix their position from vague headlands glimpsed through the scud, from soundings which brought up mud, or coral sand, or nothing, from guessing at the sun through the murky overcast. He had lent a hand at the wheel, he had helped to subdue torn canvas thrashing itself to ribbons on the yards, he had cheered his men and cursed the slow-witted and the afraid. That was what it was, to be a captain; he had discharged it heartily for five years, and he would discharge it for five years more, or ten, or twenty, whatever the burden, come hell or high water.

'Watch on deck!' called a hard voice in the darkness, to be answered, more quietly, by: 'Watch below!' as the men now relieved trooped off for'ard, towards the shelter and warmth of the fo'c'sle. The man who called 'Watch on deck' was Nick Garrett, his second-in-command, his rival; a rough-talking giant of a man who must be kept under close survey, even at the same time as he must be trusted. They had been shipmates for many years, in the good days and the bad; they had fought for the leadership, and Garrett had finally been bested, in circumstances which had not cured his bad blood. He was forever challenging Richard Marriott's place, forever plotting and talking behind his back. But he was a brave and skilful man for all that, and Richard was content to use him and to watch him. The faithful John Keston watched him also, coolly, with a grim lack of esteem which Nick Garrett could never forgive.

The ship settled down again, after the coming and going; Peter Ramsay at the wheel spun the spokes, edging their bows offwind to catch a fleeting breeze; Richard Marriott walked to the rail, and stared down at the black water, and walked back again. Out of the darkness, Nick Garrett asked: 'Anything in sight yet?'

'No,' answered Richard.

'Did you manage a star-sight?'

'No.'

Garrett cleared his throat, and spat noisily. 'We might be in the China Sea, for all we know.'

Richard said nothing; this was, for Nick Garrett, common talk – the hint of incompetence, the implication that Richard Marriott did not know his task and would, if it were left to him, run all their heads into a noose. There was a murmur of voices from amidships, and the sound of a concertina picking its plaintive way through the tune of 'Johnny's Gone Down to Hilo'. That was Tom Dowling, forever dreaming of the old days with the thrusting Baltimore clippers ... The torn mainsail slapped against a loose shroud overhead. At his side, Peter Ramsay the sea-lawyer said in his whining voice: 'Maybe the boy has brought us bad luck after all.'

Richard disregarded this; Ramsay also was a malcontent, seizing on anything that might be good for a complaint or a snarling argument below decks. But after a moment, Nick Garrett took up the lead.

'Aye, you may be right. A baby and a woman on board – that's asking for misfortune.'

'The woman alone is enough to put God's curse on any ship,' proclaimed Peter Ramsay, with ready spite. 'An old Malay bawd with a tongue like a – '

'Watch your helm!' called out Richard Marriott sharply. 'You're a point or more off your course.'

'She won't answer,' said Ramsay. His tone was cheeky and argumentative. 'There's not enough wind to fill the lashings of a hammock.'

'Watch your helm,' said Richard again. He had had enough of whining and disputing for that night. 'And keep your tongue off the boy. You were all happy enough when he came aboard. You said he would bring us good luck, not bad.'

'I never said he would bring us good luck,' put in Nick Garrett, in a harsh voice. 'I never said aught, except to damn the old woman for a witch. I shipped on board a brigantine, not a travelling circus.'

'You can ship off again, if you've a mind to,' said Richard Marriott contemptuously. 'You can swim off, for all I care.' He raised his voice, ignoring his company, and called out for'ard: 'Keston!'

'Aye, sir,' came an answering hail.

'Bring my jacket.'

The dew had begun to fall, or perhaps it was the morning mist, low-lying in these tropic seas; there was a foggy chillness in the air, which would last until the sun burned it away in an hour or so. Richard Marriott waited in the darkness, conscious of forebodings. Garrett and Peter Ramsay, known troublemakers, would always talk thus, always grumble and sneer; it was their nature, like a cat that spits at a dog – even a friendly dog. But soon, if nothing hopeful happened, if they did not make a landfall or fix their position, others would be talking too. The Lucinda D had not been so successful of late that they would all welcome a stretch of careless sea time, a rich man's pleasure cruise ... Against the gleam of the fo'c'sle lantern, a figure moved towards him. It was John Keaton.

'Here, sir,' he said.

Richard Marriott took the proffered pea jacket, and slipped it over his shoulders. The warmth comforted him, the rough blue serge had a companionable familiarity. Thus armoured, he could face the world with strength and confidence ... At his side, Peter Ramsay spun the wheel again, and the cables leading to the tiller-head rattled and clanked under their feet. Out of the darkness, Nick Garrett spoke: 'We need to take soundings, going blindly like this. Is there a hand ready in the chains?'

It was a question for John Keston, and he answered: 'Aye. James Singleton is there.'

Nick Garrett laughed, not pleasantly. 'Marvellous to hear! I thought the whole watch might be busy with fetching and carrying of jackets!'

Richard Marriott rounded on him, stung into an angry retort. 'I'll give what orders I choose!' he said loudly. 'If I want a jacket, I'll have a jacket brought. If I want to gnaw on a heel of beef, I'll have that, too. The men will do my bidding, as long as I command.'

'I have a watch to run,' said Garrett sulkily.

'I have a ship to run. My ship. And by God – '

He was interrupted suddenly, by a faraway hail from the masthead lookout, ninety feet above their heads. 'Below there! On deck!'

Richard Marriott bent back his head and cupped his hands. 'Masthead!' he shouted in return.

'A light to port!'

Richard crossed the deck in a stride and jumped up on to the port rail, steadying himself with an arm clasped round the shrouds. He searched the horizon, but he could see nothing save blackness, and pale setting stars.

'Where away?' he called out

'Port beam … Fixed light … Burning yellow.'

Richard turned inboard, and clambered halfway up the rigging, till he was well above the deck level. Then he searched again, and this time he found what he sought, a faint yellow gleam in the darkness, a pinpoint of light. It was the first such sighting, for many days and nights, and his heart brightened as he saw it. It might be any one of a thousand lights, it might mean danger or even treachery; but at least it was human contact again, it could lead them back, by slow stages if need be, to the world they had lost.

He made a swift calculation, judging courses, judging angles of approach, and the sailing skills of his ship and his men. The wind, though finger-soft, was gaining, and blowing them fair; if they went about on the other tack, they should fetch up with the light, or at least come near enough to make out what it was. And by that time it would be dawn, and they could see what their prospects were.

He jumped down again, ready for action. 'We'll go about,' he called to Nick Garrett. 'Rouse up your watch.' And then to Peter Ramsay the helmsman: 'Stand by to go about!' he ordered. 'And give her a good full, or she won't come round, in this little breeze.'

Nick Garrett had walked forward to muster his hands; already there was a stir as they prepared to tend the sheets and tail on to the braces.

'What light is that, then?' asked Peter Ramsay, as he put the wheel over to free the wind for their turn.

'We go to find out,' answered Richard Marriott curtly. 'Down helm! Bring her round sharply.'

At that moment, even with the light beckoning them on the horizon, they were still lost. This might now be the end of it, or it might be a will-o'-the-wisp, a false promise. But it did not greatly matter – such was his new mood of hope. The Lucinda D had been lost before, many times – just as had Richard Marriott himself, in ten wild years of wandering.

II

He was tougher, broader, stronger, more ruthless; compared with the youth of twenty who had left Marriott in such angry haste, the young man of thirty seemed a full generation older. The wandering had made the man; and the man, standing on the deck of his own ship, waiting for a Far Eastern dawn, was a man to be reckoned with, a hard man to cross.

It had been California first – California in the raucous gold rush days of 1850, when a quick fortune was the magnet for half the villains and thieves of Europe and America, and double-dealing was a currency almost the equal of gold itself. He was a year late upon the scene, a year behind the forerunners and the pioneers who had skimmed the cream; too young to avoid mistakes, too honest for pure villainy, he had not prospered, so that he left the gold fields of the Sacramento Valley little richer than when he arrived. Still attended by John Keston, he came back round the Horn, in a bleak, roaring winter voyage, and presently found himself in Liverpool.

The next few years had proved more profitable. He had some money saved; he invested all of it, and made two voyages himself, in a ship navigating the infamous 'Round Trip' – from Liverpool to the Slave Coast of West Africa with a mixed cargo of gin, beads, old firearms, and cheap trade goods; thence to the West Indies, loaded with twelve hundred black wretches, of whom more than nine hundred survived to be sold as slaves to the plantations; and then back to England again, their hatches crammed with sugar, tobacco, carved coral ornaments, and hogsheads of Barbados rum, as thick and as potent as treacle.

The profits were enormous (the slaves alone brought £30 a head), but the trade too risky; for more than forty years the British Navy had been fighting this stain upon the sea, and slowly they were succeeding in ridding the world of it. Blackbirding (he decided) had become too hazardous, as well as too strong for his stomach; returning to Liverpool, after a narrow escape from the law, and a brush with an American privateer off the coast of Cuba, he determined to move on. There must be easier waters, simpler fortunes to be had for the picking, without climbing halfway to Gallows Hill to enrich (along with himself) the smug merchants of the Merseyside.

He had £10,000 saved – a huge sum, but not enough for the future, for what he kept in mind. (He had cherished, for a long time, a vision of returning to Marriott, making his brother bankrupt, and taking over the great house again; or of buying some noble neighbouring estate and lording it over his poor relation. The childish dream had faded, but the urge to make his way in the world had never grown less.) With his money, he had bought his own ship, a brigantine newly built on the Tyne, in a forced sale for some debt of law; he had renamed her the Lucinda D, from a caprice which now meant nothing to him; and with her he had sailed for the China Seas, to see, enjoy, and ravish the other half of the world.

That had been five years earlier; and they had been five years of unending violence, harsh dealing, and piracy, in Far Eastern waters swarming with rogues. Richard Marriott had come to know, at first hand, every villainous character who infested the waters round the Malay Archipelago, Borneo, Celebes, the Moluccas, Java Head, and Sumatra. They ranged from crooked traders to British privateers; from Arab slaverunners to opium smugglers in ancient pole junks; from Chinese pirates to American mutineers on the run. He and his crew of twenty-three, recruited man by man over the years, feared nothing under heaven; they ran appalling risks daily, from the weather, from other freebooters like themselves, from disease and treachery; they had never met their match but once, nor were they likely to.

Nick Garrett had served four years with him; and the others – Tom Dowling, Peter Ramsay, James Singleton, Peal and Henty and Burnside; the cheerful Kanakas who worked the deck, the Negro cook who was a runaway from Charleston, Carolina – all were now welded into a crew ready to take on any task, if it promised to show the profit which they divided at the month's end. The Lucinda D was geared for anything. She had smuggled opium – the best opium, from Patna in northern India, wrapped in poppy leaves, hidden in chests of tea. She had fought Chinese pirates, she had raided settlements on the coasts of Sarawak and Cochin China and Timor, stealing gold, stealing pearls, stealing women and barrels of rice wine and arms of any kind.

She had carried for trade, she had carried for revolutions, she had carried for love of profit and for hatred of the law. She had carried consignments of dried fish, and arrack wine distilled from coconuts, and Malabar teak; legal goods which, mysteriously swollen by saltwater invoices concocted while at sea, had sold for thrice their value on arrival. She had carried an elephant for a Maharajah, and smuggled spices to beat the Dutch monopoly, and a score of sloe-eyed boys for the Foochow merchants who relished such diversions. She had fought battles at sea – in the Pelews, in the Spice Islands; battles with lateen-rigged Arab dhows, battles with East Indiamen lagging behind their convoys; battles with the picaroons who were the little lice of piracy, and with redoubtable men like Black Harris of Boston, who could claim to be the very whale of evil.

In all these years, Richard Marriott had never been bested, save once by this same Black Harris; and that had been a matter of cut-throat cunning, not of valour or endurance.

He had grown tough and hard in this progress. He ruled his crew with an iron fist; he drove his ship with the same harsh insistence. They had arms aplenty, and they used them; flintlock blunderbusses, muskets, pistols, cutlasses for the close work of boarding. They had a cannon set in the bows of the ship; they had – a great prize this, stolen in the China Wars – a repeating rifle gun which could (and often did) fire five rounds of ball before it grew red-hot. When discipline and punishment were necessary on board, it was swift and crude; borrowing from the old-time pirates, he had once keel-hauled a man caught stealing, and another time had used the old Spanish strappado – the culprit's arms tied behind his back, with the rope leading to the yardarm, and the man then pushed off the yard, to fall twenty feet or more, and to be brought up short in mid-air, with his arms jerked out of their sockets. He had little trouble now, save when – as lately – they went for weeks without meeting a ship to plunder or a merchant to rob, and the malcontents among the crew took to grumbling and shirking.

Finally there had been the boy, the year-old child whom Nick Garrett and Peter Ramsay had seen fit to whine about. The boy was his own son; he would never doubt it; and he did not regret the fact, though the manner of getting this, his firstborn, had been somewhat short of what was proper, for a possible heir to Marriott.

In Batavia, the trading settlement on the island of Java which the Dutch had turned into a bristling fortress, he had some sport, two years back, with a cheerful harlot, one Biddy Booker, a girl of the taverns who had professed to love him. When he returned, after a spell of foraging on the New Guinea coast, it was to find her dying. She had been brought to bed, and the birth was difficult, and the filthy-clawed midwife who attended her could do little save mutter spells and give her herb potions to ease her pain.

In all the deaths he had seen, in all the deaths he had encompassed, he had never forgotten that deathbed. She was in agony; the child, puny and pale, cried without ceasing; the old Malay woman who had befriended her stared at him from a corner of the noisome room with baleful, unwinking eyes. To smooth her passing, he had promised Biddy Booker many things; a decent burial in sacred ground, a sum of money for the woman, whose name was Manina, and care for the child, which he acknowledged as his own. He had been ready to forget the last promise – any man in this part of the world could get himself a dozen bastards, and sail away laughing. But when the Lucinda D was three days out from Batavia on her next voyage, Manina had appeared from below, with the child in her arms.

He cursed the crew, who must have helped them to stow away; he threatened to put Manina and the brat ashore at the next place they touched at, no matter how desolate or outlandish it might be. But then he had changed his mind and relented – aided again by the crew, who adopted the child as the ship's mascot, and made much of it, in the sentimental way of sailors. It would bring them luck, or so they claimed.

Manina, a grotesque figure in tunic and black trousers, as shrivelled, ugly, and sexless as a walnut, remained on board, making herself useful at cooking and cleaning and patching ragged clothes. The child, whom he called Adam, remained on board also. Presently it cried less, and took to laughing, and grew sturdy and brown. To love such a come-by-chance seemed weakness and foolishness, but Richard Marriott made bold to turn his back on any such misgivings. Adam Marriott was his son, and the Lucinda D was his ship, and anyone who wished to challenge him over either had only to say the word.

III

They came up with the light slowly, creeping over the black water under their tattered storm canvas, advancing mile by mile towards a horizon which held nothing but this pinpoint of hope. The light seemed elusive, insubstantial; burning bright and near at one moment, fading to pale mockery at another. Presently, after they had pursued it for two hours or more, it blinked twice and disappeared, as if, too long untended, the oil were exhausted, and could only flicker away, to nothing. Or perhaps it had been lit by wreckers who, lacking custom, had given up their designs for that night ... But whatever its origin, the Lucinda D now had a compass course to steer – west-nor'-west – and this course they held, towards the lighthouse or the land beacon or the people who they knew must be there.

It grew lighter; the sea paled, the fleecy clouds turned from grey to pink, and then to gold. On board the Lucinda D, shapes and shadows regained their lost dimension, and became spars and bulwarks and people. Men stretched, shrugging off the night, girding themselves for the day; Nick Garrett set his watch to shifting canvas and tending the slack braces; the cook, peering out of the galley in the waist of the ship, greeted the dawn with a yawning grin which split his black face unexpectedly into two halves, his teeth a startling shaft of white in between.

Richard called out to him: 'Sam!'

'Suh?'

'A mug of coffee here.'

'Aye, suh.'

'And a spike of rum in it.'

After the long night, he was stiff and cold, and conscious of the fatigue which endless hard days at sea must bring. But as he walked to and fro across the poop deck, to ease his cramped muscles, he was the very figure of command. His face was bearded now, and darkened by many suns; he walked with a roll, and his body, sinewy and tough, proclaimed its own authority. In his ear, a single gold earring gleamed – it was his affection, his badge of contempt for the dull world which was not Richard Marriott, and must conform to sober patterns ... The twin pistols, which he called Castor and Pollux, and still cherished, were carried in ornamental holsters at his belt. He had fired them many scores of times, in his ten years away from Marriott, and there was not a man on board the Lucinda D who would doubt his readiness to fire them again, at any time, whether for honour, for anger, or for sport.

Sam, the Negro cook, who was as good a man with a cutlass as with a skillet – indeed, a much better man, so the crew complained

– gave him his earthenware mug of coffee laced with rum, and he drank it in great gulps, without delicacy. The days of Sheffield plate and Wedgewood china were far behind him now … Then suddenly he cocked his head on one side, and sniffed the raw air. Mingled with the shipboard smells, of tarry hemp and brine cask, of the breakfast cracker hash and the sludge that served for coffee, of sweet Negrohead tobacco, there was now another smell, the smell of the land.

He sniffed again, and again he caught it. Somewhere, borne on the freshening breeze, was the familiar reek of Far Eastern islands; the waft of dried or rotting fish, of palm oil, woodsmoke, hot sand. It was as different from the smell of a ship as dog was from cat. He called sharply to Garrett, busy in the waist: 'Soundings!' and then, throwing back his head: 'Masthead, there! Masthead!'

A faint hail answered him. 'Masthead.'

'D'you see anything?'

'Nothing. All clear ahead.'

'Watch out to starboard – upwind.'

Now James Singleton the leadsman, up in the chains, half turned his head as he reeled in his dripping line, and prepared to make his cast again. 'No bottom – no bottom at thirty fathom!' he shouted.

'Keep sounding.' Richard commanded. 'We're closing something.'

Then, as an eddy of wind pushed aside the mist that clung to the surface of the water, they all saw it at the same instant. Their will-o'-the-wisp light had become a lighthouse, a lighthouse on stilts, two or three miles away to starboard. By a trick of the mist, it seemed to grow awkwardly, even grotesquely, out of the sea; a squat tower on spindly legs, with a fringe of bearded coconut palms at its base. Even as they stared at it, the mist came down, and hid it again.

'Back your topsails!' Richard ordered swiftly, and as the watch jumped to the task, the helmsman, knowing his business, spun the wheel to bring the ship into the wind. Within a few moments, the Lucinda D, nicely balanced, came to a gentle stop, hove-to.

'We'll stay where we are, until full daylight,' said Richard, when their movement ceased, and the only sound was the water running and lapping against their hull. 'When the sun gets up, it will soon burn off this fog.'

They did not have long to wait. Presently, parted by the breeze, thinned by the sun still below the horizon, the mist began to disperse, and the long-legged lighthouse appeared again. Now it could be seen to be stationed on a flat, low spit of sand, to which the palm trees clung precariously; but away to the right there was more land, well treed, green with vegetation, and dotted here and there with huts from which thin drifts of smoke sometimes spiralled upwards. As far as the eye could reach, the land rose in gentle sloping tiers, till the air grew hazy and it was lost in the mist again.

On their port hand there was nothing save open sea. The lighthouse, it seemed, marked the western tip of some island, their first true landfall for more than a week.

Richard Marriott studied it, first with the naked eye, then with his glass. So far, it was like a hundred other islands; it might be big or small; the huts meant that it was inhabited, the lighthouse, tended during the night, meant that it was of some consequence – a Dutch settlement, or at least a calling place for ships. But the shape of it, and the land sloping up eastwards, stirred no recollection at all. To the best of his memory, he had never seen it before.

He called out to Garrett: 'Do you know it, Nick?' but Garrett, also staring, shook his head.

'It has the look of one of the Paternosters,' he answered, over his shoulder. 'But there is no lighthouse there like this one, that I know of.'

Peter Ramsay, who liked to consider himself a navigator, said: 'There's a cape in New Britain has a light like that. Cape Gloucester, isn't it? Towards the New Guinea coast.'

'That looks north,' said Richard briefly. 'This is the western end of some island or other.'

He spread what charts he had on the cabin top, and cast a careful eye over them. The charts were cracked, and weathered by seawater, and faded to yellow ochre by the sun; they were the best he possessed, which, in these waters, even in the up-to-the-minute world of 1860, was not to say a great deal. The best charting of the Far East had been done by the Dutch navigators, who regarded these parts – against the naval might of Britain or any other nation – as their own preserve; charts were kept secret, and jealously guarded, and no ship's captain who was subject to maritime law was allowed to part with them. Those which Richard had, had been stolen from an East Indiaman wrecked on the Celebes shoals; but they were old, and often mistaken, and he had never come to trust them. Even so, they gave him no help now; there were fixed lights in abundance, all over this region; their ship might have been in China, she might have been in Timor … He looked again at the stilted lighthouse, and the land lying to the eastwards. It was clearer now, but still featureless, still unrecognized.

He made his decision. The water on their port hand was clear. He would lay a course to pass the lighthouse, leaving it to starboard, and then turn and go eastwards till he found out where they were.

'Up helm!' he ordered. 'Brace the topsails … Bring her round on west-nor'-west.'

'West-nor'-west,' repeated the helmsman. The spokes rattled through his hands as he let the wheel come over.

They had gone a mile or so, and the lighthouse was drawing abeam, when Singleton, heaving the lead at fixed intervals, shouted out: 'By the mark – ten!'

Ten fathoms … For the Lucinda D, it still meant water and to spare. The ocean bed would naturally shelve towards the lighthouse. Even the next cast – six fathoms – did not cause him any anxiety.

'What's the bottom?' he called out to the leadsman.

Singleton bent his head, examining the tallow with which the lead weight was covered. 'Clay,' he reported promptly. 'Clay and sand.'

Richard held his course. The lighthouse came abeam; he was nearly ready, having weathered it, to make his wide turn eastwards.

Then a sudden shout from for'ard brought him to urgent attention.

It was Singleton again, 'Shelving fast!' he yelled at the top of his voice. 'Three fathoms! ... Less a quarter!' And then, swiftly: 'Coral!'

Coral ... A reef ... Richard whipped round, shouting 'Up helm! Wear round!' as he did so. But he was too late. The ship, moving with smooth purpose through the water, struck suddenly, with a shuddering crash which nearly flung him off his feet. There was a sharp cracking sound, of splintered wood, from aloft – the main topmast, this time – and beneath their feet a terrible grinding of the hull as it rode up on to the coral reef – the most cruel sound a sailor could hear. Then the Lucinda D swung off wind, and came to a shaking stop, high out of the water, her keel jarring and scraping on the hidden peril below. They were fast aground, on coral rock likely to be as sharp and as fatal as a dagger.

Now all was shouting and swift movement; but it was orderly, with a set purpose. The Lucinda D had struck before – though never so harshly – and the crew knew their first tasks without any bidding. Henty, the ship's carpenter, sped below to see what damage might have been done; the cook doused the fires, for safety's sake; the watch on deck, and those others roused from their sleep, jumped cat-like into the shrouds, to take off all sail and cut away the ruin of rigging which surrounded the broken topmast. The leadsman, whose warning had come too late, began to take careful soundings all round the ship, to plot the shape of the reef and discover where safety lay. In the clear water, the reef itself could be seen, pink and green and black, encased with waving weed and mysterious sea anemones and crusted spikes of coral, as rough and cruel as it was beautiful.

Richard Marriott stood his ground beside the helmsman. He was not yet dismayed, though the solid shock and the ugly grinding beneath their feet was enough to make a sailor's heart sick. There was no pain, and no ordeal, like that of a ship ripped and tortured by coral. But the brigantine was soundly built, toughened and seasoned by years of battle with this and all other elements; she had proved her fortitude before, from the Breton coast to the shores of the South China Sea, and, unless their wound were mortal, she would do so again.

Presently a noise distracted him, a thin cry nearby which was as unlike any of the shipboard sounds as the cry of a gull in a bear pit; and when he turned, seeking the strange interruption, it was to see Manina, the Malay woman, standing at the entrance to the cabin ladder, with the child tightly clasped in her arms.

'Is he hurt?' Richard called out, anxiously.

Manina shook her head, cradling the boy who still whimpered. 'He woke suddenly,' she answered. 'It was the noise.' She looked about her, alarmed by the bustle and the strange angle of the deck; her wizened face was pinched by fear till it seemed like a shrunken nut. 'What has happened?'

'It is nothing,' answered Richard. 'We touched on a rock ... Stay here on deck, and look to the boy.' Coming closer, he fondled his son, who was silent now, looking about him with bright sharp eyes. It was only the sudden waking which had made him cry. 'Stay where you are,' he commanded again, 'till we see what has to be done.'

Henty, the carpenter, appeared now at the head of the ladder, blinking at the light. He carried a heavy caulking mallet and some strands of flax in his hand. As he approached, his bare feet left gleaming footmarks on the deck, and his legs were wet to mid-thigh.

'We are holed,' he said, matter-of-factly. In all the years on board, Richard had never yet seen him shaken or taken aback, and the moment of crisis had not dismayed him now. He might have been reporting a splinter in his thumb. 'Close to the keel, on the starboard side. Six frames back, level with the foremast.'

'How badly?'

Henty spread his hands, as a man telling the size of a fish to a friend. 'A foot, maybe. I've plugged the worst of it with sailcloth and tallow. But there's four or five planks started, and two feet of water already. You must man the pumps, before it gains any more hold.'

'Can we stay afloat, d'you reckon?'

'Aye, if it gets no worse. But there'll be more planks opening up, if we stay like this on the reef. You can feel how she's working, all the time.'

Nick Garrett, who had overheard, was already setting the pump's crew, of three hands to either side, to man the heavy levers. Above their heads, silence was falling as the canvas was taken off and the two halves of the wrecked top-mast were lowered to the deck. The Lucinda D, under bare poles, sat awkwardly upon the reef, as daylight spread and the treacherous lighthouse which had lured them on to this peril, came up clear and stark against the bright sky.

Richard considered their situation. They could not stay very long where they were; his ship, even in this sluggish sea, would grind to pieces if she continued to lie on the reef. Somehow they must coax her off into deeper soundings – but inside the reef, where shelter lay – and trust to the pumps to keep her afloat until they could find some bay or sand spit on which to beach her. Already it was clear that, before they could set sail again, she must be careened, in shallow water, so that they could patch up the hull properly and make it seaworthy.

He called out to Singleton, the leadsman: 'How deep is it, then?'

Singleton came aft, coiling in his dripping line as he walked. 'Twelve feet all round,' he answered. 'It is a flat ledge, and we are on top of it. But there's deeper water ahead, if we can reach it.'

Richard considered again. His ship, loaded as she was, drew fifteen feet of water; if she were now in twelve, she needed only a little more, in order to float off; they could, if necessary, lower a boat, lay out a kedge anchor ahead, and pull her out of trouble. With coral rock, however, it was a dangerous manoeuvre; their hull, moving against a chance cutting edge, could be sliced open like the rind of an orange. But there was another chance, of a different kind: if she had grounded at low water, a rising tide might float her off, without any effort on their part. For that, of course, they must wait their time; and waiting, while the ship pressed and worked against the coral ledge, had its own risks of disaster.

Nick Garrett, his work temporarily done, joined him aft on the poop deck. 'We should kedge her off,' he declared, with an authority which Richard did not relish, as soon as he was within earshot. 'We shall be torn to shreds else.'

Richard shook his head. 'She could be split, if we did that,' he answered. 'I've seen it happen, and so have you … I'll wait for the tide.'

'It could be falling. This could be high water, for all we know.'

'It could be … Keep those pumps manned.'

Garrett said sulkily: 'We have run into trouble enough, without waiting for more.' But he did not stay to argue, and Richard did not chide him for his insolence. In this hazard, tempers and nerves were taut enough already.

A full half-hour passed, while the men toiled at the pumps, seeking relief every ten minutes, and the groaning and creaking of the hull continued without respite. Singleton took his soundings, and called them continuously, but there was no change in the depth of water; they had gone aground, either at the bottom of the tide, or at the top – and if at the top, their situation was desperate. The cook brought coffee, lukewarm, heated up on a makeshift lantern, and biscuits and salt pork to stay their hunger; the sun climbed over the horizon, and began its burning sentry duty; the crew, freed from their turn at the pumps, lay on the deck in patches of shadow, not talking, waiting for the good news or the bad. Henty, who was still busy with his patching, reported they were holding their own against the leaking planks, but only just – it would be a continuous struggle, perhaps a fruitless one, unless they could properly repair the damage. Only the little boy Adam, warming to the sun, free from such doubts and cares, crawled happily about the deck.

Then suddenly there was a shout from Singleton. 'The tide's making,' he called out cheerfully, from his position up in the chains. 'There's three or four inches more beneath us. It's setting eastwards.'

Richard remained impassive, though his heart leapt at the news. His guess had proved right; by great good fortune, they had struck at low tide. In an hour or two, they might be afloat again, though they must still find shelter and a safe careenage for their repairs.

The water rose gradually, swirling and climbing over the top of the reef, while the Lucinda D lifted with it, and righted herself, and began to work loose from the grip of the coral. Presently her stern swung free, and she turned into the light wind, pivoting on a single point amidships. Richard set a light headsail, to steady her, and then a big mizzen sail to give her way over the reef. She began to creep forward, scraping and bumping across the rocks – but her solid, iron-shod keel, built for this rough treatment, was taking all the shock, and she was not coming to further harm. Presently she gave a shudder, as if shaking herself free of this indignity, and glided forward into deep water, while Singleton, with a new note of confidence in his voice, shouted: 'By the deep – five fathom!'

The water rippled and chattered musically under their forefoot as they gathered way. They were free at last, within a smooth, friendly lagoon which stretched before them in misty splendour. But (thought Richard wryly, as he gave orders to set the mainsail and lay a course eastwards), in their present case they were as free to sink as to swim.

They sailed eastwards all day, coasting along the same strip of low-lying land which they had first seen from seaward, and which seemed to continue endlessly. It was a thin arm of the mainland, more than fifty miles long, enclosing a bay (or so it seemed, from the sheltered aspect of the water) whose opposite shore could not yet be seen. On board the Lucinda D, no man, young or old, came near to recognizing it; it was still an island, like any other island, and they still could not put a name to it. But as they voyaged onwards, they watched it, and studied it, and learned much about it.

It was inhabited, and even prosperous. As soon as they began their eastward journey, they came upon a series of sampan villages – row upon row of fishing sampans, with palm-leaf canopies for shelter, linked and clustered like bees, clinging to the shoreline like a fringe of seaweed. There were nets staked out in the tideway, and others drying ashore, and the smoke from a thousand fires and the murmur of a thousand voices, and surly captive cormorants with lines tied round their gullets to prevent them swallowing their masters' fish.

There were groves of coconut trees, and scarlet-flowering plants, and bigger houses inland, and a road that wound along the coast, dusty and rough. Once they saw a small fleet of native canoes, called prahus, and men on board staring at them; once they saw a working elephant, pushing teak logs down a long green slope towards the sea. But they did not see what they were looking for – a sizeable village, with a sandy bay where they could safely careen their ship.

They stood to arms throughout the day, by Richard's orders; the deck bristled with the best of their weapons – pistols, and ancient muskets, and shotguns; the cannon in the bows was ready loaded. The day progressed to a burning noon, with the sun overhead like a ball of fire; watch succeeded watch, meal succeeded meal, and all the time the suck and thud of the pumps, ceaselessly manned at the cost of hard-driven muscles and hands skinned to the raw, could be heard and felt throughout the ship. The water, so Henty reported, was slowly gaining on them – a few inches an hour, but it was enough to ruin them in the end. If they did not find their careenage soon, they would not need to look for one. The Lucinda D, already sluggish, already wallowing, would slide quietly to the bottom of her own accord.

Twilight came, and with it a fitful wind which barely filled their sails; and still the long arm of the land continued, though it was higher now, with the green changing to purple, pricked by hundreds of oil lamps which flickered bravely against the coming of night. Their ship glided through the dusk like a pale ghost; once she came up with a big outrigger prahu, and a man dozing in the stern – a man who woke with a cry and stared after them as if he had seen a spectral ship. The leadsman chanted his soundings; the pumps laboured and groaned, as their hull settled inch by inch lower and lower. Then, with night not far away, and the first stars studding the pale sky, they crept past the corner of a protecting headland, and came upon an extraordinary sight – a flight of steps.

There could have been no other steps like them in all the world. They led up from the water's edge in a broad majestic sweep, tier upon tier, nobly balustraded; they seemed to be of marble; they must have been half a mile long. At the top, consummating this fantastic approach, was a palace, huge, of pink coral stone which, catching the last of the light, glowed in the dusk as if it were on fire deep within. Hundreds of windows gleamed in its façade. The steps themselves were strange enough, but the vast edifice topping them, with its lawns and palm trees and endless roofline sharp against the sky, had an unearthly quality. Only in fairy-tales, or in dreams, could there be such a flight of steps, and such a mansion to crown them.

On board, every man stared landwards with disbelieving eyes; it must be a mirage, a dream ... Nick Garrett, standing beside Richard, was the first to break the silence. He drew in his breath sharply.

'By God, I know this place!' he exclaimed. 'Or I have heard tell of it. It could not be anything else.' He pointed. 'They call those the Steps of Heaven.'

Richard, none the wiser, rounded on him quickly. He would have given much to avoid his question, but this was not the time for pride.

'And the island itself?'

'It is Makassang!'

Makassang ... For Far Eastern sailors, the very name had the ring of a curse; it stood for evil repute, lurking danger, nightmare terrors. Makassang, of all the thousand islands in these waters, was the one to be avoided; it was known to treat invaders like harbingers of the plague, and castaways like animals to be hunted to their death. Even now, when all the world was one, little of detail had been learned about it, save that it was cruelly hostile; in the last fifty years, two attempts to set up a British settlement had been starved to extinction, and, more recently, a Dutch trading station – though well armed and provisioned – reduced to the customary bloody ruin of fired houses, captured women, and the headless corpses which were still the brutal sign-manual of Makassang.

It was known only that the interior, largely jungle, was the haunt of headhunting Dyaks; that the northern coast, towards Borneo, was a nest of pirates which could not be flushed out; that there was a caste of warrior priests, and a rajah who kept barbaric state in this same Sun Palace crowning the Steps of Heaven. It had limitless riches, or so it was said; gold and silver, diamonds and pearls, teak and copra and spices of all kinds. But there were some riches which were too hard for the winning, even in these waters where no man of any nation lacked courage and endurance and (if need be) treachery.

Of what use was it (they asked) to come upon a silver mine, if your first blessing was a spear between the shoulderblades, and your next – and last – distinction to furnish the main course of a public banquet? ... There was easier game to be hunted hereabouts, easier pickings to be had, without challenging the skill of savages who would as soon make a necklace of your private parts as fashion a string of beads.

Thus mariners, by common consent, gave Makassang a wide berth, and had always done so. It lived on in its wicked isolation; all news of it was bad. Sometimes there were rumours of internal strife, of wars and expeditions, of unspeakable trophies brought back by tribal fighters. But it would take a brave man, and a foolhardy one, to dip his foot into this cauldron and find out its true nature; and though there was no stint of brave men, it was the foolhardy kind who lived the shortest lives and left the smallest imprint upon their time.

Makassang, the world said, was best left alone, to swelter, to dream evil dreams, and to feed on its own wickedness.

IV

'Makassang!' Inevitably, it was Peter Ramsay, the man with the long tongue, who was the first to speak, of all the intent men crowding the deck of the Lucinda D. His voice was high-pitched in complaint as he turned to face Richard Marriott. 'Makassang! By God, we are mad to be here!'

'We have no choice,' answered Richard indifferently. He was studying the huge flight of steps and the fantastic palace at the top, and then, with more care, the bay across which they were now gliding. It seemed to be what they were looking for; it shelved to a wide sandy beach, and there were small craft close inshore, making use of its shelter. 'This will serve our purpose, till we can be patched up.'

'It will serve our funeral, more like!' cried Ramsay. He was glancing from one to another of the crew, looking (as he always did) for allies in his perennial skirmish with authority. 'I have heard tell of Makassang, too. They have cannibals and headhunters here! They cut down the Borrowdale's crew, to the last man, and – '

'That was on the north coast,' broke in Richard roughly, 'and it was plain pirates that did it, not cannibals. Since when were we afraid of pirates?'

But Peter Ramsay was not to be put off. Around him, in the half-darkness, the men were murmuring among themselves; this was his favourite moment, his chosen stage for playing. 'Pirates or cannibals,' he whined, 'it is all one, when you finish up with the blade of a parang in your belly! I tell you, Makassang is poison for sailors. I've seen it writ in the old pilot books. "Mariners, Beware!" Aye, that was it! They warned of natives who would take a ship by treachery, and not leave a man alive to tell the tale. They are headhunters still, and proud of it! I dare swear, if we set foot ashore here – '

He would have gone on forever in the same strain, and Richard knew that he must be checked, even though what he said had, by common repute, much of truth in it. The Lucinda D had no choice but to stay where she was, and he did not want any talkative fool of a sea lawyer taking the heart out of his men. 'Ramsay!' he roared out suddenly.

Ramsay turned, in mid-sentence. 'Aye?'

'Put a dish-clout in your mouth, for the love of God!' Richard's voice was purposefully brutal. 'You talk like some damned old woman who wants to make our flesh creep! Are you afraid of a few natives who might try to steal a round of beef? No one else on board is afraid of them, I can promise you. Is it a bodyguard you want?'

'I was only saying – ' began Ramsay aggrievedly.

'Well, stop saying, and start working! We'll beach her here, and make our repairs, and be off again, before your cannibals have sharpened their front teeth.' There was a laugh at that, and the men round Ramsay broke their grouping and began to move towards their stations, ready for the orders which they knew were coming. 'Give me soundings!' Richard called out to Singleton, and then, to Nick Garrett: 'Take off all sail. We'll steer for the beach.'

Garrett, preparing to move, shrugged his shoulders in grudging resignation. He did not care for their situation, but, like Richard, he knew well enough that there was no other choice open. The Lucinda D could not put to sea again, the way the leakage was gaining on them; indeed, she would not sail another five miles, even in still water. They must ground here, and take their chance of what was in store for them.

'We'll need to mount guard all night,' Garrett said, in surly tones. 'They might have a dozen war canoes alongside, before we see a sign of them.'

'We'll row guard,' Richard corrected him. 'I'll take the skiff, and you the longboat. We can circle the ship every five minutes, if need be.'

'The men won't like it,' said Garrett. 'They need their sleep.'

'They need what I give them,' answered Richard curtly. 'Get those headsails in.'

Long after they had grounded, on a spit of sand in three full fathoms of water, and had laid out a kedge anchor and secured their ship for the night, the crew remained on deck, staring through the dusk at the mysterious land; wondering what they could make of it, and what it might make of them. They wore their sidearms ready, but, curiously, this quiet corner of the unknown carried no menace, only beauty and strangeness, and their warlike state seemed out of place. The palace grew in loveliness as the light failed; the pink of its coral stone was like a blush which faded with the quieting heart. No boats, no war prahus, no sampans approached them; they were left in isolation, while the tide ebbed, and the Lucinda D – square of keel, solid-bottomed like a wine jug – settled upright on her bed of soft sand.

There were lights in the Sun Palace, and flickering fires on the slopes surrounding it; once, the silence was broken by the cries of peacocks, and once again by a sound which might have been the ceremonial clash of spears. But for the most part the palace reigned above them in noble stillness. It had no need of clamour or movement; it was enough that it was there, commanding respect by its very majesty.

There was one brief moment, before night fell, when Richard, turning away from this contemplation of beauty and mystery, had his eye caught by a single gleam of golden light, far away across the wide bay behind them. He brought his telescope into focus, searching for his target, and found that it was indeed golden – the spire of a golden pagoda, twenty miles and more away, presiding in equal majesty over what must be the mainland of Makassang. Its dome, rounded and sculptured in purest outline, tapering to a sublime peak (being fashioned, men said, from immemorial times in the shape of a woman's breast) was the only object to be seen, in all the northern horizon. All else was now shadow, and purple dusk.

Fancifully, the pagoda seemed to challenge the Sun Palace; while the one dreamed on in royal solitude, the other stared at it with the eye of heaven ... But with night, and the coming of the stars, and the need for watchfulness, such thoughts gave way to a simple imperative, one which had seized all men since the beginning of history – the hunger to live on, to survive unmolested and unharmed, until the next dawn.

§

2

The dawn broke in ominous splendour. The sun caught first the spire of the golden pagoda, miles away across the northern bay; then the roof of the Sun Palace, and the fantastic climbing of the steps towards it; and lastly the spars and upper rigging of the Lucinda D, on whose deck weary men, dog-tired, had not yet begun to go about the business of the day. They still slept, or lay inert, conscious of stiff, awkward limbs, and uncertain hearts to match them.

They had long ago ceased manning the pumps, since their ship was firmly grounded on the sand spit, and the water was not gaining; but, as Richard had ordered – not sparing himself any more than his crew – both watches had rowed guard all night, circling the ship in the skiff and the longboat, ready for surprises of any sort. Yet surprise had not come, at any time in the course of their long vigil; nor did the dawn bring the smallest sign of change, the smallest alarm or alert. It was this which was most ominous of all.

Richard Marriott, leaning against the solid bulwarks of his ship, staring at the Steps of Heaven, tried hard to interpret this silence, this ignoring of their presence. He had expected attack during the night, or at least the probing of scout canoes; a strange ship, grounding almost within the shadow of the royal palace in sufficient daylight, must surely have excited attention ashore; they must have been closely watched, from the very moment of their first arrival.

Now, at this fresh and revealing dawn, there should again be hundreds of inquisitive or baleful eyes, wondering what their business was, trying to divine their situation. The Lucinda D, he knew well, looked what she was – a private warship manned by fighting seamen; it was likely, even in Makassang which she had never yet visited, that she would be identified, and that her reputation, never fragrant in these waters, would have preceded her. In which case – unless they were all asleep ashore, or dead, or struck by cowardice – he would have expected a counter-movement of some kind. Even a herald of peace would have been less strange than this silence, this royal blind eye which affected not to see them.

He straightened up, and stretched his stiff arms under the heavy boat cloak, to ease their aching. His servant, John Keston, who had taken his turn at rowing the skiff, along with the rest, appeared from the galley bearing a mug of coffee. At this moment, they were the only two stirring on board; it was Nick Garrett's watch below, and the rest of the hands on deck still seemed asleep, curled up in the scuppers like weary dogs, hoping to ignore the demands of day.

Richard took the proffered mug, and sipped it greedily before he spoke. He felt the coffee warming his gullet, bringing him new heart. He nodded his thanks to John Keston, and then, with a jerk of his head towards the land, said: 'It is quiet yet.'

'Too quiet for my taste,' answered Keston promptly. There was a rough comradeship between master and man which was a far advance on their former standing; John Keston, still the servant, now had liberty to speak his mind, a liberty won in a dozen desperate encounters. 'They must be up to something, or they would have sent a canoe out to see what we want here, or to sell us fruit and suchlike. But I would have wagered an attack before now, if Makassang is all they say.'

'Perhaps it is not,' said Richard. He was still staring at the land, narrowing his eyes against the brightness of the Steps of Heaven, which were beginning to catch the rays of the eastern sun. 'Perhaps it is all talk. Perhaps it is they who are afraid.'

'Peter Ramsay says they do not use money at all. Their currency is human skulls.'

'Ramsay is a fool.'

'Aye, sir.'

'And you are another, if you believe him.'

'Aye,' said John Keston again. 'But even fools can sometimes talk sense, by accident ... Do you know anything of the island, sir?'

'No. I have heard gossip of it, that's all. But whatever the truth, we must stay here until we are fit to leave. The water was gaining on the pumps, nearly a foot every hour. We have no choice. We have to careen the ship, and make good our damage. There's three days' hard work, there.'

'They could surprise us then, while we are lying helpless.'

'And we could surprise them!' Richard turned, roused from his survey. 'Come, talk sense, man! Who are we, to be afraid of a lot of prancing savages without a breech cloth among them?' He pointed, up the steps towards the enormous palace. 'With the bow gun mounted on a platform, we could pound that to rubble, if we cared to! We can have peacock pie for dinner tonight! Aye, with a soup of human skulls, if we've a taste for it! Has that prattling booby Ramsay taken your wits? I'll wager they have nothing here but a few thousand natives and some old ruffian who calls himself king, or rajah. Have they weapons to match ours? Have they – '

He broke off suddenly. He had been looking directly at John Keston, but Keston was no longer looking at him. Instead, he was staring over Richard's shoulder towards the land, his eyes wide, his face a study in surprise. Then he pointed swiftly, and his voice when he spoke was urgent.

'We need not wait long, to find out their weapons. Look at that!'

Richard turned on the instant, and drew in his breath sharply at what he saw. Makassang, the dormant island, had boiled into sudden life, touched by some giant wand. Where before the bay had been all brooding stillness, the whole of it was now engulfed in movement. From the foot of the Steps of Heaven, an advancing armada was standing out towards them. In its centre was a huge, high-powered rowing barge, and its wings, like twin horns, were composed of scores of smaller craft – sampans, prahus, outrigger canoes with slatted sails. The whole mass was bearing down upon the Lucinda D, as if directed by a single hand.

Richard crossed the deck in a swift stride, and with the butt of one of his pistols beat out a monstrous tocsin on the ship's bell. As the sleeping men round him began to stir and gaze about them, he shouted: 'Rouse up! Call the watch below! Stand to arms!'

Then he turned again, hard-eyed, coldly watchful, to see what their enemy might be.

II

Their enemy advanced towards them across the bay in a wide semicircle, keeping station on the centre ship which, as it drew nearer, could be seen to be a great ornamental state barge, propelled by sixteen ponderous sweeps on either side. The sun caught its high gilded prow, and the purple-and-gold canopy amidships. Through his glass, Richard could make out no heavy armament on board; but under the canopy were a score of men in scarlet tunics, their spears glinting restlessly as the barge advanced. They might have been a ceremonial guard, but they were armed men none the less ... His own crew crowded the bulwarks, not speaking, their muskets primed and ready, their cutlasses close at hand; up in the bows, the Lucinda D's single cannon was loaded and run out, aimed towards the centre of this motley fleet. To be thus alert was second nature; now, it was a simple question as to how near they should allow this fleet to approach, before they took steps to question its intent.

Richard waited, while the distance decreased – to eighty yards, to fifty. He could hear the steady beat of drums, giving the stroke to the rowers; he could see the helmsman, high in the stern, straining his splendid muscles against his long oar; among the scarlet guard, a figure of a different kind could now be made out – a seated figure in white, wearing a green turban. Richard held his hand, until the barge and its attendant convoy were some thirty yards off; then he called out to Nick Garrett, stationed at the gun.

'Put a shot under his bows! But aim wide!'

The slow-match came down to touch the primer; the gun roared out; as the echoes began to return to them, a tall splash of grey–green water leapt high in the air, halfway between the barge and the Lucinda D. There was a pause, while the thudding of the drum died away; then, from the barge and from all the other craft, a forest of green seemed to spring up, and to move gently to and fro, waving like banners in the wind. But the banners were tree branches, palm leaves, fronded foliage of strange shape – the traditional emblems of peace.

'Run up a white flag!' Richard called out, and within a moment the flag fluttered to the yardarm. But there was no need to warn his crew that the green symbols of peace might be a trick; the bristling row of arms along the bulwarks continued to point formidably at the oncoming craft, and the long-barrelled bow gun, reloaded, was trained now on the crowded deck of the barge. This continued to move forward with its own momentum, until it was a bare ship's length from the Lucinda D; then there was a double drumbeat, and a swirl of oars, backing water, brought it to an exact stop. It floated, in all its gilded magnificence, within easy hail.

'Watch the canoes,' warned Richard loudly. 'If they come closer, or begin to circle round us, give them a musket volley.' He jumped up and took his stand on the bulwarks, holding on to the mainmast stays. From there he called out to the barge: 'What's your business with us?'

The turbaned man in white rose from his chair under the canopy. He was a small man, and old; among the splendour of the scarlet-tunicked guard, he seemed frail and feeble. But clearly he was a person of consequence; the silver spears clashed for him as he rose, and he had no need to call for silence. He spoke in a reedy voice, though plainly: 'I bring you greetings from His Highness.'

Richard stared back at him, without speaking. He was impressed by everything within his view upon this fantastic seascape – the guard, the dignity of the old man who spoke, and the magnificence of the rowing barge which, close to, was seen to be beautifully fashioned in a great curving sweep from stem to stern, richly ornamented with gold leaf and purple hangings. Whatever else Makassang had, it had riches, and ceremonial state. He looked about him swiftly. The prahus and the other craft were making no effort to approach nearer; the forest of green branches still waved gently in peaceful greeting. He turned back towards the barge.

'What highness is that?' he called out.

'The Rajah of Makassang,' came the answer, on a note of ancient pride.

'I return his greetings,' said Richard formally.

The old, white-robed man bowed, and Richard bowed back; the tremendous lustre of the scene robbed their exchange of any hint of foolishness. Richard remained where he was, standing straddled on the bulwark, above the long line of his crew and their ready weapons; and after an interval, the old man on the barge spoke again: 'I would talk further with you,' he said. He had a curious lilting accent, as if he had learned the English tongue from someone who had been long in exile. 'I will draw near, if you permit it.'

Richard nodded his head, but his only speech was to his crew. 'Let them come alongside,' he called out. 'But keep your guns at the ready.'

The barge, skilfully propelled, edged nearer, setting its stern at an angle till it was nearly touching the Lucinda D. The oarsmen (who were likely to be slaves, in this part of the world) were below the deck level, and could not be seen; the scarlet guard numbered some twenty men, but they seemed peaceful and without guile, and their spears remained grounded. Upon an impulse, Richard hailed the old man again: 'You are welcome to come aboard – yourself alone.'

The old man, who had moved out from beneath the canopy, stared back at him. 'I go nowhere alone,' he answered, with the assurance of pride. 'My bodyguard is twenty men.'

'You need no bodyguard aboard my ship.'

'My bodyguard is twenty men,' repeated the old man.

'You may bring six,' said Richard.

'Ten,' countered the old man. Beneath its hauteur, there was a certain humorous appeal in his voice, and Richard suddenly warmed to it.

'Ten,' he agreed, and signed to John Keston and the others to rig a ladder.

When the old man stood at last on the deck of the Lucinda D backed by his bodyguard, he was indeed an imposing presence. His white robe was of the rarest silk; in the gathered folds of his green turban, a single fiery jewel which, if it were indeed a ruby, must have been priceless, flashed and glittered when caught by the early sunlight. In this splendid setting, his face, though old and shrivelled, had great pride of bearing; he looked about him as if accustomed to command. His bodyguard of ten men had formed their ranks and grounded their spears a few paces behind him. They wore, as headdress, black fezzes with bright red tassels, and their tunic-uniform was completed by loose-cut breeches and gaiters, copied (it seemed) from the Spahi regiments of northern Africa. Their captain, a tall young man whose badge of rank was an aiguillette of looped gold cords, gave his brief commands in the Malay tongue.

Richard Marriott, confronting this brave array without any ceremony to match it, was not outfaced. Nor did he mourn his lack of consequence. His men had guns, the equal of any show of polished spears and trim uniforms ... He waited for the old man, the guest, to speak first, and after the customary moment of silence, his visitor addressed him.

'I am Amin Bulong,' said the old man. 'Commander-in-Chief to his Royal Highness.'

Richard inclined his head. Titles were only titles, he thought privately; they could honour a great man, or disguise a small one. 'I am Captain Richard Marriott,' he answered, 'and this is my ship, the Lucinda D.'

'We have heard much of your famous ship,' said Amin Bulong. There seemed a trace of irony in his thin voice, but his next action belied it. He gestured over his shoulder, with a small, scarcely perceptible movement of the hand, and one of his bodyguard came forward, bearing a cushion of blue silk, with a covering laid upon its top. 'I bring you a gift of welcome from the hand of his Royal Highness.'

Richard Marriott turned his eyes towards the cushion, as Amin Bulong drew aside the covering. On it rested an elephant tusk, its ivory of purest white, exquisitely carved in filigree, and tipped with a sheath of beaten gold. Dazzling in itself, its workmanship was rarely beautiful. He stretched out his right hand to touch it – the traditional sign of acceptance. Some of his crew, attracted by the movement, turned to look at it, and there was an audible intake of breath from many of the men as they saw the offering.

Richard considered swiftly. He could think of nothing on board which could match the munificence of the gift; yet it might be necessary to match it, to preserve peace and keep a pattern of friendship. He motioned to John Keston, who took the cushion and laid it on one side. Then he spoke, putting all the warmth he could into his voice.

'Please convey to his Royal Highness my thanks for this splendid gift of welcome,' he said. 'It will be my endeavour to send him a gift in return, though I cannot hope to rival the beauty of this one.'

Amin Bulong, who had been watching his face carefully, gestured with his hand. 'That is no matter,' he answered. 'But his Royal Highness would perhaps expect you to convey your thanks in person.'

At that, Richard frowned, for with Amin Bulong's words, the climate of the occasion had subtly changed. What had seemed a gift of rare courtesy had developed undertones of something else – of gentle pressure, of enticement. He had not wanted to go ashore, to greet the Rajah or for any other purpose; he wanted, at the most, to top up the freshwater barrels, to make his repairs, and then to leave. But the magnificent present of the elephant tusk seemed likely to deny these simple plans. It was more than a present, apparently; it was at best an innocent entanglement which would delay him needlessly, and at worst a clear signal of danger. For once ashore, on whatever errand, he could become a hostage; and hostages did not fare well, in this misbegotten corner of the globe.

Richard could not gauge, with any certainty, the motive for the Rajah's welcome; but, whatever its source, he now liked it far less than the shower of spears which might well have taken its place. Some of these uneasy thoughts must have shown in his face; for as he did not reply, Amin Bulong continued: 'It is no more than our custom here, to bear greetings and exchange gifts.'

'I know that,' answered Richard. 'But I fear my visit will be too brief for me to return this call in person. I must ask you to make my excuses.'

Amin Bulong, reacting to his tone, answered tartly: 'No visit can be so brief as to exclude courtesy.'

Richard inclined his head. 'You mistake my meaning,' he said, as reasonably as he could. 'The Rajah's gift is a splendid one, and I am deeply grateful for it. But I had not intended to make a visit ashore, and my plans unfortunately will render it impossible.'

Amin Bulong looked about him, his glance supercilious. 'What are your plans?' he asked, as if so minor a person as the captain of a small brigantine would have no plans which could not be changed at will. 'Indeed, why have we been honoured with this visit, in the first place?'

'There is no special reason. My ship is on passage to the Moluccas. We have anchored here for a short while. We may take on water, and fresh fruit if it is available. Surely you would not dispute our right to do so?'

Amin Bulong's expression seemed to sharpen suddenly. 'You have anchored' – he gave ironic emphasis to the word – 'within the territorial waters of the island of Makassang. His Royal Highness takes no exception to this, as his gift of welcome shows. But in return for this accommodation, he would certainly expect you to present your compliments in person. Indeed' – the old man's tone was now almost hostile – 'he would insist on such a personal visit.'

'I regret – ' began Richard.

'Your ship is aground,' interrupted Amin Bulong. 'We were able to observe as much, last night. Our information is that you ran ashore at dawn, on the western reef, and are so severely damaged that your pumps cannot keep pace with it.'

'Not so,' said Richard easily. 'We must caulk a seam or two – that is all.'

'Your ship is aground,' repeated Amin Bulong. He tapped his foot gently on the deck. 'By the feel of this, she is badly holed. You intend to bring her closer inshore, and careen her. Of course you are free to do so – with the Rajah's permission. But otherwise – '

'Otherwise, what?' asked Richard sharply.

Amin Bulong gave a wave of his hand. 'Let us only talk of pleasant things.'

'Otherwise, what?' repeated Richard.

Amin Bulong shrugged his shoulders. 'You have seen the war-prahus which attended me,' he said. The transition to hardness in his voice was very swift. 'They are a small part of our force. If you remain here without the express permission of the Rajah – which you can only obtain in person – they will have orders to attack.' There was tremendous dignity and force in the old man's voice as he spoke thus directly. 'They will harass you by day and by night. They will make your repairs impossible. Finally they will take your ship.'

'A fine welcome for a friendly stranger!' said Richard sarcastically. 'Pray, what do you do to your enemies?'

'I have said already that a visit of courtesy is the best alternative.'

'My crew is armed, and determined.'

'We are not defenceless ourselves.'

'You will lose many men, if you try to take my ship.'

'His Royal Highness has a hundred thousand loyal subjects, who are ready to lay down their lives at a single word.'

Richard Marriott took a pace forward. He had intended only to come closer to the old man, to resolve this wordy conflict by a more direct approach; but as he moved, the captain of the bodyguard, standing a few paces behind Amin Bulong, moved also. His spear arm came up, and the glittering weapon, poised for the throw, was aimed exactly at Richard's throat. Richard made a conscious effort to disregard it as he said: 'Why does the Rajah wish to see me?'

Amin Bulong stared back at him, equally direct. 'He has a matter to discuss with you.'

'What matter?'

'A private matter.'

So that was it ... The present had been a bribe, to bring him peaceably ashore; the show of force was intended to buttress the bribe with a hint of something else; and the open threats, politely screened to begin with, now took their place in the pattern of persuasion. He was to come ashore, whether he liked it or no ... Richard could not guess what was the purpose behind all this; only the facts were clear – and the chief fact was that he and his crew could be out-numbered, and his ship, momentarily powerless, might be damaged beyond hope of salvage, by an enemy force which, most unexpectedly, seemed disciplined and well-directed. He looked past Amin Bulong, to meet the eyes of the young captain of the guard; his spear was still poised, and his appearance was more than warlike – it was unwinkingly confident and determined. If Richard reached for his pistols, that shining spear would be sunk in his throat before he had time to cock them.

He made his decision suddenly, with as good a grace as he could muster. 'I will be glad to thank his Royal Highness in person,' he said, turning back to Amin Bulong, 'and to discuss any matter he chooses. However, in view of this' – he gestured towards the captain of the guard, and then to the long line of war-prahus and sampans which confronted the Lucinda D, 'this warlike preparation, there must be certain precautions before I agree to go ashore with you.'

Amin Bulong, clearly a man of decision himself, went straight to the heart of the matter. 'You would wish me to leave some hostage behind?'

'Yes.'

'The captain of my bodyguard will be glad to remain on board, while we are absent.'

'One man is hardly enough.'

'The one man is my grandson,' said Amin Bulong.

Richard inclined his head, glancing from the old man to the proud young warrior whose spear was still lifted. 'I might have guessed as much ... He does you credit ... Furthermore, I must be attended by my own bodyguard.'

It was now Amin Bulong's turn to assent. 'Naturally. Shall we say – ten men?'

Richard Marriott smiled privately, enjoying the exchange in the same way as his adversary was doing. Ten men was nearly half his crew; he could not possibly weaken his ship's defences by withdrawing so large a number. He knew this instinctively, and Amin Bulong probably guessed it also.

'I am not so proud,' answered Richard airily, 'that I must be attended by ten men when I go ashore. Three will be ample for my needs.'

'Agreed.'

'And I will first discuss this matter with my second-in-command.'

Amin Bulong allowed himself a brief smile. 'You would be very wise to do so ... With your permission, I will await you in my barge.'

'But I must go!' said Richard impatiently, to Nick Garrett. They had drawn aside, out of hearing of the crew, close to the wheelhouse; but many glances followed in their direction, and Richard strove to seem as calm as possible, even though he had much on his mind ... 'I don't know what the Rajah intends, but I have to go to find out – he has made that much clear. I have no choice in the matter. We can do nothing else.'

'We can fight,' answered Nick Garrett, with equal impatience. From the first, he had been opposed to any contact with the shore, and he had now turned truculent and argumentative. 'You said so yourself! Or were those just brave words, to bolster up our spirits?'

'Certainly I said we can fight. And it is still true. But I can see now what the cost would be. Look at the bodyguard! Look how those boats are drawn up! By God, if these are man-eating savages, I wish I had a hundred of them on board! We could take Batavia itself!'

'Then we should put to sea again,' said Nick Garrett. 'For you to go ashore is neither one thing nor the other. Either we fight them, or we sheer off as soon as possible.'

'You know we cannot leave, till we have made our repairs.'

'We can repair her roughly, without careening. We can rig a canvas patch over the side, enough to hold the water till we reach a different island.'

'And go straight to the bottom in the first gale!' Richard faced the tall figure standing in the shadow of the wheelhouse. 'We are wasting time, Nick, with this arguing. I am going ashore, now. With John Keston, and Burnside, and Peter Ramsay. Aye, Ramsay – it will give him a taste of headhunting! What have I to fear, in any case? They are leaving us a hostage. And if they are planning some treachery, why should they waste so magnificent a gift?'

'They know they will get it back, as soon as they take the ship.'

'They will not take the ship, if you keep a good watch.' He scratched his chin reflectively. 'Perhaps it is trade the Rajah wants to discuss. He might have something the Dutch monopoly will not allow him to sell. Or he wishes news of the outside world. Or it might be a sickness – something of that sort. But there can be no harm in finding out.'

'Unless you come back in four quarters, with your head on a spear!'

'I do not quarter so easily … Now we have to match his present, if we can. That tusk is the rarest I have ever seen. We have nothing on board of that quality, except jewels, and by the look of it, Makassang has enough jewels already. Did you mark that ruby in the old man's turban?'

'I'll lay I was the first to mark it,' said Nick Garrett, with a wolfish laugh. 'I saw it snug in my own jewel box... There has always been talk of a state treasure of Makassang. I remember it now. You should find out what you can, while you are ashore.'

'I shall not be asleep.' A movement over the side of the Lucinda D distracted him, and he turned outboard to see what was stirring. He found that it was a small outrigger canoe, of the kind called a cora-cora, with a high prow and (for its size) a vast sail; it had come alongside the barge, but was now turning away again, and gathering speed towards the shore. Brought to the alert, he leant over the bulwarks, and called down to Amin Bulong: 'What was the business of the cora-cora?'

From under the edge of the canopy, Amin Bulong peered up at him, his face inscrutable. 'I have sent it ahead, with a message,' he answered.

'What message?'

'That you are coming ashore with me,' replied Amin Bulong, as if surprised by the question. 'His Royal Highness would wish to prepare a suitable welcome for you ... May I know if you are ready?'

'Shortly,' said Richard, and withdrew from the ship's side again. He caught Nick Garrett's glance, sardonic and questioning, but he did not answer it. Whatever welcome was being prepared ashore, it was his own problem. Instead he said: 'Tell those three men they are coming with me.' Then he turned, and strode below.

Down in his cabin, which was hot and airless in the morning heat, he considered the matter of a present for the Rajah. He had nothing of a value to match the elephant tusk; his offering must be something of a different sort, something unusual enough to make up for its lack of intrinsic worth. He looked about him swiftly. There were a few books, and those not worth considering. There was his sextant, which he could not part with. There was money, and jewellery, and a chest of opium, but these were poor currency with which to honour a rich man. There were guns of various kinds, but (as far as weapons were concerned) he had never yet given away as much as a

Scotsman's dirk, and this was not the moment to start such largesse.

Then his eye fell on what he was looking for. It was a musical box, won long ago in some gaming house on the Bristol waterfront; it had been gathering dust in his cabin for more than two years. It was a pretty, decorative thing, of walnut inlaid with yellow-wood; when wound up, its revolving drum played English and Scottish airs, with a curious tinkling purity. This would serve, as well as anything ... He pulled the lever and the mechanism, nearly run down, played a few slow phrases in elegant waltz-time before coming to rest. As the notes subsided, with gentle harmonious echoes, John Keston knocked on his cabin door, and forthwith entered.

Richard, momentarily foolish, pointed to the musical box and said: 'I am taking this ashore, as a present.'

Keston, nodding, said: 'I will dust it, and wrap it in a cloth.' Busy at this task, with his back turned, he continued: 'This is some great Rajah ashore?'

'Aye, so they say. Did you see the elephant tusk? He must be a rich man, to give such presents.'

'Rich men keep great state,' said John Keston. 'Have you thought of that?'

'How do you mean?'

Keston turned, and gestured. 'Sir, you cannot go ashore in those rough clothes, if you are visiting a rajah. It would not be seemly.'

'What do the clothes matter?' asked Richard scornfully. 'I am paying a call, and bringing a present. I am captain of my own ship, not a tailor's dummy! What difference does it make, what I wear?'

'You are visiting a rajah,' repeated John Keston. 'You should dress for the occasion.'

'What dress is this, then?'

'The Dutch admiral's uniform.'

Richard considered, not without amusement. He had indeed no ceremonial clothes of any sort, save a naval uniform looted from a Dutch East Indiaman which he and some others had captured, a year earlier in the Celebes Straits. The uniform was a truly glorious affair, a braided tail coat with much display of gold lace, tasselled epaulettes, and a plumed hat to match; the kind of cockatoo outfit which his brother Miles used to wear on great occasions. John Keston had altered it to fit him, but he had never yet worn it. In fact, he had not dared to.

'I am not a Dutch admiral,' he objected. 'I cannot wear it, on a call like this.'

'You are visiting a rajah,' said John Keston, for the third time. 'He will not know the uniform, except that it is ceremonial.'

'He will not expect such state.'

'All the better,' answered John Keston. 'You will take him by surprise.'

In some ways, thought Richard presently, it was far more of an ordeal to step on to the deck under the eyes of his crew, arrayed like some blue-and-gold pouter pigeon, than to face anything that lay ahead. The unknown was one thing; he could deal with it as it arose; but the amazed stares of fellow sailors who had scarcely seen him in anything more formal than yellow oilskins and a sou'wester, were real and daunting. He would not have been surprised if they had turned to dancing the maypole round him ... There must, however, have been something in his expression which discouraged comment – and he presented, in fact, a most regal figure – for as he strode across the deck, his sword clanking, his plumed hat ruffling in the breeze, no word of any kind escaped the crew of the Lucinda D. One of the Kanakas working at the foot of the mainmast dropped a marlinspike, and then stood staring at him, as if he had seen the Archangel himself. But that was all.

His armed men drew aside as he made for the ladder, forming a respectful lane for his approach. For a moment he stood above the barge, isolated, splendid in his finery; then he called down to Amin Bulong: 'I am ready!'

The old man, who had been sitting patiently on the gilded bench under the canopy, looked up at him. He was too well-schooled, or too polite, to express surprise at Richard Marriott's appearance. But there was a gratifying deference in his voice as he said: 'His Royal Highness will draw great pleasure from this visit ... Be pleased to step on board.'

III

There were special litters designed for the ascent of the Steps of Heaven; they were Chinese palankeens, with a central carrying pole supported by four bearers, save that the pole was set at an angle, high at one end, low at the other, and the litter itself, moving up the steps, was thus held comfortably level. It was a touch of luxury which, like the appointments of the state barge, impressed Richard Marriott as he observed it. But he could not help noticing that the palankeens, like the barge, were old and out of repair – as if they were toys of a rich man who had grown weary of toys, and had not troubled to replace them when they grew shabby. It seemed a clue to what he might find when he confronted the Rajah. There was decay here in Makassang, as well as magnificence.

Their two palankeens were side by side, and the curtains drawn back, as they began the slow ascent. Richard had supposed that the old man might doze off on the journey, since the noonday heat was approaching; but he was sitting up alertly, a slight smile on his face, and when Richard made a chance remark – on the grandeur of the Steps of Heaven, and of the Sun Palace above them – he answered readily enough.

'Makassang is a rich country,' he said, 'though we do not claim undue credit for that. We are blessed by nature. And the precepts of the Lord Buddha have prospered us mightily, since the very beginning of our history.' He turned to look at Richard, peering round the curtains of his palankeen. 'It is also a strong country, Captain Marriott. It is not for anybody's taking.'

'Having seen your bodyguard, I can well believe that ... You must be proud of your grandson. Surely it is a great honour in one so

87

young, to be captain of the guard?'

'He is captain of my guard,' Amin Bulong corrected him, on an appropriate note of modesty. 'But there is a Palace Guard – drawn from the Rajah's own regiment – which of course has pride of place. My own bodyguard is an adjunct of that.'

Adjunct … It was not the first time that Amin Bulong had used a word or a phrase which was curiously prosy; and Richard found himself again wondering where the old man had learned his English. It had something of a missionary ring about it … But it seemed impertinent to put the question to him outright, at this stage; instead, Richard asked: 'The Rajah – how is he called?'

'Satsang the Third.' Amin Bulong peered once more round his curtain, as the palankeens swayed together and then apart. 'You have not heard his name, Captain?'

'Unfortunately, no,' said Richard. 'I have not been in these waters before.' He smiled. 'I mean no discourtesy by what I say now. But the island of Makassang enjoys a reputation for fierceness – even hostility. It is said that you have headhunters on the island.'

Amin Bulong gestured, negligently. 'We have some few, in the interior. It is an ancient form of piety … But I hope you do not find us hostile.'

'By no means … The Rajah – has he a son to rule after him?'

A frown came over Amin Bulong's face. 'He has not been so blessed,' he answered, coldly.

His voice, as well as cold, was completely final, as if the subject, once disposed of, could not possibly be broached again. Aware that he had trespassed on some area of delicacy, Richard sought to leave it as soon as he could. This was, in part, a courtesy visit, and it was best to keep it on such a plane. A check in their progress gave him his opportunity.

They were now halfway up the Steps of Heaven; the façade of the coral palace loomed above them, taking on the dimensions of grandeur; and the palankeens now paused, so that the sweating bearers could be changed. Looking back, Richard could see the bodyguard, halted a few steps below them; then behind them his own trio of attendants, mopping their brows as they caught their breath; then, within the small curve of the bay, the Lucinda D, already dwarfed by the height they had gained; and lastly, far away across the inlet, the dome of the golden pagoda in the full glory of the sunshine. He pointed at this latter, and leant towards Amin Bulong, as their relief bearers bent to shoulder the carrying poles.

'I observed the dome of the pagoda as soon as I arrived,' he said. 'That is in the Rajah's domain?'

'Certainly,' answered Amin Bulong, and his voice was scarcely less cold than at the last question. 'Everything you see from here is in the Rajah's domain, and the island stretches far beyond that. Makassang is some two hundred miles long, and as much broad.'

'And the Rajah rules here, from the south?'

'He has strong garrisons in many parts of the island.'

'It is a handsome pagoda,' said Richard, still seeking to reach some neutral ground. 'Are there others like it in Makassang?'

'There are others,' answered the old man, 'but it is the principal one. It is a huge place, as you may see if you come to visit it. It is known as the Shwe Dagon – the Golden Pagoda. It is maintained by a priestly caste who call themselves the Anapuri.'

'The Anapuri,' said Richard, surprised at a word which, in the course of his wanderings, he had met before. 'Surely that means "the rulers", in your tongue?'

'It means "the rulers", yes.'

'How many are there in this caste?'

'Some ten thousand, I have heard.'

Silence fell between them, as their upward journey continued, and within the swaying palankeens the two men, the young and the old, kept their thoughts private. Amin Bulong seemed to have withdrawn, as if Richard's questioning, which he had intended to be innocent and polite, had touched some tender nerve. Richard himself was puzzled. There were some curious conflicts here. Priests who called themselves rulers, a rajah who had no son to follow him, a country of forty thousand square miles administered from a mere spike of land (as he had now observed it) on its southern extremity, interior tribes who were headhunters – these things did not add up to any known conception of central authority. Once again – as with the magnificent state barge with the shabby seat cushions, the gilded palankeens screened by frayed, musty curtains – there was evidence of an infection, a whiff of decay. The Rajah of Makassang might call himself paramount, but it was possible that his writ did not run very far beyond the scope of his own gaze. And if, in addition, he were an old man, as seemed likely, and childless ...

So Richard's thoughts ran, as they mounted, laboriously, twenty more of the broad Steps of Heaven, and the Sun Palace drew near. Unexpectedly, it was Amin Bulong who broke the silence, who gave voice to these thoughts which Richard had been content to keep hidden. It seemed that, after reflecting, he had come to some decision, for he leant forward and began to speak with far more freedom than before.

'You can know very little of our country, Captain Marriott,' he said, on a note of careful emphasis. 'That is no shame to you – I know very little of yours ... But it will perhaps help you in the future, if I tell you about it in more detail ...' The sun burned down, the palankeens swayed in solemn rhythm, the gecko lizards scurried from their path as they made their slow progress upwards. 'We were talking of the Shwe Dagon, and the hereditary priests of the Anapuri ... They bear that title because, long ago, they used to rule this island. It is possible that they might do so again. The Rajah, as I have said, has no son. Or, I should say, no grandson. His only son was killed in some tribal matter in the north. He has a daughter, the daughter of his old age, but daughters cannot rule in Makassang ... I said that Makassang is a strong country, but that is not altogether true. There are divisions, tribal quarrels, which weaken it fatally.'

The old man was speaking now with special care, as though striving to communicate the truth; and if (thought Richard) it were part of some studied presentation, it was not the less convincing for that. 'The country is split in two factions,' he went on, with an added note of sadness. 'There are the Sea-Dyaks, loyal to the Rajah. His royal regiment, and my own troops, are drawn from these. There are the Land-Dyaks, whose allegiance tends more towards the Anapuri, the priests. It is these who still go headhunting, when the mood strikes them ... And there are pirate strongholds on our northern coast, to add confusion.' He smiled, the thin bitter smile of a man confronted with his own weaknesses. 'You see that we have troubles,' he concluded. 'We are strong, and rich. But we are not united. And there may be worse to come.'

'I have heard of these pirate strongholds,' said Richard, after waiting for Amin Bulong to explain his last words. 'Could they not be subdued?'

'Not from landwards,' replied Amin Bulong. 'They have a hundred miles of jungle to protect them. And from the sea – well, it would take more than a fleet of prahus, however well disposed and commanded, to make the journey round the coast in open water, and then capture them by storm. Such an enterprise would need bigger ships altogether.'

They had now reached the top of the Steps of Heaven; the long balustrades had curved together to form a noble flagged plateau, and the palace gardens were in view. These, which had been hidden at sea level, now burst upon the eye in breathtaking profusion. There were green lawns, and splashing fountains, and blooms of every kind native to this part of the world – poincianas, emerald orchids, crimson cannas, and the wild beauties known as flame-of-the-forest.

There was new activity as well. There must have been a hundred sweepers and gardeners at work, though suiting their slow action to the burning sun; among them, peacocks strutted and spread their tail feathers, monkeys and parakeets quarrelled and chased one another, mynah birds brooded among the flamboyant branches. To crown this scene, there was a guard of honour drawn up at the farther end of the courtyard, arrayed in the same scarlet Spahi uniform but wearing golden breastplates; and behind them, the huge façade of the Sun Palace now rose in all its majesty, shining pink and white and grey, like some fantastic curtain marking the limits of Paradise.

Their palankeens had been halted, and set down. Richard, about to alight, turned his amazed eyes from the view, and harked back to the last words of Amin Bulong.

'You were talking of the need for bigger ships,' he said, 'to subdue these northern pirates. Is it this which the Rajah wishes to discuss with me?'

Amin Bulong, whose servants were preparing to assist him from the palankeen, looked up, and shook his head.

'No, no,' he answered. 'Pirates are little more to us than the sharks they would feed. This is a more pressing matter ... Be pleased to follow me.'

IV

When at last, towards sunset, a messenger from the Rajah entered his room and, bowing low, announced: 'Tuan – the Rajah awaits you', Richard Marriott was almost regretful at the summons. Earlier, when he had been expecting an immediate audience, he had been nettled by the delay; it had been Tuan this and Tuan that, but the honour of being greeted as 'Lord' in the Malay tongue did not compensate for the evasions and excuses of delay. He was not such a man as this, to be fobbed off with deference and double Dutch! ... But presently he had grown resigned, and then content. Eastern potentates were given to such inconsequential treatment; time here was measured differently, or not measured at all. And when time could be passed in surroundings of such peaceful elegance, without cost to anything save a Western sense of duty, it lost its eroding character and became a blessing.

Upon his arrival he had been shown, with much ceremony, into a suite of apartments on the first floor of the Sun Palace; their magnificence and luxury were balm for the fiercest spirit. But they had more than magnificence; the view from them must have been one of the fairest in the world. The palace stood at the crown of its hill, and the view was south as well as north; when his eyes tired of the northern prospect, from the Steps of Heaven down to the Lucinda D, and up again to the dome of the Golden Pagoda, he could turn away and look south to the sparkling sea. Here, the deeper water was of a different hue, purple mixed with green; the sunlight danced upon it, and upon the long lines of creamy surf which marked its nearer edges. It was a noble coastline, open to the main surge of the Java Sea. It completed the full panoply of glory, of which the glowing coral of the Sun Palace was the bright jewel.

Richard had rested first, upon a cushioned chaise longue of rattan canes; then warm water was brought, in a golden ewer perfumed with sandalwood, and after he had washed a meal was set out for him – rice with cloves and cinnamon stems, turtle flesh wrapped in mango leaves, and a dish of peeled lychees steeped in fermented syrup. The wine to accompany it was a pale, cool Javanese vintage. The repast was served, again with great ceremony, by palace servants who wore a livery of yellow; and overseen by John Keston who, impressed by his surroundings and perhaps nostalgic for the vanished greatness of Marriott, carried himself as if he were the very cup-bearer of the gods. At its close, a dark Trinchinopoly cheroot from a teakwood box had rounded out his ease.

Presently Amin Bulong had appeared, preceded by the clashing of spears which resounded strangely in the long galleries surrounding his apartments – yet not more strangely than the cries of peacocks, the monkey-chatter, the bourdon of gossip and grumbling from the gardeners in the grounds below him. But Amin Bulong brought nothing save his compliments, his hopes that Richard was comfortable and well cared for, and the announcement that the Rajah of Makassang, gratified by his presence, would give him audience as soon as certain pressing matters of state had been disposed of. After that, Richard had had a brief word with his own 'bodyguard', housed in an adjoining room (Peter Ramsay noisily proclaiming his fears that they were all being poisoned by foreign cooking); and then he had settled down to wait, and to reflect, and presently to doze off into dreamless sleep, at peace under the high gilded ceiling, lulled by a luxury he had not enjoyed for ten years and more.

When the messenger from the Rajah arrived, it was an effort to summon his wits, and to bend his thoughts towards an interview which, if it pursued the customary course, might test the most patient or the most subtle of men.

The audience chamber was a room of barbaric splendour, its vast floor tessellated in tiny, painstaking mosaic, its walls hung with curtains and canopies of Nanking velvet; the throne on which the Rajah sat was of ivory, and over it punkahs in the shape of fronded leaves, worked not by slaves but by men whose dress proclaimed their honourable rank, stirred the languorous air. At a first glance, the Rajah of Makassang did not match these splendours, save in his dress; he was a small man, as old as Amin Bulong, his face the colour of imperfect parchment, his hands straw-thin where they grasped the arms of the ivory throne. The richness of the robes, and the brilliance of the jewelled white turban, could not hide the fact that he was pathetically frail, and wasted by age or illness, and that there was scarcely a man in the room, whether they were the guards, or the yellow-liveried servants, or the bright-eyed boys seemingly serving as pages, who could not have wrestled him to the ground in the course of a single hold.

But there was more to royalty than animal strength; and Richard Marriott, approaching nearer, quickly became aware that he was in a royal presence. The face might be old and wizened, but it was lit by a fierce pride; the arm might be thin, but its gestures were regal and (he observed) instantly obeyed. A hawk-like nose, bloodless lips curved with a sardonic humour, and a pair of bright, intent eyes, completed the picture of a personality most formidable and most acute.

Here was a man who could be liberal, or cruel, or coldly detached; but he was clearly a man accustomed to have his will, come what may, a man whom no other men had denied in his lifetime, or, if they had ever dared to do so, had likely tasted peril and death as a consequence.

Richard advanced without fear, content that his own appearance lacked nothing in formality; his sword, tapping on the multicoloured floor, kept jaunty pace with his step. A hundred curious eyes gazed at him, moving as he moved, but he met only the Rajah's, whose unwinking stare had been upon him ever since he entered the audience chamber. Close to, at the foot of the three steps leading to the ivory throne, he came to a stop, with military precision, and bowed low. Then he waited, in silence, for the Rajah to give him formal welcome.

But the Rajah was in no hurry; it seemed that his patent dignity and presence allowed him to stretch out any silence to its furthest limit. For a long moment he stared down at Richard Marriott, his eyes bright and searching in the pale, wizened face; the only sound in all the room was the slow wafting of the punkahs overhead. Finally, with an inclination of his head which set the jewelled turban flashing, he acknowledged the greeting; and then he spoke, in a voice which, though thin and rasping, was firmly composed.

'Welcome to my house,' he said. His manner of speaking was closely akin to Amin Bulong's, as if they had shared the same teacher. 'I trust that you have been made comfortable, and have rested after your journey.'

'I have had every consideration,' answered Richard formally, 'and I am grateful … I would like to thank your Royal Highness for the magnificent present with which you greeted me.'

'A small token,' said the Rajah.

'A token which I cannot hope to match, from my poor resources. But I have taken the liberty of bringing with me something which I trust will assure your Highness of my regard.' He half turned, and John Keston, with a considerable air of consequence, came forward, bearing the walnut musical box. Richard took it from him, and advanced a step towards the Rajah. Then he paused, wishing at this delicate stage to preserve the utmost formality. 'I am not schooled in the customs of your court ... Have I your Highness's permission to present it to you?'

The Rajah inclined his head. Then he leant forward, his eyes on the polished box in Richard's hands, which might have held anything from a cash tribute to some infernal weapon of war. 'I am grateful for this courtesy ... Our customs, like our court, are of the simplest ... Pray bring it to me.'

There was a low footstool at one side of the ivory throne; Richard placed the box upon it, and opened the lid. Necks were craned as he prepared the simple mechanism. Upon an impulse, he said: 'This was my mother's. It is now yours.' Then he pressed the lever.

The silvery notes of the Scottish folk song filled the vast silence of the room. Though it was but the artless country air of 'Loch Lomond' its effect could not have been more remarkable. There was a curious intake of breath from nearly everyone in the room, as if they were hearing a melody cherished but long forgotten; and from the Rajah, an instant alertness which seemed to possess his whole frail body. He heard the piece to its end, with a smile almost of tenderness on his lips; when it was done, and the musical box had whirred and clicked into silence, he leant forward, a new animation in his pale face.

'That is very beautiful,' he said slowly. 'Your gift is well received ... But how does it come that you play this tune to me?'

'It is a well-known tune,' answered Richard, puzzled. 'It is called "Loch Lomond".'

' "Loch Lomond",' corrected the Rajah, with a special emphasis on the first word, to which he gave a pure Scottish pronunciation. 'We know it well here.'

'In Makassang?'

The Rajah smiled. 'Even in Makassang ... Some years ago we were fortunate to have a learned man here, a missionary who made his home with us. His name was Andrew Farthing. You have heard of him?'

'No, your Highness.'

'It is no matter. He became very dear to us. It was he who taught us your language. And this was the tune he used often to play, on a mandolin.' He turned to Amin Bulong, who was standing in the place of honour at his right hand. 'What did you think of, when you heard the tune?'

'The twelfth birthday of her Royal Highness,' answered Amin Bulong readily. 'When she first sang it for you.'

The Rajah nodded. 'You shared my happy memory ...' Then he turned, and his glance grew sharper again, as if putting away such light thoughts. 'Captain Marriott, you are welcome in Makassang, as I have said. It is not often that we entertain so distinguished a guest.'

There was something in his voice, a faint tinge of satire or sarcasm, hard to define, which Richard Marriott's keen ear caught as soon as he heard it. Schooled in these Eastern exchanges, he recognized it instantly. It was the beginning of bargaining, the preparation for the clash of wills, the descent to the bazaar. The formalities were over – so said the tone, unmistakably; now it was time for niceties of a different sort – for trading, for pressure, for disparagement and insult if need be.

'It is an honour to be here,' he answered formally.

The Rajah's sharp eyes were roving over his uniform. 'So distinguished a guest,' he repeated. 'A very high rank indeed ... I must congratulate you on the record of loyal service which it attests.'

Richard said nothing.

'That' – the Rajah pointed lightly – 'is the ribbon of the Order of Orange-Nassau, is it not?'

'Yes.'

'An unusual distinction for an Englishman.'

'I have been fortunate.'

'May I inquire what particular services led to its award?'

'It was won in battle,' said Richard hardly. He decided that he would lose his temper in two minutes – neither more nor less – and that this was the time to show it. 'I would not dream of inflicting the details on your Royal Highness, who doubtless has more important subjects to discuss with me.'

'What could be more important than deeds of bravery?'

'A fighting man is concerned only with future battles.'

Now there was a pause, while they stared at each other, gauging their strength. The Rajah's eyes, which had been so bright, were now veiled; under the lowered lids, the look was not reassuring. But Richard's returning stare was steadfast; he was not going to be put down, nor allow a joke to be prolonged till it became tedious. If the Rajah chose to make play with his admiral's uniform, which he must know to be false, then he could make play when Richard was gone.

It seemed that he had allowed enough of this message to peep out of his eyes, for after a long moment the Rajah relaxed his glance. Without a word, he turned aside, and made a sign to Amin Bulong. The latter stepped forward, and spoke a single sentence in Malay to the assembled company. It was dismissal. Within a few moments, the audience chamber, save for the three of them, was empty. The waving frond of one of the punkahs was all that stirred.

Richard waited, with sharpened attention. It was clear that he had survived some test or other, and that the Rajah was now ready to proceed to the business he had in mind. He felt very much alone – as a matter of courtesy, he had motioned to John Keston to leave with the rest – but overtopping this solitude was a feeling of intense curiosity. He was to learn now why he had been summoned, and he had still received no clue, nor could he guess anything at all of what was intended.

It seemed that even now he was not to know immediately, for the Rajah took up the conversation at a leisurely pace, as if there had been no interruption.

'You said that you were a fighting man, Captain Marriott,' he observed. His hand stroked the arm of the ivory throne as he spoke; the pale colour of the one was not far removed from the other. 'That is good news, since it is fighting I wish to discuss with you ... You have been told something of our history already, and now is the time to talk of it in more detail. I rule here' – there was more than confidence in his voice, there was an ancient pride of calling – 'but my rule has been challenged in the past, and it is being challenged now. You have heard of the Anapuri, the hereditary priests of Makassang. The High Priest of their sect is a man known as Selang Aro, an ambitious man who now sees a chance to come to power. I am an old man, and' – he glanced at Amin Bulong – 'my advisers, though faithful, are old also, and I have no son to follow me. Selang Aro sees this moment as a propitious one. He has been plotting for a long time. It was his followers who killed Andrew Farthing – but that is no matter, that is a story of long ago…' The Rajah's voice, which had seemed to tremble, grew firm again. 'I tell you this, so that you may see who are my enemies, and who my friends.'

As the Rajah paused, Richard inclined his head, to show his attention; but he did not feel called upon to venture a comment. It would indeed have been difficult to produce one which would have aided the course of the interview. For he was growing cautious, feeling that he had at last caught the drift of events. He found the Rajah's recital intriguing, even moving, but it seemed that this was purposeful, that his words were skilfully designed to engage a hearer's sympathy. Already his own sympathies were turning away. He could see – or thought he could see – what the Rajah wished of him. It was help that he wanted, help in some petty tribal struggle which had proved too much for his resources; he wanted a town sacked, or a fleet of prahus destroyed, or an important man killed. The idea beckoned Richard not at all; he had never yet been involved in such a quarrel, and he had no taste for it now, and particularly not in Makassang, which seemed to have far more than its fair share of the cross-currents of treachery and hazard.

He raised his head, to find the Rajah's keen eyes upon him. 'You are wondering, Captain Marriott,' said the old man, accurately enough, 'what is your part in this, and why I have summoned you.' Summoned, thought Richard privately; now there is another idea which I like not at all … But he did not speak his objection, and the

Rajah continued: 'The truth is that I need help, in one particular direction. The High Priest Selang Aro, and the Anapuri, are traditionally allied with the Land-Dyaks – a tribe of the interior which, in the past, have always been the first of my subjects to show disloyalty. That is not a great matter – I have disposed of it before now, and I will do so again.' There was a matter-of-fact tone in his voice more telling than any threatened fierceness. 'The help I need is in a fresh quarter. It seems that Selang Aro has acquired a new ally. When I tell you his name, you will understand the purpose of this audience. In fact, he is a man known to you.'

'Known to me?' echoed Richard Marriott, surprised in spite of himself. 'Who is that?'

The Rajah rose. 'If you will attend me to the terrace outside, I will show him to you.'

The sun outside was fierce, but only briefly so; the Rajah led the way – his passing marked by the low bows of gardeners and attendants – to a bower of flame trees which stood interlaced at one corner of the palace façade. Here, the air was cool, and the shade most welcome. But one side of the bower was open to the bay below the Steps of Heaven, and at its edge stood an unsuspected novelty.

It was a giant telescope. Richard, approaching close to it, saw it to be a star telescope adapted for land use, pivoting on a heavy metal base. It was of German make, by Liebig of Jena, beautifully fashioned and maintained; its magnification could not be guessed, but it must have been enormous. Richard, turning from it, said: 'This is a fine instrument, your Highness. It must afford you much enjoyment.'

'Thus do I draw near to my subjects,' answered the Rajah ironically. 'And to my visitors ...'

Richard had bent his head to the polished lenses, and as he looked through them he smiled broadly. The sharply-focused view of the Lucinda D was really remarkably clear ... He could recognize men working on the deck; he could even see Nick Garrett sitting within the open door of the wheelhouse, quaffing something from a tin pannikin. It was no wonder that Amin Bulong had known more of his ship, and of her situation, than he could possibly have guessed.

Richard turned, still smiling. 'An interesting view,' he said.

'Most absorbing,' agreed the Rajah.

'We have observed,' said Amin Bulong, 'that you have a woman and child on board.'

'The child is my son.'

'And the woman – his mother?'

'His nurse. His mother is dead.'

'Forgive my inquiry,' said Amin Bulong. 'It was a thoughtless intrusion.'

'You love your son?' asked the Rajah.

'Naturally.'

'So did I love mine.' The Rajah placed his thin hands on the telescope, swivelling it round to the right, and adjusting the focus. It was clearly a favourite pastime, at which he was expert. 'Now I will show you my enemy.'

He motioned to Richard, who again bent his head to the lenses. He found that he was looking at a town, on the nearer side of the bay; a bustling town with quays, and superior buildings, and people thronging the streets. A hazy blue smoke hung over it, but the telescope seemed able to pierce this. It was almost as if he could reach out and touch the man sitting gossiping on his front step, the merchant lounging in his doorway, the woman hobbling along in a blue sarong, burdened with a shabby bundle which might have been a baby.

'What do you see?' asked the Rajah.

'A town – a town of some size.'

'It is my capital, Prahang, some twenty miles from here. I hope you will visit it … Now follow the coast, to the east and then the north … What do you see now?'

Richard, whose hands were clumsier, was slow in manoeuvring the telescope, but within a few moments he had mastered its working. He discovered that the coastline to the east of Prahang led to a thin strip of land, with the sea visible on both its sides. There was a road winding along it, and on the road, a trio of elephants making a slow, swaying progress as they dragged an enormous sledge laden with orange-brown teak logs.

'I see a kind of causeway,' he answered.

'It connects this part of Makassang with the mainland to the north. It is a half-mile wide, no more.'

'It could be easily held,' said Richard, half to himself.

'It could be as easily cut ... Now turn westwards to the Shwe Dagon.'

He had no trouble in finding the Golden Pagoda; it seemed suddenly to blaze out at him, lustrous and brilliant in the evening sunshine. He marvelled at its size. It was not a single building, but a whole spreading cluster of them, clinging to the hillside, multicoloured, jumbled in dimension and shape, crowned by the great dome of burnished gold. There were gateways, and flights of steps, and a vast stone statue of the Buddha sitting smiling in the shade.

Richard straightened up; it was almost as if he had to rest his eyes, such was the brilliance of the Shwe Dagon.

'I have not seen anything to compare with it,' he said slowly. 'Is it very old?'

'The central pagoda is indeed ancient,' answered the Rajah. 'The rest of it has grown with the passage of time ... Now you have but two more things to look at ... First, look just below the Shwe Dagon.'

Richard inclined the eyepieces a fraction upwards. Within his view there was now another town, smaller than Prahang the capital, clinging to the edge of the coast almost in the shadow of the Golden Pagoda.

'It is called Shrang Anapuri,' said the Rajah, observing that Richard had it in his view. 'That is, the foster child of the Anapuri. It was a fishing village, long ago; now it has grown, as the Shwe Dagon has grown. Its people are for the most part Land-Dyaks.'

But Richard was scarcely listening to him. His eye had been

caught by something – a thin flash of white against blue – in the sea close to Shrang Anapuri; and when he inclined the telescope further, the flash of white gained sudden substance. It was a furled topsail, and it belonged to a ship anchored in deep water offshore.

She was a big ship, bigger than the Lucinda D; a three-masted barque with a black hull and yellow topsides. She was crowded with men, and there was a constant clustering of sampans and prahus around her. She was a strange focus of activity in a peaceful seascape. But to Richard, there was something about her which was familiar, and foreboding. This was a ship he had seen before.

He studied her carefully. She was at least twenty miles away across the bay, but the powerful telescope brought her within an easy glance. There was something recognizable in the sheer of the bows, and the ornate rail surrounding the afterpart ... As he watched, the barque swung slowly to her anchor, and the counter, turning, caught the sun now low in the west. Richard drew in his breath sharply. He could not see all the gold lettering on the stern, but he could make out enough.

'You know this ship?' the Rajah's voice came gently from beside him.

'Certainly I know her!' exclaimed Richard loudly, propriety and deference forgotten. 'That's the Mystic! By God, it's Black Harris of Boston!'

Black Harris ... Though it was over a year since it had happened, yet Richard Marriott still remembered it vividly, and cursed the memory. It was the first and only time, during his captaincy of the Lucinda D, that he had trusted another human being with his life – not to speak of his profits; it was the first and only time that he had been rewarded with total treachery. Black Harris had made a bargain, sworn to keep it, and then – as he had hoped and planned – thrown Richard to the wolves in order to escape with the plunder. In Richard's private calendar, there was no more hated name.

Black Harris was a Far East freebooter like himself, though with a greater fame for villainy, more men at his command, and certainly a stronger ship. He was a small and cruel man, given, not to violent rages but to cold hatred; it was said that he could never forget a grudge until he had buried both grudge and enemy in the same grave. The two of them had met by chance at Sourabaya, and agreed on a joint enterprise. It required two ships, and the enormous prize which was their target was to be evenly divided at the close.

Briefly, it was a matter of human corruption. There was a Dutch ship sailing from Batavia to the mainland of Cochin China, carrying a rare prize – fifty thousand rix dollars in gold coin, to set up a new banking house at Saigon. The transfer was highly secret, but the Dutch captain, who was in financial straits, had been bought – bought by Black Harris. At a preconcerted place and hour, his ship was to be set upon by an overwhelming force – the Mystic and the Lucinda D – and cruelly robbed of her cargo. The gold would be transferred to the Mystic while the Lucinda D kept watch. Then the two robbers would repair to their agreed rendezvous in the Lingga Archipelago, while the Dutch ship, nursing a score of honourable scars, would limp back home to Batavia with her tale of outrage.

What Richard Marriott did not know was that the Dutch captain's reward was to be the Lucinda D herself. Black Harris had privily agreed to sacrifice one ship, in order to furnish the Dutchman with some convincing evidence of valour, as well as a sizeable prize of his own.

It went according to plan – Black Harris's plan. The Dutch ship was waylaid in open water north of Singapore, menaced, holed by gunfire, boarded with more noise than execution, and plundered. The Lucinda D stood off, guarding the scene of battle, while the Mystic's longboat made five laborious journeys to transfer the boxes of gold coinage. Then, when it was done, Black Harris hailed Richard Marriott, his Boston twang sounding sharp across the water.

'We played that scene too well!' he shouted. 'He reports he is in danger of sinking.'

'Let him sink, then,' returned Richard hardly. 'We can take some prisoners for good measure.'

Black Harris, standing on the Mystic's taffrail, his speaking trumpet in hand, shook his head. 'We owe him more than that.' he called out. 'He will try to make Singapore roadstead. Stay with him tonight, till he is nearer land.'

'Agreed,' said Richard after a moment. It was true that they had reason to be grateful to the Dutchman – fifty thousand reasons, in fact. 'But what then?'

'We meet at Lingga, as we planned,' said Black Harris. His voice was growing fainter as the Mystic and the Lucinda D drew apart. 'Three days from now.'

Richard waved his hand, in agreement and dismissal. It was an extra task, but it was not an unreasonable one. So far, save for fierce looks and a threatening salvo, he had scarcely earned his share of the plunder. This would cost him little save twenty-four hours of slow sea time.

He did not know Black Harris.

At dawn next day the Dutch ship closed the Lucinda D, and her captain, a tall shifty fellow who looked as though he would sell his own grandmother for the price of birdseed, hailed him urgently.

'We are making too much water,' he said. 'We cannot reach Singapore.'

Richard examined the splintered hull of the Dutch ship, wallowing in the long South China swell. 'You are no lower in the water than last night,' he reassured him. 'You will make it, have no fear.'

The Dutchman shook his head, violently. 'We are sinking! I tell you, the water has gained nearly a metre in the night! I wish to transfer my crew to your ship.'

Richard considered. The change of plan did not greatly matter. If the Dutchman thought he was sinking, and wished to abandon his ship, then he could be accommodated without too much head scratching. The prisoners could be landed at some point near Singapore, and the Lucinda D would be fifty miles away before the alarm was raised.

He gestured with his free hand. 'Come aboard, then,' he shouted. 'I will heave-to.'

The Dutch crew came across the water in three boatloads – nearly sixty men, laden with clothing and spare gear, bearing their arms … The first that Richard knew of their treachery was when he was greeting the Dutch captain and the next dozen men to clamber aboard. While he was still speaking, his arms folded, there was a shouted command, a flash of weapons, and a musketball, fired at point-blank range, missed his ear by a hair's breadth.

It was a bloody fight – first muskets, and then pistols, and then brutal hacking work with knives and cutlasses. He did not lose his ship, because his crew was wildly enraged and fought like demons; but he lost eight good men before the fight went out of the Dutchmen, and they changed their tune and began to beg for their lives.

He spared none of them – and each one he killed was Black Harris of Boston. For the Dutch captain, mortally wounded by a cutlass thrust which had pierced his lungs, gave Richard Marriott the plot of the story, in a single sentence which welled up sluggishly with his bubbling blood.

'It – was – the – wish – of – your – friend,' he managed to gasp out, staining the deck atrociously with each word. Then he died.

'Black Harris, of Boston,' repeated the Rajah, in precise tones. He was nodding to himself, as if Richard Marriott, a model pupil, had answered some simple question which could only have baffled a stupid man. 'That accords with our own information … You know this Harris?'

'I know him well.'

'What sort of a man is he?'

'He is a thief and a rogue!'

The Rajah nodded again. 'So … We have also heard that not long ago he cheated you in some enterprise, and put your life in danger.'

Richard turned, staring in surprise. He was about to ask how the

Rajah could possibly have learned this, but he forebore. In these waters, such news travelled miraculously, on invisible wings; as in mysterious Africa, so in the Far East – stories seemed able to grow feathers and to take flight, spanning oceans, penetrating jungles, reaching alien or friendly ears in the same whispered breath. Mere bazaar talk could be borne swiftly on the wind, could veer to and fro, could fall like stray seed upon an island a thousand miles distant. It was of no use to ask of a man: 'How do you know this?' when the man himself could scarcely tell how a close-kept secret had become common gossip. Instead of asking, therefore, Richard assumed an air of indifference, and replied: 'We had a rendezvous at Lingga, but Harris did not keep it. I have not seen him for more than a year.'

'You have searched for him?' asked Amin Bulong.

'No.'

'But he tried to kill you, did he not?'

'He cheated me,' said Richard slowly. He did not like the cross-examination, and would have ended it if he could. 'It is not so uncommon in these parts … I will know better than to trust him in the future.'

'But surely he is your enemy?' inquired the Rajah.

After a moment, Richard answered: 'Yes. He is my enemy.'

'He is my enemy, too.'

There was a pause between them, while Richard fingered the polished mechanism of the telescope, and the two old men regarded him with sharp attention. In truth, it was difficult to say how he felt about Black Harris; there was hatred, certainly, and a desire for revenge, but he had no notion how to go about it, and he had ceased to give much thought to the matter. Harris had a stouter ship, and more men; only time and chance could bring Richard the advantage, and in the meantime, there was more profitable employment than plotting and scheming to square accounts with an enemy who, in almost all circumstances, could laugh at his efforts. And if that seemed to make him a coward, then he was a coward – a live and prudent coward, with other work to do and other battles to win.

Aware of the silence, and of their critical interest, Richard put his own question: 'What is Black Harris doing here?'

'I will tell you what he is doing,' answered the Rajah, with sudden energy, 'and then you and I, who have this same enemy, will decide how to defeat him ... He is plotting to overthrow my government, and to kill me – he, and the High Priest Selang Aro, and the Anapuri priests, and the Land-Dyaks!' The Rajah's voice, though controlled, was shrill with the force of his feeling. 'You saw his ship, and you saw what she was doing. Or, if you did not see, I will tell you. She is embarking, not stores, but men! It is common talk already that he has made some compact with Selang Aro, and now it is easy to guess what their plan is. The Mystic will bring men across the bay to attack the palace, and the Anapuri will cut the causeway and prevent help from reaching us. This is what we have always feared!'

'But surely,' said Richard, interested in spite of his prudence, 'you are strong enough to fight off this attack. You have the palace guard, and the royal regiment. What is so terrible about a single ship?'

'It is what we have always feared,' repeated the Rajah. 'To be cut off from the northern garrisons – they are the royal regiment – and then to have a big ship, and a company of men armed with modern weapons, to storm the palace. We are not strong enough for this.'

'What guns has his ship?' asked Amin Bulong.

It was a question which Richard could easily answer. 'She has sixteen guns,' he said. 'More than any other private ship in these waters.'

'And how many men?'

'Above a hundred.'

'And their weapons?'

Richard shrugged. 'Pistols and muskets. It is a well-armed crew.'

'This is what we have feared,' said the Rajah, for the third time. 'Trained men in league with the Anapuri, guns fighting against spears, and a ship which could bring the palace down in ruins before we could score a single hit with our own cannon!' He was now looking at Richard Marriott with fierce, intent eyes. 'I say again, this man is your enemy. He is ours, too. Help us to destroy him!'

The appeal was very strong, and the moment very persuasive; but already Richard was hardening his heart against it, for many reasons. It was an affair which he had not the least wish to engage in; it would take too long, it was too complicated, it had too many facets, both of danger and of unwanted involvement. Even with the arrival of Black Harris, this was still a tribal quarrel, in which Richard could have no interest; he did not care a jot who sat on the ivory throne of Makassang, and if an ageing Rajah were not strong enough to hold it, then he deserved to have it snatched from him … In addition, the Lucinda D was in bad enough case already; there was no reason why he should put her into further hazard, to secure a throne for a stranger and to checkmate an old enemy – an enemy who must also see this affair as a commonplace venture, and who cared as little as did Richard what the outcome might be.

He began to muster some formal sentences, by way of excuse, so that the matter need not proceed further. The visit, and the proposal, had cost the Rajah a carved elephant tusk; the price to himself had been a musical box which he did not want, and a day's idleness which mattered not at all. Now they could call it quits, and go their several ways, with no dangling strings and no hard feelings.

But it was not to be so easy. He had scarcely begun to make his excuses, pleading other plans which would take him far from Makassang, before the Rajah broke in. Clearly, to be refused anything was a novelty which the old man did not relish; he was ready to become angry, and ready also to use any pressure and any weapon to gain his ends.

It was a matter of taunting to start with, and then of naked threats. Richard Marriott found the taunting harder to endure – as perhaps the Rajah guessed already.

'But what is this?' asked the old man, with an air of astonishment almost theatrical. He was looking at Richard as if the latter were some strange animal – something in a man's shape which had turned out to be less than a man, and more of a freak in nature. 'You tell us that this Black Harris is your enemy, that he cheated you and tried to kill you. Then you say that urgent matters call you away ... One would have thought that you could not resist this chance to meet him again.' And as Richard said nothing: 'The truth is, then,' he continued, 'that you do not wish to meet him at all?'

'I will meet him at my own time and choosing,' said Richard curtly.

'When will that be?'

'I do not know.'

'You will never have a fairer chance than now.'

'I do not agree.'

'Perhaps Captain Marriott does not wish to have a fair chance,' said Amin Bulong, joining in the goading. 'Perhaps, as your Highness suggests, he would be happier never to hear of Black Harris again.'

'Why are you afraid of this man?' asked the Rajah, with contempt.

'I am not afraid of him,' answered Richard. 'But I do not choose to be caught up in this affair.'

'Harris is only a pirate, after all,' said the Rajah. 'You should be a match for him, since you are a pirate, too – a pirate in a stolen coat. But perhaps you are a smaller pirate. A picaroon, as we say.'

Richard kept silence, though anger was thickening his blood intolerably.

'A smaller pirate,' said the Rajah, 'with a ring in his ear. What does the ring signify, pirate? Is it the badge of a slave?'

'Doubtless it was stolen, along with the coat,' said Amin Bulong.

'It should be worn in the nose, not the ear,' said the Rajah viciously.

With an enormous effort, Richard Marriott controlled his rage and his tongue. He was not going to change his mind, and it would take more than the insults of two taunting old men to persuade him otherwise. Thus he faced them, with as level a glance as he could muster.

'Your Highness is welcome to enjoy this sport,' he said coldly. 'I

must inform my friends how guests are treated in Makassang …
However, nothing that you can say will alter my decision. I will not
fight Black Harris, and I will leave as soon as my ship is seaworthy.'

'You are not in a position to refuse to fight, and you are not in a
position to leave, either.' The Rajah's tone had changed subtly, from
gross insult to a harsher note of command. Outside the bower of
flame trees in which they stood, a peacock screamed angrily; the
sound was not more cruel than the look in the old man's eyes. 'I need
not remind you that you are powerless, and your ship as dead as any
hulk … We could send a message to Black Harris which would bring
him here within two hours, ready and eager to finish off an enemy
who is fast aground and cannot escape. Or we could take our own
measures.' The Rajah's eyes glittered, as if he saw the prospect laid
out in bright detail before him, and could scarcely resist its lure.
'There are a hundred war-prahus surrounding your ship. They could
take her, and burn her, and sink her, before you were halfway down
the Steps of Heaven. You would be here, watching the battle – as
long as you had the eyes to see it.'

In spite of himself, Richard felt his blood run cold as he listened.
He knew that these were not idle threats; the Rajah was speaking of
something which he could bring about with a single word, a single
gesture. Nor would he hesitate to use this power, if his evil mood
drove him to it.

Richard looked, not at the Rajah but at Amin Bulong. 'His
Highness forgets that you left a man on board my ship. A hostage.
Your own grandson.'

It was the Rajah who answered. 'We do not hold a hostage so dear
– even the grandson of a friend – that we would not sacrifice him, if
need be.'

'You would find my ship hard to take. She is alert, and ready to
fight.'

'We would not count the cost of a hundred prahus, either. In the
end we would capture your ship, and we would have you, also. We
would have – what is the English phrase? – the pleasure of your

company ... Have you heard of the water torture, Captain Marriott? It is a great favourite with the disciplinary arm of my Palace Guard. They claim that, given time and patience, they can make a man's body swell up to three times its proper size, before it bursts. Myself, I see no reason to doubt them. They also have, for grosser sport, small cages of red ants which they strap to a man's private parts. The ants become more potent, as the man becomes less ...' Suddenly, the fire died out of the Rajah's eyes, as if he thought he had said enough, and could now turn to other, more pleasant prospects. 'But how ridiculous to talk like this, when I know that we are near agreement ... It is not as if I were driving a hard bargain, or seeking a free service from you. That would indeed be inhospitable. Did I mention the matter of a fee, Captain Marriott?'

'You did not,' answered Richard, summoning, with an effort, some irony of tone. 'Truth to tell, you seemed preoccupied with other matters.'

'Forgive an old man's carelessness,' said the Rajah. 'It must have slipped my memory ... To make your ship fit for battle, I will provide a thousand men, and whatever material you need. You will find that my shipwrights, who have ancient skills, can careen your vessel in less than an hour. And on the day that the Mystic is defeated, I will give you one hundred thousand rix dollars.'

Richard could not control a start of surprise. It was an enormous sum – twenty thousand English pounds. As a fee for his services, it was fantastic; and as a bribe for changing his mind, it was still on a princely scale. With such a sum, he could do whatever he had a mind to; he could even quit the roving life, if he wished, and return to England as a rich man of leisure ... He heard the Rajah's voice as if from a long way away, as gentle and persuasive as it had formerly been brutal. 'You may have this sum in gold or in rubies, as you choose ... You may have it also in land, or in slaves, or in spices, or in opium, or in forests ... But come, my friend' – and now the Rajah's voice was positively seductive in its appeal – 'we are growing too serious. These are matters of business, matters for tomorrow. Now it is time for us to relax, and take our pleasure.'

V

I must not get drunk, thought Richard, blinking at the torchlight which wavered incessantly wherever he turned his eyes. But it was not an easy resolve; the heady wine had flowed freely, and the music had pounded and throbbed and wailed, for three hours and more, as the seven rich courses of the banquet, each tempting the appetite, had been opened before him like a Book of Delights. The Rajah had promised him pleasure, and all the gaudy magnificence of the Sun Palace had been spread for him. There had seemed no end to the succeeding dishes: spiced turtle in rice, roast sucking pig, rainbow-hued fish, fruits of all kinds – one had followed another in rich profusion, accompanied by great gold beakers of the cool Javanese wine which did more to provoke a fierce thirst than to slake it.

Richard Marriott sat, on the Rajah's right hand, at the centre of an immense table which filled one side of the audience chamber. Resin torches flared brightly all round the room; in its centre, open braziers of slow-burning wood supplied a flickering background for a hundred strange figures – wandering guests, serving men, palace guardsmen, pages, attendants, tumblers, musicians, acrobats, beggars, suppliants – who thronged the banquet. So far, Richard had seen no single woman in the room; the feast, which was in his honour, seemed an exclusively masculine occasion, like some barbaric version of the Hell Fire Club. But when he mentioned this to Amin Bulong, who sat nearby, the latter expressed surprise.

'That has never been our custom here,' he answered. For his age, Amin Bulong had shown great appetite and execution at table, and his wizened old face was shining with the effort. 'Indeed, it would be unthinkable! In Makassang, men and women never take their food together, save in the strictest privacy, and public feasting has always been the reserve of men. The women have other occupations ...' He savoured his wine with, his thin inquiring nose, while round them

113

the frieze of figures in the smoky half-darkness wound and unwound, like pictures on a turning tapestry, and the muted drums and pipes wove their curious pattern. Then he asked: 'You are fond of women, Captain Marriott?'

'Not more so than any other man, I think. But I am not indifferent.'

The Rajah, who had been listening on his other side, broke in with a gentle laugh. 'What you are eating now,' he said, 'will not make you indifferent, either.'

Richard looked down at the dish before him. It was fish, of some kind new to him, served in coconut shells decorated with vine tendrils. Delicately spiced, it had seduced even an appetite now turning jaded. 'It is delicious ... I was about to ask your Highness what it was.'

'It is trepang.'

'Trepang?'

'Trepang – the giant sea slug.' The Rajah smiled again. 'You have not heard of it?'

'No.'

'You must spend more time in my country ... We like to think that its aphrodisiac qualities are world-famous.'

Now it was Richard's turn to smile. 'Sailors like to think that they have no need of such stimulants.'

'Ah, the pride of youth!' said the Rajah. In contrast with his earlier mood, he now seemed in high good humour; though he had eaten little – as might well have been his custom – yet it was clear that he had drawn great pleasure from the banquet, and that such occasions as this were much to his taste. Perhaps he did not deserve to rule this glittering kingdom, thought Richard – and then regretted the thought, which at such a moment seemed churlish and unworthy.

Tonight, the Rajah, forgetting his cares, was playing host, in princely fashion; tomorrow he would rule again, and show that he was fitted for it ... Richard lifted his glass of wine, which a page had just replenished, and the Rajah courteously followed his movement.

But his was not a wineglass; it was a beaker fashioned from a skull, its dome hollowed out and rimmed with gold, its eye sockets aglow with precious jewels. It had been set before him ceremoniously at the beginning of the feast, and seemed to be an object of special veneration.

'I must thank you again for your hospitality,' said Richard. 'I had no thought, when I stepped ashore this morning, that I would have so royal a welcome.'

The Rajah was looking at him, his eyes bright above the rim of the grinning skull cup. 'My wish was to make amends for the small discord of our earlier meeting. I hope that I have done so.'

'Beyond question!' answered Richard – and though it might be the wine speaking, he felt that this was true. 'I can remember nothing but courtesy.'

They drank, and bowed towards each other. 'It is my feeling.' said the Rajah after a moment, lowering his jewelled skull cup, 'that you are a man who might be led to something, but cannot be commanded.'

Through the haze of the wine, Richard Marriott made bold to answer in a way he would not have dared earlier. 'I believe that your Highness and myself have much in common.'

For a moment it seemed as if the remark were too near to insolence to be permissible. The Rajah's small figure stiffened, and for a long minute he regarded Richard as though in doubt whether the latter were not presuming intolerably on his hospitality. Then his face suddenly cleared, and broke into a smile, and then into laughter, laughter so clear and unforced that everyone within earshot turned to share in it. After a moment – and it seemed an unheard-of condescension, judging by the reaction upon all their faces – he raised the skull cup again, in both his hands, and passed it to Richard.

'Drink from my cup,' he invited, still smiling, 'in token of that likeness.' And as Richard Marriott, aware of a special mark of honour, drank, the Rajah turned to his major-domo, who stood in unbroken attendance behind his chair of state, and said, simply: 'The dancers.'

At a sign from the major-domo, an imposing figure across whose yellow livery a broad purple sash was draped, denoting his rank, the music of the players faded into silence. There was a pause, as the centre of the banquet chamber was cleared, and the glowing braziers moved to one side; then the single beat of a gong was heard, reverberating with enormous power throughout the room, and to the slow percussion of drums a line of dancers appeared between the columns at the far end of the hall, and began to weave a pattern of the most insistent, sensuous beauty that Richard had ever witnessed.

They were young girls, twenty of them, their pale brown bodies naked to the waist, wearing only the traditional costume of the harem, the diaphanous folds of which shimmered as their turning limbs caught the torchlight. The dance was slow, and intricately figured; it seemed to be a dance of enticement, and their serious faces – many of them exquisitely beautiful – were in voluptuous contrast with their bending and weaving and interplay of their bodies. Richard watched with hazy pleasure, mixed with a desire too delicate to become urgent; it seemed to him, in his mood of relaxation, that the dance was not for gross appetites, that it spoke of beauty rather than of promise, it ravished the eye and the heart with more certainty than any other part of his being.

Strangely, it appeared that this was the mood also of all the other watchers in the audience chamber of the Sun Palace; here, perhaps, was a people who took their pleasure without greed, who saw the loveliness of women not as their prey but as their good fortune … Among all the faces near him, only those of his 'bodyguard' – John Keston, Peter Ramsay, and Burnside the sober Scot – betrayed any lustful intent, though it might be said that this trio, in their large-eyed, staring concentration upon the dancers, made up for the reticence of all the rest. Richard sat back in his chair and, turning, found the Rajah's eyes resting inquiringly upon him.

'You enjoy such entertainment?' the latter asked, with a touch of
irony.

'Very much,' Richard answered. 'The girls are most accomplished
… May I ask who they are?'

'They are slaves.'

The dance continued, while Richard, sipping his wine, gradually
allowed his thoughts to stray far afield from what was before his
eyes. He was in a mood to let this delicious world have its way with
him … His strongest resolve, of a little earlier, had been, I must not
get drunk; but now it seemed that this did not matter so greatly. He
had already been seduced on so many different planes – of appetite,
of hospitality, of the public bestowal of honour – that he had come
to realize that he was likely to do what the Rajah wished. The old
man had said that he could not be commanded. But it was certainly
true that he could be led – and he had now been led, by devious
stages of seduction, to a change of heart.

It was, in essence, an appeal of personality. The Rajah had in turn
insulted him grossly, threatened him with torture, and pleaded with
his sense of chivalry and pride; but these were no more than the
normal artifices of a potentate accustomed to having his own way,
either by wily or by brutal means. They could not be held against
him, any more than could the devious wheedling of a child. And it
was true that Richard was, physically, in the Rajah's power; if he
were thwarted, the old man would certainly sacrifice one noble
hostage, and the lives of countless lesser men, for the pleasure of
revenge. Richard, in his present mood, with the wine putting a
cloudy warmth of fellowship upon his brain, could not blame him
for this ruthlessness. It was ingrained in the nature of a despotic
ruler, whose will had rarely been crossed.

But behind it, also, Richard sensed something else, which now
made a much stronger appeal; the despair of an old and fearful man,
an heirless ruler concerned with the blank face of the future. The
Rajah's erratic veering between threats and cajoling was a sign of
two things – the weakness of decay, and a sense of vanishing power

which could still become obstinate and real. He was rather to be pitied than anything else. He was rather to be pitied by Richard Marriott – for a hundred thousand rix dollars in gold.

Perhaps it was this last prospect which (as the Rajah had implied) was tipping the balance in favour of action. But to put checkmate to the plans of Black Harris (thought Richard, turning back again to the dancers) might now be seen to be a duty as well as a pleasure. It was possible that his enemy, building on the alliance with the Anapuri, might have ambitions to rule Makassang himself; and Makassang deserved a better fate than Harris, or any other pirate whose thirst for blood and treasure overtopped all else.

The dance was now ended – or rather, the line of dancers, their young bodies glistening, retreated to form a semicircle some distance from the table. The gong sounded again, with a thrice-repeated, crashing reverberation; and now the single figure of a girl appeared between the entrance columns. She held herself still for a moment, caught like a jewel in the flickering torchlight, and then she began a slow dance which brought her nearer, step by step, to where they sat.

She was ravishingly beautiful; she outshone all the others as a planet outshines a hundred stars. Her face was the palest oval, beneath a headdress of gold filigree which twined in and out of her lustrous hair; her shoulders and bosom – for she was naked to the waist, like her companions – were the most exquisite Richard had ever seen. He caught his breath as he looked at her; in the whole of his thirty years, in a score of countries, he had never seen anyone to match her, in grace of form, in sensuous yet remote beauty of face. Utterly captivated, he turned to Amin Bulong.

'Who is this?' he asked, not trying to disguise his feeling. 'Another slave?'

'No,' said Amin Bulong. He seemed suddenly constrained, as though not wishing their exchange to be overheard. 'No, she is not a slave.'

'I shall have no need of your trepang,' said Richard coarsely, 'with such seasoning as this.'

Amin Bulong was now staring straight ahead of him, his manner more reserved than ever. It was the Rajah, a slight smile on his lips, who said gently: 'This is a dance which is always completed by my daughter.' Richard had never experienced a more excruciating moment of embarrassment; he felt his scarlet blush spreading, and he could have cut out his tongue. He scarcely saw the dance, which was short and formal, as if setting a crown upon what had gone before. He heard the music but faintly – drumbeats against the harmony of two pipes, in high and low pitch; he saw only that the girl danced with a studious elegance which had in it something of resignation, and that the onlookers watched her as if they were attending the close of some religious exercise. But when it was ended, with a low obeisance to the Rajah, and the girl had glided out into the shadows, he was still in the utmost confusion, and his face was burning.

The Rajah, however, seemed completely unconcerned. He motioned to have Richard's glass filled, and again for the musicians to continue their playing; then he remarked, as politely as ever: 'That is called the Dance of the Priestesses ... It is very ancient – we believe that it was a pagan temple dance, in the old days ... Of course, there have been modern variations ... I hope you found it entertaining?'

Richard nodded, still hardly able to speak. 'Yes, your Highness.'

'My daughter's role was that of the Virgin Sacrifice. I need scarcely explain to you what its significance was, in former times. However' – he smiled, gravely amused – 'we have become less bloodthirsty, with the years. She danced well, do you not think?'

'Yes, indeed.'

'Her name is Sunara ... She will be joining us shortly.'

'Your Highness – ' began Richard, wishing somehow to retrieve his crassness. He was not sure what he was going to say: still confused, he was conscious of a flicker of anger that he should have been betrayed into this position. Almost, it might have been a calculated embarrassment ... But before he could continue, Amin

Bulong interposed, like some wise old diplomat stepping in to chart a safe channel.

'We have many such dances, handed down through the generations. If you stay with us, Captain Marriott, you will see more of them. The Sea-Dyaks have a dance for blessing their nets, and the Anapuri have a rite which mimes the chariot of Phoebus Apollo, bringing the sunrise at the midsummer solstice. I do not know how they equate such things with the teachings of the Lord Buddha … But I hope you will stay long enough to enjoy these curiosities of Makassang.'

'I will stay,' said Richard, on an impulse which he could hardly define.

'That is good news indeed,' said the Rajah. He was leaning forward, in undisguised eagerness, and his fingers, touching the rim of the skull cup, were trembling. 'I hope it is the forerunner of even better.'

'And I will fight Black Harris for you,' said Richard, speaking under the same compulsion. 'On the terms which we have discussed together.'

The Rajah and Amin Bulong exchanged long glances; on both their faces was the same tremulous satisfaction, the same confession of relief.

'I cannot hide my pleasure and my gratitude,' said the Rajah. Suddenly he was a much older man, leaning upon the strength of a younger; his expression, which in repose was proud, had softened into simple thankfulness. 'You will have no cause to regret your decision.'

The major-domo, standing behind them, struck his wand of office twice upon the marble floor, and announced: 'Your Royal Highness, the Princess Sunara approaches.'

She was attended by six companions, who formed a graceful semicircle at her back; and in other parts of the great hall, Richard noticed, other women, young and old, were now joining the gathering, giving it a further relaxation, a softer texture. Close to, the Princess had a face of the rarest beauty, and her body, delicately formed, a lissom grace which, hinted at in the dance, was apparent in every smallest move she made. She was dressed now in a dark green sarong edged with gold, and she wore also a tunic of cloth of gold on the upper part of her body. Unconsciously, Richard found his eyes searching beneath its contours for the soft shoulders, the flawless breasts which, even in his embarrassment, had delighted his eyes earlier. Perhaps it was this which caused her, when he was presented by the Rajah, to appear cool and remote; for after a single glance, which seemed to take in his bold eyes, bemedalled uniform, and tall figure in an instant's sweep, she retreated to a distant detachment, to which Richard, clearly, was not to be allowed the key.

'Captain Marriott,' said the Rajah to his daughter, when they had sat down and the wine had been passed again, 'has this moment agreed to enter my service. He will fight the pirate ship across the bay.'

Princess Sunara inclined her head, but she said nothing. She sat, serene and composed, on a small ivory stool; her feet, in golden sandals, were demurely crossed. The little finger of her right hand was also gilded, Richard noticed – the traditional mark of virginity in all these islands.

'So we may expect great things tomorrow, or the next day,' the Rajah went on. He was still moved and eager; it was almost as if he were pleading with his daughter to show a like appreciation. 'And I have another surprise for you, Sunara.' He spoke over his shoulder to the major-domo, who in turn signed to the musicians to fall silent. In the sudden stillness, the musical box was carried forward, and placed on the table. It was Richard himself who set it in motion.

The tinkling melody of 'Loch Lomond' filled the air. As she recognized it, the Princess's expression changed, from indifference to unfeigned delight; it was as if she shed ten years, on the instant, and became an enraptured child again. She heard it out, as they all did, with close attention; only when the melody was ended did her air of coolness return.

But she did speak, at last, and her voice, soft and low, was as if the music were continuing.

'That is beautiful,' she said. 'Beautiful and sad…' She reached out a slim hand and touched the walnut lid of the musical box. 'It is indeed a surprise to hear it again. This must be some new gift.'

'From Captain Marriott,' said the Rajah. 'He has proved himself most generous. It is a cherished possession, it seems. It belonged to his mother.'

Sunara's eyes rose briefly, to meet Richard's. 'In that case, it must be very painful for him to part with it. Should you not be content with some smaller token?'

Richard squared his shoulders. No child like this one, however lovely, was going to mock him thus.

'The pain – if there is any pain – is as nothing compared with the pleasure of giving. Particularly when you have all shown such appreciation … I am told that the tune is a familiar one to you.'

'Of course,' answered Sunara. 'It was Andrew Farthing's favourite. He taught me to sing it, long ago.'

'He seems to have enjoyed great honour in your country,' said Richard.

'He was a good man,' said the Rajah. 'A true scholar, and a man of God.'

'I wish I had been able to meet him.'

'I do not think,' said Sunara coldly, 'that you would have found many thoughts to share with each other.'

'Your Highness cannot know that,' answered Richard with equal coldness.

'You have heard my father say that he was a man of God.'

'What am I, then?'

For the first time, Princess Sunara looked at him directly, for more than a brief glance. Her eyes, brown flecked with green, were as honest and as obstinate as a child's.

'You are fighting for my father?'

'Yes.'

'For love of fighting?'

'No.'

'For love of money, then?'

'For money.'

'Andrew Farthing would have called you a mercenary.'

'Well, I am a fighter, at least.' Richard Marriott stood up, abruptly. He was not going to change his mind or vary his decision; but neither was he going to stay to be disparaged, by this or any other chit of a girl. 'And it is flattering to be needed, Princess, for any reason under the sun …' He turned to the Rajah. 'Your Highness – forgive me, but I must return to my ship. I have much to do, before I am ready for your service.'

The Rajah eyed him carefully, conscious of constraint among their circle, wishing to make sure that it was not a vital element in their exchange.

'I had hoped that you would enjoy our hospitality for tonight also.'

'You have been more than hospitable already,' answered Richard. 'But if this mercenary is to earn his keep, he must prepare for tomorrow.'

'Tomorrow is ours?'

'Certainly!' Richard inclined his head; it gave him great pleasure thus to put on the cloak of honour. 'I have pledged my word, as has your Highness. As soon as my ship is ready, we will go to work.'

Amin Bulong, rising, said: 'I will give the necessary orders. Your ship will be taken in hand at dawn, if that is agreeable. Good luck, or skill, has already brought you within easy distance of our careenage … If you are intent on leaving, let me summon your palankeen.'

'I will walk,' said Richard grandly. 'The night air will sit well with the wine. And even better with the trepang.' He bowed, with the smallest permissible inclination, to Princess Sunara, and then more formally to the Rajah. 'Your Highness … I look forward to our next meeting.'

'Captain Marriott,' said the Rajah, 'no meeting could have given me more pleasure than this one.'

'We have an English proverb,' Richard declaimed, by way of farewell – and it was wine, pique, and self-confidence all speaking for him at once – 'which says, "Promise is a fine dog, but Performance is a better one." With your permission, I go now to review my kennels.'

Attended by torches, and by six of the royal bodyguard, and by his own stumbling trio who occasionally broke into maudlin song, he strode down the Steps of Heaven as if they were part of his own kingdom. His head cleared gradually of the wine, but he did not lose his exhilaration, nor his appetite for action. Wherever he looked – up to the stars, round him at the torchlight, below to the shimmering – he found only a vision to stir his blood. Whether he had been tricked into agreement, or cajoled, or threatened, did not matter a jot. Tomorrow would bring back all the things which were the finest fabric of his life – adventure at sea, fighting, danger, gold. He would square accounts with Black Harris. And earn his due from the Rajah. And from the girl.

VI

'I do not like this plan at all,' said Nick Garrett, with the surly look and tone he had been affecting for the past several hours. 'Black Harris is not for us – not without two more ships as big as the Lucinda to help us. Sixteen guns he has – aye, and we've seen 'em at work! He will blow us out of the water before we're within cannonshot.'

'It will be a night action,' answered Richard Marriott, good-humouredly. He was set in his mind, and it would take more than Nick Garrett's grumbling to alter it. 'What do you take me for – a damned fool fighting his first battle? I am not going to sail up to his guns in broad daylight! We'll come out of the darkness and surprise him.'

'And then he'll surprise us. What can two guns do against sixteen?

– or twenty-four men against a hundred?'

'We shall have the war-prahus to help us. More than two hundred of them. They have been promised.'

'Promised!' Garrett spat contemptuously into the shallow water at the tidemark. 'What are they worth? – save for warcries and drum-beating! The paddlers will turn tail and run at the first shot!'

Richard shook his head. 'They are better men than that.' He pointed seawards, where the Lucinda D, lying over at a hard angle, with her lower yards steeped in water, was surrounded by a swarm of native labourers. 'You have seen them get to work. If they fight half as well, we have Black Harris sewn up in his hammock already.'

The two of them were standing on the low wharf, fashioned of giant teak piles, which abutted one side of the Steps of Heaven; the Lucinda D now lay sprawled in the shallows, not more than thirty yards from them. Amin Bulong had said that she would be taken in hand at dawn, and careened within an hour, and his word had been made good, fantastic though the undertaking had seemed. At first light, the shipwright overseer – an ancient Malay who looked more likely to mouth incantations and cast spells than to repair a modern ship – had come on board with six assistants as old and decrepit as himself, while scores of prahus and sampans manned by younger, lustier men milled around the ship, and onshore there could be seen hundreds of workmen assembling on the wharf. From thence onwards, the Lucinda D was in firm and skilful hands. She had been swiftly lightened, by unloading some of her stores and gear into cargo sampans (the stevedores worked like running ants, bearing burdens twice their own size); then she had been edged nearer the shore, and naked divers – who seemed able to stay underwater for two minutes and more – had gone down to position the giant weighted rollers on which she would be brought into the shallows.

Once she was in low water, warps were led from the masts to pulleys anchored on the sea bed, and thence ashore. There they were seized upon by work gangs who must have totalled more than a thousand men. Gongs began to beat, in fierce command; the thousand men heaved and strained, chanting in chorus as they built up the surging rhythm; and the Lucinda D, overborne by this multitude of clawing humans, began to heel over sharply. Within a few moments, she was clipped down and lying on her side, and the injured planks were laid bare.

These were what the shipwrights were working on now, as Richard and Nick Garrett, out of employment, lounged on the wharf and waited for their ship to be given back to them. At their backs the throngs of men who had done the heaving down lounged also, lying in whatever patch of shade they could find, dozing, gossiping, chewing the betel nut which seemed to have stained the teeth of every man to a noisome scarlet. There was a vile smell in the air; it came from a wide-mouthed cauldron on the foreshore, in which was being boiled a mysterious kind of pitch for making good the seams of the new planks. It was a secret blend, Richard had been told, of pine resin and fish oil 'which would last forever'. He was left with the hope that the stink of it would at least disappear with the passing of time.

Nick Garrett was still grumbling and complaining. He had been awakened early, with news and plans which had come as a complete surprise, and he had set his mind against seeing any sense in any of them.

'Why should we make it our quarrel?' he asked. 'Who cares what happens to this rajah? Black Harris can rule in Makassang, for all I care!'

'We are making it our quarrel,' answered Richard crisply, 'because we are being paid for it. A hundred thousand rix dollars! We would be mad to refuse it!'

'Maybe we are mad to believe it. How do we know he will honour the bond? You should have taken a few hundreds, to seal the bargain, and then we could have sailed as soon as we were fit, with no one the wiser.'

'The Rajah will honour his bond, have no fear. He is that sort of man.'

'Peter Ramsay says he is old as Methuselah, and near his death.'

'He is old,' agreed Richard. 'But not yet feeble.'

'Peter says there are rubies and diamonds and gold, enough to sink a ship.'

'It is a handsome palace.'

'And a handsome girl, eh?' Nick Garrett leered at him. 'I hear she has a pair of breasts fit to blind a man's eyesight. Maybe they blinded yours!'

Richard, conscious of a distaste he could scarcely define, said shortly: 'I did not like her … As soon as they are finished here, Nick, have the ship kedged out into deep water, and take the stores on board again. Then look to the weapons. And tell Manina she will be coming ashore with the boy, before we sail tonight.'

'Where will you be, then?' Garrett asked suspiciously.

'I have a meeting ashore, to work out the plans. I am waiting for the palankeen now.'

'Well, make no more promises, for God's sake,' said Garrett sourly, 'or we will find ourselves fighting headhunters in the jungle.' He shaded his eyes against the glare of the sun striking the water, watching a cora-cora which had cast off from the Lucinda D and was just coming alongside the lowest of the Steps of Heaven. Behind the single paddler sat a soldierly figure in scarlet, easy to recognize. It was the hostage, the captain of the bodyguard. 'Now what is this?' demanded Garrett, anger in his voice. 'Are we letting him go?'

'Matters are changed,' said Richard. 'I need him ashore, for the planning.'

'We should take another hostage, then.'

'Matters are changed,' repeated Richard. 'We are working together. There is no need of hostages.'

Nick Garrett glared at him, openly hostile. 'You are quickly swayed,' he said. 'I must have a sight of this girl. First we are to trust some old devil who calls himself a rajah, then we are to fight Black Harris, not for ourselves but for someone else. The sun must have melted your brains!'

'We are fighting for the money.'

'And that's another thing! Have we changed our trade since we grounded on Makassang? If there is so much plunder here, why do we not take it for ourselves?'

'It is not to be had for the taking. You have seen something of their strength. If there is a state treasure, you can be sure it is well guarded.'

'We might do worse than join forces with Black Harris,' said Garrett, half to himself.

'And be robbed and swindled again? Now hark at who has lost his brains!' A palankeen, wending its way slowly down the Steps of Heaven, had nearly reached the bottom, and Richard turned to go. He could see the young captain of the bodyguard staring in his direction, and he made a sign of greeting, which was returned. 'We will do as I have said, Nick,' he declared, firmly. 'Make the ship ready to fight. Take on water and fresh fruit. I will be back this afternoon.'

'You eat luncheon with the Rajah?' Garrett inquired sarcastically.

'I hope so. He keeps the best table that I ever saw.'

'If you do not return by nightfall,' said Nick Garrett, with a rare and grisly attempt at humour, 'I will know that he has eaten you.'

In the cool of the flame tree bower which sheltered the giant telescope, the four men had taken their turn to examine the Mystic, at her anchorage across the bay. Richard Marriott and the captain of the bodyguard – called, by tradition, Amin Sang, meaning Amin the Younger – had been greeted on their arrival by Amin Bulong, who would be lending his authority to the plan of attack; and they had been joined immediately by the commander of the Royal Regiment, Colonel Kedah, whose troops would fight the major part of the action on land. Kedah was a tall, thin, hard-bitten man whose appearance was not aided by his having but a single eye; across the other, a spearthrust had furrowed a livid scar which gave his face a most devilish appearance. But he seemed a capable man, and a trustworthy one, and his words, though few, were worth hearing.

Richard Marriott had been the last to look through the telescope, and he could only agree with the others that its panorama was ominous. Around the Mystic, things were quieter now, with fewer sampans and less traffic to the shore; but her decks were black with men, and the sun caught their weapons unceasingly. By the look of her spars and rigging, she could have set sail at any time. But much plainer to be seen, and more threatening still, was the movement of soldiers along the coast, from Shrang Anapuri to the causeway.

They were not in formation, and they straggled along the road in twos and threes; but there were enough of them to stir the dust continuously, and they plodded along eastwards without pause. It was clear that two formidable forces were on the move – the men aboard the Mystic, and the men massing towards the causeway. They seemed to confirm what the Rajah had forecast; that Black Harris was spear-heading an attack designed to take the Sun Palace by storm, while the Anapuri and their allies cut the narrow causeway and isolated the arm of land on which the great centre of government stood.

Now, in an anteroom plainly furnished and screened from prying eyes, the four of them sat round a table and considered what had to be done. Richard, lacking charts, had sketched a rough plan of the bay upon a piece of white silk, and this lay before them as they talked, telling its own story of chances to be risked and dangers to be faced.

'They have given us two tasks,' said Amin Bulong. As 'Commander-in-Chief' of Makassang, he was taking the lead in their discussion, though Richard knew that sooner or later he himself must make the most significant contribution of all. 'We have to prevent the Mystic reaching here, or, if she comes across the bay, we must throw back the men she will try to land. And we must keep the causeway open, so that the palace is not isolated from the rest of the island.' He turned to Colonel Kedah. 'How many men have you there?'

'The causeway garrison is five hundred men,' answered Kedah. His single eye was bent upon the silken sketch map. 'But we shall need more, and I have sent them down already.'

'More? To hold it?'

'Judging by the number of men moving up from Shrang Anapuri, they mean to do more than stop us breaking out. They mean to break in.'

Amin the Younger nodded. 'I agree – they mean to make an attack there also.' He spoke in Malay, of which Richard knew enough to follow what he said. 'Probably they plan to storm the palace from the south.'

'It is possible,' agreed his grandfather. He also was eyeing the map – the map with many question marks and the inherent dangers. Then he turned to Richard. 'What did you think when you looked at the Mystic?'

'She is ready to move,' answered Richard. 'They must have three or four hundred men on board. And their own fleet of prahus. They might be planning it for tonight.'

'So?'

'We must plan it for tonight also.'

They were all watching him, and the attention was flattering; but Richard found that he could not yet draw much satisfaction from this. He was only important to these plans because he had weapons of a special sort – firearms, and a big ship. It was for this reason that his price was high, and he must earn it before he could sit back and play the hero.

He looked from Amin Sang, young and proudly eager, to Colonel Kedah, in whose single eye lurked a gleam of fierceness. He was not cool towards such allies.

'This is my plan,' he told them, 'and there is an important part in it for all three of us. In fact, we cannot succeed unless we each carry out exactly what we have to do.' He spoke slowly, knowing that Amin Sang, though he had mastered only a few words in English, could understand it if it were simply pronounced. 'My ship will set sail at dusk; she will be across the bay by midnight, and midnight is the time we all strike. With me will be the fleet of prahus, carrying soldiers, as many as they can hold; they will be commanded by Amin Sang. When we are near the other side, the prahus will leave me, and turn eastwards, and land their soldiers somewhere between Shrang Anapuri and the causeway.' He touched his forefinger to the map. 'There is a shallow bay there. I have seen it through the telescope. It will serve well enough.'

Richard paused, then turned again to Colonel Kedah. 'Now the three tasks come together, and the timing is important. At midnight, your men will break out from the causeway, and push the enemy back along the road to Shrang Anapuri. They are numerous, as we have seen, but they can be no match for the Royal Regiment in force … Your men' – his eyes went round to Amin Sang – 'will wait for this retreating enemy, and fall upon them as they retreat. They are likely to be confused, and thus faint-hearted. You will then turn towards the sea, and kill off the survivors from the Mystic as they swim ashore.'

'Survivors?' Amin Bulong echoed the surprising word. 'How will this be?'

'The Mystic is mine,' said Richard, with great confidence. 'Just as Colonel Kedah will surprise the men coming up to attack the causeway – who will think they have only a small garrison to deal with – so I aim to surprise Black Harris, whether or not he knows I am in these waters.'

'You have some new plan?' asked Colonel Kedah.

'It is an old plan. Nearly three hundred years old, to my knowledge. I have always wanted to see if it is as good as the historians tell us.'

Amin Bulong was watching him, amused and thoughtful at the same time. 'Three hundred years ago,' he said, 'would take us back to the Spanish wars against your own country. Perhaps to Sir Francis Drake himself.'

Richard smiled back at him. 'Was Andrew Farthing a historian, as well as all the rest?'

'He liked to tell us stories of the brave men of his country, though a man of peace himself.'

Colonel Kedah, who could not have followed this exchange, turned his single eye upon Richard. 'I understand all parts of the plan except your own,' he said, rather coldly. 'You say that our prahus will be leaving you, to land Amin Sang's men on the coast. Do you not need help, then? Will you attack this Mystic ship alone?'

'I shall need three prahus,' answered Richard. 'Old ones. This will be their last voyage.'

'You must explain,' said Amin Sang, though he had caught the note of determination in Richard's voice, and his young face was alight.

'Three prahus,' repeated Richard. 'And three brave men who can swim strongly. And three pots of oil. The gunpowder I can furnish myself.'

VII

Surprise, thought Richard, in the last moments of prickling silence before hell broke loose; it was the only thing to be achieved, the only prayer to be sent heavenwards, the only word in the language ... Thus far, everything had gone perfectly; the wind had served them, from the moment that the Lucinda D stood out from the Steps of Heaven with her three fire prahus in tow; when they came within five miles of their target, the expected uproar had been unloosed ashore as fighting broke out at the causeway. It was this uproar, this noise and yelling and clash of arms, which should even now be distracting all on board the Mystic. Let them not turn aside, Richard had prayed, let them look landwards a little longer, as the Lucinda D, creeping up on the blind side, gently launched her secret weapons on the unsuspecting foe.

He could see the fire prahus now, three vague diminishing blurs of darkness against the pale sea, propelled by determined men, closing the gap between themselves and their quarry. The canoes were linked together; in each of them was a pot of oil, a charge of gunpowder, a slow-match timed to burn for five minutes, and a single paddler who, at the last moment, would slip overboard and swim away from the holocaust. All they needed now, to achieve this careful treachery, was surprise.

By his side, in the darkness of the Lucinda D's quarter-deck, Nick Garrett breathed: 'They are there, by God! They are there!' Even as he spoke, the first prahu exploded in a sheet of flame under the Mystic's counter, showering half her hull with flaming oil.

The blow could not have struck at a better moment. Those on board who were not staring landwards, wondering at the noise now spreading along the whole coast road, were preparing to heave up anchor and get underway; the flames lit their astonished figures, and those of the men working on the yards, and the sails they were unbrailing. When the second fire prahu exploded in its turn, sending burning oil leaping as high as the barque's main topsails, a desperate turmoil broke loose; while the third, burning fiercely but broken away from its fellows by the violence of the explosions, drifted downwind among the sampans and canoes clustered near the Mystic, a fiery intruder which they were too horrified to escape.

As the second fire prahu burst into flame, Richard shouted, at the top of his voice: 'Fire!' The Lucinda D's guns and small arms, held in check until this moment, answered with a crackling roar, beginning their work of execution. They had never had an easier target.

For now the fire had taken hold. Splashes of flaming oil, mounting the sails, spread swiftly into great billows of burning sailcloth; the counter with its ornamental rail was well alight; on the deck, wreathed in smoke and split by red and orange tongues of fire, figures ran to and fro in a frenzy, and presently began to fall, as the murderous hail of shot, unanswered by a single counter-blow, took its toll of the close-packed throng. The Lucinda D, edging within fifty yards of the Mystic, poured broadside after broadside – with cannon and repeating riflegun, with blunderbuss, musket, and pistol – into her helpless quarry. It was easy; the main work had been done much earlier, when they had crept up in the darkness and launched their fire canoes; this was their reward, and there was not a man on board, remembering the Mystic's treachery which might have led to their ruin, who did not savour it fiercely.

Scattered shooting began to come from the Mystic, as a few of her crew rallied to face the attack; but from such a flaming pyre they could only aim into the darkness, and few of these shots found their mark before even this feeble counter-stroke died to nothing. Half the ship had become engulfed in roaring flame; and now groups of men up in the bows and along the bowsprit began to jump for their lives, yelling in fear and pain as they sought safety in the unknown darkness.

A lucky shot from the cannon split the mainmast and brought it down; it toppled in a fiery wreath of flame, like a great tree in the path of a forest fire. The Mystic, with her cable slipped by some distraught hand, began to drift towards the shore, a ship-of-war turned into a blazing hulk. Men with their clothes on fire continued to cast away their weapons and leap overboard, seeking to quench their agony in the murky water.

Then Richard Marriott saw Black Harris. He was standing on a hatch cover at the break of the fo'c'sle, silhouetted by a whole wall of flame; a small figure with tossing arms, shouting against the roaring of the fire, exhorting his men to turn and fight. Richard could not help admiring his spirit which, overcoming murderous surprise, refused to admit that defeat might be spitting in his very face. He had a cutlass in his hand, and with it he slashed at some of his own men as they fled from their guns and made for the only safe platform remaining – the bowsprit hanging above the water. But Richard Marriott did not hate him the less for his bravery. This was the man who would have sold him into death. He deserved the same fate, and he was within an ace of earning it.

From thirty yards away, Richard raised his speaking trumpet and shouted the single word: 'Harris!'

In the roar of flames, and the yelling of men in confusion and terror, he had to shout again before his voice carried. But then Black Harris, turning and peering into the darkness, answered him.

'Who is that?'

'Richard Marriott! Your partner!'

Harris, who must have been astonished, was quick to think and to speak. He did not question, he did not swear or shout his anger, he did not bargain. He cupped his hands, and called out: 'I will pay what I owe.'

Richard laughed, in a tone made throaty by hatred and the pleasure of revenge; it was one of the ugliest sounds of the night. He shouted back: 'Have no fear – I am paid!' Then he threw aside his speaking trumpet, and drew from his belt the two silvered pistols, Castor and Pollux, which he had carried, and used, for more than ten years. He sighted swiftly, and fired both at the same moment.

The range was long, but loathing joined with skill to shorten it to nothing. The figure of his enemy, luridly illumined as if by the fires of hell, spun round once and dropped into the sea of flame below him.

Richard laughed again, on the same animal note. He was indeed paid … Then he leant back against the mizzenmast, breathing deeply, recovering his coolness, and watched the Mystic becoming drenched by fire, and the burning oil on the water as it overtook the swimmers and the prahus and the sampans, and the doomed stragglers who, wading ashore utterly spent, tottered hapless towards the waiting butchery.

Dawn came up to reveal the scene of carnage with delicate, reluctant fingers, as though fearful of what might be discovered. The Mystic was fast ashore, a charred hulk whose sails, hanging in blackened tatters, were like the shroud of Death himself. Not a man stirred on board, among the grotesque corpses; only the stink of fire marked the burned-out funeral pyre, over which hung a fatal, everlasting peace. Beyond the Mystic, at the tidemark and higher up, countless bodies defiled the morning; some were headless, some brutally hacked to death, some – washing gently at the water's edge

– were unmarked, surprised only by the choking sea.

Blood stained the sand, often furrowed by desperate, fleeing feet; farther inland, Amin Sang's warriors were gathered in groups, their spears slaked, their fury spent, resting round campfires which faded with the sunrise, waiting like children for their modest morning rice. Here and there, like a very wraith of sorrow, a woman with black-veiled face and covered head had already crept out, and now sat, rocking to and fro, wailing in hopeless grief some distance from a body she could not yet bear to acknowledge as her own.

Half a mile offshore, the proud Lucinda D swung to her anchor, unharmed, unscathed, surveying the splendour of her total victory.

VIII

Selang Aro, the High Priest of the Anapuri, was a tall man, thin and sour-faced; his bony, shaven head topped a body whose gauntness the loose-flowing robes could not conceal. He came to the Sun Palace, and to the Rajah's audience, attended by six monks, saffron-robed like himself, who looked about them disdainfully, as if to show themselves superior to this temporal power. He came unwillingly, and showed it in his manner and his speech. But he came none the less, because the Rajah had sent for him, and had backed the request with a hundred armed men 'for safe conduct'. Disguise it how he would, with pride or with sullen looks, when Selang Aro stood before the Rajah's throne in the great audience chamber, he was a culprit summoned to account for his misdeeds.

At first he was prepared to deny all knowledge of the attempt on the palace and the causeway; and when the Rajah, whose humour in victory was excellent, gently implied that he was lying, Selang Aro seemed ready to take offence.

'Your Highness is in a position to make these charges,' he answered coldly. He stood on the lowest step before the ivory throne, facing the Rajah and his entourage, and the commanding figure of Richard Marriott; the plain monk's robes seemed almost to sneer at the

136

richness of the court. 'I can do nothing but deny them. I have not stirred from the Shwe Dagon for a month or more. I do not engage in plots of any kind, and I do not plan to rule. My mind is set on higher – '

'Silence!' said the Rajah suddenly, and his brusque tone showed that he meant it. He leant forward. 'I have not brought you here to talk, but to listen. There was a plot against my government, and if you did not take a hand in it, then your Anapuri did.' He smiled, without humour. 'We have the bodies to prove it … Are you telling me that you have so little control over your own priests that they can take up arms and storm the causeway without your knowledge?'

'Any man can put on a priest's robes.'

'And shave his head? And call your name as he goes to fight?' The Rajah's tone was scornful. 'If such a man is not a priest, then he has many talents going to waste … There were three kinds of serpent in this matter. The man Harris, and his sailors. The Land-Dyaks, hunting heads like the carrion birds they are. And the Anapuri. Your Anapuri.'

'If they took part in this, then they acted without my knowledge,' answered Selang Aro. He was still arrogant in his disdain. 'I rule ten thousand men, but I cannot rule them every minute of the day.'

'If your rule is too heavy for you, we can see that it is lightened.'

The fencing went on, while the court listened with evident enjoyment, and Amin Bulong and Colonel Kedah stared at the High Priest with a different expression altogether, and Richard Marriott gave himself the pleasure of watching Princess Sunara. She sat on her father's right hand, beautiful and cool as before; but she was aware of him, and she could not disguise it. Earlier, indeed, she had made this plain, in a brief private exchange before the audience was started.

'My father tells me that I was discourteous to you, and must apologize,' she had said, in her low voice, her eyes downcast. 'I do so now.'

'I need no apology,' Richard had answered, prepared to continue the coldness of their first meeting, 'and I have not come to hear one. My attendance is of less consequence. The mercenary is here only to collect his pay.'

'None the less, you must forgive, if I apologize,' she said. Her voice had trembled, but whether from the effort of her humility, or from some other cause, he could not divine. 'That is our custom here.'

'Do you apologize because your father orders it?'

She raised her eyes at last to his. The beautiful face was indeed moved by deep feeling; the proud princess had become the troubled child. 'I am my father's daughter,' she had answered, 'and I obey him in all things, according to custom. But indeed, I am truly sorry.'

He had relented at that, not able to resist the appeal in her voice and manner; and now, as he looked at her, he was very glad that he had done so. In the Sun Palace, he was acclaimed a hero; in the Rajah's eyes, he was a true friend; but he found, inexplicably, that he needed Sunara's approval to give significance to his triumph. He knew by now that he had earned it, and when he looked at her across the audience chamber, his face showed his contentment.

Selang Aro, continuing to argue and to deny, was growing less sure of himself, and the monks who stood at his back seemed to have lost some of their disdain. It seemed that they were coming to realize that, on this heavy occasion, their saffron robes and polished begging bowls might not afford them the protection of sanctity.

Richard could not decide whether the Rajah was having sport with the culprits, or whether he did indeed intend some punishment. There was the water torture, there were the hungry red ants; for the Rajah, the path towards these might involve no more than a change of mood... But presently it appeared that he had summoned Selang Aro, not to punish but to warn.

'That is enough,' he said, interrupting Selang Aro for the second time. His manner was still benevolent, but there was sufficient steel in it to make his words foreboding. 'I know what is in your mind, but you do not know what is in mine. I will enlighten you, and then you will go.'

A sudden silence fell all over the audience chamber; the whispering ceased; all eyes were on the Rajah, an old man with authority in every word and gesture.

'First, there will be no more plots,' said the Rajah. His voice was that of a law-giver, not to be challenged by any lesser mortal. 'I can defeat them at will, but I would rather conserve my men for worthier tasks … Secondly, any Anapuri priest found with arms in his hand will be killed. He will be killed with his own weapons, so that my Palace Guard need not soil their spears in such disgraceful blood … Thirdly, Colonel Kedah, or his emissary, will pay a visit of inspection to the Shwe Dagon on the first day of every month.'

'But that is sacrilege!' Selang Aro burst out. Gone was the disdain and the air of indifference; hatred darted out of his eyes like a snake's tongue. 'Armed men have never set foot in the Golden Pagoda, since the day it was first consecrated. The Lord Buddha – '

'The Lord Buddha would say,' interrupted the Rajah, 'that since armed men seem to come out of the Shwe Dagon, armed men may go in. That is what I say, in any case.'

'It is sacrilege!' repeated Selang Aro.

'It is justice … And fourthly' – unexpectedly the Rajah turned, and pointed to Richard Marriott – 'this Tuan is a man of honour in Makassang. He has earned the respect of all, and he has earned my thanks. If he visits the Shwe Dagon, or if he has any dealings with you or your priests, he is to be treated as if he were of my own blood.'

There was a sharp intake of breath from all who stood in the audience chamber; clearly, the Rajah's words had conferred an unheard-of distinction upon Richard. The latter, resplendent in his uniform, the gold earring gleaming in his ear, preserved an impassive face under this public gaze; but his eyes sought Sunara's, and found that she herself was looking at him, and that in her look was more than a shadow of those things which were in everyone else's – admiration, respect, a readiness to pay tribute to a newcomer who had earned it.

But Selang Aro was not of the same mind. 'I do not know this Tuan,' he said, with sour emphasis on the title. 'Is he some visitor to Makassang?'

'He is indeed a visitor,' returned the Rajah, 'and many of your friends have met him already. It was he and his ship who defeated Black Harris, two nights ago. His name is Captain Richard Marriott.'

Selang Aro's pale face came round to Richard again. 'So ... I did not know that your Highness made such arrangements with foreign intruders.'

The Rajah's eyes snapped. 'I have told you that Captain Marriott is a man of honour in Makassang. Be pleased to remember it!'

'How long are we to be thus blessed?'

The offensive question was addressed directly to Richard, and he answered it with appropriate curtness. 'I will stay as long as may be suitable.'

The Rajah, rising to mark the end of the audience, was looking at Richard with an attention almost affectionate. 'I have hopes,' he said, 'that Captain Marriott may stay with us a very long time indeed.'

§

3

'Where is the money, then?' asked Nick Garrett, ill-humouredly. 'None of us have seen the colour of it yet. Are we to take it on trust?'

'It is safe in my room at the palace,' answered Richard. 'Have no fear of that.'

'Has he paid all of it?'

'Every last rix dollar. In gold.'

'It should be here on board,' said Garrett, with the same evil grace. 'We earned it as well as you, didn't we? We should have our share of it.'

'When we leave Makassang,' said Richard curtly, 'I will share it out.'

The two of them were standing on the quarter-deck of the Lucinda D, under a burning afternoon sun which had melted the pitch between the planking into a slow, bubbling ferment. The brigantine still swung to her anchor a few hundred feet from the Steps of Heaven, as she had done for the past week; but the cable was now heavy with weed, the sails brailed up, the wheel lashed; and what few of the crew were on deck lounged about in the shade, as idle and unready as the ship herself. It was the first visit that Richard Marriott had paid to his command since the night of the attack on the Mystic: her air of disuse might have shocked or angered him to steady cursing, even a few days earlier, but now it did not seem to matter greatly.

For his thoughts were already turned ashore; and not the least of the reasons for this was the contrast between the luxury of his apartments at the Sun Palace, and the hard-lying which was his lot on board – the tarry, smelly air which stifled a man between decks, the crude makeshifts of ship-board life. Who, in his senses, would sleep in a pine plank bunk, or eat greasy crackerhash twice a day, when he could lie between silken sheets, and have his choice of the most delicate dishes, the rarest wines and spices? And if this meant that he himself was becoming softer, then let it be so ... Only a fool would leave this paradise before he had to.

As if reading his thoughts, Nick Garrett – a hulking, sunburnt figure, bare-footed, naked to the waist – put the question straightly: 'When are we leaving, then? What are the plans?'

'There is no hurry,' Richard answered. 'We are well enough off here.'

'You may be well off,' said Garrett roughly. 'But there is nothing for a man to do in Makassang. We should take our reward, and get back to Batavia or Singapore or Hong Kong, and have the spending of it where the spending is good.' He waved his arm round, his expression bitterly discontented. 'What use is this place? There's not a tavern within a thousand miles! Not a sporting house, either! The women are too proud for sailors, or else their husbands have knives ready to stick in your guts. We should get back where we are welcome, where a man can hammer on a table, and plank his money down, and buy a bottle of blackstrap or a willing girl!'

'We are welcome here.'

'You may be,' said Nick Garrett again. 'But the men don't like the place, and I don't like it either.' He looked at Richard more closely. 'It's time you spoke out. Are you planning something, up at the palace?'

'All I plan is to live ashore for a space.'

'Are you too good for us now?'

Richard smiled. 'I was always too good for you.'

But Garrett was already thinking along another tack. 'If we have to stay here, we should be using the time properly. If the old man has a hundred thousand rix dollars to give away, then he must have thousands more, lying hid somewhere. We should ferret them out. And jewels too ... I remember the talk about the state treasure?' His eyes narrowed suspiciously as they came round to Richard again. 'Are you making plans about that, maybe? Are you staying ashore to spy on it?'

Richard shook his head. 'We have made enough money here, without any spying or plotting.'

'Now by God!' burst out Nick Garrett furiously. 'You cannot be so changed! If we stay here, we should take all that they have, every last dollar of it. We would be damned fools to do otherwise!'

'We have done our work, and we have been handsomely paid for it. The Rajah is a friend. He has come to trust me. Why should I rob him?'

'For the same reason that you rob anyone else! Because he has money for the taking! And if he trusts you, so much the worse for him.'

'I do not choose to treat him so.'

Nick scowled villainously, shrugging his shoulders. 'I cannot make you see sense. But I will not stay here to rot, either. How long before we leave?'

'A week, at least.'

'A week? Why a week?'

'I want to see all the island. And there is a big banquet that I am bidden to, to celebrate the victory.'

'Banquet!' said Garrett contemptuously. 'By God, you will be the Lord Mayor, next! When is this banquet?'

'In four days' time.'

'In four days' time I shall be ripe for the madhouse...' Garrett's anger was mounting again. 'I tell you, I cannot stay here, idle, when they have all that treasure ashore! And I cannot stay, when we have money to spend as we choose, away from this Godforsaken hole. We should either rob them, or leave them, or both.'

'We will do neither,' said Richard. 'And we shall leave when I am ready.'

'I'll not wait for Doomsday,' said Nick Garrett. His eyes shifted again, becoming brooding and suspicious. Then suddenly he slapped his thigh, with a crack sharp enough to wake an echo ashore. 'By God,' he exclaimed, 'I have it! No wonder you are content to moon about, like some landsman living on a pension. It is the girl!'

II

Of course it was the girl, and Richard Marriott knew it, and did not care a jot for it either. Already he was drugged by love, already rapturous hope ebbed and flowed like a crazy tide, driving out all thoughts save those which centred on Sunara. It was not the comfort of the palace which was keeping him in Makassang; it was Sunara's ravishing beauty, which delighted him by day and tormented him in nightly dreams; it was her gentle form and voice, her softness after the hard life at sea; it was her breasts which he had not seen again, for which his eyes still searched even as he talked with her.

He did not know if she returned his tempestuous feelings, or any part of them; he could not even guess if she were aware of his urgency. Her small person, for all its sinuous loveliness, radiated a perfect detachment, a coolness which was royal as well as feminine. And they were never alone; there were always servants at hand, or her maids of honour, or a bodyguard, or her father, or Amin Sang (who Richard suspected was a suitor), or any one of the hundred souls who thronged the Sun Palace by day and by night. He could only take all chances of spending time with her; and when he achieved this, he could only summon forgotten graces to charm her, refurbishing the habits of a vanished drawing-room world which now seemed far short of what she deserved.

He had learned no more than that she could be jealous – or that she could feign it, perhaps to put him out of countenance. Once, on the day after the rebuking of Selang Aro, he had come upon her playing in the garden with Adam, his son, while old Manina kept brooding watch from beneath a scarlet-tipped poinsettia. Sunara had been ruffling the boy's hair, when Richard appeared, though Adam seemed less than appreciative of an honour which his father would have given his soul for. He was staring, wide-eyed, at one of the palace peacocks, which was spreading its tail feathers like some barbaric banner, and paying no attention at all to the slim brown hand which gently stroked and smoothed the top of his head.

Sunara looked up, as Richard approached and made his bow. Her hand dropped quickly, but there was no confusion in her manner as she said: 'He is very like you, Captain Marriott.'

'Is he indeed?' asked Richard, surprised. 'Your Highness must have a more discerning eye than mine. I had thought rather that he favoured – '

He floundered, and his voice tailed off in confusion. This was the very last subject, and the very last person, whom he wished to bring into the conversation.

But the Princess took him up without hesitation; she might have planned to do so. As Adam wandered towards the fascination of the peacocks, and Manina followed to safeguard his progress, Sunara rose gracefully from the lawn on which she had been sitting, and took a scarf from one of her attendant maids of honour. Then she asked: 'You consider that your son is more like his mother?'

'Yes, your Highness.'

'Only you can know the truth of that ... I would not, for the world, intrude on your private grief, Captain, but – was your wife an English lady?'

'I – I believe so, your Highness.'

'You believe so?' Sunara's beautiful face was a study in puzzlement. 'Surely you can remember?'

'I mean, your Highness,' began Richard, while under his breath he summoned, in cursing, all the devils in hell, 'that she was born in the border country, between England and Scotland. She had forbears from both these parts.'

'She was noble, like yourself?'

Richard managed a nervous smile. 'I am not noble, your Highness.'

Sunara frowned. 'My father tells me that your birth, in England, is of the highest ... Your wife was noble, in this border country?'

Visions of Biddy Booker, undoubtedly bred without benefit of clergy in some noisome Dublin slum, rose to plague Richard's composure. He drew out a silk kerchief, and dabbed it to his brow.

'She was of suitable birth, your Highness.'

Sunara nodded to herself. 'I am sure of it ... Lucinda is a beautiful name ... Was she very beautiful?'

'Lucinda, your Highness?' Richard was floundering again, more deeply. 'I do not understand.'

'The name of your ship is the same as the name of your wife, surely?'

'No, your Highness,' answered Richard woodenly.

'Indeed.' The Princess's voice was suddenly cold. 'I was sure that your ship was named after your wife.'

'No, your Highness.'

'But is not that a custom in England?'

'Sometimes, your Highness. Not in this case.'

'You mean – ' Sunara's face showed such astonishment that it was all Richard could do, not to fall on his knees and beg her forgiveness, ' – you mean that you christened your ship for someone else?'

'For an old acquaintance, your Highness.'

'An old acquaintance?'

'A former acquaintance.'

'Also from this border country?'

'No. From the south.'

Her eyebrows went up, in heartbreaking disdain. 'You seem to be a great traveller, Captain Marriott.'

'A man is bound to know more than one woman,' he said sulkily, at a loss how to retrieve the moment.

'Yes, indeed.' She signed to her maids of honour, and they came forward, ready to escort her within the palace. 'Perhaps you should command a fleet,' she said, and left him without a word of farewell.

He saw no more of her that day.

But there was never another occasion such as that one; and perhaps she had only been tormenting him, or placing him at a distance, for reasons of feminine strategy, for thereafter she had asked no more questions about women, but, relenting, became a companion after his own heart. They had spent much time together, though little of it at the palace; he was eager to see her country, and she seemed as eager to show it to him. Together they traversed every part of the island of Makassang that was within a day's reach of the Sun Palace.

Often they rode together, on horses drawn from the vast palace stables; splendid horses, of mixed Arabian blood, which stepped proudly and galloped like the wind. They had a favourite ride of some two hours, which they took almost daily, to the village of Kutar on the southern coast, a fishing village which was a safe harbour against the rolling Java Sea, crowded with prahus of every shape and size, and canopied sampans with strangely painted fins on the stern, and ancient sailing junks of oiled teak, burnt to the colour of the brown earth by the fierce suns of a hundred years. The two of them would dismount, and look down on the busy harbour, and stare at the ocean – or rather, she would watch the sea and he would watch her, until she became aware of it, and decided that it was time to ride on, or to pick wild orchids, or to look for seashells.

Once they went down to Prahang, her father's capital, and wandered on foot through the bazaars, teeming with Malays, and Chinese, and Negroes, and merchants of every description crying their wares – silks, mango fruits, betel nut, glutinous sweetmeats, little cakes of rice and oil, children's toys of carved yellow-wood, jewellery for the necks of women – or of princesses. Twenty of the palace servants went ahead of them, commanding a way for her by name, pushing aside the throng with bamboo staves which fell indiscriminately on head and back and shoulder and rump. But their blows were always light, and taken with a smile or a mock display of pain; it was clear that Sunara was much loved, and would have come to no harm if she had walked the bazaars without a single companion.

She was surprised when Richard commented on this. 'How else should it be?' she asked, looking up at him. 'This is my father's own town. He is not a tyrant. He could walk here, as I walk here, without fear of anything except the press of a great crowd, or perhaps a beggar too importunate.'

'But he has enemies, and they might be your enemies too, being his daughter.'

'No enemy would dare strike at him here. These are his own people.'

'He is fortunate to have such loyalty.'

Sunara nodded. She was examining some nankeen cloth, of a luminous yellow sheen, and stroking it with her gentle hand, while the old woman crouched behind the market stall smiled a toothless, almost confederate smile. 'He has earned it because he has moved with the times, as even tyrants must … As a young man, when he first came to the throne, my father was greatly feared, perhaps because of the past – for his father had been greatly feared all his life. His father, in the early days, would have a slave strangled for spilling wine at table … But that was seventy and eighty years ago. It is different now, and the people know it. My father rules firmly, of course, and he can punish evil or treachery as cruelly as my grandfather; but he is a loving and compassionate man, also.'

'And that is why the people smile at you?'

'In part, yes. Also, they smile at me for the reason that you smile at me.'

Richard laughed. 'Now what is that, I wonder?'

'If you do not know, it would be most unbecoming for me to enlighten you … They smile at you, too.' And as Richard, preoccupied with another thought, said nothing, she went on: 'Did you not know that you are a great hero in Makassang? And especially in these parts of it? They believe that you took the Mystic single-handed, and saved my father's life.' She waved her arm round about them, as if showing Richard his admirers – and it was true that those standing near them, or stretching on tiptoe to catch sight of them, were smiling and bowing, and that they looked at Richard with an unalloyed respect. 'You see how they stare at you? You hear the excited note in the voices? If they were indifferent, it would be a murmur. If they thought ill of you, it would be silence – the most ominous silence in the world. But in fact, it is hero music!'

'You make me self-conscious,' said Richard. 'I did nothing single-handed.'

'It is enough that they think you did. Bazaar talk still holds sway here. For these people, you can do no wrong now. They admire strength, strength and bravery. So does my father. And in his old age, he can admire it without jealousy and without suspicion. He does not see you as an enemy. That is why he has made so much of you.'

'And you?'

'I?' She was surprised – or appeared to be; it was perhaps the first time that he had approached, in words, such an area of intimacy, and she looked up again, and then swiftly down, as if she were not at all ready for this encroachment. 'I do not understand your question.'

'I mean, Princess,' he said awkwardly, 'that I have been very conscious of your kindness and – and friendship, during the last few days. You mentioned that your father admired strength – ' He seemed to have manoeuvred himself into a corner from which he could not escape without a direct and foolish question. 'What I meant to ask was – '

She decided to rescue him. 'You wish to know whether I share his views?'

'Yes, your Highness.'

'I am my father's daughter,' she said. And before he could draw too much satisfaction from this, she added: 'But of course, you are not all strength.'

Taken aback, he said: 'No man could be.'

'Oh, it is not a shortcoming ...' She had laid down the yellow nankeen now, and with a smile to the old woman had moved on, while the palace servants thwacked a few of the nearest backs with light, teasing blows. 'Did you know that you have a nickname already?'

'No, your Highness.'

'I heard it from Amin Sang. It is because of the earring. They call you Picanga.'

'Picanga?' The word meant nothing.

'It is a word, I must tell you, of a low class. It means, She-Pirate.'

'Now, by God – ' began Richard Marriott, nettled.

Sunara smiled, with a backward glance under lowered eyelashes. 'I can assure you, Captain Marriott, I do not altogether believe it.'

But that was all she would say, on that subject, on that day.

The longest, and the last, excursion which they made was to the Golden Pagoda itself.

They crossed the bay in the state barge, reclining at ease beneath the tasselled stern canopy, with a detachment of the Palace Guard under Amin Sang as part of their company. The rowers – the unseen, unheard slaves confined between decks – kept up a steady, powerful stroke for two hours and more, with the music of pipes to cheer them, and an overseer to give them a commanding beat on the drum; the prow quivered endlessly as it cleft the water under this martial urging.

The barge presently landed them at the village of Shrang Anapuri, and, preceded by the Palace Guard, whose bearing made no secret of the fact that they were superbly trained spearmen and would be delighted to prove the point, given the slightest excuse, they journeyed by litter to the lower portals of the Shwe Dagon. Richard was amazed by its size; close to, it seemed to be a whole community of buildings and shrines and votive arches, topped by the immense blazoned dome of gold leaf which, applied by generations of pious pilgrims (who paid outrageously for a single square inch of the precious covering) shone in fantastic splendour. They were greeted at the lowest steps by the High Priest, Selang Aro, with a sour personal welcome which had been ordered by the Rajah himself.

After the briefest of courtesies, they removed their footgear, and began the slow climb upwards. Though it was a tall structure, decorated with unremitting care and piety, Richard was struck not by its majesty but by its squalor. The steps themselves were filthy, stained by the scarlet sputum of betel juice, by the excrement of wandering pi dogs, by the urine of countless children who squatted on the steps or played among the votive shrines. There were hordes of beggars, and though they were kept at bay by the Palace Guard, they maintained a shrill whining throughout the journey, a waving of skinny hands, a showing of stinking sores which, given the kindest heart in the world, could only excite disgust.

Behind them, as the level of the steps rose, there were endless tiers of tiny shops selling drums, and candles, and lanterns, and paper flowers – all the paraphernalia of worship; and from these shops also there rose a clamour, a command to buy in the cause of holiness, a wafting of musty avarice.

At the topmost level of the edifice, under the gilded dome itself, the crowds were even thicker, for here were the shrines with innumerable images of the Buddha – Buddha smiling, staring, sitting, reclining – each decorated with a garish maze of gold leaf, and blue enamel, and green mosaic tiling, and pink sugar-plum elaboration. Here thronged the pilgrims, and the beggars also, and the proud-faced monks in their saffron robes, standing before smaller pagodas with their begging bowls ever waiting, ever held in readiness. When alms were given, a bell was struck – and at some moments the whole Shwe Dagon seemed filled by the rise and fall of a bell-like chorus, a pious reverberation sometimes deep, sometimes thin and tinkling, calling (it seemed to Richard) heaven to witness the ascent of prayer, and earth to admire human generosity.

Richard was struck also by the faces of the monks as they received these alms. They said nothing, they betrayed no emotion, either of gratitude or of simple pleasure. It was as if they were proclaiming: We hold the keys of Heaven; when you give, it is we who are doing you the honour, and you who are currying favour in the hope of salvation ... Perhaps, thought Richard fancifully, the more one gave, the more one was despised by these impassive witnesses; large alms implied a large need, a heavier load of sin.

The royal party stayed only briefly at the summit of the Shwe Dagon; Sunara seemed pale and listless after the long climb, and Selang Aro, leading the way, wore an expression of discontent, as if he would gladly be quit of this odious task, and turn again to higher things ... Halfway down the descending steps, Sunara stumbled and came near to falling; and when Richard caught her arm and supported her, unobtrusively firm, she smiled up at him in gratitude.

'Thank you,' she said quietly. 'It is so hot, and wearisome ... Tell me what you think of this place.'

'It is interesting,' answered Richard, not wishing to offend her.

She smiled wanly. 'I would rather hear what you think.'

An ancient beggar woman, her body so loathsomely crippled by deformity that one of her legs circled her neck, somehow eluded the guard and came slithering forward across the steps, almost tripping him up in her snake-like advance. Recoiling, he threw her a coin, and was rewarded by a cry of joy which pierced all other sounds – but he could feel no pleasure in the moment, only disgust and revulsion.

'I cannot like it,' said Richard after a pause. For a moment he glanced back at the enormous mass of the golden dome, towering over their heads in the sunshine. 'Oh, it has an air, I grant you, and much prayer and devotion has gone to make it a holy place. But to me, it is oppressive. There is so much filthiness, and the buying and selling – '

She smiled again. 'You speak like Andrew Farthing,' she said. 'When he first saw it, he told my father – ' suddenly she broke into mimicry of an old man's tones, precise and dry, ' – "I am bound to state, we have nothing like this in the Scottish kirk." '

Richard laughed aloud. 'That I can promise you.'

They had reached the ground level at the farther side of the pagoda, and Selang Aro, leading the party, turned round to bend a baleful look upon him. Then he spoke in the slow English of which he had a smattering.

'We are so happy to have amused you, Captain.'

'It has been most interesting,' said Richard correctly. 'I thank you for your courtesy.'

'I will be happy for you to pay us another visit, perhaps without soldiers.'

Richard said nothing; he was aware of the other man's hatred, but he could not challenge it at this time and place. Instead, he bowed, and moving out into the sunshine began to breathe the free air again.

It had been arranged that they would ride part of the way back, re-embarking in their barge farther down the coast; and relays of horses had been planned to this end. The first of these was now waiting for them outside the Shwe Dagon, and after a short, grim-faced farewell from Selang Aro, the Princess and Richard, attended by Amin Sang, took their departure. Their path, inland from the coast road, led them through forest tracks which sometimes narrowed into jungle; it was a slow progress, but pleasant and cool, and the green fronded trees formed a most grateful shade above their heads.

Sunara rode side-saddle, in the European mode, and she seemed to have recovered her spirits entirely – 'I love the Lord Buddha better than his temple,' she said, by way of explanation. They talked and laughed as they rode, and pointed out to each other flowers and birds and small animals, and answered in jest the cries of monkeys and parakeets, and enjoyed the dappled sunlight which sometimes filtered down through the trees, and, released from care, made the most of what became a mysterious and enchanting journey.

Once they passed a colony of the great bats called flying foxes, roosting head downwards in the trees till nightfall gave them back their day. Once, in a forest clearing peopled by tree stumps, they came upon a gang of woodcutters, with a pair of huge working elephants patiently manoeuvring the teak logs into a pile. Once they forded a stream, and Amin Sang, who was leading, gave a shout of warning, and a crocodile beside the bank slid off into deep water, its scaly grey back gleaming in the sunlight. Once they chanced on a deserted longhouse of the Land-Dyaks which, when they peered within, was found to be crammed to the roof trees with seemingly benevolent skulls. Once, by the roadside, they came upon a tree blown down and raised up again – its roots were bared above the level of the earth, but it was propped up with joists of wood, and its withered branches were hung with flags and ribbons, all of gay colours.

Richard reined in his horse. 'Now what is this?' he asked, puzzled. 'Who has done it – and why?'

'Tree worshippers,' answered Sunara, over her shoulder. She also stopped her horse, and dismounted, and after a moment Richard did the same. Together they walked up to the curious object, while Amin Sang watched them from a bend in the pathway. 'When a tree blows down in a storm, or is struck by lightning, this is what they do, to restore it.'

They stood close to the tree. It was old, and entirely sapless, but it seemed alive still, in the mysterious fastness of the forest. Sunara pointed to the gnarled trunk, stained here and there with some darker hue.

'They raise it up again, and smear it with blood to give it back its life, and deck it out with the flags and ribbons that you see.'

He was very conscious of her slim figure standing by his side. 'Why should they do that?'

'To appease its soul,' she answered, matter-of-factly.

'They believe that a tree has a soul?'

'Oh yes. All trees have souls. When the forests are cut down, the woodcutters always leave a few strong trees standing, for the expelled spirits to live in. Otherwise, they would be condemned to wander the bare earth forever, hopeless, without a home.'

'Do you believe this?'

She smiled at him. 'Of course!'

They were looking at each other now; Amin Sang was forgotten – and indeed, he had moved up the pathway out of sight, as if he had been commanded. Sunara was very beautiful, and serious, and she seemed to be waiting – or listening to the music which whispered between them. He nearly spoke from his heart, then; it was as much as he could do not to move forward, and take her in his arms, and tell her of his love. But the moment was not such a moment; the silence round them was too solemn, the forest too close, the beribboned tree too haunted and too holy. He could not speak of earthly love, in this green cathedral, before this altar.

He said, unsteadily: 'I will believe anything you tell me.'

'That is as it should be,' she answered gravely. Then she bowed to the tree, and turned, and walked with him back to their horses.

But it was on this night that he did declare himself, and after it was done, no day in Makassang, or in his life, was ever the same.

Dusk had fallen, by the time they returned to the Sun Palace, and after such a day they might have been glad to retire early. But Richard was wakeful, and it seemed that Sunara felt the same, for when the evening meal was done she joined him, and the Rajah, in a bower in the gardens, and they sat talking until the moon was bright above their heads.

It was her father who talked at the greatest length, and they were content to listen, for the Rajah, in a mellow mood of remembrance, seemed eager to delve into a past of the utmost fascination, producing for their delight stories – some scandalous, some scarcely credible, all enthralling – of the kind which, alas, so often died with the passing of an old man. Watching his host, and listening entranced, Richard felt that it was a privileged moment. He wondered, indeed, if ever again in his life he would sit in such magic surroundings, with such companions – an ancient ruler, a beautiful princess – and be entertained on so royal a scale.

The Rajah talked, in the custom of old men, of the days most remote in his recollection, when he was a boy growing up in Makassang, and his father was heir to the throne, and his grandfather – Satsang the First, of formidable memory – still ruled in a fashion which brooked no hindrance, and which punished treason with the swiftest cruelty imaginable. This must have been, by Richard's reckoning, at the very dawn of the modern century – 1800, even 1795 – when (according to his schooling) England's king was still, lamentably, George III, England's hero was Lord Nelson, and England's vilest foe Napoleon, who ravaged Europe with such brutal appetite and ate babies alive. Makassang, it seemed, had a comparable tapestry of discord; but she resolved it according to an Eastern mode which needed to borrow nothing from any schoolmaster in the world.

'My grandfather,' said the Rajah, looking up at the stars which could be glimpsed here and there through the bower of trees overhead, 'had one guiding precept in his life which, alas, in these modern times have gone out of fashion. It was this – that one man is set apart, to be the ruler, and that all other beings in his kingdom have been born only to obey.' With a gentle hand he stroked the shawl, of Kashmir silk, which an attendant had placed over his knees to protect him from the night air; while Richard and Sunara, like wide-eyed children allowed, by the forgetfulness of their elders, to eavesdrop upon the adult world when they should have been fast asleep, waited to hear what further strange evocation of the past he was going to show them. 'It followed from this – so thought my grandfather – that any man who challenged his rule must never be given a second chance to do so; he must be destroyed, and destroyed in circumstances which would serve as an example to anyone else who might have a like ambition. I remember being told, by my nurse, of one such occasion – ' He broke off, and looked towards Sunara. 'My child, I am talking freely, being in the mood for it. But I would not wish to shock you.'

Sunara's face was in darkness, the moon being clouded, but Richard could hear the smile which must be lighting it as she answered: 'My dear Father, as well as being a child I am also a woman, and therefore prone to be driven mad by such delays. Pray do not torment me.'

'Very well … Early in his reign – so the story goes – my grandfather discovered a plot against his life, involving a man named Costafaga, a prince – so-called – of the Land-Dyaks, who to this day are still our most determined enemies. Perhaps this happening was the reason for it … The Land-Dyaks, who as you know are headhunters, have some skill in the shrinking of their strange fetish; they remove the skull, and then render the flesh very small by the application of certain ointments and liquids. When Prince Costafaga, therefore, was trapped in his treachery and brought in bondage to the palace, it seemed to my grandfather that this was a man who would serve very well as a subject for his own tribal custom. In short, the ambitious Prince Costafaga was to be shrunk.

'They could not start with his head, of course – what my

grandfather had in mind was a living manikin.' The Rajah's voice, elaborately calm, came out of the night like a thin, terrifying ghost from the past. 'But they could certainly start elsewhere ... They enlisted the help of the Prince's own doctor – the royal head-shrinker of the Land-Dyaks, no less – on the understanding that on the day that the Prince died, the doctor himself would also die. It transpired that he was a man eager to live ... He removed first the bones of the Prince's right arm and hand, very cleverly, and then sewed up the flesh and treated it in accordance with his disgusting talents. In a month it had shrunk to half its size, and in three months to one third. Then the left arm was so treated, and then both legs. There were no mistakes, no lapses of skill. The process took three years, and at the end, Prince Costafaga presented a bizarre appearance indeed. His body remained its normal size, but his legs and arms were each ten inches long. They were still perfectly formed. He could even move them slightly, when so persuaded. The fingers and toes, in particular, were those of a new-born infant.'

The Rajah broke off, perhaps to give his hearers a respite; and indeed, Richard Marriott was conscious of a queasy stomach. But Sunara, when he looked at her face which could be faintly seen in the moonlight, appeared quite unmoved. Did the story not shock her, Richard wondered – could she really be, at heart, so cruel and so pitiless? She had been listening like a child at bedtime ... But then it seemed that this was perhaps the true answer; to her it was a story, no more and no less; it was not real because she had not seen it – only her father's words were real, and words could never be the equal of tortured flesh, pictures could not rank as screams of agony.

The Rajah's voice, continuing, broke in on his thoughts. 'So there he was – Prince Costafaga of the Land-Dyaks, reduced to the size appropriate to a man who had plotted against his rightful lord ... He was exhibited, in a litter, in a score of places all over Makassang, and he made a speech of contrition on each appearance. People could never quite decide whether he was an object of extreme pity, or a figure of fun. However that may be, there was no more rebellion against my grandfather, during his entire reign.'

'And the Prince?' asked Richard. 'How did this thing end, for him?'

'He died,' answered the Rajah, 'when his task was fulfilled. He died, shall we say, a martyr to experiment – for my grandfather, as well as being an unforgiving man, was an inquisitive one as well. He had some gross sport with that part of the body of which the Prince was, by reputation, proud. Then the doctor was given the task of reducing, if he could, the whole lower half of the trunk, in the same fashion; and there, alas, his skill failed him, and his patient – by now there could be no other word – died.'

'And the doctor?'

'He died also,' said the Rajah. 'My grandfather was a man of his word. The doctor, under sentence of death, was offered a chance of demonstrating his art on his own person – a limb at one time, for as long as he cared to continue – but he chose rather to take poison.'

The recital, macabre, horrifying to a Western mind, was ended, on the same matter-of-fact note with which the Rajah had begun it. He added only: 'It was with such stories that my nurse lulled me to sleep when I was a little boy,' and then he clapped his hands lightly and called to the major-domo: 'A glass of wine!' Richard sat silent, as the wine was brought and served to them all; he was beginning to feel as perhaps Sunara was feeling – that this had been no more than a story, a recollection of the evil past, and its reality and truth existed no longer. But there was a point which, for some reason strangely connected with his peace of mind, he wished to establish.

'Your Highness has a notable memory on which to draw … But I would like to think that, in this beautiful country, the happier aspects of history have now overtopped the rest. Times have changed, have they not? Cruel blood runs thin, and some worthier strain takes its place. After all, this is the nineteenth century! Your father, for example, was not so – ' he searched for a word which would not offend a possibly devout son, ' – so determined a ruler?'

'By no means,' agreed the Rajah. 'Of course he was subject to sudden rages. I saw him once, on board the state barge, walk down to the rowing benches, and seize a parang from the overseer, and strike off the hands of one of the slaves, as they rested on the oar. The man had ceased working, or had fainted, and the result had been a delay which, for some personal reason, was intolerable. But such anger, as I have said, was only a matter of impulse. He was not a cruel man by nature. I myself am even less given to harshness. And my daughter' – he gestured carelessly towards Sunara, but it seemed that there might be more to his words than a simple jest – 'is a very model of gentle behaviour. Of course, much of my father's reign was taken up with repelling adventurers and invaders from the outside world. Thirty and forty years ago, Makassang had more than headhunters to deal with. Every pirate saw a quick fortune here. Every trader had ambitions to barter glass beads for prime rubies. And more than pirates and traders! There were many expeditions from other nations – including your own – who had conceived the idea that Makassang would make a desirable addition to their possessions.'

'I had not heard that,' said Richard.

'Perhaps because the outcome was total failure … Nay,' added the Rajah, raising his hand, 'I intended no insult. It was not your country which made the most determined effort, in any case. The English, so Andrew Farthing taught me, do not fight hard in the first instance. They conquer by accident, and then they hold on to their conquest like the claws of death himself … In fact, it was the Dutch who came nearest to making this country their own.'

Richard smiled. 'I had not heard that, either.'

'The Dutch would not boast of it now … They made many such attempts, and they sent an expedition here, in the middle years of my father's reign, which was planned to be the final one. It was commanded by a determined fellow who, on landing, told my father that, since most of the islands hereabouts belonged to the Dutch, there was no reason why Makassang should not belong to them also.'

Richard smiled again, enjoying a story which he knew must have a happy ending – happy for Makassang. 'What befell this determined fellow?'

'My father welcomed him,' answered the Rajah, surprisingly. 'It chanced that the Royal Regiment had been weakened by some contagious sickness, and was not ready to take the field. It was therefore a time for thinking, not for fighting. It was a time when my father did not give way to foolish anger … He welcomed the Dutch expedition – and I must tell you that it was a well-planned affair, intended to endure as well as to succeed. In addition to a strong ship, and plenty of fighting men, there were carpenters to build houses, and gardeners with the choicest plants, and bankers to count money, and women to breed children. They made their landfall in this very bay – like yourself, Captain Marriott – and the commander came ashore with a show of force, and some cannon shots to frighten the ignorant, and said to my father: "I am now the ruler of your country."

'My father made them welcome,' went on the Rajah, 'and was at great pains to point out the best choice of a landing place – not on this side of the bay, naturally; this is unhealthy swampland, as anyone can see – but across the inlet, to the west of the Shwe Dagon, where the jungle meets the sea. I cannot tell you,' said the Rajah, who was now enjoying himself, 'the number of misfortunes which fell upon this Dutch expedition. That part of the island which my father recommended turned out, alas, to be fever-ridden; it is safe to say that within a year, fully half the expedition – especially the women and children – perished of malaria, and tick-bite fever, and those diseases of the lung which our moist climate encourages. There were also losses from snakes, from crocodiles, and even from tigers which, though very rarely seen so far from the interior, somehow made their way towards this tempting bait … There were forest fires in the dry season, and rivers which burst their banks at the time of the monsoon. There was a stampede of elephants. Crops were destroyed by evil spirits in the course of a single night-time hour. The

Dutch ship's anchor cable parted during a storm, and she was driven ashore and wrecked, so that they could not escape, or send for aid; and another ship which arrived in the spring was set upon by the largest number of pirate-prahus ever seen in these waters, and not a single Dutch seaman lived to tell the tale or take back the news.'

'My heart bleeds for this expedition,' said Richard cheerfully. He sipped his wine, restored in his spirits; there were fearful tales to be told of Makassang, but there were brave ones also, and he was happy to be sharing this moment of memory. 'How did it end?'

'It ended cruelly,' answered the Rajah. 'Cruelly, but justly. These were, after all, usurpers. They had come to steal something which did not belong to them; if they had succeeded, they would have drunk our blood. But the undertaking proved too difficult … There came a time when the expedition was reduced to a handful of men, and one woman, and a dozen children. But the children were of equal strength with their elders; they were all of them scarecrows, weakened by fever, and half starved, and praying only for rescue. It was now that the Royal Regiment made ready for action. They had recovered their strength, they were eager to slake their spears … They made a stockade of their shields, circling the Dutch settlement which had its back to the sea; and each day they advanced the stockade by a few feet, so that the space it enclosed grew smaller, and nearer to the water's edge. No one could pass by it, not even the smallest of the children. In course of time, the only space left to the Dutch expedition was a few yards of sand, enclosed by a double ring of shields made of elephant hide, and behind them, men with sullen faces and glittering spears, ready to kill.'

Richard waited. There could be only one end to such a story, and, as the Rajah had said, it was indeed a cruel one; he was less happy now with the recital, which seemed to have degenerated into a second version of the story of Prince Costafaga, having the same vein of brutality running through it, the same lust for revenge, the same cheapness of human life. Of course the Dutch had been wrong, to try to steal this fair land; but surely there were other ways

161

of pointing out their wrong-doing, less terrible methods of defeating them ... Or were all these Eastern seas dyed with the same stain, infected with – the same wickedness? – was this ruthlessness, which he himself had practised, in a lesser degree, for the past ten years, an inescapable part of the fabric? Perhaps it was wrong to blame the Royal Regiment, taking such pleasure in stalking their wretched prey, when Richard Marriott, a few days earlier, had fallen treacherously upon the Mystic, with the same lust to exterminate.

But the Rajah was speaking again; and it might be that he had sensed Richard's disquiet, for he concluded his story quickly, as if to point the fact that no man of any commonsense could have devised a different end to this tale of misfortune.

'In fact,' he said, 'it never came to killing, for the Royal Regiment – not with their spears. Perhaps their bearing alone was fierce enough to win the victory. But whatever the truth, there was an evening when the remnants of the Dutch expedition had been reduced to a few miserable yards of beach, hemmed in by the shields; and there was a morning when there was nothing left of them at all. No men, no forlorn woman, no children. There were some footprints in the sand, which was smoothed over by the next tide. But no living humans ... My people are now inclined to ascribe this disappearance to magic. But the truth of course is simpler.'

'What is the truth?' asked Richard.

'They decided to swim away,' answered the Rajah. 'Back to Holland, I have no doubt. But I would not wager any money that they reached their homeland.'

There was silence now; the story was ended; the last Dutch pioneer had been drowned, the last fair-haired child had been throttled by the sea. But there was one thing which Richard became aware of, in all this variety, and that was the silence of Sunara. She had not spoken a word since her father had begun to tell the story of Prince Costafaga; she sat between them in the bower of trees, staring seawards, keeping her counsel. Richard could not divine what was in her mind; he could not even guess it. She might draw pride from such stories as these – they were, after all, victories for men of her own name and blood. She might draw shame, being the heir of such gross cruelty. She might, in total indifference, be thinking of love, of perfumes, of shades of silk ... Rather to provoke some comment from her, than to answer the Rajah, he said: 'So perish all the enemies of Makassang! ... Of course, one cannot truly blame them for their enterprise. This island is a temptress in all things. It is a most beautiful country. And, by all evidence, it is a rich one also.'

It was, indeed, Sunara who answered him, stepping delicately out of her silence as if passing from one room to another; but she did not give an answer which he could have expected, nor one which he understood.

'You have not yet seen our riches,' she said, in a quiet voice.

He was puzzled by her choice of phrase. 'I have seen much of Makassang,' he answered hesitantly. 'Your Highness has been kind enough – '

'You have not seen our riches,' she repeated, with a special emphasis on the last word. 'There is a common talk, we have heard, of the state treasure of Makassang. It is not a fable. If you are interested in such things' – there was no irony in her voice – 'I would like to show you the treasure vault of the Sun Palace.'

'I would be more than honoured – ' began Richard.

'With my father's permission.'

Richard had been taken by surprise; the Rajah, clearly, was not. Though he exchanged a glance with his daughter, it seemed to Richard that this was something they had spoken of before, and agreed upon. It was part of a pattern, natural and ordained. He was to be shown the state treasure of Makassang. He had not asked to be thus complimented. He could scarcely have done so without impertinence, or worse. It was something freely offered, making him a privileged friend – the reverse of a marauding pirate ... In the surprise and confusion which swept over him, he hardly heard the Rajah answer: 'I am happy to give my consent.'

'Thank you ...' Sunara turned to Richard. 'You are still wakeful?'

'Yes, your Highness.'

'Then we will visit it now.' She rose, small as a jewel, graceful as a doe; within the starlit bower, her beauty glowed like a candle in the dusk. 'Will you come with us, Father?'

'I think not,' answered the Rajah. 'I have talked long. It is time for old men to sleep.' But he seemed far from sleep; he was looking at them both with alert eyes. 'Say good night to me now, Sunara ... The servants will light torches for you. Do not lose yourselves in the vaults.'

'If we are not here in the morning,' said Sunara lightly, 'pray send searchers for us.'

'I will send searchers,' answered the Rajah, with dry irony, 'at ten o'clock precisely.'

Alone, holding their torches which the servants had brought, standing poised at the top of a flight of steps which led down into total, underground gloom, they exchanged half a dozen brief sentences which seemed to point their private solitude as nothing else had yet done.

'I do not care,' said Sunara, 'for such stories as my father has told us. He is an old man, and I love him. But these memories belong to a wicked past.'

'I agree,' said Richard, and it was now true. 'There is more to life than fighting and hatred.'

'More to your life?'

'My life is changed.'

She nodded, in grave concord. 'That is why I am showing you the state treasure.'

Thus they stepped, together, out of one world, and into another they had never shared before.

He was conscious of tremendous excitement as he followed her down the stone steps, where the flaring torches cast giant shadows against the darkness of the walls. For the first time, they were alone together, in extraordinary circumstances which he did not yet understand. There was no reason why she should be showing him these riches of Makassang, unless she were judging him to be a different kind of man from the one who had stepped ashore, a few short weeks ago.

She knew, or could guess, his past; she had called him a mercenary, and it had been true when she had used the word; she must be aware – from his looks, from his bearing, from his taut ship and warlike skills – that he was nearer to being a pirate than many a man who had stamped his footprints upon the sands of Makassang. And yet she was showing him the treasure … Was it foolishness? Was it guileless innocence? Was it a test of his honour? Was it love? Did she think that he could be brought to candour and integrity by her own display of these qualities? Or did she think nothing at all, except that such a joint errand would be an agreeable climax to a day which had had a special quality of enjoyment?

He speculated thus, as step by step they went down the winding staircase to the vault below. But within a few minutes, such questions faded to nothing before the wonder of what she had to show him.

At the bottom of the steps, in the gloomy, echoing darkness, there was a small antechamber bare of adornment, and at one end of it, a great door of unpolished teak, studded with nails, and supported by ornamental hinges extending to its full width. To Richard's surprise, it was unbarred; and when, following her gesture, he raised the latch and began to push back its ponderous weight, he spoke of this. Above its slow, laborious creaking, he asked: 'Is your treasure vault left unlocked? Are you not afraid of thieves breaking in?'

She shook her head as if the question were all but meaningless. 'It is the royal treasure,' she answered. 'By tradition, it is holy. Also, its protection is a matter of honour. No one except a palace servant could approach even as near as this. They would come only to sweep, and to brush away the spiders, with their eyes cast down. Anyone in the household who stole from it would be torn to pieces.'

'But if it were done secretly?'

'There are eyes watching.'

He ceased to probe, though he did not understand. Whether she meant that the vault was in fact guarded in some latent fashion, or that anyone approaching the head of the stairs would excite instant attention from others in the Sun Palace, was not clear. And in a moment it mattered not at all. The door swung open under his thrusting hands. Sunara, waiting upon his efforts, stepped to his side to join him, and together they crossed the shadowy threshold.

It was a vault so huge that their torches, though flaring brightly, were as candles in the dead of night. But there were other torches, unlit, set in ancient mirrored sconces all round the vault; and when – crossing and recrossing like fireflies in the dusk – they had set flame to a dozen of these, the fantastic treasure house emerged out of the darkness and shone with a thousand lights.

Richard, who had known much of plunder and riches during the past ten years, caught his breath as he took in the scene; it had a barbaric extravagance such as he had never before witnessed, nor even imagined. There was row upon row of chests, open-mouthed, crammed and heaped with gold ornaments which gleamed dully in the torchlight. He saw gold cups, and chalices, and jewelled pectoral crosses fit to grace any prince of the church; there was bar gold in stacked heaps, and coins which he could recognize at sight – English guineas, Dutch rix dollars, Spanish pieces-of-eight – and others less familiar dredged up from the glittering past – Portuguese moidores, French pistoles, even coins with stern Roman heads upon them. Ancient iron boxes, which Sunara opened casually, revealed crimson rubies, yellow diamonds, emeralds as green as the sea at sunset. There were silken altarcloths, and tapestries with forgotten battles marvellously worked in Persian thread; there was a statuette of the lovegod, exquisitely formed of bronze, with silver wings and a bow encrusted with a hundred tiny diamonds.

Round the walls were hung rows of blazoned banners, trophies from long ago, standing sentinel over the staggering wealth below them, for which, it seemed, the seven seas must have been ransacked for many hundreds of years.

Richard was spellbound; he wandered from shelf to shelf, from chest to chest, examining, fingering, touching gold bars and silver boxes, allowing a rain of rubies to drip through his fingers like liquid fire, holding an ice-blue diamond up to the torchlight till its myriad facets confused his eye. Sunara was watching him rather than the treasure; her face was grave, as usual, but there was a hint of amusement in her eyes as she saw this pirate wandering at will among fantastic riches. At the end of this strange day, there could be nothing more strange than to see him thus beleaguered by what he had striven for and pursued, for so many ardent years.

He turned from examining a heap of uncut emeralds, whose fire shone even through their rough, unpolished surface, and caught her eye.

'But this is stupendous!' he exclaimed. His face and his voice were both boyish in their wonder. 'I have seen nothing like it – there can be nothing like it, in all the world! Where did such treasure come from?'

'We have always been a nation of warriors,' answered Sunara. 'Warriors, pirates, raiders, wreckers of rich ships ... Most of the jewels are from our mines in the north – their working is a personal privilege of the Rajah of Makassang. The coins, as you can see, are from many lands; there have been treasure ships in these waters since the beginning of history, and sometimes they do not reach their homeland.' She smiled; in the flickering torchlight, she was very beautiful, and Richard was conscious again of their solitude, at the hour of midnight in this cavernous vault. 'But I need not teach you what can happen to a treasure ship.'

Richard, about to answer, found that his eye had been caught by something else, perhaps the strangest object in the whole room. It was a suit of armour, of a pattern long forgotten, rusty and mildewed, standing by itself in one corner. He raised his torch and peered at it, and as he did so, he caught his breath afresh. The pattern of the armour could be recognized from a score of prints and pictures in his father's old library; and the faded coat-of-arms on the breastplate was unmistakable. It chanced that he had some amateur knowledge of such things; his father had taught him the language of heraldry, and, long ago, brother Miles, at the age of fourteen, had not been too young to wax pedantic about fesse gules and vert, lions passant and salient. Now, confronted with the fleur-de-lis on a blue ground, and the three golden lions on a red, he pointed in great excitement.

'Those are the Tudor arms!' he said. 'Our own Queen Elizabeth!'

Sunara approached, and with him examined the pale colours engraved on the breastplate. 'You know that, also? We did not know it, until Andrew Farthing told us. It was from the ship going round the world.'

'The ship?'

'The first English ship to do so.'

'But that can only mean – this must have been one of Sir Francis Drake's men-at-arms!'

'Even so.'

'Of course!' exclaimed Richard. His awe and excitement charged his voice with deep feeling. 'That was the voyage which compassed the whole world, before he returned to fight the great Armada! In fifteen hundred and eighty – nearly three hundred years ago. I recall that they touched at many places hereabouts, in the Spice Islands, the Moluccas. This man must have died on board, or he was killed. A gentleman adventurer ...' He was still wonderstruck at the sight of the armour standing alone, its breastplate bespeaking the pride of valour across three hundred years, its leather joints creased and stained with age. 'He was a small man, seemingly ... I hope he died well.'

'My father drinks from his skull,' said Sunara.

Richard looked at her. She had used a matter-of-fact tone, as if it were no great subject for comment, but he could not help remembering that he himself had drunk from this same ceremonial cup, and had not known what pale ghost from the past had furnished it. Now he learned that it had been one of Drake's own men ... He reached out, and touched the armour, asking forgiveness for hapless sacrilege, and answered: 'Well, God rest his soul, in any case.'

Sunara turned aside, and took up her torch again from its mirrored sconce. There was sudden urgency and meaning in her voice as she said: 'There is another room.'

She led the way, past the treasure chests and the heaped jewels and the banners. At the farther end of the vault, opposite the entrance door, there was an archway in the wall; and as they passed through it, the light from their torches began to fall upon some objects which reflected the fire, but which burned also with pinpoints of red against a vague whiteness. They were like eyes in the darkness – and as the light increased, Richard found that they were indeed unearthly eyes, rows of them, staring out at the intruders. For the white patches in the gloom were human skulls; and the red points of light were huge rubies set into the eye sockets. Sunara put down her torch; then she advanced, and bowed low to the skulls, which stared and stared back with their sightless, unwinking gaze. Richard shivered involuntarily, and turned his glance away. There had been enough of death and decay, for one day … He saw that the room, which was small, contained only three things; the rows of skulls, ranged on marble shelves, another row of some dozens of rubies, neatly sorted into pairs of different size and quality; and a golden couch with a magnificent lion-skin draped over it.

He turned to her. 'Who are – they?'

'My forefathers, and my family. It is a burial custom in Makassang. The skulls are set with rubies, and enshrined here forever.'

He remembered her earlier words. 'These are the watching eyes you spoke of?'

'Yes. Would you dare to rob this vault, with such guardians as these?'

He shook his head. 'No.'

'I do not know them all by name,' she said. She seemed at home in the room, but warmed also by a special quality of feeling; for some reason, he had never before been so conscious of her sensual beckoning. Standing in the stillness of the skull room, with the eyes staring down at them, they might have been the last man and woman left on earth. She pointed a slim hand. 'That was my grandfather, and that my great-grandfather. That is my own brother, who was killed fighting – you may see the spear furrow at the temple – and that, my mother, who died when I was born. The others' – she swept her arm around – 'are honoured ancestors. I also will rest my head here, some day.' She turned to the lowest shelf, with its rows of matched rubies, and pointed once more, at a pair of the stones which lay on one side. 'These are my eyes,' she said.

Now he did more than shiver; he was seized with that terror which springs most fiercely from love.

'Oh God!' he exclaimed. 'I cannot bear that thought.'

She seemed surprised. 'But it is not sad. I shall be at peace, and these my eyes will join the other watchers.'

'It is horrible!' he said, uncontrollably.

'Why so?' She had sat down on the curved golden couch, a couch such as Cleopatra might have graced; she looked more lovely than any woman in the world. He noticed suddenly that she was wearing the same clothes as on the evening they had first met; a green sarong edged with gold, and a tunic of cloth of gold which hid what his eyes had then so greedily searched for. Now there was no greed, only longing and worship. The gilded fingernail on her right hand, the mark of virginity, was challenging and moving at the same time. But because of love, she was indeed inviolate. 'Why so?' she repeated. 'Death is only a stage on our journey. That is all we need to know.'

'It is the thought of your eyes,' he said. He did not dare to speak directly of love. That moment had not yet come, in this room with the watchers on guard. But he had to reveal something of what was in his mind. 'It is because, living, you are so beautiful, and I could not bear the thought of your living eyes being stolen away, and exchanged for cold jewels.'

Now they were staring at each other; he had declared himself enough; she was a princess seated upon a golden couch, he was a strong man who thought her ravishing. It was a moment of charged feeling, of overwhelming compulsion. But it was Sunara, not Richard Marriott, who responded to it.

She still held his gaze with her own steadfast look; though hers had softened wonderfully, to a compliance he had never guessed in her.

'I am glad that I am beautiful,' she said. She spoke very slowly, with pauses filled only by the thudding of his heart. 'I am glad, being a woman, that you should think so … I have learned much about you, during these many days … I do not know all that you want – perhaps you do not yet know yourself – but I know one thing that you want … You want to see what your eyes have been seeking for, ever since I first danced in the Dance of the Priestesses.' He cast his head down, in swift confusion, and she noted it, and asked: 'Why should that not be? You are a man … Why need you be ashamed? Why need I be ashamed?' She rose from the couch, softly small, flawlessly beautiful; her eyes alone were drawing them both past all return to the divided past. 'Shall I dance for you again, my lord?'

He could not answer her; the constriction of his throat was overpowering. In a graceful, unconcerned movement, she took off her golden tunic, revealing the small and perfect breasts. Then she looked straight at him, and began to sing, a small wayward song in a small true voice; and then she began to dance.

It was a dance not like the Virgin Sacrifice, lulling some god into slothful benevolence; indeed, it was not formal at all, it fulfilled no pattern – it was Sunara speaking to Richard Marriott, for his private pleasure, and for hers. By the light of their twin torches, her pale body moved with exquisite grace, shadowy one moment, glowing at the next; as she danced, she spoke with her hands, with the offering of her bosom, with her eyes which never left his. The dance answered his wondering heart, and the question which had struck him with the first astonishment – why she was dancing for him.

She was acknowledging his love, bending to the precious compliment, rising to the ardour which prompted it. She was saying as much as he had said, and more – and saying it without pause for reticence. If he could be brave, her flickering body told him, then she would be braver still – candid in answer, loving in intent, honest in desire, generous in all things.

It could not take her long to give him this simple message. Presently she was very near to him. The small tune died away, and her smile died also, and the last flowing movements of her shoulders. She ended her dance, not with a bow – as to her father formerly – but with upraised arms which dropped gently on to his shoulders. Then there was nothing left in the world but the rise and fall of her bosom, and her eyes engulfing his.

He did not hesitate; her honesty must be matched, or he would be a coward forever.

'I love you, Sunara,' he said.

She was grave and direct, as always. 'After you have seen my body?'

Once again he must match this. 'Yes. And before that. And now, when I see nothing but your eyes.'

'What do you see in them?'

'The answer.'

She broke into a slow smile. 'Then you do not need to hear it.'

'I need to hear it.' He was trembling now. The thudding of his heart was enough to shake his whole frame.

On the verge of all their shared desires, she dropped her hands, as if, at last, they did not need to touch each other in order to be closely entwined. Her voice was as soft and as clear as her gaze. 'I can love no other man but you,' she said, and stood on tiptoe for his embrace.


They lay together for a long time on the golden couch, enjoying a new world of sensual wonder; their kisses were untrammelled, their caresses as free as the air they breathed. But, in spite of his storming need, he did not take her, nor did he, after the ebbing of this first wildness, mourn his denial. For though she allowed him much, and would have allowed him all, yet he felt in her compliant body a shyness, a hope that she would be spared until tomorrow, or another day – until some new dawn made it more fitting. It was as if the gilded nail of her virginity, proud and appealing in the same moment, did in truth protect her. He did not press his will, because his will was not exactly matched by hers, and it was this matching which, for the first time in his life, his love demanded.

When this became understood between them, and her loving smile and gentler kiss acknowledged his forbearance – though they did not greatly aid it – he took her hand, and pressed it, leading them both back to the world they had left.

'You are beautiful, Sunara,' he said tenderly. 'Too beautiful for one man ... Tomorrow I will – '

'We speak of tomorrow already?'

'Better so ...' He took her golden tunic from where it lay, and placed it about her shoulders, and – with hands not yet steady – fastened the jewelled clasp at her bosom, hiding the shape on which his eyes, and indeed his hands, had dwelt. Then he stood up, and drew her to her feet. 'Do not think me the less a man,' he said, 'for talking of tomorrow, when today is still so much with us. It is part of a man's love, for all that. At least, it is part of mine.'

'It might be the dearest part ... You are strangely mingled,' she said thoughtfully. 'A pirate at one moment, a man of gentleness at another. But it is easy to love you the more for it. There are times – and tonight is one – when you put me in mind of Andrew Farthing.'

He was astonished; it was the last name he would have expected to hear. 'Andrew Farthing?' The touch of his hand caressing her cheek was ironic. 'I understood that he was an old and godly teacher.'

'Even so. But he could change his nature also – or show another side of it. He once told us, with disapproval, of a great prince of the Roman Church, who used to pray: "Oh Lord, grant me the gift of continence – but not yet." Then he smiled and said: "Honesty is a virtue also." '

They had begun to wander back slowly, their hands clasped, out from the room of the skulls, past the shelves and chests and counters of the treasure vault, towards the gaping doorway which led to the stairs and the upper air. Richard's blood was cooling, and his thoughts with it; he was content in love, happy, utterly at peace, as if he had in truth possessed her body, and slaked his fierce hunger. That could be his happy lot tomorrow, he knew, or the next day – and in that assurance he found enough delight to carry him past a hundred burning temptations. He could not feel his body denied, when his heart sang with promise, and when her hand-clasp was his warranty of fulfilment ... To ease the moment of its last tension he asked: 'What became of Andrew Farthing? Did he die in Makassang?' Then he remembered. 'Nay, your father once told me he was murdered. How did that come about?'

'It was the priests, the Anapuri,' she replied. She was answering more than his question, matching his step towards normality with a considered coolness of her own. 'They feared his influence, which was very great, all over the island. One day he was found stabbed, on a forest pathway, going towards one of his mission houses.'

'Did he make many converts here?'

She shook her head. 'No. Our belief in the Lord Buddha is too strong; he could not turn it. It troubled him, at first, but towards the end he was satisfied with simple teaching. He used to say, "Men can come to God in different hats ..." Is that an English saying?'

Richard smiled at the thought. 'I never heard it before,' he answered, 'from a Scottish minister ... I wish I had known your Andrew Farthing.'

'One day I will give you his journals to read.'

'He kept journals?'

'He wrote of his hopes and his fears for us. They are sad to read – full of loving, and regret.'

'But what did he regret?'

'He called it, our want of a good shepherd.'

They were making their way up the stairs now, still going hand in hand; Sunara's walk, which he felt rather than saw, was graceful and swaying, the walk of a woman in love with a man close by her. Richard had a last pang, for what had so nearly been, and had now faded; and then he tossed away the thought, without repining, and said: 'It seems to me that these priests of the Anapuri have much on their consciences. Do you think we shall see them more quiet now?'

'No. Not while Selang Aro lives. He is the spring of all this. He will bide his time, and watch, and try again when he feels strong enough.'

'Fear nothing!' answered Richard cheerfully. 'I will protect you. You are safe with me.'

Sunara, checking her step, turned to look at him. For the first time in the jointure of their lives, he saw her face lit by a feminine guile, mocking him in love.

'I can swear to the world that that is true,' she said mischievously. Then she turned and ran ahead of him, up the stairs and away, before he could think of a fitting answer – or a fitting action either.

III

On the following morning, being the morning of the great banquet – for which the preparations were so lavish that many parts of the palace had been in a continual stir, from the earliest dawn – it was John Keston who, to Richard's surprise, brought him the tray of fruits and the silver jug of Amboina coffee with which he began his waking day. Richard lay, as usual, in the canopied bed, under a light covering of silk; without stirring, as soon as he awoke, he could look past the open window of his private balcony, to the seaward slopes of the palace grounds, and the restless Java ocean which, pounding in upon distant beaches, was always to be faintly heard, a reminder of outer majesty, at any hour of any day or night.

He felt deeply at ease; he had slept well, the day was fair, he would meet Sunara, by accident or design, within an hour or two. Seeing

John Keston unexpectedly at his bedside, Richard greeted him jovially.

'Well, now, John! You put me to shame with your early rising! I thought you would still be aboard the Lucinda. Did you sleep ashore last night?'

'No, sir.' Keston put the tray with its savoury burden down at the bedside table, and propped the pillows behind Richard's head; then, turning, he began to gather up his master's clothes and set the room to rights. 'I came ashore at first light, and told the servants here that I would wake you.'

'You are welcome,' said Richard, in the same careless mood. He stretched his arms out wide, greeting the new day, pushing aside the languors and confinements of the night; when he was refreshed, with his hand poised over the coffee pot, he looked up at John Keston again. 'There's nothing gone amiss on board, is there?'

'I would not say that all is well.'

Richard, not in the mood for long faces and gloomy words, smiled at the tone. It was true that he had left John Keston on board the Lucinda D, in order (as he had phrased it) to keep an eye on Nick Garrett; but he could not believe that this surveillance had uncovered any dark secrets or plots. Sailors were always grumblers, and Garrett was one of the best of them; but now that Richard had sent down two chests of rix dollars – more than ten thousand gold coins – for the general sharing onboard, he did not expect any serious disaffection. The days were too handsome, Makassang was too happy a place ... Pouring his coffee, reaching out for a slice of the paw-paw fruit spiced with cinnamon, he said: 'Tell me of these great disasters.'

But John Keston had his solemn tale to impart, and he would not be turned aside by joking.

'You said to watch the ship and the crew,' he began without preamble. 'It's as well that I did ... They've nothing to do on board but talk, and they're making the most of that, I can tell you!' His hands were busy now with the folding of clothes, but his look was directly towards Richard. 'And there's drinking all the time, and women coming on board in canoes after dark, and the hands fighting for their favours – not that they're worth the fighting! It's time you came back aboard, to knock all their heads together.'

'I'll do that, if need be,' said Richard easily. 'But talk and drinking is cheap – it does no harm. And they're welcome to make free of the women, if the women are so free already ... Is that all the bad news you have?'

'It is bad news,' said John Keston obstinately. 'You had a good crew, a while back. Now you have a gang of idlers. They say you won't be coming back, and they might as well take the ship, and sail off home again.'

'Who said that?' demanded Richard.

'Peter Ramsay was the first to say it. Now it is common talk, and Nick Garrett has not been backward, when it comes to talking, either.'

'I would not expect any miracles from Nick ... What does he say?'

John Keston hesitated; then he threw back his head, as if in determination. 'He says you are planning to keep the rest of the prize for yourself.'

'So? What harm does that do? I will prove him wrong, when I come on board with the money in gold, and he will look a fool.'

'He has other plans, maybe. He told some of the crew that this was no time to think of leaving Makassang, whether you came back or no. He said he could promise them a change for the better, and he has been visiting ashore.'

'So?' said Richard again. He was savouring his coffee, allowing nothing to spoil the delicate flavour. 'Let him visit, it will give him an appetite.'

'An appetite for what he has no right to. He has been visiting up at the Golden Pagoda.'

'It is worth a call.'

'He came back drunk, the last time. Drunk, and full of schemes. He said – it was to Peter Ramsay, down on the orlopdeck, but I overheard them – that there would be a new captain before long. And new guns. And – these were his own words – "another try".'

'Another try at what?'

John Keston shrugged. 'He did not say more.'

'I'll be bound he did not!' Though the news might have its ominous side, Richard was still not at all disturbed. He had known Nick Garrett, and the others, for a long time; he knew how they talked, and also how their talk ran dry, and was forgotten, as soon as work took its place. It was a fit time to worry, when sullen silence fell … But John Keston still meant much to him; it would be wrong to scoff at his fears, or to dismiss as idle gossip something which had so clearly troubled the other man. He sat back against the pillows, and tried for a more reasonable tone.

'Nay, John, do not give way to worry. This is just so much talk – talk and liquor. New guns? Where would they get them? And if they did succeed, they would still be my guns … A new captain? – ' he laughed, dismissing the idea, ' – that is no more than Nick Garrett himself, scheming to take over from his betters. He has done that for five years, and he is still my first-lieutenant! And as for "another try" – if he means another try at the Golden Pagoda, he is welcome to it. There is no profit to be had there, except gold leaf and tawdry ornaments. If he means another try to win this country, or to get his hands on the treasure, he is welcome to that also. He will run his head into a noose, and I will be the first to take a strong pull at the slip-knot!'

John Keston, his hands now idle, looked at his master. Conscience struggled with the habit of trust; he had come ashore to warn, but in the face of such confidence, how could he labour this point, which the bright morning, and the sunshine casting bars of shadow along the length of the balcony, were rendering foolish? Yet he was an obstinate young man, and a loyal one also. He put forth a last effort to say what was in his mind, whether he was seemingly made a fool thereby, or not.

'Sir,' he said, more formally, 'can I speak my mind?'

Richard, brought up short by the change of tone, stared at him. 'You know that you can. Why do you ask such a question? We have shared too much in the past, for you to grow delicate all of a sudden.'

'But it is not the same now.' Clearly, Keston was struggling with deeper thoughts than any that had troubled him during the years of which Richard spoke. He gestured round the room, richly appointed, replete with all the trappings of ease. 'You are a great man again, now that you have come ashore. And you are soon to be greater, maybe.'

'How, greater?'

'Oh, there is talk here, too ... What we would know, sir – what I would know, is – when do you plan to return to the ship?'

'In due time,' answered Richard. 'I have set no day for it. What is the harm in living ashore? I can be back on board in thirty minutes!'

Keston swallowed; talking thus plainly, he had become ill-at-ease. But he was determined to persist to the end. 'Sir, you will lose the ship, unless you return. The men will not follow someone they cannot see, the ghost of a man who has forgotten them.' He gestured round the room again. 'Perhaps it does not matter to you, giving up the Lucinda. It does not matter to me, if I know what is in your mind. But you should not lose the ship by default, for want of a word of warning. Or for want of energy, either.'

Richard sat up at that, stung out of his calm, prepared to give way to ill-temper. 'What is this, energy? What sort of word is that?'

John Keston, once he had ventured past the edge of boldness, saw no merit in retreating. 'There is more to do here,' he said – and his country burr was strong, and his tone rough, 'than pick flowers.'

Glaring at his servant, within an ace of dismissing him for insolence, or ordering him from the room until he could learn his manners, Richard Marriott found himself dissolving into laughter instead. It was no use wearing such a grim mask – he could not, on this morning of love and sunlight, hold a grudge or sustain a quarrel. He knew John Keston for what he was – a faithful servant, an honest man, a friend. The fact that he had been betrayed, by fear or rumour, into this rare display of feeling, could not alter his worth.

Nor could it alter what he, Richard Marriott, the sudden darling of fortune, felt and thought and hoped, either ... He waved his hand, in most genial dismissal, to John Keston, and settled himself back on his pillows again, preparing to take the half-hour of ease which remained before he need be up and about. Later, he might worry – but not now. Later, he would return to his ship – but not today. Later he would pronounce the name of action, but not before he had kissed Sunara, and put the sign of love on all that lay ahead.

Yet he was to have another reminder, that day, that there were other things beside love in Makassang; and this from an unexpected quarter.

The Rajah summoned him to audience at sundown, an hour before the time set for the banquet. The old man seemed troubled and fretful; at first Richard thought it might be the matter of Sunara – the Sun Palace, like the treasure vault, had many eyes, and he and the Princess might well have been observed, in circumstances likely to affect a father's composure. But this apparently was not so. Though the Rajah did mention his daughter, it was in quite another sense from that which Richard might have expected. His thoughts, though indeed dynastic, were directed to a larger canvas altogether. His theme and his preoccupation, it seemed, was the future.

'I have been thinking much today,' said the Rajah, when the civilities were done, and Richard, with permission, had sat down on a couch opposite the smaller throne in one corner of the audience chamber. They were alone, save for the two drowsy slaves pulling slowly at the mechanism of the punkahs; the heat of the day was diminishing, leaving behind it the promise of a cool, scented dusk. 'Indeed, I have had much in my mind, for these many days past.'

Richard, wary and formal, expressed the hope that the Rajah's thoughts had been happy ones.

The Rajah shook his head. He seemed especially old, on this

evening; old and frail and scarcely able to fend for himself; his hands, clasped together on his lap in an attitude of resignation, were almost transparent in their delicacy. 'Happy thoughts are rare,' he answered, in a melancholy voice. 'They are for the young and hopeful who, alas, often live too swiftly to enjoy them ... I would like to hear, Captain Marriott,' he continued, turning off at a tangent, in the manner of old people, 'what you think of Makassang?'

'It is very beautiful,' replied Richard, with the same wariness. Faced by the Rajah's unheralded question, he could not escape the thought that he was being stalked, like some quarry in a quiet forest – or, if that were too fanciful an idea, that he was being brought under examination, for some special purpose. He felt the need for care, even though he could not see the reason for it. 'It is the most beautiful island I have ever seen, in many ways.'

'You are drawn to it?' asked the Rajah. His eyes, the most notable feature in a face inscrutable and shadowed, were now closely fixed on Richard. 'You feel happy here?'

'Very happy, your Highness.'

'I thought as much ... And my daughter?'

'I beg your pardon, your Highness?' answered Richard. He was far from ready to declare himself – he had not seen Sunara for more than a few minutes, on that busy day, and they had not spoken a word of the future – and the sudden query had seized him with the need to temporize. There were rules to be observed here, customs of which he knew nothing; it was probable that he had already stepped far beyond the permissible limits of protocol, and had the prospect of a royal wrath to face, as well as a father's. 'I do not understand.'

The Rajah gestured, with minor impatience. 'You are drawn to Makassang, you say. You are happy here. Are you drawn to the Princess Sunara?'

The Rajah's tone contained no hint of anger, only of the desire to be informed. He might have been speaking of day-to-day matters. But such unconcern was not dependable. Perhaps the honest answer was the best one.

'I am very much drawn to her.' Richard replied, as bravely as he could. 'When you summoned me, I was of a mind to speak to your Highness – '

The Rajah, raising one of his frail hands, interrupted him. 'Later,' he said, with a return of his fretful manner. 'These are not things to be settled as between a father and a suitor. They are affairs of state. All that matters to me is to know that you have a certain intention.'

'I have that intention,' said Richard. It seemed a foolish form of words, to cover the urgency of his feeling for Sunara – to describe, for instance, the magical happenings of last night – but he saw, or thought that he saw, the path which was being indicated to him. It now became, as the Rajah had said, an affair of state – another, even more foolish phrase to disguise such living, breathing wonders.

'Excellent!' said the Rajah, with an abrupt change of spirit He sat up suddenly, and clapped his hands together. 'Wine!' he called to the servant who appeared at the head of the long room. 'Bring wine!' In the silence that followed, he surveyed Richard Marriott as if he were indeed a favourite son; and when the wine was brought and served, he raised his glass as if he were already toasting the bridegroom himself. 'You have made me happy,' he said, when he had set down his glass. 'This can only mean that you plan to remain with us in Makassang.'

It was a statement rather than a question; it left Richard with little room for anything save agreement. 'Why, as to that,' he began hesitantly, 'I have made no plans. Your Highness will recall that I undertook to fight Black Harris and his allies. Now that this is done – '

'Now that this is done,' the Rajah interrupted, 'we can all of us settle down in peace. Until danger strikes again, as well it may.'

It was clear, thought Richard, that he must tread delicately here. There were some promises he was very ready to make, others that he still shunned. He wanted Sunara – that was undeniable; but he wanted her alone, he did not want the island of Makassang caught up in the girdle at her waist; he did not want other men's cares, other men's quarrels … Yet this was not the moment to make his thought clear; the best that he could do was to display a general goodwill, without commitment.

But before he could speak, he was forestalled. 'I cannot live forever,' said the Rajah, with a swift return to his former manner. It was something which Richard had noted of late – the way in which the old man's mood could change, within the course of a few moments, from dejection to joy, and back again. 'I want peace – I want to see the future clearly, and to be content with it … I need someone to help me, a strong man, a young man. During the past weeks, I have come to hope that this young man would be yourself.'

'I should feel most honoured – ' began Richard.

'I thought that you had been sent by the Lord Buddha to help us,' said the Rajah, almost bad-temperedly. 'Surely you wish to stay in Makassang? And if not, what can persuade you to stay? Is it money? You may have all that you wish … Is it a matter of honours? There need be no limit to them. What is it that you are seeking?'

The swift questions, irritably thrown in his direction, could not be answered with any particularity; indeed, Richard scarcely knew the answers, and he could not venture upon such seas without careful preparation. 'I need no honours,' he said slowly. 'I need no money, either.'

'What then?'

'Your Highness, please believe me when I say that I have planned nothing.'

'But you are planning to leave?'

'I have planned nothing,' Richard repeated. He dared not show his impatience, but he made his tone as firm as possible. 'I am happy here, and that is enough for the moment. But – ' he hesitated, uncertain how much involvement in argument he should risk, ' – I am surprised that you should think that you need more help from me. The country is quiet and orderly. You have your own advisers.

Amin Bulong, Colonel Kedah – ' he gestured. 'They are your strong men, surely?'

'The country is not quiet,' said the Rajah peevishly. 'It is never quiet. It was not quiet in my father's time, nor in his father's either. We are always being plagued by rebellion from within, or by attacks from outside. You know that all the islands hereabouts are Dutch. They have proved cruel rulers, cruel and grasping; I would as soon be ruled by crocodiles … The Dutch would have taken Makassang too, if they could but we have been strong in the past, and there are such elements as headhunters and pirates to discourage colonists. However, they will always have envious eyes … If anyone is to take us,' said the Rajah more thoughtfully, 'I would wish it to be your own country. But that is because of Andrew Farthing's goodness … Amin Bulong sits at the head of my Council of State,' he said, going off on another of his bewildering tangents. 'But he is old. I am old, too. I have no son to follow me. Sunara, being a woman, cannot rule in her own right. Kedah is a brave soldier – nothing else. Makassang needs more than this. And I need more. I need a man to stand at my right hand. A young man whom I can trust. A young man bound to me by ties that go beyond paid service, or self-interest.'

He ceased, and there was silence, while the punkahs creaked and swung to and fro in the heavy air. Richard did not know what to say. If the Rajah were proposing anything at all, he was proposing a mighty change in Richard's circumstances; not only that he should stay in Makassang forever, but even that he might come to rule the country when the Rajah had gone. How else to interpret the words: 'I have no son to follow me'? And the talk of Sunara? And the talk of England? … With a sense of growing confinement, unwilling to commit himself to so bizarre a future, Richard sought, once more, to temporize.

'I will give thought to it, your Highness. Much thought. But I am scarcely fitted – '

'There are men,' said the Rajah, breaking in, 'who can grow to be giants, if need be, in order to fulfil their destiny. You are such a man

184

...' Then he looked up suddenly, almost suspiciously. 'You said that the country is quiet and peaceful. Yet you know that the Anapuri once ruled here, and would do so again, if they could. And I – ' his eyes sparked with brief cruelty, ' – I would hang them all from their own pagoda, if I could ... Have you heard no rumours?'

'None, your Highness. Rumours of what?'

'Of Black Harris.'

'How can that be?'

'It is bazaar talk,' said the Rajah. 'It may be true, it may be false. But they are saying that he is not dead, after all. They are saying that he slipped ashore after the battle, and took refuge.'

'I saw him killed.'

'You saw him fall. He has been seen since, by many people.'

'Seen?' Richard was astonished. 'Seen where?'

'At places a hundred miles apart,' answered the Rajah ironically, 'on the same day at the same hour. But there is much talk in the bazaars, none the less. They say also that some of the Mystic's guns have disappeared.'

'But she was wrecked, and burnt.'

'Do guns burn?'

Richard shrugged, at a loss for an answer. He could not credit any of this, nor see its purpose either; he guessed only that it was part of a general subterfuge, to persuade him that there was still danger, and thus to keep him in Makassang. But he could not say so, in so many words; though the old man was amiable enough, yet there were risks involved even in implied contradiction, risks which no prospective son-in-law in his senses would choose to run ... Observing that the Rajah had risen to his feet, to mark the end of the audience, Richard followed suit.

'Well, we have talked enough,' said the Rajah, with a return to his cheerful mood. 'Let the rest of the day be given to pleasure, and to happiness ... The Princess will be joining us at the conclusion of the banquet.'

Richard murmured his satisfaction.

'I would talk of a father's blessing,' said the Rajah, 'but in these modern times, I might seem to be out of date... Let us say that you may look for surprises, at the banquet.'

'I have had enough surprises already, today,' answered Richard, meeting his mood. 'I doubt my capacity for sustaining many more of them.'

'I have no fears for your capacity,' remarked the Rajah, with sly emphasis. It was even conceivable that he was making a broad jest, and Richard, in spite of himself, felt his cheeks warming. Perhaps the Sun Palace held no secrets, after all. The Rajah continued, on this same rallying note: 'Tell me, Captain Marriott – you still have your fine uniform?'

The admiral's coat, with its brave array of medals and orders, had already become a joke between them. 'I have it still, your Highness.'

'Wear your fine uniform tonight,' said the Rajah, nodding in high good humour. 'It will suit a fine occasion.'

IV

There was no doubt that the occasion was a fine one. Though Richard Marriott had by now become used to the splendours of the Sun Palace, it seemed unlikely that the first banquet he had attended on his arrival – now so long ago, in everything save the realm of time – could be surpassed. But it did not take him long to realize that, by comparison, that first banquet was no more than a poorhouse supper, when matched with the barbaric magnificence of this night's entertainment.

To begin with, there were many more people present; there must have been fifty at the high table alone, and in the body of the room, upwards of a thousand guests ate, drank, and took their ease. There were also many strange faces among Richard's immediate neighbours; by their bearing, and the number of their personal servants, they were men of importance, but he had never seen them at court before. Their attendance intrigued him, and presently he leant across to address a query to Amin Bulong, seated nearby. The old man, busy as usual with the pleasure of eating, shrugged his shoulders as he answered: 'Every chief in Makassang is here tonight!'

'Why is that?'

'They have been summoned,' said Amin Bulong briefly, and went on to speak of what was clearly uppermost in his mind – the dish of gulls' eggs spiced with cloves and nutmegs, which had just been laid before him.

These strangers – most of them old men, grave-faced and withdrawn – had on their arrival greeted Richard with respect. They seemed to know him already, or to have heard of his deeds and to acknowledge his consequence, without reservations. Many of them bore the same badge of office, superimposed on their other regalia; a broad sash of purple silk, worn across one shoulder and held in place by a jewelled emblem. It put Richard in mind, irreverently, of the wine waiters of certain glittering establishments in Paris, who were also thus distinguished. But when, again, he asked Amin Bulong for enlightenment, the answer was short and pointed.

'They are members of the Council of State,' said Amin Bulong. Then he motioned to the dish of gulls' eggs, nestling in their bed of scarlet sea moss. 'Help yourself,' he said, with very good humour, 'before it is too late.'

A second oddity was the presence of Selang Aro. The sour-visaged priest sat in a place of honour, almost at the centre of the table; by turning slightly, Richard had the other man's face in full view – and the full view was not reassuring. Above the saffron robes and the severe black collar which was his sole mark of rank, the face of Selang Aro reflected nothing save a supercilious disengagement. He might be there, in the unwilling flesh, but in the spirit he was many worlds away. *I am a priest,* the thin, high-boned face seemed to declare; *I witness your gluttony, I listen to your unholy music; but my way of life is different, and my way of life will conquer* ... Richard wondered why he had been invited at all, and why he had consented to attend – unless it were a matter of command, as on his last appearance at the Sun Palace. His air of reserved power, of being preoccupied with higher matters, made him an uncomfortable neighbour. He ate nothing. He spoke to no one. He was simply present – a dry skeleton at a profane feast.

Certainly the entertainment was not designed to accord with priestly withdrawal from the world of the flesh. Once again, there were no women yet to be seen, but every other focus of appetite was indulged to the full. The whole audience chamber had been newly hung with tapestries, which Richard recognized as coming from the treasure vault below; against this background of magnificence, the banquet ran its course on a scale scarcely to be comprehended by a single set of man's senses. The wine flowed in rivers; the dishes were of an extraordinary variety, ranging from such gross offerings as a wild pig roasted whole, standing upright on a golden salver which must have measured four feet across, to tiny brilliant fish not much bigger than a finger's length, seeming to swim in their bowls of scented oil.

The flickering torchlight fell on a riot of colour and movement. Servants brought new dishes, in endless relay; beakers of wine circled the room without pause; there was constant visiting from table to table, prefaced always by deep and formal bows towards the Rajah, both on rising and sitting down again. There were tumblers in multicoloured finery, with bells on their ankles, and magicians whose deft hands conjured tendrils and wreaths of flowers from the very air. An Indian with a filthy matted beard charmed a snake from its basket, with such sweet notes upon the pipe that it seemed no miracle to see a lowly serpent unable to resist them. A pair of naked wrestlers, both larded with a thick covering of pig's fat, slid in and out of each other's grip like great flopping fish, while roars of laughter rang through the room at their efforts to subdue one another. Their contest ended with a wild chase among the tables, in which many others joined, until the whole roomful of a thousand people seemed rendered helpless with laughter. Then the musicians took up their task once more, filling the air with an insistent yet melodious beauty; and the company fell to eating again, and pledging each other in wine, and bowing towards the high table, restoring to the banquet the sense of a great occasion.

The Rajah was in fine spirits. He had placed Richard on his left hand, and saw that he was plied with food and drink; the skull cup – which now held so devout a meaning for Richard – constantly passed between them. But he would say nothing of the purpose of the evening – if it had a purpose, beyond this bountiful enjoyment. When Richard expressed his curiosity, the Rajah answered him only in vague terms.

'Let us say that we are celebrating the victory, Captain Marriott. Your victory.'

Richard looked round him at the fantastic scene. 'It was not worth so much honour,' he protested.

'It was worth so much to me ... Come ... let us drink a toast to victory, and to the future.'

Richard, looking over the rim of the skull-cup as he drank in response, suddenly found that he was gazing directly into the eyes of Selang Aro, seated a few feet away. After the Rajah's expansive good humour, it was a shock to encounter the very reverse, within the space of a moment. For the High Priest's expression, though veiled, was unmistakable; there was envy in it, and bitterness, and something akin to hatred.

Taken aback, Richard sought to ease the moment with a friendly exchange of words. Still holding the skull cup, he leant across towards Selang Aro, and said with all the politeness he could muster: 'I hope you are finding amusement here tonight.'

As if one curtain were succeeding another, Selang Aro's face changed swiftly, from its cast of malevolence to a customary sour disdain. Though he bent forward with an equal formality, his tone was cold as he answered: 'Such occasions as this are far removed from the life of the Anapuri.'

'But you must agree that it is a great celebration,' said Richard carefully.

Selang Aro glanced pointedly at the skull cup. 'Greater for you than for myself.'

Richard, brought up short by the words, which were so uttered as to border on the offensive, decided that politeness had had its fair day. He frowned as he said curtly: 'I enjoy such hospitality, and I am honoured by it.'

'No doubt.' Selang Aro's thin smile was devoid of humour. 'I understand that you will be full of honours, before the evening is out.'

'I know nothing of that.'

'Yet I hope,' said Selang Aro, disregarding entirely Richard's answer, 'that you will not receive more honours than one man can safely bear.'

'You talk in riddles,' said Richard coldly.

Selang Aro lowered his head, masking his eyes completely. His voice was scarcely above a whisper as he said: 'Such honours can be heavy enough to kill a man.'

Richard was about to probe further, to satisfy both his curiosity and his anger at the words, when his attention was distracted. It seemed that the long feasting was at last done; there was now a general movement at the centre of the floor, as the tables were cleared away and the guests withdrew gradually to the steps and porticos flanking the audience chamber. Something nudged uneasily at his memory, and then emerged into clear thought; reminded suddenly of the first banquet at the Sun Palace, and what had taken place when the formal repast was done, he turned aside to speak to the Rajah.

'Is there dancing tonight, your Highness?'

'Certainly,' answered the Rajah. 'There will be a special dance in your honour. We call it the Dance of Heavenly Exaltation. It is our rarest entertainment.'

Richard hesitated, at a loss how to phrase his next question. But he had to know the answer.

'Will her Highness be dancing also?'

'Certainly,' said the Rajah again. He turned on Richard a bland look of innocence which, if it were assumed, was well done indeed. 'On this night of all nights, she could not fail to take her appointed place, could she?'

Richard's peace of mind was unequal to the moment; he experienced a sudden pang of foreboding, mixed with a wild jealousy. He remembered the first time that Sunara had danced, and her dress which had so fired and pricked his imagination. Would she dance thus again, before a thousand pairs of eyes? It had not mattered at all, on that first occasion; he had been a stranger then, free of thought, careless of glance, tasting all delights with equal appetite; but now all was changed. There were things that a man, a lover, could scarcely bear to witness ... He waited in silence, sick at heart, as the dancing floor was cleared, and the musicians, after a pause to allow quiet to fall, began the first notes of a new melody.

Richard, no connoisseur of the intricacies of the dance, and momentarily too disturbed to form a judgement of any sort, found himself unable to distinguish the dance of Heavenly Exaltation from the earlier dance of the Virgin Sacrifice; to his heavy heart, they both seemed designed to culminate in the appearance of Princess Sunara, in circumstances which he remembered far too vividly for his composure. He watched in brooding anticipation as the line of twenty slavegirls, diaphanously clothed as before, embarked on their graceful measure; he found himself listening with dread to the music, as it worked towards its climax, and the beat of the gong which must herald her appearance. It was shameful that she should be thus exposed to the public gaze ... Turning slightly, while the music rose to its appointed crescendo, he saw that the Rajah was watching him; there was in the old man's glance a hint of sly mockery which in Richard's present mood seemed intolerable.

He dropped his glance, determined not to feed this unseemly curiosity. Within a few moments, the music ceased; then the iron beat of the gong reverberated throughout the room; and at that, perforce, he raised his eyes again, as Sunara made her entrance, gliding through the curtained portico at the far end of the chamber.

Instantly, his spirits leapt upwards, to a peak of love and longing. For Sunara was, after all, unrevealed; indeed, she was clothed from head to foot in a simple, even severe dress of yellow silk, so modest and so demure that it might have been designed to send him a direct message of reassurance. She looked beautiful, and remote, and set apart from the gross world; the 'heavenly exaltation' of the dance could only be the exaltation of purity. Watching her, Richard felt ready to shout aloud for happiness; and when, for a brief moment, he glanced again at the Rajah, and saw that the old man's mockery had become a broad smile, as at a good-natured joke happily complete, he nodded his assent and acknowledged with an answering laugh that he had been fooled – and did not care who knew it.

Sunara ended her dance with a bow to her father, as before; then, instead of withdrawing, she began to ascend the small flight of steps which led to the high table and the ivory throne. As she drew near, her eyes sought Richard's, in candid eagerness to restore their loving communion; her look of warming happiness was not lost upon those who stood at the high table awaiting her approach, and there was a murmur of interest which spread gradually, like a lapping wave, until it had reached the far corners of the room. When finally Sunara stood at his side, and Richard bowed low over her hand, the public concentration on their meeting was obvious. Many smiles were bent upon them; goodwill seemed to flow in their direction; there was even some hand clapping from the humbler parts of the room. Only Selang Aro, remote and grudging, remained apart, not choosing to bless with his approval this evidence of a romantic confederacy.

On this formal occasion, there were certain presentations to be made; Sunara moved gracefully within the circle of the Council of State and the high table, greeting her father's old counsellors with a blending of the regal and the feminine which was a delight to see. But her concentration, to a discerning or a loving eye, was not perfect; at times, as she made her progress from guest to guest, her glance turned towards Richard – across the space of a table, over the broad shoulder of a stranger, in a small space between one man and another – and in her glance, the recollection of last night's tempestuous intimacy was lovingly apparent. To receive this private message in the midst of such mannered exchanges was more exciting than any direct communication could have been.

Presently, her duty done, she rejoined Richard and her father, and took her seat on the smaller throne which her maids of honour now brought forward. The Rajah, still relishing his joke, could not forbear to enlarge on it.

'You danced well, my daughter,' he told her. 'As always, it was a pleasure to watch you … Don't you agree with me, Captain Marriott?'

'A great pleasure,' answered Richard.

'It seemed to me,' said the Rajah, 'that you appeared nervous, before the Princess made her appearance.'

'Nervous?' said Sunara, with seeming surprise. 'Now why should that be?'

'I cannot imagine,' said her father.

'Perhaps it was anticipation,' said Richard. He did not mind the raillery; he was happier, at that moment, than at any time he could remember. 'One is inclined to suffer when someone personally known is to make a public appearance.'

'I noted the suffering,' said the Rajah, 'but I could not guess its cause.'

'You have a most handsome dress, Princess,' said Richard.

'Thank you, Captain Marriott.'

'It has a certain merit,' said the Rajah. 'Even to a father's eye.'

'The merit of great beauty.'

'And of great modesty?'

Richard nodded. 'That, also.'

Sunara looked from one to the other. 'Modesty is a matter of behaviour,' she said, affecting a severe tone. 'It needs no dress to aid it.'

'Perhaps you have discovered the core of Captain Marriott's fear,' said the Rajah, and relapsed at last into open laughter; while Richard and Sunara, whom nothing on this night could provoke or disturb, smiled at his antique pleasure, and then at their shared amusement, and then for themselves alone.

As on the earlier evening, other women had followed Sunara's maids of honour into the audience chamber, and were now joining the gathering; soon the room was thronged, and the company fell to drinking and talking again. But there was an air of preoccupied expectancy about the whole room, which heightened each moment beyond mere enjoyment; people would break off from their talk, and stare with interest at the Rajah and the other dignitaries, keeping their movements under survey; often they looked towards the centre of the high table, where indeed certain unusual preparations had been set in train.

A canopy, like a great golden umbrella with ornamental tassels, had been brought, and raised above the Rajah's ivory throne; and now a kind of portable altar, of the most delicate workmanship – ivory and ebony intermingled – was carried out, and placed on the trestle table under the same majestic covering. Selang Aro, not less grim and withdrawn than before, had come forward, and was busy with the arrangement of certain objects upon this altar; they were a scroll of parchment bound with leather thongs, a tiny chalice of gold supported on a slender stem, and a dagger with a brilliant jade hilt. There was also the skull cup, freshly brimming with wine, which was so placed as to furnish a centrepiece for this strange array.

Richard, as on so many occasions before, turned to his mentor, Amin Bulong.

'What is this?' he asked the old man in an undertone. 'If I am to take part, I must know the formalities. I do not wish to make any error.'

'You are to take part,' answered Amin Bulong, surveying him with eyes unexpectedly moist with feeling, 'and you will make no errors.'

It seemed that he would have said more, but at that moment the Rajah walked forward until he stood underneath the golden canopy, and throughout the vast room an instant silence fell.

The old man's bearing was proud and stately; his slight figure had gained in presence, drawing nobility from its regal setting, and especially from the motionless attention of all in the room. When he spoke, after a pause, it was in his own tongue; but he pronounced the words simply and slowly, so that it was easy for Richard Marriott to follow.

'I will not interrupt your pleasure for long,' said the Rajah. 'Indeed, I hope to add to it, as well as to my own ... You are bidden here for two purposes tonight. One of them you know – it is to celebrate the defeat of our enemies, at the hands of a brave man. The other one, you do not know – though it is possible that some of you have guessed it. It is to witness my adoption of a son.'

A gasp went round the room; it was clear that, in spite of the gossip and the whispering which had filled the Sun Palace for many days, most of those present had no foreknowledge of the Rajah's true intention. Richard, preserving an impassive face, felt his heart beating loudly. So this was the answer to the puzzle ... He knew that there could be no greater honour, for any man in this country; such an adoption was a most signal mark of favour, placing him at one stroke on a pinnacle of distinction. What else it might carry with it, either now or in the future, he could not guess, and did not wish to ponder; it was enough, at this moment, to relish the award for what it implied, in terms of approval and open recognition.

The low murmur of voices was stilled as the Rajah began to speak again.

'You all know this man,' he said with simple directness. He had no need to point at Richard, or to indicate him by name; every eye in the room was bent on the tall figure in the imposing uniform, standing just outside the golden canopy. 'He has proved himself a true friend of Makassang. He has fought our battles. He has overthrown our enemies. It may be that he has saved us from utter destruction. He is therefore worthy to be called our son. It is the greatest honour in our power to give, and we give it to him freely.'

He motioned for Richard to come forward, and the latter joined the Rajah under the canopy of state. He felt rather than saw that, along with all the rest, Sunara was staring towards him; he knew what he would read in her eyes, if he should turn to look. But he gazed straight ahead, as the Rajah motioned again, this time for Selang Aro to join them.

The High Priest, who could not be liking the moment, or anything connected with it, came forward until he was standing between the two principal figures. He seemed to know what was required of him, though this must have been a rare ceremony, if indeed it had ever been witnessed before by anyone in the room. He took up the jade dagger in one hand, and the small gold chalice in the other; then he signed to Richard to bare his arm, and when this was done, he made a tiny incision at the wrist, no more than a deep pinprick, and drew a few drops of blood which he let fall into the chalice. Richard bore the small wound without flinching; at the moment of the broaching of his flesh, he thought he saw, deep in Selang Aro's eyes, a brief shadowy stirring, as if, when he wielded the knife, the High Priest might be wishing that he could wield it to more purpose. But it might have been a trick of the light, and in any case it was so swift a flicker of feeling that it had vanished without trace before Richard could well recognize it.

Within a few moments, the Rajah's blood joined Richard's in the chalice. Selang Aro raised it high above him, and intoned: 'The royal blood is mingled. With this act, you shall be father and son.' Then he lowered it, and allowed the few drops to fall into the skull cup; and this, in turn, he presented to the Rajah.

The old man held it poised a few inches from his lips, dwelling on the solemn moment. 'We take you as our son,' he said, in a moved voice, and drank briefly of the wine. Then he held out the cup to Richard.

With nothing to guide him, Richard spoke the first words that came into his mind, by way of worthy answer. He said, in Malay: 'I take you as my father,' and also drank. Then he set down the cup, and, on an impulse, leant over and embraced the old man with both arms.

He made no mistake; his instinct had been true, as his movement had been natural. Murmurs of appreciation came from every quarter of the room; be was suddenly surrounded by smiling faces; the Rajah clasped his hand in a warm grip, folding into it the parchment document which was, it seemed, his patent of nobility; and when at last Richard turned to look at Sunara, her face also was alight with happiness. Quickly the tableau moved on; Amin Bulong and the chiefs of the Council of State crowded round to give him their good wishes; he noticed that all of them now addressed him as Tunku – meaning, Prince – as if this were a distinction which had been settled on earlier. He felt himself to be surrounded by friends and well-wishers, by public honour, by a benevolent esteem which, flowing towards him, was as heartening as a rising tide.

The Rajah, it seemed, had one more thing to say; and when the general movement was subsiding, he held up his hand for silence, which was quickly accorded.

'The ceremony is finished,' he said. There was a lightness in his tone, displacing his former solemnity. 'I now have a son, whom it is my pleasure to name the Tunku of Makassang. You know that I have a daughter also, the Princess Sunara.' There came into his voice and his look an added touch of humour, almost of roguishness. 'I should make it clear to you all that they are not, in truth, brother and sister.'

There was a startled silence; then the allusion was caught, and the whole room seemed to dissolve into delighted laughter. Richard looked at Sunara; her eyes were downcast, but into her pale cheeks a warm blush had crept, which nothing could disguise. After a moment she looked up, bravely, under the probing of a thousand amused and speculative glances; then she put her hand into Richard's, and together they faced the great audience, to acknowledge the truth of what the Rajah had hinted. The murmur of the throng swelled to acclamation, carrying with it an earnest of unstinted loyalty; there seemed no one in the room who did not wish them well.

It was upon this moment of love and triumph that there now burst a most unseemly intrusion.

It came first as a confused flurry of sounds from a distant portico, and the heavy trampling of booted feet; then as a voice, raucous and rough, shouting: 'Out of my way, you damned yellow dog!' on a note of crude brutality. A spear dropped clattering on a marble floor. Then, at the far end of the room, the crowd stirred, and wavered, and drew back, allowing entrance to three figures who stood out from their surroundings like hawks in a flight of doves.

They were white men, and arrogantly so; as they advanced, they cleft and elbowed their way through the assembled guests, and on to the floor of the audience chamber, striding with great insolence, as many Europeans did among Asiatics. Truculent and uncouth, perhaps full of liquor, they struck a note of the utmost vulgarity. With a sudden sense of shame, Richard Marriott realized that they were his own men. They were Nick Garrett, and Peter Ramsay, and Peal, who had been a tinker and was now, it seemed, a drunken sailor on the loose.

A cold silence fell; the trio reached the middle of the floor, halfway to the high table. Nick Garrett was in the lead, dressed in his rough working clothes, a cutlass at one side of his belt, a pistol on the other. Amin Sang, the young captain of his grandfather's guard, came forward a few steps, as if preparing to intercept them; but Garrett halted twenty paces off, and looked slowly round him, first at the high table, and then directly at Richard Marriott.

In the warm night air, he was sweating, and the smile on his face was heavy and mirthless. When he had looked his fill, and the taut silence had stretched to intolerable limits, he stuck his hands in his belt with a gesture of contempt, and called out to Richard: 'We were not bidden to your banquet, but you see we are here, just the same!'

And then, with particular venom: 'Well now, Dick! Where's your greeting? Have you forgotten your old shipmates?'

By contrast with the heartening scene of a few moments before, it was a most shameful moment, and Richard was at a loss how to deal with it. He stood in confused silence, while Amin Sang, and some members of his guard, started down the steps towards the intruders, their spears grasped and ready. But it was the Rajah who made the first effort to meet the situation on a plane of normality.

He called out sharply to Amin Sang: 'Wait!' and then he turned to Richard. 'These are your men?'

'Yes, your Highness,' said Richard. Recovering from the first shock of surprise, he felt anger and the need for action flooding in. 'I will express my regrets to you later. But at the moment – '

Like Amin Sang, he made as if to start towards the intruders, and the menace in his bearing was unmistakable. Once again, the Rajah intervened.

'Let them be made welcome,' he said. 'On this night, there are no strangers in my house.'

'You hear that, Dick?' Garrett called out to him mockingly. 'You may be too good for us, but others think differently! What about a draught of wine, now? We have climbed a long way to get it!'

Richard, once more at a loss, looked about him. He saw disgust and anger on many faces; a rightful disdain in Sunara's expression; a cold courtesy in the Rajah's. Only Selang Aro seemed unconcerned, as if he were not at all surprised by the turn of events. Earlier, the High Priest had stood aside from the well-wishers who had crowded round to clasp the hand of the newly-adopted son; but now he had drawn close again – indeed, he was within a few feet of Richard, his face expressionless, his hands hidden in the folds of his monk's robes. Suddenly, Richard's sixth sense of danger came to life, but before he could react to the stab of warning, the silence and the stillness burst into ugly violence.

Nick Garrett bellowed loudly: 'Wine, I say!' and, having spoken these three words, which must have been an agreed signal, he whipped the pistol from his belt and levelled it at the Rajah. As in a dream, Richard watched the wild uproar unfold. Garrett fired, but not before old Amin Bulong had thrown his body in front of his master, to receive the ball in his own chest. Ramsay and Peal both aimed and fired at the same moment, finding their marks among the guests at the high table. Then a great shout from John Keston, who had been attending Richard throughout the evening, made the latter whip round.

He was almost too late. Selang Aro, that impassive man of peace, had his long-concealed dagger raised to strike. It was aimed, treacherously, at Richard's back; turning, he received the thrust on the heavy gold epaulette which covered his left shoulder. The padded braid turned the weapon, though it could not deflect it completely; Richard felt a shaft of pain as the blade seared the flesh above his collarbone. He threw off Selang Aro, and then staggered back against the table, his right hand clutched to the bleeding wound.

Sunara rushed to his side, her face distraught; while all around them a wild turmoil exploded. Amin Bulong had fallen insensible, his body still shielding the Rajah; young Amin Sang was pillowing his grandfather's head in his arms, cherishing the last moments of his life. Colonel Kedah and some of the Palace Guard made for the assassins, their weapons poised, their faces contorted with fury; Richard saw both Ramsay and Peal fall, under half a dozen spear thrusts, before a worse confusion invaded the room.

This must be more than a simple attempt at assassination, thought Richard bemusedly – for now general fighting began to break out on the fringes of the audience chamber, and to erupt towards the high table. Bands of armed strangers made their appearance, shouting, brandishing spears and heavy cutting parangs, cleaving a way towards Nick Garrett, who still held his attackers at bay; among them – a vile mark of treachery, this – was one of the grease-daubed wrestlers who had lately been entertaining them. It was strange to see this figure of fun transformed into a demon with a flailing axe. He also was making for the high table, and perhaps for Richard himself, but a spearthrust from one of the guards took him under the heart, and his larded body toppled and slithered down the steps again, as indecent in death as it had been comical in life.

Not only the enemy strangers, the Land-Dyaks, were now fighting. By the misfortune of this occasion, each of the chiefs who formed the Council of State had brought with him his own small bodyguard. Many of these, coming from different parts of Makassang, were unknown to each other; some, on the other hand, came from smaller tribes, or families, which had been traditional enemies in the past, and were not more than wary truce-keepers at the present time. With the whole room now in an uproar, with women screaming, men fighting and dying, tables overturned, wine spilled, tapestries torn from the walls, it was not long before these men of the bodyguards caught the infection of fear, and took to fighting among themselves.

Richard still stood under the golden canopy, supported by John Keston and a weeping Sunara who clung to his unhurt arm. He had lost some blood, but his brain was clearing from the misty confusion which the shock of the attack had brought. Presently he said: 'Let me be ... I am well enough ...' and he straightened his tall body and looked about him. Selang Aro, the would-be assassin, had slipped away; in the main part of the room, the fighting ebbed to and fro; Nick Garrett, shouting obscenities, was still on his feet, the centre of a knot of his allies who kept Colonel Kedah and the guard at a long arm's length. At the high table, Amin Sang had released his grandfather's dead body, and was standing sentinel over the Rajah, whose frail form was menaced by the hand-to-hand fighting which now threatened to engulf the entire room.

Richard had come unarmed to the banquet; he cursed the niceness which had made him leave his pistols in his room, and reduced his armament to the ceremonial sword which went with his admiral's uniform. But he now drew this from its scabbard, wincing at the pain of the effort, and set to work to bring order out of the chaos surrounding him.

He shouted to Amin Sang: 'Take your men, and help Kedah! Rally the guard! Clear the floor, and we can see what we are doing!' And as Amin Sang hesitated, looking behind him at the defenceless Rajah who had now almost collapsed upon his throne, Richard shouted again: 'I will see to him! I and John Keston! I give you my word! Get down among those devils, and push them back to the walls!'

Amin Sang raised his hand in acknowledgement, and took his men under command, and made for the main fighting in the centre of the audience chamber; it was good to see the small, tough spearhead of his guard cleaving its bloody way through the throng. With no other word necessary, John Keston stationed himself in front of the Rajah, his cutlass at the ready; while Richard turned to Sunara, who, regardless of her safety, still had eyes only for him.

'I love you!' he shouted. At that moment of stress and danger, it seemed the only appropriate thing to tell her. 'But I want you alive! Leave us – go to your room – lock yourself in with your women!'

'I will not leave you!' she panted. 'You are hurt. Do not make me go!'

'Then stand by Keston, under the canopy.' He found time to smile, in the midst of the turmoil. 'I will return, Sunara ... I am off on a mission of peace.'

At that, with his ornate, blunted sword in his hand, he began to move among the guests and the warring bodyguards at the high table, ordering them to put up their weapons, threatening them with hanging if they did not. His tall figure, which had been such a focus of honour and fealty a few minutes earlier, carried its own authority; and his fierce bearing did the rest. In this corner of the room at least, peace began to return, especially to the men of substance who already began to see the struggle in its true outlines. Presently they started to join him in his efforts, imposing their own discipline on those who would still fight, outfacing the determined, in a few cases shedding blood to enforce their will. Calm gradually settled; the person of the Rajah was made safe, as some of his Council joined to form a circle round the ivory throne; and Richard could turn his attention to the main struggle.

His practised eye, which had gauged many a close fight, told him that the worst was over, the day was almost gained. Amin Sang and Kedah, working in a pattern of unison which was a professional delight to see, were quickly clearing the floor, pushing back the mob into the more confined space of the colonnades which flanked the room, where those who still chose to fight could be cornered and subdued, a single segment at a time. There were already signs of weariness; there was less shouting, more hard-breathing concentration on simple survival; the enemy, whoever had composed their cohorts – and what an inquest there would be, thought Richard grimly; what an inquest, and what an execution afterwards – the enemy had lost the momentum of treacherous surprise, and were now more simply matched, sword for sword, wound for wound. He noticed that, as victory seemed near, the Palace Guard was beginning to run wild in the lust to avenge; there was much headlong pursuit, and aimless slaughter, of people who could be nothing except innocent – slaves, punkah-workers, attendants who had come to pour out wine, and who remained to spill their own blood.

The avenging troops were scarcely to be blamed for this excess. They had seen their Commander-in-Chief killed, their Rajah menaced, their comrades slaughtered; if the treachery had been successful, it would have been their own blood now darkening the mosaic floors, making the marble steps slippery and loathsome. The wailing screams for mercy, which began to take the place of fiercer battlecries, were a measure of this relief, now turned to sullen fury; and Richard knew that he could not have stemmed it, even if he would. The bloodletting must run its course. Peace would only come when enough dishonoured graves had been filled.

Meantime, there was one grave which must surely be furnished … Nick Garrett was not yet numbered among the slain or the fugitive; indeed, his hulking figure, towering over friend and foe, dominated that corner of the audience chamber where the fighting still raged. With no time to reload his pistol, he fought two-handed, a cutlass in his right hand, a sailor's dirk – honed to a razor-sharpness – in his left; at close range, he was too formidable to be overcome, and in the constantly changing movement of men around him, he was a difficult target for any other kind of attack. Richard saw one of the Palace Guard circling stealthily, with a short throwing spear poised in his hand, waiting for an opening; but when he did launch the spear, it flew past Garrett's jerking shoulder and killed one of the thrower's own comrades, in useless slaughter.

But as Richard watched, he felt a touch on his arm. It was Sunara, and in her hand she carried his two pistols, Castor and Pollux, already primed and loaded. Unseen, she must have slipped away, and made the dangerous journey to his room, and returned with this most timely aid.

He looked at her, wordless, his admiration overflowing; and she smiled back, with fine spirit, and said: 'Here – finish him!'

He took the two pistols in either hand – though his left hung nearly useless – and strode down the steps towards the fighting men. In all the press and uproar, Nick Garrett saw him coming, and saw also what he carried. Clearing a space round him with a whirling arm, Garrett bellowed his anger and his defiance; he seemed within an ace of rushing headlong towards his main enemy, ready to match his blade against the chance of a bullet. But when Richard's arm came up, sighting the pistol carefully across the tangling bodies and tossing arms, Garrett's nerve wavered. On an impulse which could not be questioned, he ducked swiftly out of the line of fire, and jumped for the steps and the nearest portico. Richard's shot, changing its aim swiftly, shattered an ornamental jar of magnolia blooms, a foot above his head. Then Garrett was out of sight, and, with him gone, the heartbeat of the battle swiftly died.

Richard turned, racing for the doorway leading to the gardens and the Steps of Heaven; swift as he was, another panting figure caught up with him and ranged alongside in pursuit. It was Amin Sang the bereaved, spear in hand, intent on the same execution. Running together, they left the lighted uproar of the palace, and emerged into what seemed, by contrast, a pitch-dark night. But there were torches set in iron holders at the edge of the gardens; Richard seized one, and Amin Sang another. Ahead of them, a shadowy figure sped away into the gloom, and leapt out of sight down the first flight of steps.

Others joined the pursuit, with torches or without them; as their eyes gained strength, the moonlight gained also, showing them Garrett's figure hurtling down the steps, the lights on the water far ahead, and the comet-tail of flaming torches flaring out in pursuit. Richard and Amin Sang ran side by side, and step by level step; the pleasure of the chase had restored Richard's strength, and for Amin Sang, his grandfather's blood must be spurring him on to pious loathing of the murderer. Halfway down the Steps of Heaven, in full cry among the streaming torches, it was clear that they were gaining on their quarry, and must soon overtake.

For Richard, it was paramount that he should gain most of all, and be the first one in the racing pack to catch up with the outlaw. For Garrett was his own man; it was Richard who had brought him to the island, it was Richard who shared the guilt, until Garrett was destroyed. There was dishonour by association, also; in later accounts of this night, in the myths and folk tales which would assuredly grow up round it, men must never say that it was the Tunku of Makassang's right-hand man who had attempted to murder the Rajah, to procure the succession for his own lord, and that they were both party to the same base plot, an infamous return for honour ... He himself must be Nick Garrett's executioner, and no one else.

Pricked by this need, he forgot his weariness and his loss of blood, and began to charge full tilt down the sloping steps, expending every ounce of energy in the effort to outstrip the others and to close with the figure ahead. Already they were nearing the water at the lower end of the Steps of Heaven; already Garrett's form began to be silhouetted against the pale expanse of moonlit ocean. He was labouring now, his energy sapped as much by drinking and wenching as by the hard, hour-long fight he had waged and lost in the audience chamber; and Richard, though gasping himself, could hear the other man's loudly sobbing breath, and his heavy footfalls slurring and stumbling their way down the last remaining steps.

Then suddenly they were there, at their journey's end ... It was the foot of the Steps of Heaven; there was nothing beyond save darkness and blank water. Richard, beside himself with the hunger to kill, hurled his torch at Nick Garrett; when it missed, and fell hissing into the sea, he swiftly sighted his pistol, and fired his only shot. But his aim, ruined by the uncertain light and the pumping of his heart, was wild, and the shot missed also. Now he had nothing – nothing save his bare hands, which would have to be enough.

Nick Garrett had turned snarling, at bay. It must have been a fearful sight, with the water lapping greedily at his back, to see the stream of torches closing in on him, to hear the hoarse breathing and the wolfish cries, to have the avenging figure of Richard Marriott as the focus of all this. But he was a brave man, and a desperate one. He stood up straight, and gasped out: 'Come on then, Dick!' A gleam at his right hand showed that he still had his sailor's dirk.

Richard came on; as he did so, the circle of torches closed in at his back, a fiery ring of witnesses; in front there was nothing save the hated figure who must be destroyed, whose grave – the sea itself – was palely gaping for him. He feinted to the right, and as Garrett brought the dirk across, probing savagely for Richard's chest, he clawed at Garrett's arm, and secured an iron hold on it. No man alive could have loosed himself from such a grip; the dirk, falling with a clatter on to the lowest step, was the evidence of this.

Now they were man to man; the one near to exhaustion, the other wounded and weak from loss of blood. In such a struggle, Richard had always been able to hold his own. But it must be done quickly, he thought, or this time his strength would not last him out.

Nick Garrett had his life to lose; Richard Marriott, beside the same stake, had an enormous rage that one of his own men could have behaved with such treachery. Even thieves' honour should hold back from this margin of shame ... He forgot his pain, he felt himself briefly and invincibly strong; not even Garrett's knee, coming up to crash into the pit of his stomach, could turn him aside. While the watchers with their ring of torches closed in, he seized Garrett in the murderous grip which Cornish wrestlers used to make a man cry out for mercy, and forced him to his knees, and then backwards till his neck and shoulders overhung the void at the bottom of the steps. Then Richard, sitting astride the lower half of Garrett's trunk, raised his hands, and locked them together, and brought them crashing down on the other man's face and temples.

There was nothing for Garrett's neck save to give way, and this it did, with a sharp crack which could be heard half a mile off. With that sound, and a rattle of breath, the man beneath him became a corpse.

Richard, utterly spent, was near to fainting; only the helping hand of Amin Sang at his back saved him from toppling into the water. But then strong arms lifted him clear, and Nick Garrett's body, released, fell over the edge of the last step with a ragged-sounding splash, and sank, and rose again, and drifted sluggishly away.

Richard would have no litter to carry him back. He crouched and rested within the circle of torches, and took a long draught of wine, and then raised himself and began to climb the Steps of Heaven again, slowly, with Amin Sang at his side. Above them, the Sun Palace, though still ablaze with light, was quiet now, and cleansed of strife. In his soul, he had but three things left to do that day; to make his duty to the Rajah, to hold Sunara in his arms, and then to sleep and sleep … He stumbled, in utter weariness, and Amin Sang caught him by the elbow and supported him for a step or two.

'Thank you,' said Richard, in a throaty voice. His wound, stiffening, made his head swim with pain; his thoughts seemed to be wavering to and fro, like his body on the long climb. 'I am not the strongest man in the world, at this moment … I hope his Highness came to no harm … Your grandfather saved his life, at the cost of his own … It was bravely done … And you yourself have earned nothing but honours tonight.'

'I could have hated you, Tunku,' said Amin Sang, astonishingly, out of the night. In a flash of understanding, Richard realized that the young man was speaking, for the first and the last time, of Sunara, and of his love for her which he had not declared, and would now never do. 'But I cannot hate you now ... You have avenged my honoured grandfather ... From this night forward, I am your man, for ever.'

V

Their two hands had been bound together with a silk scarf, in token of their uniting. They had eaten rice from the same bowl. They had bowed in obeisance to their elders, and the Rajah had asked for, and received, their vows. Later, a Buddhist priest – who could take no direct part in the marriage, since earthly love was too profane a matter for men of God – had read from the Lotus of the True Law, and a children's choir had chanted their praises. But all the solemn ceremony of a state wedding had been only a prelude to the feast, which Richard found intolerably prolonged, and the feast only a prelude to the seclusion of their wedding night, which was proving, as yet, even more of an ordeal than what had gone before.

Richard Marriott stood by the open window of his apartment, looking towards the sea, watching the moonlight cleaving a pathway to the far horizon, hearing plainly the surf of the Kutar beaches, miles away to the south. Round him the Sun Palace was sunk in a deep night-time silence; though in the audience chamber the merriment continued, yet it could not penetrate here, where the coral walls were thick, the teak doors as solid as rock, the solitude absolute. His thoughts were the thoughts of a bridegroom, yet they were mingled with other thoughts, ranging from the strange past to the shadowy future.

He had taken many women in that past; but Sunara was not to be 'taken', save with tenderness and reverence. For the first time since the youthful escapades, he had doubts of how he would acquit himself; his desire for her was most potent, yet beyond this there was the need for gentleness, the need not to shock or hurt her, the loving awe which might inhibit manhood. She was adored above all. It had been a long and trying day. His shoulder was still stiff and painful from the dagger wound. He wanted nothing more from this day, from this life, save to lie in her arms, but he wanted this with the fiercest hunger he had ever experienced.

They would find their joy or their embarrassment soon enough ... He shifted his position, leaning on the sill of the wide window, staring out into a star-pricked, perfumed darkness which answered no questions and gave no hint of what was real and what was a dream. In many ways, Sunara was his only certainty. This was their marriage day, because he loved her. He had remained in Makassang, because he loved her. He was an adopted son, and a prince, because he loved her. But none of these things helped him to divine the future. Rather did they cloud it almost beyond discovery.

Within a few moments, perhaps, such thoughts would not matter; drowning in love, in Sunara, all doubts and puzzlements would melt away. Or perhaps they would matter more strongly still, perhaps they would be all he would have left, if the tide of love were out, if she turned from his rough and intrusive body and left him alone once more.

By the light of reason, he was alone in any case; as much alone as if he had been shipwrecked, or marooned. The Lucinda D had disappeared, most strangely, on the night of the banquet and the fight; she had been there at anchor, when Nick Garrett had made his attempt, but in the morning she was gone. Under whose command? He could not guess. Selang Aro had also disappeared, fading into the shadows without trace. He was not hidden in the Shwe Dragon, which had been invaded and turned upside down by the Palace Guard; nor had the most painstaking torture of captives revealed his whereabouts. There were plenty of rumours, and endless talk in the bazaars, but all trails had run dead, like rivers trickling into sand.

Only Richard Marriott, a captain without a ship, a fighter without an enemy, remained in Makassang, at the centre of a private maze which returned a blank face to all questions. Why was he here? – why should he stay? – what was in the future? – what fate ruled him? It seemed that, in fantastic faith, he was looking, for all these answers, towards a single, lovely, and studious brow.

And she of this brow was here ... Behind him the beaded curtains stirred and rustled, and a soft, hesitant voice said: 'Tuan.'

My lord ... He turned, his throat suddenly constricted, and looked at Sunara. She was standing in the arched doorway between the two halves of the dimly-lit apartment; she was dressed for the night, for sleep, for love, in a modest robe of silk which matched her submissive face – and yet belied it. For she was beautiful, and her small form was undisguisedly shaped for joy. He remembered how he had seen her half wanton, half shy, on the night in the treasure vault, and how it was for this present moment that they had both held back – though they had not known it then. As he came towards her now, he prayed that his touch upon her soft body could carry her past all fears, and that she would presently concur in readiness, and welcome him as the glove welcomes the hand.

At his gentle pressure on her shoulder, she said again, in the same submissive voice: 'Tuan.' But she was trembling; through the thin silk he could feel the uncontrollable shaking of her body; her eyes were downcast. He pressed her to him lightly, and said what was in his heart.

'Do not be afraid, Sunara. I love you. I will never hurt you. Not tonight. And not ten years from tonight. You can be sure of that.'

'I know it.' She had dropped her head on his shoulder, trustfully, as if she knew that before long it would come to be at ease there. 'I am foolish ... But it is only my body which is trembling ... I was waiting for you, as I have been taught by the old ones ... What were you thinking of, staring out of the window?'

'Only of you ... No, that is not true. I was thinking a little of the past, and a great deal of the future. And I was asking myself some riddles.'

'Such as, the reason why you are here?'

'Yes.' Wondering at her perception, he pressed her body again, feeling it becoming calmed, divining that it would soon be warmed, as his own was warmed. 'Yes, that was the chief riddle. But it does not matter now.'

'Why not?'

'Because I am holding you.'

'That is why you are in Makassang.' She made a slight movement towards him; and suddenly, it was enough to set his blood on fire – fire which she swiftly caught. 'You have made me brave, now,' she said. 'I knew it would be so ... You are here because of love, and you are here' – she let herself be drawn closer still – 'because I am yours. Do you remember, in the vault?'

'Yes,' he said. 'Oh yes.'

Before they knew it, their fingers were intertwined, fumbling at the fastenings of her robe; and then, as he held her away from him, she was revealed, and her pale exquisite body glowed in the lamplight.

She raised a beautiful, untroubled face. 'Do you remember? This was what your eyes sought. And then your hands. Your gentle hands.'

'And now I seek all the rest.'

'It is yours ... Now I am very brave. I will never be more brave, in all my life. Take me now. Tuan. My lord. Take me now.'

There was a time in the night, at a sighing moment when she was his, that she said, again: 'Ah, Tuan!' But that was different, as, by then, all the world was different.

# BOOK THREE

## The White Rajah: 1861

She was with child, and he had never been happier. It was a joy to watch, at close quarters, her grave preoccupation at this strange station halfway between wife and mother, and to see how she neither said goodbye to the one nor lost sight of the other. It was a joy to make love, gently yet ardently, with her when she carried the hallowed token of this love already. To lie with her, which before had been a wild rapture, was now a deep contentment.

Yet for much of each day he was restless, and out of employment. There were moments when he seemed to be surrounded by toys – he had a toy to make love to, in a toy kingdom, whose small resources and pigmy honours could be manipulated with two fingers, like the chocolate pennies of children. His occupation, like Othello's, was gone. While he played the man in bed, he seemed to have become, within the space of six months, a mere courtier out of it.

Such were Richard's uneasy thoughts, as he sat in the garden of the Sun Palace, on an afternoon in May. The servant who had just set a sangaree of spiced Madeira at his elbow, with a low bow and the customary murmur of 'Tunku', had now withdrawn, leaving Richard to sip the wine and stare at the view – the perfect view which he had surveyed for hundreds of idle hours already. He wore now the Malay dress which was common in Makassang – a longhi of striped cotton, a braided tunic of silk, and a green turban as a badge of rank.

The dress was well fitted for leisure in a hot climate, as the view was well fitted for slothful eyes to enjoy. Below him was the bay, and across the bay was the golden dome of the Shwe Dagon, and beyond that the green jungle and purple hills where Selang Aro lay hid, and where, men said, another enemy, dark and faceless – Black Harris, no less – still roamed, when he was not roaming the sealanes like the pirate he was. It was likely that Harris had seized command of the Lucinda D, which had twice been sighted by the Sea-Dyak garrison, coasting up past the western seaboard; it was likely also that he had never left Makassang, but had made some mysterious, interior part of it his home – an attic lair from which he would fall upon and plunder the rest of the house, when the time was ripe.

But Richard Marriott, alas, did not spend his time hunting these, or any other enemies. He spent it by killing it – the most unworthy of all pastimes.

He killed time with love, which was wonderful, and with eating and drinking, which was not. Like the Rajah, he kept tremendous state, with retinues of liveried servants, and a glittering ceremonial to govern affairs at court; and outside the Sun Palace, there were royal progresses to be made, state visits to Prahang and Shrang Anapuri and those Sea-Dyak garrisons whose morale required it, parades and reviews, regattas and foot races, fêtes champêtres for the rich and the distribution of largesse for the poor.

Dressing for such functions alone might account for three or four hours of every day; and this, it turned out, was a matter of love also. For in the fond belief that Richard's wearing of the Dutch admiral's uniform betokened an interest in such matters, Sunara and the palace major-domo had put their heads together, and designed for him a truly gorgeous range of ceremonial dress. He was an admiral one day, a commander-in-chief the next, a peacock princeling on days of celebration. He could not tell her that this aspect of a Prince Consort's life occasioned him the greatest boredom of all.

Of course there were excitements to be had, but they were

contrived for sport, not to test a man's courage in a good cause. There were tiger hunts from the safe and massive vantage-point of an elephant's back; Richard would have taken part, but Sunara's loving eye (once again) discovered an ancient statute forbidding any member of the royal house to hazard himself in this fashion, and when the converging ring of javelin men closed in upon the quarry, Richard could only be a far-off spectator. He could fish for shark, of course; he could watch teams of oxen straining mightily in a tug-of-war; he could even wrestle in the midsummer games – though there was some doubt as to whether he could lose. But he could not venture into danger, nor into any role that was more than decorative and formal.

Above all, he could not fight, and he could not rule – not by so much as a finger's snap. If he had had a ship, he might have had some useful sport with the pirates, who still infested certain parts of the northern coast, and whose fleets of two hundred or more prahus lay in wait for ships in the narrows between Makassang and the Celebes, and tore their prey to pieces like the piranhas of the Amazon. But Richard had no ship of his own to fight such a sea battle; and as for land battles, the Rajah would have none of them. The country, he said, was quiet; Selang Aro was driven into hiding, and as for Black Harris – Black Harris knew better than to turn soldier and make a second attempt on the Sun Palace. Things were best left as they were, in guarded peace.

The Rajah was equally adamant, and irksomely so, about Richard's position in the royal household. His bearing daily proclaimed that there was only one Rajah, and therefore only one ruler; the Tunku of Makassang, though a favourite son and honoured son-in-law, was not to trespass beyond this, into the realm of kingship. The Rajah had, on one occasion, made the fact plain, with mortifying clarity.

It chanced that Richard, on one of his visits to Prahang, the capital, had been approached by a suppliant who claimed that he had been unjustly threatened with imprisonment, for a debt that was no debt at all, but an arrant swindle by one of the city's thriving moneylenders. Richard, impressed by the man's story – though wretchedly poor, he had the stamp of honesty in his bearing – made some inquiries, and brought the two disputants face to face in his presence. He had no difficulty in deciding which was the swindler and which the honest man, and he gave a ruling which set the suppliant free and put the moneylender under pain of severe penalty if he practised such iniquities again. The reaction of the spectators left no doubt that the matter had been justly dealt with.

He thought no more of it. But reports of his intervention reached the Rajah that same evening, and when Richard returned to the Sun Palace, he was called to account, in an interview which set his temper on edge.

'I do not understand how this came about,' said the Rajah, coldly, in the manner of a schoolmaster, when Richard had answered his queries and set out the facts. 'You exceeded your authority – indeed, you have no authority in these matters. There are courts of law, and in certain cases there can be petitions to the Rajah – myself. But these private hearings – there is no such procedure in Makassang.'

'The man came to me for help,' explained Richard reasonably. He was in good humour, as he always was when he returned to the palace and to Sunara. 'Why should I deny him? He said he had been wronged –'

'Every debtor has been wronged.'

'But this was an honest man.'

'An honest man should approach the courts.'

'He was too poor for that.'

'He was too clever.' Richard suddenly realized that, behind the cold façade, the Rajah was violently angry, and he sharpened his own mood to meet it. 'He could not face the court with his story, so he came snivelling to you. He knew that from you he would win, not justice, but a verdict which would sit well with the crowd.'

'But that is ridiculous!' said Richard, astounded.

The Rajah froze. 'You forget yourself.'

'I ask your pardon, your Highness ... I meant, of course, it is unfair to suggest that I would come to such a judgement, in order to court popularity.'

'You had no right to come to any judgement.'

'But I was acting as your agent, your own representative. After all – '

'You are not my agent. You are my son-in-law. You have married my daughter,' the Rajah went on cuttingly. 'You have not married Makassang ... So we will have no more of these courts and judgements.'

'Can I take no part in ruling, then?' asked Richard, near to anger himself and determined to do his share of plain speaking. 'Does the title of Tunku mean nothing?'

'While I live, no one else rules,' answered the Rajah. 'And Tunku means prince, as you are well aware. It does not mean rajah. We have no other word for rajah,' the old man added sarcastically, 'and no other man, either.'

The ill-tempered snub ended the audience, and Richard was left to salve the wound to his self-esteem as best he could. A few months earlier – even a few weeks – he would not have tolerated such treatment, nor listened to a lecture such as had not been read to him since brother Miles used to voice his disapproval, in the old days at Marriott. But now it seemed to matter less; he had other things to set in the balance, against the jealous dominion of a royal father-in-law; and whenever his pride was thus lacerated, he had Sunara to anoint it ... There were necessary excuses to be made, also. Where the Rajah was concerned, he knew, such outbursts were largely a matter of mood; the old man was given to sudden rages, and this interview – estimating it fairly – was a likely occasion for rage. Richard realized that, in assuming the office of judge, he had probably overstepped convention and, also, the law; his motives had been pure enough, but that would weigh nothing with an old man whose life had held more than its share of intrigue and manoeuvre.

The mention of 'popularity' had been the key to this. The Rajah had come to feel safe and secure on his throne; he had, at this stage, no enemies for Richard to fight; he must be thinking himself far above the vulgar need for rescue – he could even be regretting the fact that he had heaped unnecessary honours on a man who might, in certain circumstances, take advantage of them. Richard's following among the people was beyond question; and it was reflected – though not by his own wish – in a palace faction which already led to occasional quarrels among the servants, minor wrangles over precedence among the retinues of courtiers. The idea that Richard Marriott might come to usurp even a small part of the royal prerogatives would certainly set the Rajah to thinking troublesome, nagging thoughts.

Richard, taking his customary ease in the garden, shrugged resignedly. The outcome was the same, in any case, whether he chafed at the restraint or let it run off his shoulders. His part in Makassang was limited. In this toy kingdom, he had become something of a toy himself. He ruled nowhere save in the marriage bed. There were times when the role irked him intolerably, and other times – such as now, with Sunara approaching him across the lawn – when only a fool would be discontented.

He had never ceased to marvel at her grace and beauty, newly revealed to him every day; not his eyes, not his body which had come to know hers so well, could ever tire of this enjoyment, or reach satiety. Now, as she moved across the green carpet of turf towards him, and he stood up to greet her, he wondered anew at the perfections which could be found in so small a frame. Now three months with child, her body was still unaltered in its outline; and her face, the focus of her loveliness, had gained from marriage and from love a glowing happiness which shone, not for him alone, but for all the marvelling world. Its pallor, which before had seemed remote and cool, had been translated by some sensual alchemy into radiant animation. Especially, she moved in a fashion which declared one pleasure above all others – her pleasure in being a woman.

She came near, and they smiled at each other in loving welcome. Her eyes moved swiftly from his face, to the garden chair he had been sitting on, the tall glass of sangaree conveniently placed, the angle of the sun and the shade of the palm tree overhead. It was part of her love, to see that the rest of the universe cherished him as he deserved. She bent down, to brush away a leaf which had fallen on the table. Then, straightening, she said: 'Are you comfortable? Have you all that you want?'

'I have everything, Sunara ... Did you take your proper rest?'

She smiled again, sitting down in the chair next to his. 'I have rested, I have even slept. I have pretended to be an invalid. I have drunk my milk and eaten my boiled fish. I have done all that you ordered, Richard.'

To call him Richard was in the middle range of their intimacy. To the world, she spoke of him as 'the Tunku'; at all other times, in public or private, he was Richard. Only in bed did she use, with fervour or with contentment, the word 'Tuan'. It was often the most strangely exciting part of their passion, thus to be called 'Lord' at a moment when he was in fact the lord of so sweet a dominion.

'These things are important,' he chided her gently. 'The child must be strong, from the moment he is born.'

'Alas, I thought you were concerned about me,' she said, in pretended ruefulness.

He put his hand over hers, and caressed it. 'Until the day I die,' he assured her. 'But he can only be strong if you are strong.'

'Spoken like a man,' she answered. She looked round her, shading her eyes against the glare which the bay below them threw back at the afternoon sun. 'Another wonderful day ... If it were not for the crops, one could pray that the monsoon never comes ... I cannot tire of this view.'

'It is perfect, as usual.'

She was quick to catch something from his voice. 'Too perfect, Richard?'

'How could that be?'

'One grows tired of perfection.'

He nodded: what she said was too much in agreement with his

secret thoughts to be passed over. 'I suppose so ... I was thinking yesterday of one thing I would greatly love to see. As a change, as a surprise.'

'What would that be?'

'Snow.'

She turned to him, searching his face in amazement. 'And I have never even seen it once ... Is that what you miss, in Makassang?'

'I miss nothing, my darling. It was just a stray thought – a wish for contrast, I suppose. In truth, the country is beautiful, whether it changes or no, and if I have you, I have everything.'

She persisted. 'But you miss England?'

Suddenly he had to tell her, without dissembling. 'I miss – I miss doing, Sunara! I was not born to sit in the sun, drinking sangaree and gazing at the view! I am thirty years old, not eighty ... There are times when I feel myself growing older by the hour, with nothing done and nothing to show for all the years going by.'

'But you have done so much. And surely there are many diversions, here in Makassang. You need not sit idle, unless you choose.'

'Diversions!' He could not help his forceful emphasis on the word. 'Oh yes, there are diversions enough. I suppose I should not complain. After all, I am only out of employment until the next banquet!'

There was silence. He had hurt her, as her face showed plainly; she was staring out across the bay with deeply troubled eyes. He would have recalled his words if he could, for he loved her too much to inflict such careless wounds; but he could not recall his mood, which remained constant in its mixture of boredom and frustration. It was the word 'diversions' which had sharpened his discontent intolerably; it was the gross idea of killing time again – as if a man should be satisfied to squander the heavenly gift of life on the sweet nothings waiting to be plucked from the languorous air ... He turned towards her, and found that she was already regarding him, her expression changed from pain to a loving thoughtfulness.

'You have never said such a thing to me before, Richard.'

'I am sorry,' he said contritely. 'It is a bad mood, nothing else. Please forgive me, and forget it.'

She shook her head. 'I think I was waiting for you to say it. And it is more than a mood, or you would not have spoken as you did. You must have been thinking of this for a long time. Is not that so?'

'Yes,' he admitted. 'It is something that has been growing.'

'You must tell me these things … I know that you have little to do, these days, save to enjoy life, and that is not enough for a man like you. Of course, it is in the air here … Andrew Farthing used to call it Makassang fever – the urge to do nothing in perfect surroundings.'

'I am sure he was not subject to it.'

'Oh, indeed he was! But as soon as he felt it coming on, he would be up and doing.'

Richard sighed. 'Fortunate Andrew Farthing.'

'It was his cure for sadness.'

'What sadness was that?'

'Principally, the death of his wife.'

'His wife!' exclaimed Richard, astonished. 'I knew nothing of that. I had been thinking of him as a solitary figure. So Andrew Farthing was married?'

'He came here when he was thirty-five,' answered Sunara, 'long before I was born, with his wife. They were newly married, and very happy. She was lively and pretty, they say, and singing all the time … They built a mission house here, and had permission from my grandfather to preach the Christian gospel, if they wished. But then Andrew's wife died, within three months, in childbed.'

Richard shivered involuntarily, and pressed her hand. 'Nay, Sunara, do not tell me such stories, and do not think of them either!'

'Oh, I shall not die. I love you, and life, too much … But when Andrew Farthing's wife died – I had the story from my father – he was mad with grief, and inconsolable. He cursed Makassang, and everything in it, and he planned to sail for home immediately, having buried all his hopes, all that he loved. Then he changed his mind suddenly, in the course of one night, and stayed on with us.'

'Why was that?'

'It is said that some children came at dusk to place flowers on his wife's new grave, and he saw them, and asked them roughly why they did it, and they answered: "If we love her, she still lives." It touched him beyond belief, and he told my grandfather: "I came to preach the love and the pity of Christ, and here they are preaching it to me," and so he stayed, and worked here for more than thirty years.'

'And his work?' asked Richard. He had been deeply moved by the story. 'How did he spend his working day? With more than preaching, surely?'

'Oh yes. He came as a preacher, but in the end he was everything to us. Schoolmaster, doctor, judge, comforter. He started a mission school in Prahang, and he taught generations of children their letters, and much else as well. He had a little hospital, and the garden round it was thronged from morning till night. People would even bring their children to be touched, though it made him very angry, and he pretended to curse them with Scottish curses. And he went among the lepers ... He was a saint, Richard, and he did so much for us. And yet, to the very end – this was when I knew him – he was a disappointed man, not a happy one.'

'Why so?'

'Because there was so much left undone.' She turned to him again. 'And it is true, Richard. A man of ideas, a man of energy, could do great things for Makassang.'

'I am sure of it.'

'You could do these things.'

'I do not think your father would like that, Sunara.' His tone was light, but underneath it his mood had grown suddenly sombre; the contrast between the dedicated labours of Andrew Farthing, and his own butterfly existence, was mortifying, even disgusting. 'He has made that much clear, as I told you. I am not to take any part in ruling.'

'There are other things besides ruling.'

He laughed shortly. 'I am not fitted for teaching, or for curing lepers with a touch!'

His tone was bitter, reflecting his mood; the story of Andrew Farthing had shamed him. Now, perversely, he did not even know if he wished to exert himself, to do anything for Makassang. It was not his own country; it had been made clear that he was a stranger in it. A far-off echo from the past came to mock him – the words of his old tutor, Sebastian Wickham, as the two of them said their goodbyes at Marriott: 'When you find your kingdom, make sure you use it well.' He had found it, and he was indeed using it well – as a plaything for a thousand idle hours.

Perhaps he had contracted Makassang fever already.

Sunara, watching his troubled, angry brow, touched his arm, and said: 'You are fitted for everything that a man can do. And I love you.'

In the distance, at the edge of the lawn leading to the Steps of Heaven, a small figure appeared, followed by a watchful larger one. It was Adam, and his attendant nurse Manina. The boy had grown sturdy; he ran and jumped with the best; he had settled into the strange world of Makassang as if he had been born to it. Only the palace peacocks – he was staring, in fascination, at one of them now – still caused him to marvel and, perhaps, to quake … He saw that Richard and Sunara were watching him; but he surveyed them without recognition, unwinkingly, until Manina bent and prompted him, and he waved his hand, and the two of them waved back. Then he turned to his study of the peacock again, and, when the peacock strutted away, to the absorbing mysteries of a gardener's barrow full of plants. He was alone in his private wonderland, talking to peacocks, talking to plants and leaves.

'He is waiting for his brother,' said Richard.

In the succeeding days and weeks, each one so dismally the twin of the last, Richard had endless leisure for the confused, uneasy thoughts which he had partly revealed to Sunara. The things he might have wished to do seemed to be denied him; yet he was not sure if he would really welcome a change, or if he were sinking, gently yet decisively, into the fatal pleasures of indolence. He still dressed and comported himself royally; he walked through his magnificent, facile role as Tunku of Makassang; he treated his father-in-law with respect, and kept his counsel on any matter save the most trivial. He played with Adam, and made love to Sunara as often as they chose, since they took an undiminished delight in this. But loving, however sweet, and talking, however soft, and the watching of one son and the waiting for another, was not enough for a man. All it did was to make him wonder whether, in fact, a man was what he still remained.

It was a relief when the nearly headless survivor from the East Garrison staggered across the causeway, a fearful bearer of fearful news, and once more plunged their small world into bloodshed and horror.

II

It chanced that both Richard and Amin Sang were at the causeway when the messenger of death stumbled in; they had ridden down together to inspect the garrison, and had planned to spend the night there. During all these days, they were finding each other excellent company; Richard liked the tall young man who was so good a soldier and so firm a friend, and Amin Sang had at least one other strong admirer in the royal household – the boy Adam, who had attached himself to the guard-captain and consumed, as of right, much of his off-duty time. Among other pastimes, Adam was at present being taught the intricacies of ceremonial spear drill, with a miniature (and blunted) weapon, under the disapproving eye of his nurse Manina.

In the late afternoon Richard and Amin Sang had ridden out beyond the fortification with a small troop of horsemen; and it was when they were turning for home that one of the outriders shouted a warning, and pointed northwards. His attention had been caught by the single figure of a man stumbling and staggering his way across the bare plain; the stranger seemed in the last stages of exhaustion, weaving from side to side like a drunkard, his feet stirring slow puffs of yellow dust as he laboured onwards; both his hands were curiously clasped about his head. As Richard and Amin Sang spurred their horses and started towards him, his leaden feet tripped for the last time, and he dropped to the ground, and lay motionless.

When they reached him, and dismounted swiftly, his hands were still clamped rigidly to his temples, and the frightful reason for this immediately became apparent. He had a gross wound on one side of his neck, and his head, in fact, was nearly severed from his body; if he had walked far, with that lolling burden thus held in place, his strength and courage must have been superhuman. It was Amin Sang who reached him first, and who cradled his shoulders and gently turned him over on his back, only to catch his breath at what was then displayed. The whole of the upper part of the man's body was glistening black with blood from the hacked wound; exuding already a vile stench, he crawled and hummed with blowflies.

'By God, I know this man!' said Amin Sang, his voice tense. 'He is one of the guard from the East Garrison regiment!' He bent low over the fearful, noisome, gasping figure. 'What has happened, my brother?'

It took many long minutes to piece together even the outline of the story; the man, who was in the last extremity, could only croak a few words at a time from his gurgling throat, and water, when tipped into his mouth, ran uselessly out from the hole in his neck. But, seeing his captain's face above him, he was determined not to die before he had delivered his message; the same spirit which had brought him, holding on to his own head, through a hundred miles of jungle, now brightened and possessed the last moments of his life.

He was from the East Garrison (the story came slowly, with agonies of waiting, and agonies of pain also). It was the time of the year when the wagon train of silver, the output from the mines which the garrison safeguarded, was sent on its annual journey down to the Sun Palace. To make this transfer, the East Garrison had been split, as usual; half to act as convoy, half to remain in the garrison camp.

'I was with those left to guard the camp,' gasped the man, staring up at Amin Sang as if his salvation depended upon never letting go his glance. 'We had been alone for two days, with the wagon train on its way, when a ship came into the bay, and anchored ... She had heavy guns, and many men, but they took us by a trick ... They came ashore under a flag of truce, asking for water, and we agreed, and they landed some twenty water barrels ... The barrels were full of guns, and gunpowder too ... They breached the walls and stormed the fort at dusk, while we were off our guard.'

Standing behind Amin Sang, Richard said, with a sense of foreboding: 'Ask him, what ship?'

The dying man heard the question, and answered it, without turning his eyes from Amin Sang.

'I do not know what ship ... It was a white man in command – a small man with a black beard, a shouting man ... He took the fort, and began to shoot the prisoners, and then other men – Land-Dyaks from the tribe of Latangi – came out of the forest on a signal, and began to cut us to pieces with axes and spears ... I had this wound' – his head moved loosely, terribly – 'and I lay for dead two days, and then I escaped, and crawled out, and began this journey.'

His voice ceased, with a rattling gurgle, so that Richard thought he had at last given up the ghost. He had just begun to think, with anger and amazement: It must be my own ship – it must be Black Harris, when the doomed man made a supreme effort, and took up the remnant of his tale.

'That was many days ago ... I kept a count of them, but then I lost it ... I passed the wagon train in a clearing ... They had been slaughtered, to a man, and the silver taken. The ship's captain with the beard must have followed them swiftly, as soon as we were put down ...' His eyes suddenly opened very wide, burning with the last of the flame of life. 'We have lost many brothers, my captain,' he said clearly, and on the words 'my captain' he died, with a final convulsion, and his head fell aside, and his neck parted like a ghastly gaping mouth, opening his wound to the sky.

Amin Sang raised himself slowly, and looked at his men standing in a ring round him. There was a glitter of tears in his eyes, but his face was as if made of stone, and so were the faces of his men, and of Richard Marriott too. None of them were strangers to death; and the picture of this man crawling and stumbling through the jungle, carrying his own orchestra of loud-buzzing blowflies, holding his head on his shoulders like a bloody water pot, was a picture which, though briefly daunting, persuaded them towards one end, and one end alone. That end was not sackcloth and wailing ... This their dead comrade had been valiant in agony, because he was a soldier with a report to bring back. When the time came, they must not do less; and if the time were now, so much the better for their resolve.

Amin Sang, brushing a tear from his cheek with unashamed, indifferent fingers, summed up their feeling: 'This was a brave man, and a brother ... Now it is our turn to be brave.'

But it was one thing to make a stern resolve, with a dead comrade lying at one's feet, and another to come to grips with an enemy whose whereabouts could not be determined, even to the nearest hundred miles. Though Richard and Amin Sang returned with all despatch to the Sun Palace, this proved to be the only swiftly-moving part of the affair. For there was no agreement in counsel; uncertainty, and divided opinion, ruled from the very beginning of their discussions.

The Rajah, whom the theft of a year's tribute of silver had put into a vile temper, wished to take the offensive at once; and Colonel Kedah, his single eye blazing with a like fury, was of the same opinion. Amin Sang, a dutiful soldier who was also a vengeful man, was inclined to agree with his colonel and his rajah; but he had come to trust Richard's judgement in all things, and Richard, for once, was wary. Certainly they must attack – so ran Richard's argument; but where and when, and whom should they fight?

'Your Highness, we cannot march off into the blue, on the chance of coming up with Black Harris.' Richard put forward his objections as reasonably as he could, in the face of a climate of opinion which was clearly against him. 'We do not even know for certain if it is Black Harris who has done this – though it is very likely – and we do not know where he is to be found, in any case. If we attack to the north, he will melt away into the jungle, before we reach the East Garrison camp. Or he will take to his ship again, and land at our backs. We must wait, until we find out more about him.'

'Wait?' repeated the Rajah scornfully. He looked round the small audience chamber, where they were gathered, as if he could not believe his ears. 'What sort of talk is this? How can we wait, when a whole garrison has been wiped out, and a wagon train of silver stolen? Are we to be the laughing stocks of Makassang?' He turned his gaze on Colonel Kedah. 'What do you think of this plan of waiting?'

Kedah's tone was as cold as his single eye was hot. 'I have lost four hundred men,' he said, staring fixedly at Richard. 'I am not in the mood to wait. No one could wait, who has a spark of pride in him!'

'I have a spark of pride,' said Richard, equally cool. 'I also have my wits.' He could not resist a caustic comment. 'I am sure your Highness realizes that I would welcome employment of any sort. And when it is a matter of fighting Black Harris, that is doubly true.'

The Rajah chose to ignore the main sense of Richard's remark. 'Then fight him!' he commanded. 'Give him no chance to go free! Seek him out, wherever he is! Destroy him, and recover the wagon train!'

'In good time, we will do all those things. But we have waited for many months for Harris to show his hand. A few more days, or weeks, will not matter.' He saw this thing, Richard realized, on a

227

different plane from the others; as well as a sense of caution, inherited from hazardous experience, he had a special feeling about Black Harris – Harris who was his betrayer, his nemesis, the dark mysterious enemy who had roamed the seas round Makassang, or lurked in the interior, refusing to give up his own chance of vengeance. Black Harris was Richard's own man, his own hated spectre from the villainous past, and this time he was never to escape. They were bound together by chains of loathing and suspicion, forged in blood, linked in treachery; to have such a close enemy was like having someone to cherish, almost to love.

Amin Sang had been watching Richard, intent on his words, and now he made his contribution. 'What do you suggest, Tunku? That we should send out scouts?'

'Scouts?' interrupted the Rajah. 'We shall be sending out women next!'

'The guard-captain may be right,' said Richard. He still kept his tone as reasonable as he could, though his patience was not far from its end. 'Certainly we should take time to consider what Black Harris' next move will be. For myself, I am almost sure that I know.'

'We are all ears,' said Kedah sarcastically.

'He will come here,' said Richard. 'For the treasure.'

The Rajah gestured impatiently. 'He has one treasure already. A year's silver!' The old man's voice was strident with spite and anger. 'What more would he want? He can live like a pirate king for the rest of his days!'

'He will always want more,' Richard insisted, 'and he will come here to get it. Your Highness, I know this man! I know what drives him, and what the scope of his greed is. He will never leave Makassang, while the main prize is still to be taken. That is why he has stayed on here, for more than half a year. The wagon train of silver is one thing – and not a small one, either. But the state treasure, here in the Sun Palace! He would give his life for it!'

'Would you give your life to stop him?' asked Colonel Kedah.

Richard had had enough of such transparent insolence. 'Hold your tongue!' he snapped, with sudden harsh authority. 'You forget your position – and mine!'

'Your position?' said Kedah, taken aback.

'I am of royal blood,' said Richard. 'A son of the Rajah. I need no army colonel to teach me my business. And when it comes to stopping Black Harris, I am worth more than rank to Makassang, and I have proved it already!'

Kedah, recovering his cold composure, appealed confidently enough to the Rajah. 'Your Highness, I am sure you will not permit such insulting – '

The Rajah held up his hand for silence, and Richard knew without hearing his next pronouncement that, within the turning of a few words, the Rajah had reversed his position and conceded his status. He needs me, thought Richard, in surprised perception; he needs me, and now he knows it.

'My son is right,' said the Rajah, and his voice was icy enough to quell the most rebellious heart. 'Whoever questions his authority, questions mine.' He allowed a long moment for the rebuke to sink in, and then he turned to Richard. 'We will hear you. What is your plan?'

'That we should wait, as I said.' Richard spoke now with calm authority; the tide had turned, and in the space of thirty loaded seconds he had ceased to be a toy prince, and was a valued fighting man again. 'We must find our enemy first, make certain of his position and strength, muster our forces, then work to destroy him.'

'But if we do not fight Black Harris immediately,' said the Rajah – and there was now suggestion in his voice, not command, 'then should we not go against the Land-Dyak village in the interior, and punish them for their part in the storming of the fort? The Latangi tribe have always been the backbone of revolt, and now they have joined in this outrage, like jackals. We could at least execute justice there.'

'The Latangis are little men,' answered Richard. 'In this matter, they are like dolls jerked by a string. We are after bigger – the biggest of all – the man whose hand is on the string – Black Harris. Certainly we should reinforce the West Garrison, to make sure that the ruby mines do not go the way of the silver. But we should not mount any attack, anywhere, at this stage. We should keep watch, and wait for Black Harris to join his ally.'

'His ally?' It was Colonel Kedah who put the question, in a voice much subdued. 'But who is that?'

'Who else but Selang Aro? There is another man who is not dead …' Richard did not look directly at Colonel Kedah, or try to outface him further; it was enough to know that the proud, supercilious soldier had, for the moment, been taught the lesson of hierarchy. 'In due time, these two will join up together, as they did before, and make another attempt on the palace. They still have a ship, don't forget – ' he laughed, without mirth or pleasure, ' – my ship, and a good one, with extra guns retrieved from the Mystic. But it is important to know when they do come together, and where.' He looked towards the Rajah. 'You have spies, your Highness?'

'I have spies.'

'Let them watch the Shwe Dagon. That is the point where this thing will fester, and ripen, and burst out. Then, when we have sighted our enemy, and judged his plans, we can strike – once, for all time.'


They lay in their broad bed between silken sheets, drawing from each other the comforts of love and nearness. Sunara's head was pillowed in the crook of his arm, and her small body patterned closely to his; it was at such moments of warmth and gentleness that they were most happy, and most glad of each other. But tonight, at this moment, Richard's thoughts were not of her, and through the taut-muscled frame and the encircling arm she could easily sense this. When presently he sighed, she divined without difficulty that it was not a lover's sigh. She waited, but since he did not speak she brought her free arm across, and touched him gently on the shoulder, and said: 'Tell me your thoughts, Richard. You are not easy tonight. Is it Harris still?'

He nodded, to her and to himself, in the darkness. 'Yes, it is Black Harris, our friend, our enemy ... But do not take on my worries, Sunara. I can bear them myself.'

'If you worry, I worry ... For my part, I cannot imagine how he comes to be alive.'

Richard smiled, sardonically. 'It was my bad aim, and nothing else. I could have sworn I dropped him, but he was only winged, it seems. He must have jumped, not fallen, and swum ashore.'

Her body stiffened within his grasp. 'I wish he were ten times dead!'

'You speak like the gallant colonel.'

'I am not Colonel Kedah!'

He caressed her slim flank. 'Agreed ... Kedah is becoming an enemy, I think. Or at least, a critic. I will not tolerate it! Nor, it seems, will your father.' He smiled again, in memory of that afternoon's scene. 'Your father changed over, and took my side of the argument, within a few moments. It was extraordinary.'

'Why did he do so?'

'He saw that I felt insulted, and angry enough to act on impulse. He feared that the next thing I would say to Kedah would be: "Very well – fight Harris yourself!" Your father could not afford that. He needs me, Sunara. It is the same as when I first arrived in Makassang ... But sometimes I wonder what his real opinion is.'

'Of you?' She felt him nod his head. 'He trusts you, I am sure of that.'

'Only because he has to.'

'No, it is more than that. It is a kind of admiration, admiration touched by his own pride ... He is becoming old, of course; he changes from day to day; at one time he is happy to lean on you, at another he is jealous of what you have become, of what he has made you. But he trusts you, I know ... Are you so sure of what Black

231

Harris will do?'

'I could not be more sure! I told your father, I know Harris as I know myself. He is greedy, and determined, and he never forgets. And I know him so well because he is the man I might have been, myself.'

'You could be like Harris? Never say it! He is no more than a pirate!'

'Exactly so.'

'But you are different.'

'I have become different, with your help … But before we met, and before I settled in Makassang, Harris and I might have been twins. We each had a ship, and a fighting crew, and a great hunger for gold, and as much conscience as a shark in the shallows. I agree that many things are changed now, Sunara. He has become worse, and I have become better. But at one time we were the same man.'

'I do not believe it.'

He chuckled. 'I would be disappointed if you did… Well, I will do my best to bring him to ruin, in any case. I owe it to myself, because it is an old score which I must pay off, for honour's sake, and I owe it to you and to your father, for many other reasons.'

Her arms tightened about him. 'I pray for success! I want my father to love you.'

Richard laughed again, more intimately. 'You want your father to love me?'

She stirred, in languor and response. 'So that he may be more like me.'

'This love of your father's may take some time.'

'Alas, yes.'

'In the meantime …'

Her turning mouth was soft. 'Yes. In the meantime. Tuan, you are the only true man in the whole world. Tuan!'

By night, he had such pleasures and such rewards, such balm for an uncertain spirit; but by day, he knew only sombre waiting and speculation, in an atmosphere at once brooding and suspicious.

For a week, there was nothing, and for another week, nothing, either by report or by observation. The Rajah's agents were everywhere – Richard had little doubt of that; but they brought back no word of Black Harris, nor of Selang Aro, and nothing at all of the Lucinda D, which seemed to have vanished from the East Garrison beaches on an outgoing tide of blood. There was much 'coming and going' at the Shwe Dagon, so the spies said; and Shrang Anapuri, the town below it, was reported more full than usual. But one could find nothing notable in any of this. There was always countrywide marketing before the monsoon season, and a choice of half a dozen religious festivals could explain the activity at the Golden Pagoda. From all the sum total of the gossip, the whispering, the bazaar rumours, no clue as to what might be happening, or what dangers threatened, had emerged into the light of day.

There was no clue, either, from that other weapon of observation, the Rajah's giant telescope. Richard, ill-at-ease with his gradually growing doubts, and chafing at the delay which had been of his own advising, spent long hours in the bower, restlessly sweeping through an arc of vision which included every foot of ground, from the causeway at the eastern limit to the coastline west of the Shwe Dagon. He was looking for his ship, which he felt must be the focus of this new danger, as the Mystic had been of the last one; but there was never a sign of her – not a fluttering topsail, not a flash of white canvas, not a ripple on the water. There was nothing to be seen round the Shwe Dagon, either. The golden dome still ruled in majesty, the town below it seethed with its usual throng. But of attack, of suspicious concentration, there was not even a shadow, to bring him reassurance that his guess had been correct.

He was finding his position uncomfortable. Though the Rajah preserved an impassive mien, Colonel Kedah did not; he was already beginning to look down his nose, to inquire several times a day, with sardonic formality, if there were any news, to talk of the pitfalls of too much prudence. His men took their cue from their commander.

There was murmuring among the troops, both in the Sun Palace and down at the causeway; they wanted revenge for their dead comrades, they wanted a bloody and victorious battlefield, they did not want to practise arms drill, and stand guard duty, and loaf about in barracks … All over the palace, especially among the servants and the courtiers and the hangers-on who warmed or cooled the climate of repute, there was whispering, and side-glances, and that kind of deference which is made ironic by its emphasis. Richard, holding his head high in the midst of these pinpricks, was beginning to have serious doubts of his own. Nothing was turning out according to his forecast. His judgement might have been at fault; and if his judgement, then his whole course of action was fatally wrong.

Then, suddenly and overwhelmingly, it was proved right. In a swift culmination of spy reports, rumour, and the small, significant drift of action, the dubious pause boiled over into the fact of peril.

It began with a report from one of the fishing fleets. This one, consisting of a dozen outrigger prahus from the sampan village by the western lighthouse, had gone up the coast after a school of flying fish, and had been compelled by bad weather to run for shelter far from home. In a cove not ten miles from the northern coast of the island, they had come upon the Lucinda D. She was careened on a sand spit, and out of action; indeed, she seemed to be deserted save for a pair of shipkeepers living in a hut on shore, who fired warning shots to discourage further intrusion. The fishing fleet gave her a wide berth; but one of the prahus, more enterprising than the rest, and with a keener nose for a reward, had come flying down before the gale to bring back the news.

It was news which meant two things: that Black Harris was somewhere ashore, and that the assault on the Sun Palace, if such were planned, would come from landwards.

Secondly, there was the matter of the pilgrims. Suddenly, in the space of a week, the word 'pilgrim' became a title, and an idea, which appeared to have obsessed the whole of Makassang. All over the island, and especially from the dark interior round the Land-

Dyak villages, men were on the move, impelled (they said) by piety and the wish to pay their respects to the great Lord Buddha. With the choice of half a dozen large and small pagodas, they were making only for the Shwe Dagon.

They travelled by boat along the shoreline, they slipped through jungle pathways, they rode by bullock cart along the winding coastal roads which ringed the island. They seeped and flooded in, in their hundreds and presently their thousands; they crowded the streets and the hovels of Shrang Anapuri; they thronged the slopes round the Shwe Dagon. By day, the smoke of their cooking rose like laden incense, and by night, the twinkling lights of a thousand campfires could be seen through the big telescope, a huge shadowy billowing carpet embroidered with pinpoints of fire.

Spies, mingling by the dozen with these devout strangers, reported that they kept a remarkable silence. They were crudely armed, as a pilgrim outside his tribal area had a right to be; and they returned uniform answers to all questions. Was it a holiday? No, it was a pilgrimage. Was it part of a planned movement? No, it was a pilgrimage. Was it war? No, a pilgrimage.

Then, there was the matter of the Shwe Dagon itself.

At about this time, a detachment of the Palace Guard under a young captain named Sorba presented itself at the Shwe Dagon, for the routine monthly inspection which had been decreed by the Rajah. This was never a close search, nor was it a formality: the platoon of twelve men was accustomed to enter the pagoda, walk round the various levels and stairways and see that public order and decency were being maintained. On this occasion, however, they were baulked even of this modest supervision. They found the lower gates locked and barred, and when repeated knocking brought a face to the grille, it belonged only to a young monk, disdainful and surly, who affected to know nothing save that the gates could not be opened to anyone.

Captain Sorba, a small and not notably warlike man, inquired as sharply as he could what was standing in the way of their entry. On the other side of the grille, the shaven head and slit brown eyes of the monk confronted him, immovable as a painting, impassive, unimpressed.

'It is a matter of repairs,' answered the monk briefly. 'The pagoda is closed to all visitors.' And he made as if to shut the grille again.

'It is not closed to the Rajah's inspection,' said Captain Sorba, taken aback. 'Come, you know the decree. Open the gate immediately!'

'Repairs,' repeated the monk. 'The gate will not open.'

'Open the northern gate, then!'

'That is shut, too. The pagoda is closed.'

'Why?'

'Repairs,' said the monk, with scarcely veiled insolence. This time, he moved to shut the grille in his visitor's face, but Captain Sorba brought up his short spear and wedged it in the opening. Through the narrow gap, the monk surveyed him malevolently. 'This is a holy place,' he said. 'You cannot force your way into it with arms.'

Captain Sorba, at a loss for his next move – for though he knew his military rights, he knew also that they could be whittled down by considerations of piety – withdrew his spear hurriedly, as if he would wipe out the evidence of sacrilege.

'When will these repairs be finished?' he inquired uncertainly. At his back, his men were regarding him with appropriate, if cautious amusement; the spectacle of a small, proud officer outfaced by a humble monk could not fail to make a good soldier's joke. 'I shall have to report this to my superiors. When will the gates be opened?'

This time, the insolence was plain. 'Shall we say, next month?' answered the monk, and slammed shut the grille with a sharp, mocking thud. The outsiders were left only with the nail-studded teak gates, and that smell of ancient privies which was the true odour of sanctity.

It was a rebuff which the Rajah, when appraised of it, could not stomach. But before action could be taken – and action, clearly,

236

would involve some degree of force, and many more men than had made up the inspecting guard – the last report came in, and the matter of the locked gates assumed its place in a pattern which, at last, vindicated Richard Marriott's judgement to the hilt.

This time, it came by the hand of a trusted spy – a monk who was no monk, but one of the Rajah's own household. He had spent a month or more within the Shwe Dagon, as a pretended novice, and then, seizing his chance to escape, he had brought out the news – news which could be distilled into a few, foreboding sentences.

Selang Aro had returned to the Shwe Dagon. Black Harris, and all his crew, were there also. Every monk, and every dubious visitor to the pagoda, was armed. And every 'pilgrim' in Shrang Anapuri had sworn an oath – of a strength and holiness matching his pilgrimage – to give his life, if need be, in the storming of the Sun Palace.

Faced with the truth, all their doubts resolved, the Rajah and his advisers might have looked forward to an easier meeting, with decisions speedily agreed. But this was not so. When they reassembled in the audience chamber, it was to find that, in their deliberations, a fresh area of disagreement had been opened up, at least as profoundly as the last. It concerned the sanctity, or otherwise, of the Shwe Dagon.

Richard Marriott, and to a lesser extent Amin Sang, were in favour of an instant, full-scale attack on the pagoda, which had clearly become the core of revolt. But when Richard proposed this, expecting ready agreement, he met opposition which was not less ready, for a reason which had never before been part of his calculation.

'We cannot do that,' said Colonel Kedah, in a dismissive voice, as if one short sentence from himself were enough to dispose of the suggestion out of hand. 'There can be no attack on the Shwe Dagon.'

'No attack!' echoed Richard, astonished. 'What are you talking of? The Shwe Dagon is the very first place we should make for. It is their battle headquarters!'

'We cannot attack it,' said Colonel Kedah, in the same tone of finality. His single eye was bent on Richard with a steady determination. 'It would be sacrilege.'

'Who cares for sacrilege? This is war!'

'The pagoda is a holy place.'

'It is a holy place full of soldiers and armed ruffians. They threaten our lives. They must be destroyed, wherever they are to be found.'

'And if we destroy the pagoda?'

'I would destroy ten pagodas, if I had to.' Richard, truly amazed at Kedah's objections, turned to the Rajah. 'Your Highness, will you rule on this?'

'I will hear both sides,' answered the Rajah coolly.

Baulked, Richard summoned his arguments swiftly. 'Sir, with respect, I cannot see that there are two sides to this. We have no choice! The Shwe Dagon is now the centre of revolt. All our greatest enemies are there. It is a nest which must be wiped out, if we are serious about beating off this attack. Once more, he was saying 'we', with the utmost sense of participation. 'These people have plagued Makassang for years – for a hundred years, if what I am told is true. Let us put an end to it, now! We will never have a better chance.'

At his side, Kedah's voice was heard again, as uncompromising as before. 'It is not a simple matter of attack and destroy. There is more to this than military action. If we commit sacrilege, we invite disaster.'

'And if we don't commit sacrilege, we invite disaster.' Richard rounded on him, ready to be angry. 'What is this sudden tenderness?' he asked scornfully. 'The pagoda is inspected every month, with armed men, and for a very good reason – to make sure that they are not plotting against us. Is not that a form of sacrilege? Yet we commit it cheerfully. And now that we have proof that they are planning an attack, are we to back away like a dog kicked in the muzzle?'

'Inspection is one thing, fighting and the shedding of blood is another. An armed attack on the pagoda is an impious idea which would only occur to an unbeliever.'

Richard laughed, shortly. 'Have it as you like. I am not afraid of names and labels. Of course I am an unbeliever. The Shwe Dagon is not a shrine to me. It is a building. It is a building now taken over by enemies who plot to kill the Rajah and end the dynasty. It is an enemy stronghold, a barracks full of traitors, and I do not care a brass farthing what holy name it goes by.'

The Rajah broke into the pause that followed. 'What you say is true,' he told Richard. 'But Kedah has right on his side, also. Such an attack could be called sacrilege. We have to consider the effect on the people.'

With these words, Richard saw his loophole. Whatever had impelled Kedah to his objections (and they might be grounded in a true religious instinct), for the Rajah it was not a matter of piety. It was a question of reputation, the 'effect on the people' which might cause them to falter in their loyalty, or turn faint-hearted at the prospect of heavenly wrath. This was a very different matter, and one to which Richard was sure he had an answer. In effect, he must take the hazard of sacrilege on his own shoulders. He was not afraid to court unpopularity, and in the present circumstances he might be the only one who could do so, without ill effect to their cause.

Furthermore, it was not difficult to divine, cynically, that the Rajah would have no objection to Richard's thus running the risk of public censure.

He turned to the Rajah. 'Your Highness, if we win, there will be no murmuring from the people. And if we lose, the murmuring will not reach us, wherever we have been consigned to ... And we will lose, unless we strike without mercy at the very heart of this insurrection.'

'It is still sacrilege,' Kedah interjected.

'Not for me,' answered Richard instantly. 'You will recall that I am an ignorant infidel? I cannot tell a pagoda from a parrot cage ...' Deliberately he made his voice as light-hearted as he could, as if this whole matter were something so trivial that it could never stand in the way of serious planning. 'There will be plenty for you to do, Colonel, without embracing these religious dilemmas. There is the whole of Shrang Anapuri, full of our enemies, who must also be disposed of. If you will see to that, I will take care of the Shwe Dagon, and take care of the sacrilege too.'

His tone was just short of offensive, and though Colonel Kedah stared at him with cold dislike, he did not put his feeling into words. It was possible that he saw the truth of Richard's argument, and was glad to have this necessary source of embarrassment taken off his hands. Without exactly resolving the clash, they went on to discuss other details, and here there was a fuller measure of agreement. It was a formidable force, and a determined effort, which they had to crush, and to do this, every loyal man must be pressed into service.

Richard was especially emphatic about this. 'We will never have a better chance,' he said again. 'We can crush every last shred of revolt, and settle the affairs of Makassang for fifty years … But to make sure of that, we will have to gamble, and it will be worth it. We need more men than at any time before. We must bring back the garrisons, wherever they may be – from the west, from the east, from the causeway – and have them converge on Shrang Anapuri and the Shwe Dagon. There can be no idle hands, no grounded spears. Every man in every regiment must be fighting, that day!'

The Rajah fingered his chin. Richard's enthusiasm was infectious, as the rapt face of Amin Sang showed; but the old man was more prudent in his thinking.

'It is indeed a gamble,' he said. 'If the day goes badly, everything we value will lie open to the enemy.'

'The day will not go badly!' In his eagerness, Richard set one foot on the flight of steps leading to the ivory throne, and the Rajah, even at this grave moment, was forced to smile at his vehemence. 'First, we will strike before they do. Second, whatever their numbers coming against us, our troops are trained men, and will cut them to pieces. Third, think of the opportunity we are given! Every enemy of Makassang will be collected in one place at one time, for us to fall upon with all the force we can muster.'

'I do not like to leave the mines unprotected,' said the Rajah, though with less certainty in his voice. 'They are altogether too tempting.'

'Sir, there will be no one for them to tempt. The main bait is here. The treasure vault is worth ten ruby mines! And with all the Land-Dyaks gathered for an assault on the Sun Palace, as we know them to be, the men guarding the mines are going to waste, if they stay on guard against nothing. We need them here! For if we fail – if the palace falls – then the garrisons will perish in any case, like fruit withering on the vine. Far better that they should be here, under our close command, so that they can play a proper part.'

After a long interval of thought, the Rajah raised his head. 'Kedah?' he queried.

It was a difficult moment for Kedah, and all those in the room were aware of it. In the last few days, his personal and professional opposition to Richard Marriott had become clear: they had had more than one open collision in council, and Kedah's temper, never sweet, could not have been improved by the fact that Richard seemed to have come off best in every argument. But Kedah was a realist, and a professional soldier, and above all a man fanatically loyal to the Rajah. He had the highest of all the ancient virtues – devotion to his king. He might dislike what Richard proposed; he might dislike Richard himself; but if a certain course of action meant victory for the Rajah of Makassang, then no personal considerations would be allowed to stand in the way of making that victory come true.

He showed this very clearly when he answered: 'Your Highness, I have no objection to make.'

'Very well.' The Rajah, an excellent judge of men, exhibited no surprise; it was as if he had foreseen, and approved, Kedah's eventual agreement. His frail body and withered old face seemed to gather majestic strength as he rose from the ivory throne, and walked towards a side table where certain maps and sketches had been spread out. 'Join me here,' he commanded, 'and we will make our plans in detail … This is our strategy, in general terms. The garrisons will be brought back, to encircle Shrang Anapuri under the command of Colonel Kedah. The Tunku will lead an attack on the Shwe Dagon, where the leadership of the revolt is gathered. Amin Sang will remain here in the Sun Palace, with a small body of men, to guard our own person.'

Richard, catching sight of Amin Sang's crestfallen face, was emboldened to propose something more adventurous than mere guard duty for his friend.

'Your Highness, there can be no question of danger to the palace, or to yourself, if we strike first, as we plan to do. I had in mind a two-handed attack on the pagoda, one from the northern gate, one from the southern. It would be an assistance to me if Amin Sang can lead one of these.'

'Am I to be left unprotected?' inquired the Rajah, with a touch of hauteur.

'By no means,' answered Richard. 'I suggest that Captain Sorba be assigned to command the Palace Guard. As you know, he is a trustworthy officer.'

'He is a fool,' said the Rajah, 'but perhaps a fool will do … This talk of a two-handed attack on the Shwe Dagon – you must take care that there is no destruction of the fabric of the pagoda, or of the various statues and relics. They are, after all, part of our riches. It should be possible to capture it without harm to the building.'

'It is bound to become somewhat stained, in the course of the action.'

'There is no harm in that. The monks can clean it… And this time, Tunku' – the Rajah's voice took on an odd note of venom, quite unlike his former cool tone – 'I would like some evidence of victory, in the form of prisoners brought back. Shall we say – five hundred?'

III

The view from the top of the Golden Pagoda was the finest that

Richard Marriott had ever seen. To be sure, his gaze was turned inwards only; he did not look below the Shwe Dagon towards Shrang Anapuri, where under a brazen sun Colonel Kedah and his lines of disciplined troops were conducting the methodical slaughter of hordes of panicked, fleeing, hemmed-in Land-Dyaks. Richard's view was his personal prize, the view of the platform at the summit of the pagoda, lined with painted shrines and smiling Buddhas, and slippery now from the blood of the countless corpses which marked their victory.

He had fought his way up one of the towering staircases, step by step, man by man; Amin Sang had done the same, entering by the northern gate on the opposite side. They had met at last on this hard-won pinnacle, both wounded, dripping with sweat and blood, near exhaustion from the desperate effort. It had been hand-to-hand encounter ever since the gates were first breached, with teak logs for battering rams, and the hardest-fought battle of Richard's life; there had been many moments during that day when he had doubted their success – when the enemy rallied with screams of defiance, when his own men were sent toppling by the score down the stairway, when it seemed impossible that he could force his way a single step higher. But he had triumphed in the end, and Amin Sang had done the same.

The divided uproar of the two battles, the faint converging shouts of 'Makassang!' had drawn closer together, until at last the two commanders and the remnants of their men had met at the top with a great cry of victory. Then they had set to work on the last grim moments of execution. The harvest of that execution lay about their feet now – sprawling grotesquely, ungainly and awkward in death. The smell of blood, drying and baking in the sun was everywhere.

The attack had begun at dawn; it was now nearly midday, and, save for one guarded cage of prisoners for the Rajah's pleasure, there was not an enemy left alive within all the labyrinths of the Shwe Dagon. It had been methodically cleared, level by level, shrine by shrine, hiding place by hiding place, until the whole edifice reeked of slaughter. The trail of corpses led upwards to this elevated offering of death, under the shadow of the golden dome itself.

Selang Aro was dead; his head, severed by a single stroke from the avenging Amin Sang, had rolled a dozen steps downwards until it came to rest, gory and sightless, obscenely bald. There were men from the Lucinda D, dead also, some of Richard's own runaways who had chosen to follow Black Harris, and had been led to this murderous ruin. There were armed monks by the score, their saffron robes stained by the last of their treacherous blood. But of Black Harris himself – arch-villain, arch-enemy – there was now not a sign. Richard had glimpsed him briefly at the height of the battle, but then, after discharging his pistols and gauging the struggle which was clearly going against him, he had melted away, and was not to be seen.

Richard looked round him, leaning on his cutlass. He was wearied to exhaustion, but his body and jaded spirit still had the spur they needed.

'Black Harris is somewhere here,' he said. 'He cannot have escaped … I will find him, if the pagoda has to be pulled down stone by stone.'

His voice was low and hoarse; he spoke the words to Amin Sang, who was perched with cheerful irreverence on the arm of a reclining Buddha, binding up a spearthrust which had furrowed his thigh. The guard-captain knotted the strip of silk which served him as a bandage before replying: 'Is he not among the dead?'

'No.' Richard let his gaze wander round the high platform on which they stood, but he knew the answer well enough. 'No. His is a corpse which I would recognize from fifty yards away at midnight … You are sure he did not slip past your own line of men as they mounted?'

Amin Sang's weary, sweat-streaked face split into a grin. 'No one slipped past my line … I would not be bold enough to ask you the same question, Tunku.'

Richard smiled also. 'You would have the same answer … I saw him at one moment, then he fired, and turned away. He wore a red scarf. I have seen it before.' His eyes went up to the golden dome, burnished and brilliant in the sunshine, massively smooth, not to be scaled by any living thing save lizards and monkeys. 'He cannot be there, he is not dead, he did not break through to the stairways. He cannot fly, nor jump down a hundred feet. Therefore he must be hiding, somewhere on this very platform.'

Silence had gradually fallen all over the level where they stood; the groans of the dying had ceased, the battlecries of wildly-excited men had given place to the wordless relief of rest. There were some fifty men – all Richard's – alive on the platform; a few of them stood, slaking their thirst at a fountain in the peaceful sunshine, most were crouched in the shade of the images and shrines, staunching their blood, binding up their wounds. Here and there a man bent over a sorely wounded comrade, easing his hurt, doing what could be done for his comfort. Richard had just begun to say that they would rest, and then take up their search, when the silence was split asunder by a single harsh cry which rang and echoed round them: 'Marriott!'

Richard jumped, as if he had felt a lash across his back. He knew the voice, which seemed to come from behind him, at the edge of the platform where the gaily-painted shrines made a wall against the outer world. But when he turned, stung to hot anticipation by that hated voice, he could see nothing save smiling images, tongueless, benign.

The voice said again with the same fierce desperation: 'Marriott! If you move you are dead.'

Richard stood stock-still. He, and his men, were now all staring in the same direction. At one side of the platform, where the shadow cast by the dome gave place to glaring sunshine, there was a small shrine, a pretty thing of pink mosaic tiling, and miniature gold baubles which copied the shape of the dome itself, and blue enamelled fretwork, and yellow railings – a very wedding cake of a shrine, sentimental and rustic. Its centrepiece was a representation of the Lord Buddha; not a stone or wooden image, like the hundreds which decorated and sanctified the Shwe Dagon, but a painting.

The work was crudely done, on poor canvas framed in yellow-wood. The colours were garish, the pose banal, the Buddha's features almost fatuous in their benevolence. Above the plump and smiling mouth, the eyes in the canvas had been cut open, as was sometimes done, for the insertion of beads or jewels. But today, a day of hot sunshine and the smell of blood, there were no jewels – and yet the slits of the eyes did not gape sightless, for all that. The eyes of this Buddha were living, and they stared out of the benign face in implacable hatred. They were fixed on Richard Marriott, a few feet away, and glowing with a mad intensity.

Richard stared back, almost hypnotized. He had never seen anything more blasphemous, more horrible, than the wicked eyes set in this face of blissful holiness. It was, of course, Black Harris – but in what a fearsome guise!

The voice came again, throaty with fear and hatred: 'I have you covered! There is a gun pointed straight at your belly. If you move a muscle, you lose your guts!'

Richard made as if to speak, but Black Harris barked again: 'Tell your men! I want no mistakes!'

Without turning his head – for he knew he had all their attention – Richard called out to his staring men: 'There is a gun aimed at me. Make no move to help!' Then he looked again into the gleaming eyes of the Buddha, and said: 'What do you want?'

'My life.' The words were like a curse. 'A safe conduct out of this place.'

Richard found that he could laugh, even in the midst of nerve-racking tension. 'It would not be worth a string of cash! They would tear you to pieces!'

'Don't laugh at me, you damned dog!' roared Black Harris, with fury in his voice. Then he said, more controlled: 'They won't tear me to pieces, if you are with me. They won't put a finger on me. I will take you as cover, with a gun in your back. As soon as we are free, you can go.'

Richard shook his head. 'I would not, even if I could. I have sworn to kill you, and so have a thousand others. We will keep our word.'

The eyes behind the smiling mask glittered. 'I mean what I say. It is your life or mine. You will take me out, if you want to save your skin.'

Richard raised his voice. He was continuing to talk because of something he had remembered. 'They will kill us both,' he called out. 'Do you think they would let you go now, because I am with you? They would laugh, even as they cut the two of us down ... Come out, Harris,' he commanded. 'You have no hope, on this side of hell.'

He was talking, spinning out the time in desperate subterfuge, because he had remembered Amin Sang – the faithful Amin Sang who was his forlorn and only chance. Amin Sang was directly behind him, or he had been a few moments before; sitting on the stone arm of the image, binding up his thigh. Black Harris, from where he stood behind the painted Buddha, could not see him, or what he was doing; Richard himself blocked the view. Amin Sang was the only man on the platform who might, unseen, aim a spear and launch it at their last enemy.

Richard's blood ran cold as he thought of the odds. For Amin Sang himself was unsighted, until Richard moved aside. If he moved, it must be in a single instant – and in that flash, Amin Sang must aim and throw.

Sweating, he wondered if Amin Sang would see his advantage, and act upon it. How could he be prompted? Would he be willing to take the chance – both for himself and for Richard? He remembered, as if from a hundred years ago, the young guard-captain saying: 'I will be your man forever.' Would he steel himself to prove it now? Had he the wit, as well as the resolution? Above all else, how was Richard to give him a signal, to show him the way?

He could not even remember if Amin Sang, sitting on the Buddha's arm, intent on his wounded thigh, had had a spear within his reach.

In the prickling silence, Harris's voice came again, hoarse and determined in evil. 'Enough of talking! Will you walk out with me?'

'No.'

'Then, if I am to die, I will take you with me.'

'I do not care, as long as you are killed.' Richard was straining his ears for the slightest sound behind him. He heard nothing. Amin Sang might have fallen asleep. He might even have moved away when Harris first spoke, and be among those standing by helplessly.

'Brave words,' said Harris. 'I will count three, and then fire.'

Richard summoned his wits, for the cast of fate. He spoke in a loud, clear tone. 'Rather than agree, I will fall where I stand.'

'Save your heroics,' sneered Black Harris. 'I tell you, I will count to three.'

'Count to three hundred, if you will,' said Richard, in the same charged voice. 'Three will be enough for me.'

'One!' said Harris.

Richard stood his ground.

'I mean what I said,' the voice behind the Buddha's mask was venomous. 'You will get me safe conduct, or you will die on that very slab of stone ... Two!'

There was not a sound anywhere, save Richard's thudding heart. He tried to listen for the warning intake of breath, but he did not hear it. Then, as Harris barked out: 'Three!' he flung himself on the ground.

There was a shout, and a whistling hiss which was the spear hurtling past his crouched back. It flew straight as a die, and impaled the picture of the Buddha where the full belly joined the casing of the ribs. Sacrilege indeed, thought Richard, shaken to his soul. A scream of agony broke the silence, as if the Lord Buddha himself had been foully murdered, and a gun went off behind the picture, discharging harmlessly into the air. Then the picture itself crashed forward amid its ring of tawdry decoration, revealing Black Harris, with a face of torture more terrible than the ancient lineaments of martyrdom, plucking at the spear which had cleft his right kneecap, splitting it like kindling, and buried itself deep in a baulk of timber behind his back.

'At your service, Tunku,' said Amin Sang calmly, and came sauntering forward, a huntsman ready to retrieve the fallen animal which has run the last course of its life.

The canopied state barge, which had been sent across the bay to carry them back, put out from the shore with its load of weary, happy, and triumphant men. The overseer's drum gave out its commanding signal, followed by the sweet music of the pipes; the hidden oarsmen took up their steady beat, the huge curved prow dipped and rose as the barge met the thrust of deep water. With a fair and favouring wind, they left the small bay of Shrang Anapuri and, crossing the threshold of the sparkling sea, set their course towards the Sun Palace, and home.

Richard and Amin Sang reclined at ease on couches under the velvet canopy; below them in the sumptuous well-deck the fifty men of the Royal Regiment who had stormed their way to the top of the Shwe Dagon – the Fifty of the Brave, as they were already coming to be called – also took their ease, as honoured passengers in the royal barge. Not for them the dusty homeward trudge of common soldiers … Both the commanders were tired to the bone, after the wild and relentless struggle which had taken such toll of nerve and sinew; and Richard's wound, a slash across the forearm, had swollen and stiffened in the last few hours, so that he could not settle easily even in this cushioned retreat. But victory was the great salve for such troubles; it was victory which bound up all wounds, eased all pain. The warriors might not be whole in body, but they were returning in triumph from a battle which would become part of the folklore of Makassang, to be told and sung and remembered wherever men gathered to gossip of bitter fighting and brave deeds.

John Keston appeared at Richard's side with a tall glass of sangaree, for his further comfort. John Keston was disgruntled, as perhaps he had a right to be: at Richard's insistence, he had been left behind in the Sun Palace, as part of the Rajah's personal guard, and this voyage in the state barge, to bring back the fighting men, was the nearest he had come to taking part in the battle. His tightened lips and heavy silences made clear his displeasure. Richard, well aware of his servant's mood, tried to bring him some cheer.

'Thank you, Keston,' he said with great heartiness, accepting the sangaree. 'This is all I have need of, to round off a beautiful morning … I hope it will do more for my arm than it will do for my liver.'

John Keston, impassive as a clergyman who has strayed into some dubious entertainment, said nothing.

'Does the arm trouble you, Tunku?' asked Amin Sang from the other couch. His wounded thigh, which had opened painfully during the night, was propped with pillows, but he wore a look of deep contentment none the less; his quick wit, coupled with his skill, which had saved Richard's life in fantastic circumstances, was already a legend among his men, and he won a hero's acclaim wherever he went. 'That stroke went deep. Would it not be better to have it covered?'

Richard shook his head. 'I never knew a wound that was not the better for the sun on it.' He was looking up at John Keston, still wanting to improve his grumpy spirit. 'Isn't that so? – fresh air is the best ointment?'

'I couldn't say, sir,' answered Keston.

'Well, I will say!' exclaimed Richard, exasperated. 'Come, man – cheer up, for God's sake! We are bringing home victory, not going to a funeral. My arm will never mend, with all these sour looks on it.'

John Keston pursed his lips primly, not to be wooed from his sulkiness. 'Maybe, if I had been by, you would not have had the wound.'

'You could not be with me.' Richard made a last try for persuasion. 'If you had been on this side of the bay, then the palace would have lacked its proper protection. Don't forget, you were guarding what I treasure, above all else … Now, Keston, we have had this talk before, and settled the matter. There was duty to be done at the pagoda, and duty to be done at home. They were of the same importance. I had to leave someone behind whom I could trust. You know that.'

'Duty, is it?' exclaimed Keston, with overflowing bitterness. 'Standing guard, twenty miles from the battle! Is that all I am good for? I thought my place was to be by you. It has been so for the past ten years. Let others do the guard duty, and act as messenger boys!'

'What messages are these?' asked Richard, his attention caught by the strange word.

After a pause full of wounded feeling, Keston said: 'Her Highness sent you her greetings.'

'Then it is high time I heard them!' said Richard, in fresh exasperation. 'Have I to prise them out with a crowbar? What greetings? What did she say?'

'That she looks forward to your return.'

'Is that all, then? Is she well?'

'As well as can be expected.'

Richard rounded on him, thunder in his brow. 'What do you mean, as well as can be expected? Stop this stupid play-acting! Is she well, or isn't she?'

'She is well,' answered Keston. Though his face was still wooden, he was, at last, relenting, and beginning to enjoy himself. 'She told me to say, she is as well as can be expected, when she is separated from you.' He was investing the loving words with a sickly emphasis which was enough to drive Richard to fury, and to make Amin Sang smile behind a covering hand. 'She said that I was to see that you hurried back to her. She said I was to assure you that she was miserable when you were away, and would only be happy when you returned.'

'Is that all?' asked Richard, discomfited.

'She said,' concluded the stolid John Keston, with relish, 'that I should put on the wings of love, to bring you back to her again.'

There was a muffled snort from Amin Sang, for whom this tender recital had proved too much. Richard glared at him, but, meeting a pair of innocent eyes, he was forced to give way to mirth himself. The Fifty of the Brave, lounging in the well-deck, turned in amusement to hear their commanders dissolve into loud laughter.

'Thank you, Keston,' said Richard presently, as gravely as he could. 'I will tell her Highness that you delivered her messages most movingly.'

'I would rather have had other duties,' said Keston. But he was mollified at last, having done something to square the account, and relieve his disappointment.

They were well set upon their course; the waves rippled musically as they ran against the thrusting prow, the sunshine on the water danced and sparkled, as far as the eye could see. There could not have been a fairer day for their journey; and, wounds or no, they were a thousand times better off than the wretched men they had vanquished.

They carried one of these men, perhaps the most luckless of all, in the state barge itself. Black Harris was on board, bound hand and foot – though the gross wound in his knee had put him out of commission entirely – and consigned below decks like a piece of valued cargo – which, in fact, he was. Harris was bearing both his wound and his situation stoically; no word of regret or remorse, no plea for mercy, had crossed his lips; he had lain in silence as he was carried on board, and his eyes as they met Richard's were expressionless. Of all the captives, he was the only one to be thus transported; the rest – some six or seven hundred unfortunates – were at this moment embarked on their long march back to the Sun Palace, and to the death, torture, or servitude which awaited them.

Earlier, Richard had witnessed the start of that melancholy pilgrimage. Colonel Kedah was in command – Kedah who had acquitted himself so well in the containment and slaughter of Shrang Anapuri, and yet had missed the more spectacular assault which had brought the Fifty of the Brave to such glory. The prisoners were shackled together, in droves of thirty or more; overseers with ox-hide whips, freely used, added to their miseries. Most of them were young men, who had sought to blood their spears in a pretended 'holy war'; some were monks, impassive and resigned: some Latangis; cunning and vicious; some country boys with broad flat faces and drugged eyes. The dust of their progress could be seen now from the state barge, as the long and hopeless columns wound their way down the coast road.

Richard watched them with a sense of foreboding, which not all his feeling of triumph could alter. Surrounded by luxury, reclining at ease, listening to a soldier's song which some of the Fifty were singing in chorus, he found it impossible not to think of the miseries of that march, and of what awaited the captives at their journey's end. He realized that he was thinking of Black Harris with the same sense of pity. For all the treachery and cursed spite which had landed Harris in his present situation, his punishment was likely to outweigh it most cruelly.

Richard stared out across the water, where far ahead of them the pearly morning sun was slanting down on the noble coral of the Sun Palace. For himself, this prospect meant home, and the warmth of loving arms; for Black Harris, the future was by contrast unspeakable. Richard thought to himself: Whatever he may have deserved, and however much I hate him, I should have put him out of his misery.

He knew by now, better than most, that there were things he could do in hot blood, which the Rajah preferred in cold.

IV

From morning till night, the sound of hammering, the thud of mallet on crosstree and wooden peg, rang up and down the Steps of Heaven. To make a showing worthy of the occasion, explained Colonel Kedah (who was in charge of the operation), there must be no scamping of any sort: it was necessary to make use of the best craftsmen, the finest materials, the most painstaking attention to detail. Six hundred and fifty immense barrels had been constructed by the palace coopers, and weighted with stones, and filled with earth; in them had been planted six hundred and fifty crosses of seasoned teak, sufficient to bear the weight of a man, be he never so heavy, be the sun never so hot, hang he never so long.

When the carpenters had done their work, the barrels were rolled into place down the Steps of Heaven, and there set up in careful symmetry: ten to a step, for sixty steps down, with a circular fringe of fifty to contain the whole. It took a week to erect this descending forest of crosses, and a day to erect the proudest cross of all, and the tallest – a cross of polished ebony, set in the place of honour on the topmost step. But after a week it was all done, and the stark grove stood waiting, in the utmost silence, like some venerated shrine of the woodland god, for human visitation.

'My garden,' said the Rajah, pleasurably, on the morning of the seventh day. He pressed his dry palms together. 'Let us now plant our vines.'

The prisoners were brought out from the underground cages, a shuffling throng who blinked at the sunlight, but made no other sign. With shouting, but with little whipping or cuffing – for they had by now grown docile – they were led to their appointed stations, overflowing down the Steps of Heaven in a dejected human tide. The first man to come to a cross took his place before it, and then the next, and the next; when one step was fully tenanted, the column of shuffling men moved lower to the next level, and filled that one; and the remainder passed on, seeking their vacancies. After an hour, before each tub of earth, and each implanted cross, a man stood in an attitude of humility, waiting for attention. Then the trumpets sounded and it was the turn of the soldiers.

The cries were few, for the pain of the nails piercing the hands and feet of half-starved men was not great – and they knew their fate in any case, and were stoic. The crucifiers, fortified with liberal draughts from a cask of rich wine, set to with a will; as the work progressed, it became a matter of lusty efficiency – the cross lowered, the man impaled with fewer than a dozen strokes, the cross raised again, the barrel brought into exact line with its fellows, the steps brushed free of blood and earth – all within a few minutes. The teams vied with each other in their despatch; there was even some wagering, though it had to be discreetly done, being against the regulations.

The prisoners did not watch each other being crucified; it was as if some convention of modesty made them look elsewhere; it could be said that none could truly bear witness to the punishment of another, for their eyes were downcast throughout. As each man's turn came, he lay down on his cross as quietly as a dog curling up for sleep. When the garden was fully planted, there was still no sound above a whimper from the hundreds of men who were now its terrible fruit.

Some formality attended the raising of the ebony cross of honour, which was the cross of Black Harris. He was carried out last of all – his wound made walking impossible – and his litter grounded at the foot of his cross. The Rajah had signified that he would be present at this final ceremony, and, to honour so impressive an audience, Black Harris was given his best possible appearance. His naked body had been washed with spiced almond oil, his beard cut and trimmed; his red scarf was neatly knotted at his throat. He looked almost jaunty as he was tipped from his litter and laid upon the cross.

In the cool of the evening, the Rajah had walked out to see justice done. But he was in no hurry to complete the planting of his garden; he first made a tour of some of the higher levels, staring with interest at his victims, pointing with a light cane to where one of the barrels had been imperfectly aligned with its fellows. Finally Colonel Kedah, who was accompanying him on his inspection, asked if they should now proceed with the raising of Black Harris.

'By all means,' said the Rajah agreeably, and began to walk back towards the ebony cross. 'Let us not keep our most distinguished guest waiting.'

Black Harris was giving no entertainment to his captors. He lay with his eyes closed, his face and body gaunt, his limbs unmoving; even when the nails pierced his hands and feet, there was no more than a contracting tightness round his mouth to compliment the onlookers. But if the Rajah were disappointed, he did not show it, nor did he betray emotion of any kind as the cross was raised; it was the eye of a connoisseur, not of a victor or an avenging judge, which followed closely the raising of the cross, and the position of Black Harris's trunk as his shoulders approached dislocation under the weight of his body. When finally all was in place, the Rajah stood back, shading his eyes, to review this centrepiece.

'Well done, Kedah,' he said finally. He might have been praising a winning stroke in some game of skill. 'The workmanship is really excellent ...' His gaze turned from the cross of Black Harris towards the Steps of Heaven, and the serried rows of the damned. 'What is the final tally?'

'Six hundred and fifty, your Highness,' answered Kedah. 'Some thirty died under questioning, and I thought it best to bring the remainder to a round number.' He gestured below him, his single eye gleaming. 'It is a matter of symmetry, of course. I spent some time planning this pattern.'

'The pattern is admirable,' said the Rajah. 'I am pleased with my garden.' He turned back to Black Harris, and for the first time seemed to project his personal interest upon the haggard figure suspended in agony above their heads. 'And this is the choicest flower of all ...' He raised his voice slightly. 'Well, dog!' he called out, with a perceptible edge of spite. 'How do you like your command now?'

At the sound of his voice, Black Harris at last opened his eyes. The position of his sagging neck was such that he was looking straight down on the Rajah, and with a painful effort he raised his head until he was staring straight ahead. But he said nothing. He might indeed have been king of his own private domain, and set above all vulgar intrusion.

'I spoke to you, dog,' said the Rajah. 'Let us hear an answer. They tell me you swore to reach the Sun Palace. How is it, now that you have kept your oath?'

There was still silence from the cross; though the taunting

question must have reached Black Harris, he gave no sign of it. The Rajah signed to Colonel Kedah, who drew from his belt the kris which was part of his ceremonial uniform, and handed it to his master. Delicately, with no change of expression in his pale eyes, the Rajah advanced the wavy blade of the dagger, and pierced the flesh of Black Harris above the ruins of his shattered kneecap. The pain must have been excruciating.

'Answer, dog,' said the Rajah softly. 'Tell me how you enjoy your conquest.'

An answer came, but it came not in words. It came as the only gesture of contempt of which Black Harris was capable.

The Rajah had to step back swiftly to avoid the stream of water; and perhaps it was this indignity, rather than the few drops defiling his shoes, which overthrew his composure. With a furious gesture he thrust back the kris towards Colonel Kedah, and said, in a voice suddenly snarling: 'Prick me this wineskin.'

A scream of pain split the air as Kedah pressed home the undulating blade into the offending organ, and turned it, with that deliberate, almost formal flick of the wrist which devotees of the kris customarily used. Black Harris writhed in uncontrollable agony, inflicting unimaginable torture on his nailed hands and feet. Then, with a rending sob, his body grew still again, and his head fell forward on his chest.

'In the days to come, dog,' said the Rajah, 'I will ask you many more questions.' He breathed deeply, regaining his former calm. 'See that politeness rules your answers.'

With a cold stare of farewell, he turned, and his entourage with him, and began to make his way across the lawn towards the Sun Palace. The soldiers collected their tools and drifted off to their barracks, arguing about certain details of the final wager. Behind them, silence and a terrible calm settled upon the Steps of Heaven; and that was the end of that day's work.

Richard Marriott was watching from afar. Though he had been

invited to join the party of inspection on the Steps of Heaven, he had made his excuses to the Rajah, pleading that his wound was still painful (which was true enough). But truer still would have been his real reason – that he would have drawn no pleasure from such a viewing, and would indeed have been sickened by it. It was one thing (as he had forecast in thought, on the journey back from the Shwe Dagon) to kill in hot blood, to hate a man for what he had done, and for what he might do in the future; but it was another matter altogether to carry this hatred over into the realm of peace, and, having such a man at one's mercy, to take pleasure in his prolonged punishment.

So Richard, outfacing the Rajah's doubting look, had declined the invitation; instead, he had remained in his apartments on the first floor of the Sun Palace. But he found that he could not so easily dismiss the crude world; the prospect troubled him, without respite; and on this last day especially, when hour by hour the waiting crosses received their load, he had been constantly drawn to the windows on the garden side, overlooking the Steps of Heaven. What he saw, and what he heard, were scarcely less disgusting than if he had stood at the foot of each cross, and, like the Rajah, given greedy attention to all the processes of crucifixion.

Now, leaning on his elbows on one of the wide window-sills, staring out into the dusk, he could not fail to be aware of the terrible carpeting of the Steps of Heaven, where, upon a forest of crosses pointing to the sky, the dregs of their enemies were hung out like tattered linen. Not all the sweet smells of the night could disguise the smell of fear and of death; not all the melodious sounds of a Makassang dusk could overcome those other sounds – the creak of straining timber, the restless muttering like a wind stirring dry leaves, the occasional cry, no louder than a man might cry out in his sleep if that sleep were troubled by hopeless dreams, but which spoke loudly and clearly of pain and torment.

The tall cross of Black Harris was in the forefront of this dreadful picture, and his collapsed figure could be readily seen; though

Richard could not distinguish his eyes, he could imagine them all too easily. He could even imagine that they were staring directly at him, sunken eyes pleading out of a gaunt face, condemning him for this unspeakable cruelty, scorning his comfort when other men hung in such torment. The triple themes of pain, punishment, and forgiveness seemed to be racing round the prison of his head, making careful thought unbearable. He and Black Harris had long been tied together by malice and by treachery, by the urge to repay wickedness in the same ruthless coin; but he could not wish the knot to be sundered in this grisly mode – he would rather remain tied forever.

Behind him, a light step and the stirring of a silk sarong told him that Sunara had joined him. He half turned, and she came to him without a word and nestled into his arms, bringing the sensual tenderness which was love, and the perfume which was hers. He pressed her closely to him, feeling the child, feeling the glow of that love. But the contrast of their joy and closeness, in the private heaven of their room, and the desolate scene outside, was enough to turn all such thoughts to ashes. Who could be happy, even in paradise, when ill-starred suffering was also near enough to be touched, loud enough to be heard, vivid enough to be felt?

Sunara looked out of the window, towards the dusk and the unconcealed pain, and then she turned aside again, and laid her head against his shoulder, veiling her eyes as if such limitation of her view were all that she could bear. She said something, so low that he could not catch it; but he caught the feeling in her voice, and answered it.

'You should not be watching, my darling.'

'No one should be watching.' He could feel her troubled spirit in the very texture of her skin. 'There should not be a man in the world who could witness this without shame, without being cursed for it.'

'What about Adam?' he asked, on a sudden thought.

'I have moved his room, to the other side of the palace. Instead of this, he can look at the sea, the innocent sea ... And Manina has forbidden him the garden. He can play and walk on the other side, also.'

'Thank you for that thoughtfulness. Perhaps the two of them should go down to Kutar. Perhaps you should go also, till all this is done with.'

She nodded. 'I will think about it. Not for myself – I stay with you. But it might be better to send the boy away, for a little while.'

Richard looked from the window again. It was darker now; the dusk was almost black, waiting for the moon which would make it luminous again. But the blackness could not hide anything, from any eye which was privy to this shame. The bedevilled scene of punishment was still there, and the muttering, and the small hopeless cries.

'This is a monstrous project!' he exclaimed suddenly. 'I would shoot a man; I might even maroon a man, and leave him to starve. But by God, I would not hang him up, till he was decaying meat! And I would not do it six hundred times, if God Himself commanded me.'

She said, in a low voice, to his surprise: 'Do not hate me for this.'

'Hate you?'

'You understand my thought, Richard. My blood is the same. But I am yours now, not his.'

'You have nothing to do with this.' Even to gesture towards the Steps of Heaven was to take part in this wicked charade. 'This is your father's iniquity, not yours ...' He sighed, deeply moved, wishing above everything that the moment could pass away, and that the precious innocence of Makassang – sometimes only briefly glimpsed, but real none the less – could be re-established. 'There is one thing that can give us comfort – and them too. They will die quickly.'

Sunara waited a long time before answering him with a small, guilty shake of the head.

'I do not think that is my father's plan.'

It was not her father's plan, and in the succeeding days Richard felt himself a childish fool even to have imagined it. Next morning, the Rajah was early upon the scene, walking about his 'garden' like some benign landowner seeking to enjoy and perhaps improve his property. Colonel Kedah followed him, and took note of his suggestions – a cross to be moved here, some steps to be swept clean of blood droppings there, a nailed arm which had worked free during the night's restlessness and must be made secure and symmetrical again. There were even arrangements for the cultivation of this plot. Each cross was to be dowsed with water once a day, to cleanse it and perhaps to revive its burden; and each prisoner was to receive a daily allowance of water, as much as he could consume at one administering, for as long as he lived. But he was not to receive it on the first day. The first day was to be experimental, and punitive.

Colonel Kedah, dismissed, returned to the palace to make his arrangements; while the Rajah, still in his mood of large benevolence, continued his stroll about the Steps of Heaven. Already he had favourites, among his planted flowers; and upon these he gazed with a connoisseur's delight. There was a tall lanky priest, on whom the dread intimations of his mortality had already settled: his face had become a mask of horror and pain; even his shaven head, lolling downwards, managed to add something to this extremity of holy agony, proclaiming that it had begun to destroy even his pious fortitude – that the portals of heaven, or whatever he hoped for, suddenly, seemed too strait for human endurance. There was a fat man, a veritable balloon of woe, whose writhing, jerking flesh, most pitiful in aspect, could not fail to make him a monstrous figure of fun. And there was always Black Harris, in his position of honour, to which the Rajah returned again and again, reserving his most baleful scrutiny for this arch-enemy.

Black Harris's wiry body, brutally mishandled as it was, seemed likely to endure for a long time. He had lost some blood, and the wound in his groin – more of a branding than a wound, and already the target for marching armies of ants – presented a frightful aspect. But over the years he had been hardened to endure many such wounds, many such nights of torment; though it could hardly be said that he had ever been in a worse case than this, yet pain and wounds were no strangers to him, nor desperate ordeals either. The Rajah noted with approval that, keeping his wits even now, Black Harris was doing his best to distribute the fearful strains of his position equally over his whole body, so that his legs and feet took their share of the burden, and no one limb was called upon to outlast another. Such prudence, thought the Rajah, argued a will to live which was just what his garden needed ... Taking his farewell at last, the Rajah bent a final gaze on Black Harris, and found that the pirate's eyes had opened, and that the gaze was being returned.

'I wish you long life,' said the Rajah, using the traditional Malay salutation which implied a real and warm interest in the welfare of the person addressed. Then, with a stately nod, as if to a valued acquaintance who would never be wholly absent from his mind, the Rajah left the Steps of Heaven, and walked across the lawn to the Sun Palace.

It chanced that Richard met him under the entrance portico – Richard who, sick of the infected air, had taken a dawn ride down to the Kutar coast and back, in search of relief for a most uneasy night. The brisk movement, and the clean wind rushing past his face when his horse was stretched to full gallop, had been briefly exhilarating; but now, drawing near to this shrine of cruelty again, he found his spirits ebbing once more. It was with a sombre look that he noted the Rajah coming from the direction of the Steps of Heaven. So early in the morning – the old man must have the stomach of an ox. Richard, greeting his father-in-law with formal courtesy, found him, as he had suspected, to be in the highest spirits.

'I bid you good morning, Tunku,' returned the Rajah, with something like heartiness in his manner. 'You have enjoyed your ride? I hope it will give you an appetite for whatever the rest of the day provides.'

'I have little appetite,' answered Richard, not disguising his low spirit. From where they stood under the arched portico, he could see the topmost crosses on the Steps of Heaven, and in particular the gaunt ebony cross of Black Harris. The sight, after the freshness of the morning on the Kutar beaches, struck him with sudden disgust, and he spoke what was in the forefront of his mind. 'Who could have an appetite,' he asked, with bitterness, 'when he has a sight such as this set before him as well?'

The Rajah's eyebrows lifted, in what seemed like genuine surprise. 'Do you not like my new garden?' he asked. 'The utmost care has gone to its planting ... Surely you are glad to see these traitors undergoing their punishment? They have deserved every moment of it! And Black Harris, your oldest enemy of all? Would you not rather have him where he is, than playing the pirate in your own ship?'

Richard frowned. 'Oh, I am glad enough that they have been brought to book. But I have no taste for punishment like this. A quick end is what these wretches deserve. Anything else is needless cruelty.'

'It is not cruelty at all,' said the Rajah, in the same surprised tone, as if he could not comprehend Richard's objections. 'It is justice ... They tried to kill us, and they failed. Now we will kill them.'

'Then let us kill them,' returned Richard. 'Not play with them.'

'I do not understand you, Tunku,' said the Rajah, with his first touch of asperity. It was as if his pleasure were endangered, and might be spoiled altogether if the manner of it came under criticism. 'Why should we give these carrion a merciful death? Would they have given it to us? They would have taken the two of us, and boiled us, to make cooking oil for a Land-Dyak feast! I tell you' – he pointed, with vehemence, towards the Steps of Heaven – 'not a man there shall die until he has learned his lesson! And the longer the lesson, the better I shall be pleased.'

Richard shrugged. His muscles were stiffening after the dawn's hard riding, and the sweat drying on his silk shirt was clammy and unpleasant. He wanted peace, and a scented bath, and solitude with Sunara. Yet it was difficult to turn his eyes and his mind, away from the agonies of the Steps of Heaven, towards such promised ease. Some men deserved to live, and some to die. But none deserved to have their death eked out over ten thousand miserable pulse-beats.

'It is your Highness's affair,' he said at last, using a formal phrase. 'I have said what is in my mind.' He looked once more, briefly, towards the tall grove of crosses. 'Those poor devils are quiet enough, in any case.'

'These are early days,' answered the Rajah. The word 'days', in this connection, conveyed a latent, terrible significance, though Richard tried to ignore it. 'They are quiet, because they are resigned. But it is a mistake to become resigned too early.' His old face, in the fresh morning sunlight, took on a seriousness almost holy in its contemplation. 'I have had some experience in these matters, and I am not surprised that our friends are quiet now. But I look forward to a change of tune.' His head was inclined to one side, as if he heard the promised subtleties of that melodious change already. 'I fancy that they will begin to cry out tomorrow evening, after the heat of the midday sun.'

It was as the Rajah, that cunning judge of men and affairs, forecast. The climbing sun next day, unrelieved by cloud, smiting downwards in burnished wrath, began to drive men mad. There developed, slowly at first, and then in terrible crescendo, a wailing and a sobbing on the slopes of the Steps of Heaven, a cursing and a screaming, a low-pitched groaning of strong men, a high piercing appeal from the weak and the tormented. It grew and grew, towards twilight, until the whole of the steps was filled with its monstrous clamour.

It stilled somewhat as dusk fell, though during the night it was never less than a sad, prayerful muttering, most penetrating on the night breeze. In the morning, it grew again; it even seemed to be revived by the attention of the gardeners, unmoved men who sprayed their withering plants with a miserly hand, while the Rajah, walking abroad, watched their ministrations and took full enjoyment from the delights which had been set before him.

Thus the noise rose and fell; brutally loud by day, stilled to a hopeless sighing by night. It was a noise which could not be excluded from Richard's apartments, nor indeed from any part of the Sun Palace; in its terrible penetration, it became as much a part of their lives as the coming of day and night themselves. Such continued and pitiful appeal was truly unendurable; and it was on the third afternoon, when, by the Rajah's attentive reckoning, there were still more than five hundred crazed wretches left alive, that Richard found he could tolerate it no longer.

After talking with Sunara – a wan and pale Sunara, now near her time, shielding the precious life within her from the dominant ugliness without – he strode down from his chambers, and confronted the Rajah, who was sitting contentedly with Colonel Kedah in one of the lawn bowers, listening to the rise and fall of his villainous orchestra.

The Rajah looked up as Richard approached and made his bow. If he saw anything amiss in the younger man's expression, he took no notice of it; instead, he motioned to one of the rattan cane lounging chairs by his side, and invited him to join their company.

'You are welcome, Tunku,' he said, in the customary words. 'I had been expecting you to change your mind, and decide to enjoy our simple pastime. Look at that fellow there!' He pointed with his stick at his favourite, the fat man, who had now been reduced to a jelly of quivering pain. 'Is not that the most ridiculous sight imaginable? He looks for all the world like a pig hung up by its trotters!'

Richard stared straight at the Rajah, not meeting his mood, not accepting the proffered chair. 'Sir, he is a man, after all.'

'He thought he was a man,' the Rajah corrected, though still ignoring Richard's unusual manner. 'But fate has decided otherwise. Just as it has for all the rest. They have all come to their point of change.' He gestured round the disgusting landscape, with all its hideous clamour. 'Hear that homage!' he exclaimed. 'Listen to those loyal voices! Could you wish for anything more satisfying?' His eyes flickered upwards, surveying this young man whom he knew perfectly well to be divided from his own thoughts and feelings, by a chasm of instinct. 'Could you wish for anything more just?'

Richard contained himself with an effort, as duty warred with distaste. 'Justice should be swift,' he answered. 'Or so I have been taught.'

Now Colonel Kedah spoke, for the first time. He had been watching Richard carefully, as a man watches another man who may be a hidden rival, and who may also betray some flaw which will repay careful scrutiny. In the last few days, Kedah had continued his coldness towards Richard; but it had remained on a basis of prudence, as if he were feeling his way towards a settled enmity, making sure of his allies – and the greatest of these could be the greatest in the land, the Rajah himself – before committing himself to the alienation of a powerful friend. Now it seemed that he had grown more sure of his position, or more adventurous; for his words, aimed at Richard, conveyed a clear contempt, from which it would be difficult to retreat with any sort of grace.

'I do not think the Tunku is at one with us over this matter,' he said – and with the slight emphasis on the word 'us' he made clear his own alignment. 'I fancy he finds us lacking in such Western qualities as mercy and forgiveness.' His cold eye came round to Richard like the beam of a searching light, probing for weakness or self-betrayal. 'Is not that so? You would be happier if this' – he gestured before him – 'this punishment had never taken place at all.'

Richard decided to make the plunge, and his tone was purposefully cold. 'It is true that I do not care for senseless cruelty. In fact, it sickens me.'

'Sickens?' queried Kedah, with an equal coldness. 'That is hardly fit talk for a fighting man, surely? Is a fighting man sickened by blood? Not by the blood of his enemies!' Kedah smiled round about him, calling the Rajah's attention to his sarcasm – and to his loyalty also. 'This is a strange moment to show a weak stomach!'

'Call it what you will,' answered Richard indifferently. 'I take no pleasure in cruelty, and I am not ashamed to say so, before all the world.'

'And your son also?' It was Kedah again, pressing his advantage. 'Are you teaching him to be squeamish?' He used a vile word which had connotations of cowardice as well. 'I understand that you have sent him away.'

'I have sent him away.'

'Perhaps,' said Kedah, with pointed malice, 'you should also send away the Fifty of the Brave. One cannot be certain, can one, even where such resounding titles are concerned? Your Fifty may prove to be squeamish in the same way, and for the same reasons.'

He spoke, as Richard well realized, from the fullness of a bitter heart. Though Kedah had played an essential and gallant part in the battle of a short time ago, he had not been in the forefront, at the storming of the Shwe Dagon; the public champions of that action were Richard, and Amin Sang, and the fifty men who had met at the crest of the pagoda; and Colonel Kedah, assigned to a more pedestrian role, resented fiercely the fact that other men had won the laurels of the day and become the acknowledged victors.

In fact, the designation 'The Fifty of the Brave,' which had come into being naturally and innocently, had excited Kedah's special jealousy from the very beginning, and this was not the first time that he had used it in an odious sense, as if the fame it advertised were false and the reputed action far in advance of reality. Richard, stung to anger, was about to return a trenchant answer, both for his son and for the Fifty; but before he could do so, the Rajah intervened.

He might have made such a move before, thought Richard swiftly, if he had not perhaps been enjoying the exchange, taking malicious pleasure in this added spectacle. Now he raised his hand commandingly.

'I have heard enough,' he said. Though he did not address either of them by name or by glance, it seemed clear to Richard that the rebuke was intended for himself. He stiffened to meet it; his own anger had been directed at Colonel Kedah, but perhaps the time had come to bring it to bear on others as well. 'I have heard enough,' the Rajah repeated. 'These are my prisoners, convicted of treachery against my person, and the penalty for that is what you see. And what you hear,' he added, with a faint smile, as a long wailing cry came from one of the nearby crosses. 'I do not want to listen to talk of mercy. I prefer to listen to this.'

'And I,' said Kedah. 'Treason must be punished, rooted out.' His single eye was grim and intent as it rested on Richard. 'In the highest, and in the lowest.'

Richard decided to ignore him; instead, he addressed himself to the Rajah. 'I would ask your Highness to hear me,' he said, and his tone was not humble or suppliant. 'These are your prisoners, certainly, but I have done my share towards their defeat. I ask that, having been vilely punished for three days, they now be executed.'

'No,' said the Rajah.

'Sir – '

'No!' repeated the Rajah, with sudden venom. 'Do I have to say a thing ten times, before it becomes clear? I am not used to argument … Their punishment will continue, for as long as I please. Let us have no more of this. It does not concern you.'

'It concerned me very closely,' answered Richard tartly, 'when there was fighting to be done.'

The Rajah stared back at Richard, in icy anger. 'Silence! Did you not hear me say that I have had enough? You become arrogant – arrogant, and interfering. And why are you suddenly so tender? Is it because that man' – he pointed towards the cross of Black Harris, a drooping, motionless emblem of death – 'is in fact near your heart? Did he try what you did not have the courage to try?'

'That is absurd!' exclaimed Richard, provoked to fury. 'Who can doubt my loyalty? I have shed my blood in your service! I have as much sympathy with Black Harris as your Highness himself! Of course he deserves to die. But – '

'Then let him die,' interrupted Kedah, 'at his own pace – and ours. Do not come to his aid, like a woman nursing a sick child.'

'I am not "coming to his aid",' said Richard, almost snarling. 'I am the one who brought him to his cross! If you can match that service, you have a right to speak. If not, be good enough to hold your tongue!'

They had come to the verge of open warfare. 'One man did not defeat Black Harris,' said Colonel Kedah, and it was clear that he was speaking once again with bitter feeling. 'Not even one so exalted as yourself. Not fifty men so exalted ... I have as much right to speak as you ...' He was coldly, enormously angry; his breath and his speech were forced from him with an effort, as if they were dammed up within. 'More right, because I follow his Highness in all things, without question, without lagging ... If you cannot bear to see your friend suffer, you should join your son down at Kutar.'

If he had had a sword or a cutlass, Richard Marriott would have drawn it at that moment, so enraged was he by this insolence. But he was unarmed, as was Colonel Kedah; all they could do, having reached the limit of words, was to glare at each other with the hatred of men whom nothing could now reconcile. Into this furious scene, the Rajah stepped once more. But as their anger had grown, his own appeared to have ebbed; his tone was good-humouredly chiding, nothing more.

'Enough, enough,' he said. 'You spoil my day with your wrangling ...' Far down the Steps of Heaven, among the lowest of the crosses, a distant wailing broke out, borne on the summer air like the wafting of smoke. The Rajah, his attention caught by it, rose from his chair. 'Kedah, we must not neglect those lower slopes. They are as fine, sturdy fellows down there, as those in the places of honour.' He turned to Richard. 'You will join us, Tunku?'

'I thank you, no,' muttered Richard, still robbed by his anger of words to suit the occasion.

'You are in danger of missing the rarest of pleasures,' observed the Rajah. 'But I will not press you ... Come, we waste a fine evening. Let us walk.'

Now the cries from the Steps of Heaven came in short swelling bursts of agony, in concerted wails which were taken up by every man who still had a voice, as if the jointure of their appeal might melt some stony heart. But always, at each awakening, the sound would waver away to nothing, as the torture sapping the prisoners' strength showed its terrible toll. Often silence would reign for an hour or more, a settled stillness more frightful than sound itself; and then some tormented slave would snatch back his soul and find his voice, and give a sobbing cue to his companions. At this signal, the clamour would mount, and burst into desperate entreaty, and dwindle down to silence once more.

Gradually the bloody turmoil simmered away into a hopeless endurance. Taunted by draughts of water, taunted also by the holidaymakers who were allowed by the Rajah to spend their daytime leisure and enjoy their family meals on the steps, the prisoners clung to the last of their lives, in grisly belief that even this skeleton survival might be sweeter than death. More than a hundred still remained, hung upon nails, suspended in this idiot delusion of hope. It was the evening of the fifth day.

On that night, Richard could not sleep. He would doze, and wake sweating from some monstrous nightmare of pursuit and slaughter, and lie listening – listening to Sunara's light breathing beside him, and to the silence, and then, time and again, to the thin far cries of men in their last extremity. Sometimes he rose, and went into a neighbouring room, and drank deep from a carafe of the heavy rice wine, seeking to drown the pitiful clamour, which sounded louder each time it was heard. He could have wished for company – not the company of Sunara, who was too loving and too tender for this brutal hour, but John Keston (who had gone down to Kutar with the boy Adam and Manina), or Amin Sang, faithful friend, valiant soldier, whose guard duty had taken him elsewhere in the palace.

But he was doomed to be alone; alone with the wine which could not drug his senses, and with his rank and power, which could neither save life nor snuff it out, and with the silences, which did not endure long enough to bring even a hint of the mercy of peace.

Towards morning he rose from his daybed, sending a half empty wineglass crashing to the polished teak floor, and stretched, and listened, and stared about him, stupid with sleeplessness, possessed by an unplanned impulse of action. Then he said, aloud: 'It is enough,' and he sought out his pistols, and loaded them, and strapped them on. Then, walking as lightly as he could, with the wine and his heavy spirit weighing him down, he descended the wide staircase, and went out into the garden.

In the sleeping palace, he had been the only one who stirred. But now, as he crossed the threshold of the main portico, and stepped on to the velvet lawn, a shadow moved, and barred his way, and a voice challenged him: 'Halt, and speak!'

It was Amin Sang.

Richard answered: 'Peace! The Tunku!' making himself known in the custom of the Royal Regiment; then he looked towards his friend, dimly seen in the darkness, and said: 'You are watchful, Amin.'

'I have the guard, Tunku.' Amin Sang lowered his short stabbing-spear, on which a flicker of reflected starlight burned briefly, and eased his determined stance. 'You are watchful also. Could you not sleep?'

Richard stared out towards the Steps of Heaven, silent now save for a snuffling and a moaning, which might grow, or might die away, as the passion for life dictated. 'Who could sleep, in this swinish place?'

It was only in speaking to this trusted man that he, the Tunku of Makassang, could venture such a form of words, which approached a traitorous edge; and Amin Sang acknowledged this confidence when he answered: 'Sleep will come, for all of us, and all of them. Do not bear it too heavily.'

Richard leant back against one of the pillars of the portico, deadly tired, deadly sick of the guilt of the punishment. 'I bear it heavily, because of the part I played, in making prisoners of these wretches.'

'You played an honourable part.'

'I wish I had played no part at all!'

There was silence; and then Amin Sang spoke, in a reasoning voice, as one might speak to a child who must be brought to know the shocks and shifts of the adult world. 'Tunku, you do not mean that. Or, if you do mean it, you are wrong. These men were enemies. Black Harris was an enemy. It was necessary to bring him to justice.'

Richard said: 'It was not necessary to torture him. Or all the rest.'

'This is a cruel land, Tunku.'

'It is people who are cruel.'

There was another heavy silence. Richard had come nearer still to treason in his speech; and this time Amin Sang, loyal and dutiful in all things, could not voice his agreement, nor even hint at it. The silence stretched, long, loaded with wild thoughts, loaded at the last with a pitiful, faraway cry in the night. At the sound, Richard collected himself, and stood upright. He knew what he had to do. It was not the whole answer; it was not even rational, or sensible, or calculated. But it was a step, a gesture: the only one he could make.

He spoke the military phrase: 'I pass your guard, Amin Sang.'

Amin Sang's voice was careful. 'You are armed, Tunku.'

'Yes.'

'Yet we are alone. My men are making the first rice, in the forecourt.'

'Yes.'

'On my life, I have not seen you.'

Almost before his voice was gone, Amin Sang was gone, withdrawing like a ghost from a world he did not wish to rule. At his going, Richard stood alone, in the garden, near to the pale dawn. It was the coldest moment of the night, the moment which could rob the fiercest warrior of his spirit. But he was prepared at last to play the man.

He walked out towards the Steps of Heaven, and the sobbing, urgent cries which by chance broke out at that moment. A sweet bird sang of the dawn, but its trilling melody was drowned and lost in ugliness and pain. The prisoners' cries grew pitiful, unbearable, then ceased on a strangled note of despair. The stench of blood and excrement was appalling. He drew near, not by chance, to the ebony cross of Black Harris. In the dawn's revealing light, the gaunt wasted figure hung like small meat in a giant slaughterhouse, awaiting, not a buyer, but a deliverer.

Richard moved forward as in a dream, and stood stock-still as in a dream. He willed the next action, the next sound; and the next sound was the sighing, croaking voice of his enemy, Black Harris, falling from above him like dew wrung out of tattered rags, saying: 'I knew you would come ... Put me away, Dick.'

Though it was what he had been expecting, though it was what he had come in search of, yet it was still a shock. He stood looking at his feet, just as the man above him looked at his feet; they were two luckless beings caught in the same agony, the captive and the free. Richard sighed; the turmoil of anger and disgust which had brought him into the garden had given place to a dull despair. His very life now seemed irrational, and overturned; here, within his grasp, was this treacherous enemy to whom he owed nothing but hatred, and he was about to show him the greatest blessing in his power – and that was only a swift passport to death. Was this what it was, to be a pirate transformed into a prince? – to command neither the ruthlessness of the one, nor the benevolent generosity of the other?

If he had remained a pirate, he would have left Black Harris where he was, to bleed out his miserable life. If he had become in truth a prince, he would have lifted him from his cross, and bandaged up his wounds. But he was trapped between these two worlds; halfway from a bloodthirsty malice, halfway to loving kindness and great mercy.

Richard shook his head. He could only do as much as fate allowed. But he knew that he was bound to this man, so much like himself, by more than hatred and a lust for revenge. They remained brothers, in spite of all the past. For a brother, one must do the best one could.

Dawn was at hand. It was light enough to see the fearful wreckage of the garden, with its multitude of drooping victims, and to see also the man above him, a figure of unnameable filth and pain.

Richard drew one of his pistols, and stepped back, and aimed. In his resolve, he had grown deadly calm, and his hand at the last was firm as a rock. He shot true. Black Harris slumped into death with no more than a rattling sigh. His jaw, now gaping, seemed to sketch the wraith of a smile as it fell.

The single shot had rung and echoed up and down the Steps of Heaven. First it was the turn of the peacocks to scream in savage surprise. Then monkeys set up a scandalized chatter, and men came running.

'Upstart!' screamed the Rajah. Robbed of his pleasure and his prey, he was beside himself with ancient fury; it seemed that he could scarcely remain seated on the ivory throne, as he cursed and upbraided Richard Marriott for his interference. 'How dare you take the law into your own hands? Who are you, to decide when a prisoner is to die? By God, I have had a man whipped to death for less than this! And do not think that I will not do so again!'

'I told your Highness what was in my mind,' answered Richard stonily. He had endured nearly an hour of questioning and probing, insult and threat; he was wearied to death of it; there was a temptation to say: I did it, and I am glad of it – now do your worst. But he could not quite bring himself to such a point of defiance: too much was at stake – he had a life to lose, he had Sunara, and the boy, and John Keston, and Amin Sang to defend. Even if he had stood alone, he would not have delivered himself over to the malice of this furious man. 'I told you I did not care for cruelty. Black Harris was dying, like all the others. All I did was to give him his death before it was due.'

'By whose authority?'

Richard shrugged. 'My own.'

The Rajah glared at him. 'You have none! There is only one man

274

who has authority in these matters. Myself! Are you seeking to take my place?'

Richard shook his head. 'I meant, the killing of Black Harris was of my own choosing. I took it upon my own conscience. I told no one what I planned.'

The Rajah's eyes bored into the man standing before him, with the most malevolent concentration. 'I am not so sure of that. There might be a plot here – a plot to challenge my rule. If there is, be sure I will find it out!' His glance became suspicious, veiled, as it had done many times during the past hour, when his mood swung like a weathercock, and rage gave way to brooding doubt. 'I will have the truth from you. How did you pass the guard?'

'I met no guard.'

'They were on duty, surrounding the palace. You must have passed them.'

'I saw no one.'

'Then Amin Sang, the guard-captain, is at fault. Or is he part of this cursed plot?'

'Sir, there was no plot.' Richard spoke warily, conscious of delicate and dangerous ground. 'I was alone. It was near dawn, and the guard were standing down, in the forecourt, making their first rice. I saw no one, and it is clear that no one saw me.'

'You lie!' shouted the Rajah, in renewed fury. 'There were voices heard. Do you think I have no loyal servants in the palace? You were heard to speak to someone. It was reported to me. Who were you speaking to?'

'I saw no one,' Richard repeated, 'and I spoke to no one. If there were voices heard, it was the prisoners crying out. God knows there was enough of that, to fill the whole palace! Or else I was speaking to myself.'

'What did you say to yourself?' asked the Rajah, in sneering contempt.

Richard stared back at him, not prepared to dissemble. 'If I said anything, I said that I had seen and heard enough of cruelty and torture.'

'The guard will be punished,' muttered the Rajah, taking up a new line of thought. 'And the guard-captain will lose his rank, if not his life. The prisoners were in his charge. I do not care what name he bears, nor to what honoured family he belongs. Treason is treason!'

'Sir,' protested Richard stoutly, 'there was no treason here, and Amin Sang is innocent. He knows nothing, and he saw nothing. He is a loyal soldier, and he has proved it, times without number. I tell you again, the killing of Black Harris was not plotted. It was my own decision.'

Now the Rajah rounded on him, working himself towards a fresh outburst. 'Do you feel yourself so strong, that you are ready to take all this blame? Have a care! I called you an upstart, and by God you are proving it true! Do you think you can escape punishment, because I took you for my son, and named you Tunku?'

'Surely a son may advise his father. Surely he may speak out, if he sees injustice.'

'He cannot advise, and he cannot speak out!' The old man's anger was reaching its peak again. 'Perhaps you have risen too quickly, to have learned the conduct of my court. A son remains a subject none the less. All my subjects, high and low, do as they are bidden. If they do not, they pay for their disobedience with their lives.'

Richard at last had had enough. He regarded the Rajah with cool temerity. 'I am ready to die,' he said, 'if you are ready to kill me.'

'Not so fast,' answered the Rajah, obscurely delaying his judgement. 'I will decide who is to die, and when ... I wish to know why you took it upon yourself to kill Black Harris, the enemy of us both.'

'Because I kill my enemies, whenever I can.'

'Do not trifle with words,' said the Rajah venomously, 'nor with myself, either ... You know well enough what I mean. Why did you cut short his punishment?'

'It was a matter of pity.'

'What has pity to do with war?'

'Your Highness, this is not war.' Richard, alone with his antagonist, made a last effort to show what was in his mind. He looked round the great audience chamber, where only the tireless arms of the punkah slaves moved, where the two of them faced each other in charged, monumental solitude. Though there were still men left alive on the Steps of Heaven, they no longer cried out; this was the last hour of the last day of punishment; death or terror had stolen all their voices. 'The war is over. It is won. Now we have nothing to fear. Now is the moment to show pity.'

'Are you teaching me how to rule?'

Hearing the barbed, blood-chilling tone, Richard sighed again. Clearly it was no use. He was wasting his time, and his wits; he might as well have bowed his head and taken his browbeating without a word of answer, like any truant schoolboy. Wearied of the futile contest, he spoke his last sentences with resigned calmness.

'I would not presume to teach your Highness anything … But for myself, I can feel pity for those I have defeated… It is not a sign of weakness, nor of treason either … Indeed, it is a measure of strength. I truly believe that compassion is a part of government.'

'Is it, in truth?' The Rajah rose from his throne; Richard noted, with concern but without surprise, that the old man was visibly trembling, as if a sudden seizure of rage had possessed his whole body. 'Let me tell you that I need no lessons in government!' He glared down at Richard, like a veritable avenging God. 'You have taken upon yourself to pardon – ' the Rajah positively spat out the absurd word, ' – to pardon a criminal who was undergoing punishment. For that you will bear the responsibility … You will be told later what my decision is, in this matter … But in the meantime' – the Rajah, descending the steps of his throne, had the murderous look of a swooping bird of prey – 'it will be my pleasure to teach you one lesson, at least. I will teach you how to govern Makassang. And that without pity, Tunku – without pity!'

'I angered him,' said Richard, in the miserable knowledge of his guilt. He was aware, now, that his enterprise of killing Black Harris had been stupid and ill-advised; he had acted on impulse, under pressures of feeling which now seemed foolish and childlike; if he could have gone back over that fatal ground, he would have blocked his ears, forgotten his nature, and done nothing. But how could he have guessed this hideous outcome? 'I angered him, and this is the result.' He took Sunara's hand, needing above all her comfort and her understanding. 'If this is what happens when one counsels pity, then God help us all!'

It was a true prayer, spoken from the very heart. Richard had never been so shocked as he had been, during the past few days, when the royal anger had reached its odious peak. The Rajah, baulked of the pleasures of one particular revenge, had set himself to seek other avenues; it seemed that he must compensate for what he had lost in the untimely death of his principal enemy, by all the means which a harsh nature could devise. Wanton cruelty had run its gamut: appointing Colonel Kedah as his chief executioner, he had embarked on an unspeakable programme of torture and punishment. As the crucified flowers in his garden one by one withered and died, he had replaced them by others; there had been vast forays in search of enemies and 'spies'; the palace dungeons resounded to the cries of men, young and old, who had been brought there by the capricious will of a tyrant, and detained in agony and fear to slake his pleasure.

Richard had not entered any further protest, nor even indicated his aversion; he was convinced that he had done enough harm already, and must be content to watch the reaping of the vicious harvest he had sown. To be such a spectator was made unexpectedly easy for him; within a short space, the Rajah seemed to have forgotten his earlier, furious rage over Richard's interference; in manner he had grown jovial and benign, as if, feeding on blood, he had become full of good humour also. Or it might be that he was beginning to discount Richard, and his thoughts and opinions, as elements which need not be taken seriously in the adult realm of kingship.

He did not seek his adopted son's company, nor did he avoid it; he seemed to take it for granted that all was well with the world, and that any misgivings of Richard's had been matters of small moment, short-lived qualms which might be overlooked in an accepted climate of retribution and terror. For his enemies, real or imagined, the old man reserved his most vicious scale of reprisal; for all others, a royal goodwill now seemed to be the rule.

'It is not your fault,' Sunara now told Richard, returning the hungry pressure of his hand. 'You did what you thought right – it was an act of pity – it was right!' Her lovely face, which now, towards the end of her time, was often frail and transparent, glowed with sudden warmth and feeling. 'I am proud of what you did, in spite of what followed. It was merciful, and brave!'

'It did no good.'

'It did good to one man, and that is more than all the sum of what is happening now.' She leant against him, seeking to give every comfort in her power. 'You know that I was awake when you went down to the steps, Tuan?'

He was surprised. 'I thought you fast asleep.'

She shook her head. 'I knew what you had in mind. You had been crying out in your sleep, as if you could not endure your dreams. Then you were wakeful, and restless. I knew that you would do something.'

'You should have prevented me.'

'I would not have prevented you, for all the wealth of Makassang!'

He put his arms round her, in thankful tenderness. This was the most loving woman in the whole world. 'But what now, Sunara? Will it always be like this? Is this how he will rule?'

'I fear so. I think it will be rule by terror, as it was in the old days – by terror and by spying. Perhaps it has reached us already. You know that it was a spy who reported what you did?'

'I thought something of the sort. There was a watchfulness about the whole palace, that night. But I was not in the mood to creep about, or to dissemble.'

She looked up at him. 'We may have to dissemble, in the future.'

'What do you mean?'

'If my father has spies, then we must have spies of our own.' Her words struck him with astonishment; this new world, suddenly glimpsed, of calculated plotting and intrigue was alien to all his nature, and to all his expectation too. The peace and happiness which he had hoped for seemed to be receding, rather than drawing nearer; at this strange pace, the longer he stayed in Makassang, the less likely he was to achieve the contentment on which he had set his heart ... But because he loved Sunara, and because she was so deeply involved in all these affairs, he softened the expressions of dismay which had all but sprung to his lips.

'I had hoped, my darling,' he told her, 'that we could live together, and be happy in our love, and enjoy our lives, without ever being troubled by such matters. I hoped that we had reached our safe haven.'

'You cannot have hoped it more than I.' It was clear that she had given much secret thought to what she was saying; her tone was full of brooding contemplation. 'But lately I have lost heart ... We know that Kedah is working against you. And my father is changing, too – now he prefers to govern by fear ... It may be – ' her voice trailed into silence, as her latent doubts multiplied.

'What may be?'

'It may be that it will come to a struggle.' She was speaking to herself rather than to Richard. 'Of course, we are not powerless. We have spies of our own, and friends too. We have Manina, and John Keston, and Amin Sang. We have the Fifty of the Brave. There are countless men who will follow you without question. We need not – '

'Sunara, Sunara!' he interrupted her. 'You cannot be serious! You talk as if we were still at war. This is not the life we have planned together. What have I to do with spies and followers? I want peace, and love, and you, and the children!'

'You may yet have to fight for all of them,' she said stubbornly. 'Do you think they will be served to you on a golden platter?'

He was taken aback. 'I have fought already, for peace and for all the rest. Surely it is over now? Surely I have fought enough?'

'This is Makassang,' she declared. He had never heard her voice so bitter; he knew that it must relate to the child she carried, and her primal need to guard its life. 'You are not living in some sleepy, comfortable English world ...' Catching his look, she softened momentarily. 'Forgive me, Richard – my thoughts are too much for my tongue ... But you were my father's favourite, and now you have lost favour. You know what that means? It is as if you had landed in Makassang this very morning. You heard him tell how such invaders were dealt with. That was in the old days. But do not be so sure that the old days have changed.'

'He cannot have such things in mind.' Richard was appalled, not only by these astonishing thoughts, but also by the fact that Sunara could think them, and voice them, with such rare freedom. It was something in her which he had never suspected, and now could scarcely comprehend. 'He has made me welcome, he has done me the greatest possible honour, he has blessed our marriage – '

'And he has changed his mind!' Now it was her turn to interrupt, and she did so with passionate fervour. 'I know him, Richard. In his old age, he has been taken with the mood to surprise and to shock even me, his only child ... When all these punishments and tortures have run their course, he will turn to something else. I have a terrible fear that this something else will be – '

Her voice broke off, on a single instant of time, as her acute hearing caught a soft footfall outside their apartments. Silence, suspect and dangerous in its falsity, fell between them; and then Richard, turning, was in time to see Colonel Kedah brush aside the light silk curtains, and present himself on their threshold.

Though his face was impassive, his single eye, sardonic and calculating, surveyed them in a manner which might have brought disquiet to the most innocent.

'Forgive me for intruding on your privacy,' he said. The silky voice was an insult itself. 'But I bear a message from his Highness.'

Richard stared back, not disguising his cold dislike. 'You do not intrude … We are not private here, as must be obvious … What is your message?'

'It is an invitation,' answered Kedah. Insolently sure of himself, he gave not an inch of ground. 'His Highness invites you to witness the punishment of the last of the Shwe Dagon traitors.'

'What punishment is this? And what traitor?'

'The fat man. You remember the fat man?' Richard could readily have strangled Kedah, for his tone of voice and the disdainful look which accompanied it. 'You must have noted that he has been his Highness's favourite, for a very long time.'

'I thought by now that there was no one left alive, on the steps.'

'Care and skill have preserved this one … But he is the very last. It is his Highness's opinion,' said Kedah, vilely matter-of-fact, 'that there will be sufficient time to flay him alive.'

§

2

It was a boy, a pale petal of a child with Sunara's enormous eyes and the promise of his father's sturdy frame. Richard Marriott, possessed by wonder, gazed down at it with a bursting heart, near to tears. The tiny puckered face and the soft limbs were infinitely moving; as the infant lay cradled in Sunara's arms, the two of them together seemed to sum up all that he hoped of life, all that he most loved and most cherished. In this broad bed, he thought, lay everything a man could desire, and more than he could deserve.

Then he remembered Adam, his firstborn, and thought: There is room for him, too, in this close-coupled private world – thanks be to God, and to Sunara.

Richard was near to tears for another, more potent reason. It had been a most difficult birth: Sunara's small frame, apt for love, was not apt for child-bearing; she had been more than a day in labour, and her lovely face, grey with exhaustion, seemed to become the more drained of life as she strove to give life to the world. Manina, attending her, using a woman's skill in a woman's dolorous world, had not slept for forty hours or more; she suffered even as the Princess, her mistress, suffered, bearing in her dried up, wizened old body all the writhing pains which Sunara herself had to bear. Richard, feeling foolish and guilty at the same moment, underwent an almost unbearable torment of spirit as he watched his wife enduring her prolonged agony.

Her time had come upon her, as the monsoon was at last about to break. The skies were laden and lowering, the air heavy, the heat monstrous; every normal movement, much less every pain of labour, was enough to start a drenching sweat. In this tense and oppressive stillness, it seemed as if nature herself could not relent, as if the world would grow hotter and hotter, and heavier and heavier, until its very fabric melted and the people gasped and died. But then there had been a rolling crack of thunder, and a terrifying play of lightning about the palace rooftops; and then came sudden swamping relief.

With the skies streaming, and the parched earth resounding to a million pattering drumbeats, the child was delivered, and gave its first cry.

Now, looking down at them with tenderness and joy, Richard bent and kissed her brow. Sunara was still drowsy from her first exhausted sleep; her violet eyelids fluttered against the light before her eyes opened. Then she saw him, and her mouth curved to a loving smile.

'Tuan … We have our son.'

'Yes, Sunara.' Richard brushed the tears from his eyes with a candid, undisguised movement. 'He is beautiful, and you are beautiful too.'

She was looking down at the tiny body nestling in the crook of her arm. 'He is in your image, I think. But after all, he is so small.'

'He will grow to a giant … But tell me how you feel, my dearest one.'

'Tired. Though very happy.' Her brow wrinkled. 'What is that strange noise?'

'The monsoon rains.' The steady drumming on the roof had increased to a hissing roar; from the garden, the rain streaming down upon a thousand leaves was to be heard everywhere. 'It broke at last, a few hours back.'

She sighed. 'May it wash us all clean again.'

He too, aware of the sluicing downpour of the rain, had been thinking of the Steps of Heaven.

'With the new child,' he comforted her, 'comes a new beginning.' He sat down in a low chair by the bedside, and reached over to take her hand. His forearm rested momentarily on the tiny form of his son; it seemed the sweetest contact of his life. 'You must think of nothing except to rest, and be strong again. Then nothing can mar our happiness, and no force in the world can take it away from us.'

He would have said more, from the fullness of his heart. But the old nurse Manina, who had been crouching in one corner of the room, a forbidding presence in their loving Eden, now came forward to the foot of the bed.

'It is time for sleep,' she said. Her croaking voice had a strange, undeniable authority. 'The Tunku must be pleased to leave us now.'

'But the Princess is resting,' protested Richard.

'Resting is not enough.' Manina regarded him with fierce, resentful eyes. You men! her glance seemed to say: you take your pleasure in us, you wear us out with labour, then you would kill us with talking … 'It is not enough,' she repeated. 'The Princess must have the sleep she deserves, after all she has suffered.'

'Very well,' answered Richard. He could not argue; this was a woman's barred realm; he had no place in it, and no rank either. He pressed Sunara's hand in farewell. 'I will return, later this evening.'

'Tomorrow, at noon,' said Manina.

Sunara smiled. 'You see how I am guarded … Has Adam visited

his brother?'

'Yes. He came with me, the first moment he could.'

'What did he say?'

'He said, "When will he walk?" '

Sunara's eyes fluttered and closed again; she was once more drowsy with the healing drugs which were Manina's secret. 'Bring him with you, the next time,' she whispered sleepily, turning her head on to the pillow. Her voice, fading, seemed to come from some faraway country where all was deep relief. 'Bring him to see us ... He must be sure of our love ... It is important that we are all one.'

For a space, it seemed as if it were indeed a new beginning. On seeing this, his first grandchild, some flicker of ancient pride took possession of the Rajah's spirit, and fired it with a dynastic fervour. At this first flush, he could not do enough to honour the new birth.

The instant it became known that a boy had been born in the line of succession, benevolent commands began to flow from the palace. All captives were set free, in a general amnesty which for several hours thronged the streets of the capital with a horde of miserable wretches blinking up at the sun. Three days of public holidaymaking were decreed; and to aid in their observance, a hundred casks of wine and a thousand bushels of rice were distributed to the poor. At the Sun Palace, a week of feasting culminated in a vast ceremonial procession to celebrate the naming of the child.

Makassang had not seen such a show in a generation. There were eighty elephants painted in gold and scarlet; bullocks with ochre muzzles and silvered horns drawing wagonloads of the palace slave dancers, who showered the crowds with magnolia and poinsettia blooms; and towering golden shrines in the shape of the Shwe Dagon, each carried on the backs of a hundred bearers, like a vast litter for the Lord Buddha himself. Basketfuls of silver coins were flung to the mob at each fifty paces. The procession wound for three hours, like an enormous brilliant serpent, through the streets of Prahang, while the gongs sounded and the pipes played their sweetest melodies. Then it made its slow ascent to the Sun Palace, honouring the firstborn grandchild with all the barbarous pomp which the island kingdom could furnish.

At the final ceremony, the child was named Presatsang, which was the name of the Rajah's own son, long dead in battle. In the public proclamations, the title Rajah Muda – that is, the Young Rajah – was used.

Later, on the evening of this great day, when dusk had fallen upon the scene of rejoicing, Richard Marriott looked down on the vast throng of celebrants in the palace gardens, and watched the multitude of flickering torches, and heard the shouting and the laughter, and felt his heart swell with pride and happiness. At this moment of honour, the omens seemed all good, all auspicious. Presatsang had come to a fine inheritance; from now onwards. Richard himself, and Sunara, and the two boys might hope for happiness, in a country plainly fashioned, like paradise, for such joys and such fulfilment.

He was to remember that night later, with mourning and a sense of loss, for there was never another like it, in all his days in Makassang.

For a full week after the naming ceremony, it was noted that the Rajah kept to his apartments; he received no one save Colonel Kedah and his major-domo, and he paid no visits, not even to the nursery suite where Presatsang was installed in the customary state of new babies, surrounded by his idolaters. But Richard thought little of this – the old man was doubtless tired after the festivities, and would make his appearance when he had recovered his strength. When he did make his appearance, however, it was clear that his mood had swung, as it had done so many times in the past, away from a brief benevolence and towards its brooding opposite. His time in seclusion seemed to have been fed on suspicion and jealousy, and on nothing else.

There had been no inkling of this; a week earlier, the Rajah had appeared as eager as anyone in the palace to take part in the joyful ceremonial. A most trivial occasion, which was magnified into wretched embarrassment, served to mark the turning point.

It was a late afternoon in the royal nursery, shortly before one of the day's important occasions – the baby's evening bath. Richard and Sunara were there, and Amin Sang – the 'double-uncle', as Adam now called him – and Adam himself, and Manina, giving grudging leave for the spectators to witness this act of worship. It was very much a family party, relaxed and intimate; and the parents watched amusedly as Amin Sang instructed Adam in a new form of 'guard duty' – a formal patrol round the curtained crib in which Presatsang lay.

Adam, now a sturdy five-year-old, was taking his martial duties seriously. He marched with small, swaggering steps round a designated square, halting and grounding his miniature spear at each corner; from time to time Amin Sang called out appropriate orders, in the manner of a guard-commander disposing of his men. Intent on the play, none of them noticed the Rajah enter silently and stand by the doorway, watching the scene. Indeed, it was Adam himself who first discovered his presence, and that most unfortunately. The little boy was over-excited, and he was, in the manner of children attracting too much grown-up attention, 'showing-off' to his audience. Suddenly he broke off his march, with a look of theatrical alarm, and ran over to the doorway, his small spear thrust forward in a position of attack. Then he shouted: 'On guard – an enemy!' and brandished the spear in the Rajah's face.

In a certain mood, the Rajah would have laughed, while scolding him, and the others would have joined in without hesitation. But it was obvious that the Rajah's mood was not of this quality. He remained standing in an attitude of frozen dignity, staring down at Adam who, aware now of an enormous breach of etiquette, stood stock-still in sudden fright. Under the Rajah's bleak gaze, the innocent game became transformed and ugly; the comfortable ease of the room was swiftly destroyed, and danger put into its place. Richard, rising to greet the Rajah, was aware of sharp discomfort.

'Good evening, your Highness – ' he began.

The Rajah gestured for silence, which was itself an unlooked for insult. He remained staring down at Adam, whose lips, in a face turned scarlet, were already trembling. Then he said, in a soft and terrible voice: 'What did you call me, boy?'

Adam stood transfixed; his toy spear dropped to the floor with a clatter; he would have turned and run, if he had been able. Richard made as if to step forward, angry, ready to rescue and protect his son; but it was Sunara who put an effective end to the scene. She gave a swift sign to Manina, who gathered up the baby and bore it towards another room. Then she called out firmly: 'Adam! Go with Manina.'

It was a very ready small boy who bowed quickly to the Rajah, and turned, and scurried after his nurse.

Sunara, who had also risen from the daybed on which she had been resting, tried to guide them all past the dangerous corner, towards safety.

'Forgive him,' she said to her father. 'He was over-excited with the game.'

The Rajah looked round the room, slowly and deliberately. From his manner, Richard now found it easy to imagine his mood, and the elements which had gone to its making. He had come upon them unawares, and had watched their innocent enjoyment as a happy family circle. Surveying them in secret, he had seen a daughter, a son, two grandsons, and a guard-captain who, with the status of uncle, was clearly admitted to special privileges. Their unity must have seemed so obvious that, like many a grandfather before him, he had felt totally excluded. Adam's foolish utterance of the word 'enemy' could only have seemed especially pointed, at the moment of its use.

Richard was about to make his contribution towards smoothing over the moment, when the Rajah himself spoke. He addressed Sunara, in freezing dignity.

'I gave no leave to withdraw.'

'I am sorry, Father,' said Sunara. She did not sound sorry, but rather detached from the scene, as if it could be of little importance. 'I thought it best to dispense with formality. Adam was frightened.'

'He showed good sense in that.'

After the grim comment, the Rajah's eyes moved on; now it was the turn of Amin Sang to submit to their scrutiny. The young guard-captain was standing at attention, as palace etiquette required; and the Rajah stared at him for a full minute before breaking the silence. When he spoke, it was in a voice of silky disdain which Richard had heard many times before, and never on any happy occasion.

'You have been giving some additional training in guard duty, Captain?'

Amin Sang looked straight ahead. 'Yes, your Highness.'

'With what purpose?'

'It was a game, your Highness.'

'A game?'

'We were pretending to guard the – the Rajah Muda.'

'The Rajah Muda.' The old man mouthed the phrase as if it were indecent. 'Since when did the Rajah Muda stand in need of guarding? And from whom?'

'It was a game, your Highness,' said Amin Sang again.

'Was it a part of the game, to teach him to call me "enemy"?' Amin Sang drew in his breath; there was such sudden spite in the Rajah's voice that he did not know how to answer. The silence stretched to ominous lengths. Richard made as if to intervene, and then checked himself. Once again, he would do more harm than good, if he took any part in such a scene. However unjust or offensive it became, it was something which must run its course.

'I do not like your game, Captain,' said the Rajah at last, 'and I do not like to see my officers so foolishly employed. Have you no present duty?'

'Not until sunset, your Highness.'

'We must devise something ... You will report yourself to Colonel Kedah.'

'Yes, your Highness.'

'Tell him of my displeasure.'

'Yes, your Highness.'

'Tell him also that I am dissatisfied with the cleanliness of the stables.'

Amin Sang saluted, his face burning, and strode from the room without another word. Richard clenched his hands tightly, finding it difficult to let pass what had been said and done; the insulting tone, and the promise of the insulting task, were alike intolerable. But if he tried to intervene, worse might befall his friend ... Holding his temper in check, he presently looked up, to find that the Rajah's eyes were now fixed balefully on himself.

'I am astonished,' said the Rajah, 'that you should encourage such behaviour in your son.'

Richard still held his tongue, fearing to speak anything at all. But Sunara, who had returned to her daybed, raised a pale face towards her father.

'You make too much of it,' she told him bravely. 'It was a game, as Amin Sang said. Adam was playing at guard duty. He meant no harm.'

'No harm, to call me "enemy", and threaten me with a spear? Is that how these children are to be brought up?'

Sunara, watching the working of his furious face, knew, like Richard, that no word from her could benefit the situation. 'I am sorry, Father,' she said again. 'Richard will talk to him tomorrow. He will not be so thoughtless again. But please remember how young he is.'

'He is young, and I am old,' answered the Rajah, speaking with cold and careful effect. 'But I am not so old that I am ready to give place to an insolent boy, or to anyone else. I will rule for a long time, you may be certain of that. And as long as I rule, I will be treated with due respect.'

He waited, as if expecting argument, and Richard felt that he must break the silence.

'I hope your Highness's days of rule will be many,' he said formally.

The Rajah glared at him under lowered lids. 'Be sure they will, Tunku. Be sure they will!'

Early next morning, Manina, whose access to palace gossip was unrivalled, brought them a piece of news which Richard had been expecting, though it was none the less disturbing, for all that. Amin Sang had been summarily transferred from the Palace Guard, to a tour of duty with the far-away West Garrison. He would be absent for three months at least. He had left at dawn, too early to say any farewells.

'Adam will be sad,' said Richard, when he had digested this intelligence.

'I think we will all be sad,' answered Sunara. 'From this day forward.'

II

In Richard Marriott's dressing-room, a workmanlike apartment containing little save cupboard space and linen presses, John Keston was busy with the Tunku of Makassang's principal and most elegant possession, his wardrobe. This was a weekly task, which he would delegate to no one else; no matter how great the number of Richard's personal servants – and they now ranged, in a descending scale, from military aide to punkah-slave, via secretary, major-domo, butler, wine steward, cook, launderer, bath boy, shoe boy, head groom, and head sweeper, each with his own smaller retinue – yet the care of his fabulous array of clothes remained as John Keston's prime and private responsibility. They must be brushed, aired, pressed, and cleaned; camphor must be sprinkled with a free hand; gold leaf and silver thread must be protected from the tarnishing which the moist monsoon climate encouraged; turbans must be wound to a hair's-breadth, linen must be spotlessly laundered and displayed.

It was a whole day's work, and John Keston made the most of it. Indeed, he clung tenaciously to this office; for it was, in truth, all that now remained of his honourable role of bodyservant.

Lately, Keston's frame had grown comfortable, even portly; a year and more of soft living ashore had changed the ruddy, tough young sailor into something less admirable. He had rusted, as a man must rust if he eats three copious meals a day without a day's work to justify them. He found it difficult to pass the time, in the Sun Palace or anywhere in Makassang; in theory, he stood nearest to Richard Marriott, and ruled his household; but the multiplicity of office-bearers, the division and sub-division of even the smallest tasks, and Princess Sunara's own overseeing, had largely stolen his responsibility.

For the most part he strolled the corridors and passageways, greeting those he met, watching other men work, nagging at sweepers and gardeners and all those of menial rank. Sometimes he loitered in the nursery, until Manina, jealous of her own domain, bustled him out again. Sometimes he played with Adam, but Adam had many other friends, and attendants also – he was being taught his letters by Sunara, the head groom schooled him in riding, Captain Sorba of the Palace Guard now instructed him in the military arts; there was little room, and no need, for an ex-sailor whose skills and energy had wasted away through lack of employment.

Only on this, the first day of the week, did John Keston find something to turn his hand to; and he spun out the task of brushing and tidying, mending and folding, for all that it was worth.

He was busy now with a leather cloth, slowly perfecting the high polish of a silver shoe buckle, when Richard came into the dressing-room.

It was mid-morning, and Richard was not yet arrayed for the day; his magnificent brocade robe proclaimed the man of taste and leisure whose only preoccupation was the elegant passing of time. He had taken his morning coffee, he had shaved and bathed, he had visited the nursery, and talked to his major-domo about the preparation of a wild pig for dinner, and sent a message to the stables concerning a horse which might be lame. Now, walking into his dressing-room, he crossed to the window and admired the view, which was to the southward, towards the rolling surge of the Java Sea. Then he turned, and studied John Keston, and said finally: 'I am not riding this morning … I will wear the black longhi, and a lawn tunic … It seems to me you have gained weight lately, Keston.'

'I know it.' John Keston, standing up, continued to rub and polish the shining shoe buckle. 'I have gained more than a stone, in the past few months. The food is too rich, to my taste. And I lack exercise, to keep in trim. But there is one good cure for all that.'

'And what is that?'

'A long sea voyage.'

Richard smiled, divining the direction of John Keston's thoughts. 'And where would that voyage take us, pray?'

'Back to England.'

In the ensuing silence, Richard turned again, and stared out, across the slopes to the sea. With the monsoon rains blown away to the northward, the waves sparkled and beckoned, as bright and happy as laughter; and yet they were not close, they were a lifetime away … He knew the feeling behind Keston's words, and sometimes, in a certain mood, he could share it; he could feel homesick, as deeply as any yearning bride who pined for the family bosom again. But, as on all other occasions, he knew he must thrust the thought away; a hundred reasons made it impossible to entertain.

With his back still towards John Keston, he said firmly: 'You know we cannot return. Our life is here now. We are settled in Makassang.'

'We can settle where we will; we have the world to choose from … There would be more to do in England, if we travelled back; a great estate to run, maybe.' His voice took on a careful note. 'The Princess and the children would be more secure there, too.'

Richard turned, in surprise. 'More secure? What do you mean by that?'

Keston was looking down at his feet. 'We would all be safer, away from here.'

'What kind of nonsense is this?' scoffed Richard. 'You talk like old Manina!'

'Manina hears much.'

'She hears too much! She will be hearing voices in the air, next!' But he was intrigued, in spite of his scoffing tone. 'Now speak out, man. What have you and Manina been talking of?'

'Nothing, sir.'

'Then tell me of this nothing.'

'Well...' John Keston put down the shoe and the polishing cloth, and faced his master; with his legs straddled, and his hands on his hips, he suddenly looked like a sailor once more – a sailor in an attitude of watchfulness. 'Sir, we think there is danger here.'

'What danger?'

'We think there are spies watching.'

'Watching whom?'

'Yourself, and the Princess, and the children.'

'Have you seen these spies?'

Keston shook his head. 'No. They are too careful for that. But there's whispering, and moving behind curtains, and shadows out in the gardens, all the time. One cannot say a thing, or do a thing, without it being all through the palace in half a day.'

'The palace has always been like that.'

'But this is something new. It is growing all the time. The whole place has sprouted ears and eyes! And it seems as if we are losing friends, too, every day.' He came out, suddenly, with what appeared to be his most pressing question. 'Why was the Captain sent away from here? Is it true that it was because he spoke out about the child, saying it should be guarded instead of left defenceless?'

Richard frowned, wondering at the foolish way in which gossip could twist and turn and stretch the truth, beyond a shadow of its proper shape. 'It was nothing like that. It is true that he was sent away because he angered the Rajah. But it was for a different matter altogether.'

'Well, he is gone,' insisted John Keston stubbornly. 'And he is not the only one. What has become of the Fifty of the Brave, that you used to drink with, when you went down to the barracks? Do you still drink with them?'

'The battle we drank to was a long time ago. These reunions lose their savour by and by. And the Fifty are dispersed now, in any case.'

'Aye, they are dispersed! Do you know there are not five of them left in the palace?'

Richard shook his head. 'There is nothing there, man. They have been sent to join the garrisons. It is the system of exchange. You know it well. They make these tours of duty, every year of their service.'

'They have been sent to join the garrisons, and they have never returned.' John Keston thrust out his chin, determined, sure of his facts. 'They have gone, and now Amin Sang has gone. It is Colonel Kedah's doing! He would not stand for you to have your own faithful following. So they have been dispersed, and none of them have come back. In the end, we shall not have a friend left here, to raise an arm in our defence.'

But Richard did not care for this kind of talk, and he felt that he must say so, without dissembling. It was one thing for him to have his own doubts about Kedah, and quite another for John Keston, his servant, to retail idle gossip about a man who held high office under the Rajah. That was not how the Tunku of Makassang should conduct his household ... He put on his stiffest manner, and turned away from John Keston, with a gesture of displeasure.

'Enough!' he said curtly. 'You forget your place. Colonel Kedah is a loyal officer, and his example should serve for all of us.'

John Keston shrugged, recognizing the inflection of rank, and the division of it also. 'Aye, sir.'

'There is no danger, from him or from anyone else. You and Manina should watch your tongues.'

'Aye.'

'And my place is here in Makassang, and it will remain here. We are taking no long sea voyages, to England or to anywhere else.'

'Aye,' said John Keston again. He was unimpressed, and unmoved, but he could not pursue the subject. He had said his say, and he might as well have left it unsaid; that was the way of the world. He picked up the polishing cloth again. 'Well, I thought I would mention it.' There was the ghost of a grin on his face. 'We two are the last of the old Lucinda's left. I thought maybe we should stand together.'

Richard, staring out of the wide window, found his mood softening again to meet John Keston's words. The mention of the Lucinda D struck a chord in his heart; and it was answered by what he saw in the far distance – the sparkling sea, deep green, noble, and tempting. It was true that a great part of his life had lain there, and another great part in England; by contrast with those stirring and strenuous years, their present ease was futile. Though he could not bring back the past, even if he had truly wanted to, yet there was no great harm, occasionally, in sighing for it.

'The Lucinda days are over,' he said, almost to himself. 'They will not come again. But I agree that they were good days, when all is said.'

'They were better days,' John Keston corrected him, without anything in his tone to give offence. 'And there's one good reason for that – we did more work!'

III

The two strange individuals who asked for audience, and were presently received by Richard Marriott in his private apartments, might have been sent by Providence in direct answer to his discontent. He had been musing, long and uncomfortably, upon his interview with John Keston; it was not the talk of danger, and spies, and the curious disappearance of the Fifty, which had disturbed him, so much as Keston's last satirical words about their days on board the

Lucinda D: 'We did more work!' There was a reproach therein, and a verdict of guilt, which could not be gainsaid.

It was an old reproach, which had never faded or been wholly lost; it centred inevitably on his lack of worthwhile employment. Keston's thickening figure had recalled it (Richard was not yet over-fleshed himself, but how long would that be true?), and the phrase 'We did more work' had been a most pointed endorsement. For now, plainly enough, he did no work at all; it had been true for many a long month; it was likely to continue forever. In such circumstances, a man could only wonder disconsolately as to what, at the age of thirty-two, had brought him to such a pass.

There had been a time, a brief time, when he had thought that Makassang would turn out very differently for him; but now, all that remained of that time were rueful questions. What had happened to those golden days of hope? What had happened to the Rajah's broad hints that he might one day succeed to the throne – or at least come to wield some tangible power and authority? Richard could guess now that the Rajah, with his promises, had been making sure of an ally, at a time when an ally was desperately needed. But was that truly all that he was worth – a stop-gap friend whose friendship shed its worth in the space of a few months? Or was it the birth of the child, and the spectacle of a ready-made dynasty prepared to take the Rajah's place, which had daunted the old man in his last years? Or was it simple jealousy, an ancient onset of spite and fear, so deep-rooted that nothing could now dissolve it?

Richard had told John Keston, curtly enough, that they must stay on in Makassang; and it was true. He had made his place there, at great risk and effort; he was bound to Sunara and the child, and Sunara especially was a true flower of Makassang, who might wither and die if she were transplanted. He tried to imagine her in England, presiding as châtelaine over some broad family acres in the west, and he could not do so. He could not even see himself in the conventional squire's role; he had ventured too far out, into an alien world which had now become his own. When he had married Sunara, he had finally married all these Far Eastern waters, all the mysterious beauty and decay of the islands; he could never leave, because now – for better or for worse – he had no home in all the world save in Makassang.

In this musing, he had reached the point – the somewhat desperate point – of wondering what he could do with the rest of his life, of knowing that, to save his face and his self-esteem, he must devise some useful and innocent employment which would not provoke the Rajah's wrath, when the double doors of his apartment were opened, and Durilla, his major-domo, with that supercilious look which only an upper servant could convincingly wear, announced: 'Tunku, the Jews are here.'

They came in, loaded like packmen, the old Jew and the young. They were both bearded, though the old man's beard was grey and straggling, and the young man's black and trimly cut; they both wore the kaftan, of rusty black calico belted at the waist, and embroidered skullcaps set far back on their heads. The packages they bore were mysterious – bulky objects wrapped in Nankeen velvet shawls; the young man, whose bearing had that pride of race sometimes to be found among Jews of an ancient culture, carried his burden with scornful ease, while the elder, in whom the blows of life seemed to have implanted a respectful humility, was bowed down under his load.

Together they advanced towards Richard, who regarded them with amused attention, while Durilla the supercilious, disdaining to help them in any way, gave them a glance of the purest disgust before he withdrew.

The old man, whose face was seamed with a thousand crafty wrinkles, was evidently the spokesman of this strange embassy. When he had set down his burden, he bowed low, his hands within the folds of his kaftan, and said: 'Your Excellency, we thank you for the honour of receiving us.' His voice was musically soft, almost too ingratiating, and his bright eyes were fixed on Richard with a suppliant attention. 'Allow me to make the presentations. I am

Mendel da Costa, and this is my brother Nahum.'

Richard, sitting at ease in his formal, high-backed chair, looked at them closely as he acknowledged their greeting. They were Jews, as Durilla had said: furthermore, they were Portuguese Jews, a sub-species not highly regarded in this part of the world. Too many of the Portuguese nation, arriving in these Far Eastern waters to pursue, ostensibly, some noble colonizing role, ended as pirates, or slavers, or brothel-keepers, or worse. Of all the oily rascals who came to these parts, the Portuguese bore the worst reputation of all. But something about this pair intrigued him; perhaps it was the aspect of the younger man, who, having also set down his strange package, was looking at Richard as if it were no part of his bargain with life to be impressed by rank or wealth. Richard, inclining his head, answered: 'You are welcome ... You asked for audience, and I am ready to give it ... What is your business?'

'Your Excellency, we are factors.'

Richard raised his eyebrows, as indeed he might, at the inflated word. 'Factors? I did not know we used such a term in Makassang. Or that we had such elevated persons doing business on the island.'

Mendel da Costa spread his hands, and shrugged apologetically. 'Forgive me, your Honour, I thought to use an English term. If it is wrong, I withdraw it. Let us say, we are traders. Traders in a small way of business.'

Richard, turning his eyes, looked at the young man, Nahum da Costa, who seemed to be paying no attention to what his brother was saying; instead, he was staring about him as if appraising the contents of the royal apartments. Something made Richard determined to catch this wayward attention, and he said, with sudden curtness: 'And now you wish to be traders in a large way.'

The old man opened his mouth to answer, but he was forestalled by his brother. The younger Da Costa, as if to prove that his attention could perfectly well be in two places at once, answered with an equal precision: 'Exactly so. We have plans to be the largest traders in Makassang.'

At this, Mendel da Costa gave a gesture of warning, discouraging so bold an approach; his face assumed a look of dramatic consternation, as if their whole plan might be ruined by this crassness and candour. Richard, who had not ceased to examine them, had the sudden conviction that they were acting a part, for his benefit and for their own; Mendel da Costa was clearly cast as the crafty elder statesman, and Nahum as the irrepressible youngster who must be restrained from his own good-hearted folly. Richard, wrapped in a mood which welcomed distraction, saw nothing to which he need object, at this stage; if his unusual visitors wished to entertain him in this fashion, he was prepared to enjoy it. He put on his most statesmanlike look, as he answered: 'That is a praiseworthy ambition. But why do you come to me?'

Nahum da Costa, the younger, answered immediately: 'Because you have the Rajah's ear.'

Once more Mendel da Costa rounded on him, gesturing for silence with such exaggerated dismay that Richard had to raise his hand to hide a smile. After taking a moment to regain his composure, he said: 'I have not the Rajah's ear, in the sense you mean ... But I am interested in these packages.' He pointed. 'What do they contain?'

The two brothers spoke at the same moment, as if they had rehearsed their answer – which might well have been the truth. Nahum da Costa said baldly: 'They are gifts,' while Mendel da Costa said: 'They are samples of our wares.' Then they frowned at each other, and the older man said, with smooth unction: 'They are samples of our wares, which we offer to your Honour as tokens of our respect.'

Richard said, more sternly: 'You have not told me what they contain.'

'Samples of our wares,' repeated Mendel da Costa. He was now busy, as was his brother, with unwrapping the velvet shawls, which were in several protective layers. Finally the unveiling was completed, and they both advanced, each with a laden wicker basket.

'The choicest Edam cheese, from the Low Countries,' announced

Nahum da Costa.

'Selected neats' tongues, from England,' said his elder brother. Then they both fell upon their knees, and chorused, in unison: 'They are offered to your Excellency, with our best wishes for a long life.'

After a moment of startled silence, Richard Marriott obeyed his strongest impulse, which was to laugh. He laughed long and loud, partly from the relief of tension, partly because of his lively delight; this was the most absurd moment of all his time in Makassang. It was clear that laughter was not what the Da Costa brothers had been expecting, and into their expressions there crept a genuine hint of concern; but after a moment, gauging Richard's mood to be benevolent, they both joined in, with unfeigned pleasure. Before long, the room rang with their united merriment.

Richard, giving further reign to his impulse, had a fleeting urge to summon Sunara; she would enjoy this so much – they had not laughed together for a long time – laughter was the most blessed balm for all the cares in the world ... Finally he collected himself, though not so abruptly as to affect their entente, and said: 'I accept your presents, in the spirit of their offering. And I thank you for your entertainment ... Now tell me why you are here.' And seeing Mendel da Costa's face turning crafty and calculating again, he added: 'I mean by that, your real reason.'

Their real reason, it seemed, was commercial. 'Sir, we are traders,' said Mendel da Costa. He had begun to shed his false unction, as if he judged that the time for such nonsense was past, and that they could now move on to adult pastures. 'We have a small business, and, as my brother said, we would make it a larger one. We have in mind' – he fingered his straggling beard, eyeing Richard with real speculation – 'to secure a contract, to supply the palace with such delicacies as these we have brought you.'

'An excellent idea,' agreed Richard. He glanced again at the basket of golden Edam cheeses, which looked most succulent, and the small hogshead of tongues, which were labelled, he noted, 'Produce of Bristol, England'. 'But it merits no special embassy, surely. You do not need the ear of the Rajah, in order to sell foodstuffs to the palace kitchens. Even by contract. That is to say, unless you have some larger project in mind.'

'We have a larger project,' said Nahum da Costa.

'State it,' said Richard.

But it was the elder brother who now assumed the task of exposition. 'We plan to import many such things,' he said, 'but we wish to make sure of our market before we venture. Stilton cheeses, spiced English beef, wines from Provence, sherry from Spain, oysters from Whitstable, smoked eels from Italy.' As he recited his possible wares, his voice took on a dreamy, dwelling intensity. 'Makassang needs such things; Makassang needs to enlarge its knowledge of the world ... We had it in mind,' he went on, 'that we might be appointed to supply the palace with the very best of this produce. Think what they have to offer in Europe alone!' he exclaimed. 'Makassang needs to know of such things. But it cannot know them, unless a lead is given by the palace.'

'A royal warrant,' said Richard, translating fancy into fact. 'The Da Costa Brothers: By appointment to his Highness the Rajah of Makassang.'

'Exactly,' said Nahum da Costa. His eyes at last were sparkling with a genuine enthusiasm. 'That is what we had in view, when we came to see your Excellency.'

'I am with you,' said Richard, reacting to a sudden impulse. 'But why should we stop at foodstuffs?'

Mendel da Costa looked at him warily, as if his own thoughts were in danger of being exposed before they were fully ripe for the light of day. 'Why should we stop at foodstuffs?' he repeated. 'I do not quite understand your Honour's question.'

'You understand it well enough,' returned Richard. He felt easy now; easy, and well content. This project was likely to answer his mood exactly; at long last, it promised something to occupy his time. 'You say that Makassang needs to know more of the outside world, and I agree. But it is not a matter of foreign delicacies alone. It can be everything, everything which might follow the development of trade! It can be new kinds of farming tools. It can be looms for weaving. It can be railways! We need to open up this country; to bring it forward. It should not be allowed to fall behind, as our present danger is.' He looked at the two brothers, trying to gauge two elements in them – their worth, and their enthusiasm. If he were any judge of men, these Da Costas might be the answer to his hopes. 'Tell me what your resources are. You have agents abroad? You must have made contact with other countries. And you must have offices, and clerks to work in them.'

'We have agents abroad, your Excellency,' answered Mendel da Costa. 'And though we are small traders, as I said, we plan to increase as soon as the time is ripe. As to our offices, we have a warehouse – as we say, a go-down – in Prahang, close by the harbour. But it is only a poor place, at this moment.'

'In poor places, heavenly flowers grow,' quoted Richard. 'I would like to visit your go-down. And then we can see about such things as appointments, and royal warrants, and the opening up of Makassang!'

Nahum da Costa, the younger, was staring at Richard as if he had, for the first time in his life, found a man in authority to suit his temper.

'It seems that you have plans, your Excellency.'

'I have plans.'

The go-down of the Da Costa brothers was indeed a poor place; perhaps the poorest and shabbiest ever to be dignified by such a title. It was no more than an immense lean-to shed by the wharf at Prahang; it had been built, at least sixty years earlier, of teak and yellow-wood which had now weathered to a dry and dusty monotone. Partitioned off from the storage space were a number of small counting houses with high stools, and desks scored and stained by use, and innumerable bills of lading impaled on iron spikes. The rest was given over to what looked like the forgotten dross of the world's commerce. This shabby shell notwithstanding, its abundance and variety were fantastic.

A ship chandler's smell overhung everything, a tarry odour of hemp and manila which Richard sniffed with nostrils made keen by recollections of the sea. Indeed, there were countless things here which anyone fitting out a ship would have to place on his stores manifest: coils of rope and cordage, hardwood blocks, ships' lanterns, tallow candles, casks of brined beef and hardtack biscuits, Negrohead tobacco wrapped in tarred twine; rum jars, bottled lime juice, salt pork by the barrel, dried cod and kippered herring.

There were other things designed to catch a sailor's eye when roving ashore: elephant tusks, brass Benares ware, skins of tiger and shark and crocodile, embalmed watersnakes with arched necks, shrunken human heads with lacquered hair; scarab amulets, ornamental daggers, conch shells made into lamps, giant moon moths impaled on pins, model ships in bottles, phallic coral fingers.

There were household stores to delight or confuse a woman's eye: silk rugs, Manchester goods, bales of striped tarlatan, muslin curtains; japanned chests of tea, canisters of cloves and nutmegs and cinnamon sticks; kettles, and cooking pots, and iron soup ladles. There were straw hats with college ribbons, strapped Pathan sandals, elastic-sided boots, celluloid shirtfronts, whipcord trousers such as English navvies wore in their bleak northern midwinter. There were whole shelves of medicines and dubious specifics: herbal remedies, phials of coloured liquids, powders ground from dried insects and reptiles; laudanum pills, sal volatile, tasty infusions of sassafras, tinctures of quinine bark and aromatic tansy.

The goods were ranged on shelves and dusty counters; or strung from the rafters on cords; or piled higgledy-piggledy wherever space could be found. Anyone who could make his way through this confusion, or could put his hand, with any certainty, on a required object, must have been on the premises since they were first stocked. Perhaps this was true of Mendel da Costa, thought Richard, looking round him in wonder and a boyish delight in this jumbled cornucopia;

but Nahum, so much the younger, must have served a long and confused apprenticeship ... He brushed aside a string of Chinese lanterns which hung tinkling from the roof tree, avoided tripping over an elephant's foot made into a fern pot, and, fetching up at the farthest counter, came face to face with a representation of Queen Victoria and the Prince Consort at Balmoral Castle, tastefully done in seashells and plaster of Paris.

'We have a number of fine lines,' said Mendel da Costa.

But there was less than complete confidence in his tone. Both the brothers, in fact, kept glancing at him uncertainly; their go-down could never before have received so distinguished a visitor, and Nahum da Costa in particular appeared shamefaced as he watched Richard's expression. It seemed important to reassure them – important, and also easy, since Richard found himself perfectly content with his surroundings. The place was shabby, but it was busy also; Malay and Chinese clerks bustled about or scratched industriously with their long quill pens; customers argued and bargained, with expressive fingers; there was a welcome contrast between the activity here, and the stagnating luxury which marked his own life.

This go-down also was a treasure vault, the harvest of men's eager hands, no less than the underground caverns of the Sun Palace. Lacking intrinsic wealth, its very diversity was a kind of riches.

In Mendel da Costa's inner office, Richard took the wicker chair which was brought forward, and the dark Trinchinopoly cheroot which Nahum da Costa offered with a bow. He sat back, and contentedly blew a smoke ring towards the shadowy ceiling. Then he said: 'I am glad to have seen your go-down. Tell me how many men you employ.'

'Some fifteen,' answered Mendel da Costa.

'Those are the inside clerks,' explained Nahum, eager to elaborate. 'We also have Sea-Dyak coolie gangs out on the wharf, but that is only when we unload the lighters.' The young man was still watching Richard's face, with anxious attention; his pride was more touchy than his elder brother's; he searched for signs of disappointment or disdain. 'May I ask if we have your Excellency's interest?'

'Certainly,' answered Richard. For a moment he watched an old clerk in a faded blue longhi shuffle past outside the glass partition; when he intercepted the glance, the ancient bowed and quickened his pace. Then Richard turned back to his hosts. 'We were talking of supplies for the palace, and I said that we might consider greater matters than this. Tell me what you would do,' he commanded, 'if you wished to open up Makassang to all the world's trade.'

It seemed that they already had many plans, for just such a scheme; the sunbeam shafts moved steadily across the floor, the dust drifted and settled, as the floodgates of their thought were opened. They both spoke with equal facility, catching each other's ideas, adding to them, seldom correcting; they had great dreams, but the dreams were lucid also, founded on fact and probability as well as the fragile web of speculation. Richard had been right in estimating that these were men of large hopes, who had been awaiting their chance to transform them into action.

For the most part, they told him with growing confidence, it was trade with Singapore which was the key to the rest of the world – Singapore, the great clearing house for Far Eastern commerce which another dreamer, Sir Stamford Raffles, had long foreseen and long laboured to translate into fact. But to welcome big ships from Singapore, or from anywhere else, an improved harbour was needed; a deep-water harbour with quays and wharf space and proper docking, where ships could come alongside, instead of – as now – anchoring offshore and discharging into cumbersome lighters and leaky sampans.

Such a scheme would cost money, but there was plenty of money in Makassang; the Da Costas had money, though not as much as they wished, the Rajah had money, the Tunku himself was not a poor man ... If necessary, credits could be arranged with the European banks ... With a new harbour, and more roads to the interior, and inns to accommodate travellers, Makassang could be transformed.

'One day there will be steamboats here!' declared Nahum da Costa, eagerness in his voice, pointing out of the window at the rundown wharf close by. 'They are no match for the Blackwall frigates and the China clippers – not yet – but the day will come when they can carry the heaviest cargoes, and show a profit. And the day will come when we have our own fleet, plying all the world!'

'That may be too ambitious,' said Richard doubtfully. 'Makassang is a small island, after all.'

'It can be made greater!' This time it was Mendel da Costa taking up the tale, his old eyes suddenly shining. 'Your Honour, now that the East India Company is dead, there are many places to be filled. Already there are other big houses of export and import – Jardine Matheson – Godeffroy of New Britain – great names both ... Da Costa of Makassang could be such a name! With a deep harbour, and a fleet of ships; cranes and warehouses and go-downs; a comprador for each cargo – '

'And a customs service,' put in Richard, with studied carelessness.

'A customs service!' Brought up short, Mendel da Costa gazed at Richard as if he could not believe his ears. 'That indeed may be too ambitious ... What would be the merit in such a thing as that?'

'The collecting of taxes,' answered Richard, prepared to enjoy himself.

'But your Excellency – ' began Nahum da Costa.

'You are asking me for a trade monopoly,' said Richard. 'It might be that I would be prepared to grant one. But a big export-import house – if that is what you have in mind – should certainly pay its share of taxes, and for that a customs service would be needed.'

'Taxes,' repeated Nahum da Costa, scratching his chin doubtfully. 'It would mean the inspecting of books – a government accounting system – an army of civil clerks with special training ... We would not put your Excellency to such a mountain of trouble.'

'With care, the trouble would be sufficiently repaid, I have no doubt.'

Now Mendel da Costa shook his head, in a most elaborate pantomime of disbelief. 'Inspectors – new laws – taxes – by these, Makassang would be completely changed! And not for the better, your Honour. It would mean that we would lose our – our innocence.'

'I fear that is a risk we must be prepared to run.'

'It would be a tragedy,' insisted Mendel da Costa – and indeed, he looked as if he believed this, with all his heart. 'Contrary to the natural law … Has not your Excellency heard of the philosopher Lao-Tzu?'

'I have heard of many philosophers,' said Richard gravely.

'This was the greatest of them all – the father of Taoism! Lao-Tzu said – ' the old man's face lit up with a fervour which might have been holy, ' – Lao-Tzu said: "The secret of good government is to let men alone." Is not that a truly wonderful saying?'

'It is a saying so wonderful that I doubt if we can live up to it.' Richard rose, ending the interview which had covered much valuable ground, and had satisfied him well. 'But I will think of the philosopher Lao-Tzu,' he promised, 'and you will think of taxes. Then, when we meet again, we will have more to discuss.'

Nahum da Costa, a young realist, went to the heart of the matter. 'If I may ask your Excellency, how great would these taxes be?'

'Ten per cent,' answered Richard promptly. He had little idea of an appropriate figure, but he felt it best to produce one.

Both brothers clasped their hands to their heads. 'Ruin!' they exclaimed in unison. And Mendel da Costa added: 'Such a charge would eat up our profits entirely!'

'Ten per cent,' repeated Richard. 'To pay for the new harbour, and the roads. Perhaps a railway also.'

'And when these were paid for?' inquired Nahum da Costa cautiously.

'To pay for other things … Houses, streets, hospitals, homes for the aged, schools …' He smiled. 'If we truly have this dream of Makassang,' he told them, 'we must not skimp it. It will cost money.

Some of it will be your money, and some will come from the royal treasure. But for ten per cent I might be prepared to follow the precepts of Lao-Tzu, and leave you alone.'

There were many such meetings, which Richard Marriott found it no hardship to attend; in truth, he discovered pleasure and inspiration in the go-down at Prahang, such as the Sun Palace had not been able to show him for many months. On these visits, he came unescorted, or with a single groom who waited with the horses outside; he stayed long, often through the course of an entire day, sipping wine, smoking the Da Costas' excellent cheroots, gossiping, planning, thinking, feeling. Sometimes he shared their meals, Jewish dishes of stuffed fish and highly seasoned meat which (to him) seemed heathen and delicious at the same time. Always he shared their thoughts, and found in them a matching delight.

He enjoyed their company, without reservation. They were Portuguese Jews, people whom he had only heard of, by repute, as arrant rascals and swindlers; he now discovered them to be the very reverse – witty, subtle, good-hearted; a link with the civilized fulcrum of Europe which he had all but forgotten. Their world was wide; they could talk as easily of Montaigne as of the mud flats which must be dredged to make a deep-water approach to Prahang. They could bargain, finger to nose, about customs duties, insurance of cargoes, forward rates of exchange, the cost per foot of building a properly equipped market place – and then break off, with sly laughter, to quote Shylock as the source of their artful energy. To spend time with them was to be provoked, at last, to the pleasures, preoccupations, and itching cares of manhood.

Richard became a familiar figure in the go-down of the Da Costas, wandering at will, examining books and ledgers, asking questions, learning the outlines of this novel universe. The clerks and office workers came to know him well; often, when he was talking and questioning, they loitered nearby, to hear what the Tunku of Makassang had to say, on any matter under the sun. Between himself and the brothers, anything and everything was meat for hopeful speculation.

In their discussion and dream of a model kingdom, their talk ranged like a turning, all-seeing eye. Sometimes they spoke of details – of the 'houses, streets, hospitals, schools' which Richard himself had cited, at their first meeting; sometimes it was of larger themes – the function of commerce, the merit of one kind of colonizing over another, the patterns of dominion which were still shrouded in the misty future. Sometimes it was of those intricate, twin tides of trade – export and import – on whose ebb and now the prosperity of Makassang must be founded.

'We have much to offer,' said Mendel da Costa, on one occasion, when they were trying to estimate the future position, and strike some kind of balance. 'There are many markets we cannot hope to invade – we know the Dutch monopoly in spices, and the Java pepper trade is closed also. But we have teak, we have fish, we have copra, rice, rattan, coffee, rubber, antimony – now there is something the world wants! At the moment, the quantities are small, and everything is spread out over the island, like a thin patchwork. But if we can bring in modern methods, increase our crops, make the day's work of one man the equal of what it is in the Western world, then Makassang has a great future.'

'Makassang can have a great future of a different sort,' said his brother. 'In time, we can make things, as well as grow them. If we have teak, we can make furniture to sell. If we have coconuts, we can weave matting, and ships' fenders. We can set up a guild of silversmiths – '

'We should leave silver out of account,' Richard interrupted him. 'And the ruby mines also. They are in the Rajah's personal domain.'

After a silence, Nahum asked: 'But will that always be so?'

'Why should it not be?'

The young Jew, aware of delicate ground, chose his next words carefully. 'Are not the silver and the rubies part of the riches of Makassang? It is true that they are a royal perquisite, at the present time. But' – he glanced at Richard – 'some might say that they are going to waste, when they disappear into the palace treasure vaults.'

There was another silence, which Richard did not feel called upon to break, and then Mendel da Costa disposed of the subject with skilful ease.

'That is in the far future,' he said smoothly. 'We will have enough things to sell, and things to make, without intruding on the Rajah's preserves.'

'Even if they disappear into the treasure vault,' said Richard, conscious of wishing to make an honest evaluation, 'they are not lost.'

'They are lost to Makassang,' Nahum ventured.

'Not so,' said Richard. 'The silver and the precious stones can provide the backing of our currency. In that sense the palace treasure belongs to all Makassang.'

A servant, bringing tea and English biscuits, interrupted the topic, and their talk went off at another tangent, questing, speculating, eyeing the hopeful horizon. Each plan led to another; each idea had its lively offspring, its footbridge into the future. On paper, in their heads, and within their hearts, there seemed no limit to the glowing promise of this new world.

It was Mendel da Costa who, at the last, sounded the note of caution.

'Remember, there is danger in this financial growth,' he told them. They were in one of the smaller counting houses, sketching a plan for the excavation of rice terraces to replace the haphazard cultivation of the past; the clerks moved round about them, soft-footed, eternally busy. 'The rest of the world will come to hear about Makassang; its reputation will spread, wherever ships put into harbour; it will seem a small, rich country, without allies, and therefore desirable ... Unless we are careful, we will be opening Makassang to enemies as well as to friends.'

'We must be strong, then,' declared Richard. He was in a mood of high good humour, as so often happened after a day spent with the

Da Costa brothers; viewing the world from such an elevation, he felt there were no problems which could not be solved. 'We must confront these enemies – and throw them into the sea, if need be!'

Mendel da Costa smiled at his vehement spirit. 'And I know who will be leading the charge ... But a modern state, such as we hope to build, needs a modern defence. We have the men, and they are well-trained, but their arms are pitiful, measured against what the rest of the world has access to. There are new weapons which can make us look like children playing at war in the nursery.'

'Then we must have these new weapons ourselves.'

'Such things are expensive,' said Nahum da Costa dubiously. 'And hard to come by.'

'None the less,' said his brother, 'we cannot leave them out of account. We should turn our thoughts in that direction, when we are planning all the rest.'

'Agreed,' said Richard. He took a fresh sheet of writing paper, and laid it on the sloping desk in front of him. 'Some field guns, perhaps? A shore battery, to guard the harbour and the palace? Even a small ship-of-war, to keep down the pirates.' He smiled. 'The Royal Navy of Makassang ... I will be an admiral yet!'

'I was thinking rather of small arms,' said Mendel da Costa. 'There is word from England of a new repeating rifle, the Enfield. If the Royal Regiments were equipped with that, there's no country in the world that would not think twice before launching an attack on us.'

'But the cost of it,' objected Nahum.

Richard nodded. 'It might prove too much, for all the regiments to be armed so. But we could make a start with the Palace Guard, surely? Suppose we gave them these rifles?' His eyes brightened; already the fresh dream was outstripping slow reality. 'That is the answer! We will begin by equipping the Palace Guard with rifles, the best rifles in the world. As a compliment to the Rajah!'

'The Rajah might object to such a change,' said Mendel da Costa.

'Why should he? It will make them better soldiers, and a stronger guard. What use are spears and daggers, in these modern days? His Highness will be delighted!'

'You would not consult him?'

'No.' Richard, in a spirit almost of birthday largesse, saw the project as a rare surprise, for an old man who would be pleased and flattered by such attention. 'Let it be our secret, and then our pleasure to surprise him with it.' He straightened up from the desk, and thrust the piece of paper with its scribbled list of arms, into his waist belt. It was evening, and time to return up the hill to the palace; the westering sun cast straggling shadows on the quay outside, as his groom began to walk the horses again. 'Three hundred Enfield rifles,' he said cheerfully. 'Can you find them?'

'I believe so,' said the elder brother.

'Then do so ... I will pay for them out of my own purse.' Pausing in the doorway to take his leave, he said again: 'But not a word of this, remember. Let it be a surprise for his Highness.'

IV

Richard faced Colonel Kedah across the width of the stone balustrade between them; his natural, long-continued hatred of the other man, combined with a deep anxiety, made his manner brusque and forceful. They had met at the head of the Steps of Heaven, by chance; Richard, storming out of his apartments, had been on his way across to the barracks to seek out Kedah, when the other man made his appearance, strolling to and fro at the top of the steps as if he had not a care in the world. Their ill-omened meeting place cast a further shadow on the occasion; a piercing peacock scream from nearby seemed to lay a curse on all that might pass between them. Without greeting or formality, Richard said: 'Kedah! I was looking for you. I have some questions to ask.'

Colonel Kedah's single eye was still expressive enough to convey a supercilious carelessness as he checked his step, and turned to face

Richard. He answered, with a coldness matching his manner: 'I am not surprised.'

The curt phrase, and the absence of a formal mode of address, might have warned Richard of hazard, but in his disturbed mood he scarcely noticed anything amiss. He took his stand before the balustrade, and asked baldly: 'What has happened to the Da Costa brothers?'

Kedah's face became theatrically blank. 'Da Costa?... The name is for some reason familiar, but I cannot place it. The – Da Costa brothers, you say?'

'The Da Costa brothers. I think you know them, or have heard of them. Where are they?'

Kedah flicked at a tall blade of grass with his riding switch. 'I would answer that question by asking another. What is your interest in them?'

'I think you know that also.' Richard drew a deep breath, holding his temper with difficulty. 'Come – do not fence with me! You said that you were prepared for questions. These are questions ... The Da Costas, as you know well, are merchants in Prahang. I have had some dealings with them. Today, I went down to meet them, and they had disappeared, no one knew where. Or they affected not to know.' As he spoke, he relived again that strange, unreal moment of discovery; the shuttered and deserted go-down, the vanished clerks, the passers-by who, covertly watching him, turned away as he approached to put his question, or spread their hands in faceless ignorance of what he asked.

The conspiracy of silence had been complete, the wall utterly blank; he might have landed upon another planet, seeking a friend once rumoured to be there. 'Where are they?' Richard demanded again, more harshly, as he remembered that impenetrable blankness, that spoor erased without trace. 'People do not disappear in Makassang, without your knowledge. Nor without your playing some part, either.'

Kedah allowed himself the thinnest of smiles. 'You flatter my powers ... In this case, all such questions should go to the Rajah himself.'

Richard stared back, on the verge of fury at this fresh check. 'The Rajah will not see me. Did you know that also? He sent a message that he is receiving no one. Whether that is true or not, I was refused audience.'

'I believe he is indisposed.'

'For how long?'

'Until he mends,' said Kedah.

There was such a subtle, silky confidence in his tone that Richard looked at him more closely. It was difficult to discern exactly what made up this new authority; it was certain only that Colonel Kedah had changed. On the surface, the change was a composition of small things: his failure to use the formal 'Tunku' in addressing Richard; his manner, which had never been more cold and collected; the fact that he did not back away before Richard's anger, and seemed prepared to outface it. But there were other ingredients, secret and remote ... He had become utterly sure of himself, in a way that Richard had never encountered before. Of all the strange and furtive happenings of the day, this was the most ominous.

But Richard, who had his own share of confidence, momentarily brushed aside his doubts. He assumed his bleakest expression, and said: 'It is not like the Rajah, to refuse me audience. Unless he has been persuaded to do so. I fancy you know something of this, also. I order you to tell me what is happening, what has become of the Da Costa brothers, and why their go-down has been closed.'

Kedah, by no means impressed, drew himself up. 'In this matter, I recognize no such order. I answer to the Rajah alone.' His eye, burning in a face of mordant determination, bent on Richard a most baleful look. 'But you cannot be surprised at this turn of events.'

'I do not understand you.'

'You cannot be surprised,' said Kedah again, 'by the Rajah's deep displeasure at your dealings with these – these Da Costas.' He brought out the name as if it were inexpressibly vulgar. 'His Highness does not understand – and neither do I – why you should consort with such riff-raff – and on such disgraceful terms.'

'I will choose my own friends,' answered Richard furiously. 'The word riff-raff is absurd – absurd and insulting. There is worse riff-raff close at hand!' He took a step nearer to the stone wall and to Kedah, ready for any desperate action in his determination to reach the truth. 'It seems that you are in the thick of this matter, after all. Well, you will stay in the thick of it! Tell me where they are!'

'They are dead,' said Kedah.

It was a mortal shock. The look of grim triumph on Kedah's face showed both that he knew it, and that it gave him pleasure to break the news thus suddenly and brutally. Richard, seeking respite from the blow, put his hands upon the sun-hot surface of the stone wall, and leant against it. But the warmth did nothing to aid his chilled spirit; rather did it seem to point the difference between benign nature and cruel humankind. He knew, even better than Kedah, how deep this wound might prove, how shattering to his confidence.

In this one swift stroke, he had been told, not of the loss of old friends, but of a worse bereavement – the loss of hope. Snatched from his world were two men who had been able to confer a matchless blessing on him; two trusted messengers of the future, two bright spirits who, though despised Portuguese Jews, had reached down to draw the Tunku of Makassang from his mire of despond.

He had been building higher than he realized on these foundations. Now, it seemed, they had been destroyed out of hand.

An old gardener with a watering pot shuffled past, glancing at him curiously. The peacock screamed again, completing its fundamental curse. Richard straightened his shoulders, and faced Colonel Kedah with burning eyes. There were still things to be said, and, perhaps, to be done.

'What do you mean, they are dead? What befell them?'

'Death.'

Richard had no weapons, and Kedah knew it; if he had crossed the wall, it could only have been to claw and club the insolent soldier with his bare fists. He made an enormous effort of will – against his rage, against desolate sorrow – and brought himself upright, and said: 'I will not be mocked in this ... How did they die?'

'They were executed.'

Richard frowned, aware of a forest of confusion, of words and thoughts which were shapeless and nonsensical. 'Executed? How, executed?'

Kedah answered him in precise, almost mincing tones; having dealt one blow, he had the pleasure of a second one, more vicious yet, which was his to administer. 'After due trial, they were tied back to back, strangled with the same cord, and thrown into the sea.'

His eyes were glittering, his breath shorter than before; without any proof, Richard guessed that Kedah had witnessed this execution, that his own hands were likely to have knotted those bonds, tightened that noose. But something else besides Kedah's gruesome relish plucked at his attention, something more unspeakable still.

'Back to back?' he said, in stupefaction. 'But that is the punishment – '

Kedah nodded. 'Just so. It is the punishment for unnatural acts between men. We have ample proof that the sentence was justified.'

'But they were brothers,' said Richard hoarsely.

'They were — ' Kedah used a loathsome term, which Richard had never heard save among the vilest; it galvanized him to action. He summoned all his strength, as a man striving to escape from a nightmare of pursuit, to reach the shores of reality again.

'This is monstrous!' he cried. 'I knew them. They were honourable men. Such charges are insupportable! It is shameful that they should die in this fashion. And why should they die, in any case?'

Kedah was smirking. 'What does it matter? They were Portuguese Jews!'

Richard felt the rags of his patience falling from him. 'What was their real offence?'

'They were Portuguese Jews.'

The contemptuous laugh which accompanied this was too much for Richard's self-control. Now he did mount the balustrade which divided them, and leapt down, and confronted Colonel Kedah, his fists clenched, his face full of menace.

'I warn you, Kedah,' he said, in a voice thick with anger. 'Do not play the fool with me. You have committed a disgusting crime – '

Kedah did not even allow him to complete his sentence; once more, the new authority was apparent in every look and word. 'You warn me!' he said contemptuously. 'Who are you to warn me? If I had not interceded for you, you would have shared the fate of the Da Costas!'

'Interceded?' repeated Richard, stupefied.

'Yes, interceded! These men were plotting, and you were closely involved. Can you deny that they came to the palace to see you, and that you spent hours of every day talking and scheming, in their go-down at Prahang? Do you think we are fools? What would you have in common with this sort of scum, except plotting?'

'There was no plotting,' said Richard. He had fallen back a pace, as if to give himself room to answer this absurd charge. 'We did everything openly – '

Kedah gave a barking laugh. 'I took good care that this was so! Every word of what you said was brought back to me, by more faithful men. And when the time was ripe, I plucked these Jews of yours from their lair, by their own beards, and dashed them against the stones!'

Something in his voice made Richard's blood run cold. 'Were they tortured?'

'Certainly they were tortured!'

'With what result?'

'They revealed nothing of consequence.'

'There was nothing to reveal.'

'That is not true,' answered Kedah. 'But it was no great matter. We had enough proof already. The torture was part of their punishment for treason – and part of my pleasure in uncovering it.'

Sickened by the inhuman words, Richard said: 'It was a wicked crime. There was no treason. And as for the other charge – ' he looked at Kedah, seeing in him the sum of all the unspeakable cruelties of Makassang. 'Why did you have to shame them like that?'

'For the best of all reasons – because they deserved nothing but shame … It seems to me, Tunku,' went on Kedah – and his very use of the title was now satirical and contemptuous, 'that we shall never agree, because of our differing standards. We have disputed this Western conduct before, have we not? – your sacrilege in attacking the Shwe Dagon was an example of this, the worst until now.' And as Richard made to interrupt: 'You will hear me out, Tunku! I speak for the Rajah, I can promise you … If you see no harm in meeting and plotting with such greasy filth as the Da Costas, then I cannot teach you to avoid guilt. But I can prevent it, and punish it, and I have done so. It will be worth your remembering.'

'You have no proof of plotting. There was none.'

Kedah looked at him as if he were a servant caught lying. 'No proof? Do you take us for children? I have enough proof to hang a hundred Da Costas! And proof of your own guilt!' Suddenly his anger was blazing, and he spoke in a full and bitter flood of accusation. 'I will tell you what was heard. I will jog your memory! … You said that the palace treasure belongs, not to his Highness, but to all Makassang … You said that men should not be governed, but should be left alone … You said that you would be an admiral, with your own fleet … You said that you would raise your own taxes, and set up your own customs service, and for this you would take bribes from these Jews … You have taken bribes already! Cheeses and meats! Are you so hungry, Tunku? … You said that Makassang must be changed, and become like a western nation, and that anyone who resisted would be thrown into the sea … And lastly – ' Kedah suddenly whipped a piece of paper from his belt, and flourished it, ' – do you recognize this? It is a list of arms – guns, cannons and rifles for your traitors. Three hundred rifles! What do you want with three hundred rifles, if not to overthrow the Rajah and rule in his place?'

Richard shook his head; the torrent of accusation had all but overwhelmed him. 'The guns were to protect Makassang. The rifles were to equip the Rajah's own guard.'

'They were to equip a revolt ... Don't deny it! You were heard to say – and we have a dozen witnesses to this – that all these arms were to be kept a secret, until they were procured, to surprise the Rajah.'

Kedah fell silent at last, and Richard, sick at heart, did not know how to answer him. The ridiculous charges, the phrases set in isolation, the twisting of words, had indeed been skilfully marshalled; in a sense, he could not blame this wicked man for imputing a worse wickedness to himself. He realized, with a bitter conviction of guilt, what stupidity had governed his actions of the last few weeks, and how his hope of employment, leading him to idiotic folly, had also led innocent men to a vile end.

He knew now that it was his mood of elevation which had betrayed him, and betrayed the Da Costas at the same stroke. The time spent with the brothers had transformed his own feeling and mood altogether; but no such time had been spent by the Rajah, in whom suspicion and spite naturally remained unaltered. Living his days in a dreamworld of hope, Richard had forgotten the envious eyes forever fixed on him, forever spying out his smallest action, and the ears privily alert for a single word which might be out of tune with the general song.

In despair, he muttered to himself, accusingly: 'I did not think of this.'

'I find that hard to believe.'

Kedah's words were spoken with their customary blend of coldness and disdain. But when Richard. after a silence, raised his head, it was to find that Kedah had done an extraordinary thing; he had turned slowly on his heel, and walked away some twenty paces, his head bent, his whole manner thoughtful and preoccupied. At the limit of his steps, he turned slowly again, and walked back. It was as if he were deliberately softening the climate of their meeting, allowing the bitterness of charge and counter-charge to recede, relieving the terrible pressure which thoughts of murder, treachery, and lying had induced. When he reached Richard again, at an unhurried pace, his manner was perceptibly easier, and his words no longer threatening, merely inquisitive. He said, softly: 'Why the arms, Tunku?'

'I have told you,' answered Richard, without spirit. 'They were to make Makassang stronger, and to bring the Palace Guard, and later the Royal Regiments, up-to-date with the rest of the world.'

Kedah shook his head slowly from side to side: but he did not cease to watch Richard's face with the most careful attention. 'No, Tunku ... I mean, the real reason for the arms. I would like to hear what your true plans were. Believe me, I am interested.'

His manner was subtle and secretive; it had also an air of intimacy which Richard found at least as distasteful as the former hectoring, and which placed him on his guard immediately. He answered in a brief sentence: 'I gave you the true reason.'

Kedah sighed, prepared to be patient, to spend time if need be in overcoming this stubborn spirit. 'We are alone, Tunku,' he murmured. It was true that they were alone; the Sun Palace stood silent and withdrawn, no gardeners loitered nearby, their meeting place at the top of the steps was open to heaven, and to nothing else. Only the spirits of the dishonoured dead could be serving as spies. 'Remember that I stood between you and the Rajah's anger. We need not be enemies, if we open our hearts, if we resolve our differences ... How were you planning to use the arms?'

'I have told you.'

Richard's tone was final enough. But Kedah had not done. The mysterious, loaded exchange continued, like men talking at cross-purposes in a dream, with the key always hidden, always an inch beyond the grasping.

'You have told me what perhaps you told your Jews, your agents ... How were the arms to be used?'

'To strengthen the defences.'

'And to strengthen yourself?'

'No.'

'A new supply of arms might be necessary, if the rule became weak.'

Richard frowned. 'Why should it be weak?'

'It might be weak, until his Highness mends his health. If he mends his health.'

'If he mends?'

'He is an old man, as we know … What was your plan with the arms? What would you have attacked first? The palace? Or one of the garrisons?'

'I have told you. There was no plan.'

'The palace attack might have favoured you. A swift stroke, with the Rajah ill, confined to his apartments, perhaps not knowing what was happening until it was too late. Then would come the turn of the garrisons. Or perhaps they would surrender, with a strong ruler installed here, and ready to march. Or perhaps they already prefer loyalty to someone such as yourself, in the line of succession. Perhaps they would acclaim you, without a weapon raised except in homage.'

'I know nothing of these things.'

'Soldiers often prefer a strong ruler, an armed man who knows his own destiny.'

'His Highness is a strong ruler.'

'Beyond a doubt. But we must remember the great age of the Rajah Tuah.'

At that, Richard, whose wits were laggard, awoke to the true tenor of the exchange. It was the title 'Rajah Tuah' which was the key to this dream. It meant, in strict terms, 'Old Rajah,' but in this part of the world it had undertones also of withdrawal or supersession – it could mean the 'retired Rajah', even the 'ex-Rajah' … Colonel Kedah, the loyal commander who believed he had smelled out a plot, was ready, after all, to come to terms with treason. This single phrase was his offer of complicity.

Every instinct of Richard's recoiled from the prospect. It had been delicately done; under the clear sun, the sword had flickered once from its scabbard; the pass could be forgotten, or denied. He stared at Kedah as if he understood him for the first time; though in truth all he understood, at this moment, was his treachery and utter disrepute. He would as soon have made a compact with some mangy tiger, prowling the edge of the jungle, seeking hyena's meat.

He said: 'I hope his Highness will enjoy good health and a long life.'

It was enough. Kedah's face, which had been expectant and confederate, now became veiled again. Perceptibly, his bearing grew taut and trim; the conspirator was now the polished soldier, resplendent in honour and duty. Answering in his turn, he said: 'So do we all...' After a pause, he spoke again, and his tone had become cold, regaining that austere authority which Richard had noted earlier. 'I have brought you your news, Tunku ... You now know the Rajah's mind ... He will not tolerate plotting, nor plans to turn Makassang into some Western paradise for Jews ... He will be slow to forgive, and he will take all precautions against traitors, wherever they may be found.'

'Good luck attend his search,' answered Richard ironically. Then the spectacle of Kedah became odious, and anger overcame prudence as he added: 'I do not need these lectures from you, nor from anyone else whose nature makes him suspect a traitor under every stone! Who are you to tell me what the Rajah is thinking, and what he plans?'

'You will learn,' said Kedah, and with that he turned on his heel, and marched off, his manner as different from that other turning-away as blood was from oil.

It was the same ceremony as before, and yet how altered! The Council of State must have been summoned some days earlier, at short notice, and many of the outlying chiefs had not reached

Makassang in time; there were not more than ten of them present, and the invited guests were numbered by the score instead of by the hundred. A strong guard of the Royal Regiment ringed the audience chamber; at the high table, only the Rajah, Kedah, Richard Marriott, and Sunara had been accorded places of honour. The oath was administered by a priest of the Anapuri, a small fat man looking and sounding like a backsliding abbot in some absurd medieval morality play. Nervous as a circus wire-walker, he gabbled through his liturgy as though he were playing with gunpowder, and he knew it.

The whole occasion had an air of political purpose, rather than of celebration. When the Rajah lifted the ceremonial wine-cup towards Colonel Kedah, and announced: 'We take you as our son,' he seemed to sound a note of defiance, not of benevolent accolade. There was no answering murmur from the crowd, no smiling acclaim; they had been brought there to witness a dictated act, and, like the fat Anapuri priest, they knew it well enough.

But it was only when the Rajah, holding up his arm for silence – which was deep enough already – continued: 'We name you also First Minister and Commander-in-Chief, in the place of our trusted Amin Bulong,' that Richard Marriott realized the full measure of his defeat.

No wonder, he thought savagely, that Kedah's authority and assurance had blossomed in the last few hours! This ceremony explained everything – even his treachery. The attempt to suborn Richard had been his first stroke of policy, his first essay in active treason, and Richard himself designed to be the first instrument of it.

On the words 'Commander-in-Chief', Richard caught Sunara's eye, and their glances locked, expressionless and yet closely communicating. She was the only woman present, in all the gathering; she sat on the side of the dais opposite from him; he could not even press her hand ... Sunara was pale – as pale as he had become when he had last spoken to her, an hour before. He had barely had time to tell her of the murder of the Da Costa brothers, before they were summoned to audience, and to this farce of adoption.

Richard caught other glances, as the ceremony reached its close, and the guests mingled sparsely in the vast room. They were discreet glances, of mystification, of astonishment, often of sympathy; though Kedah was receiving his share of formal congratulation, the covert attention of the room was on the man who seemed to have been supplanted, even insulted, by this new appointment. Rumour, flying from mouth to mouth, spoke of arrests, imprisonments, and disappearances, all within the last few hours, increasing the secret, speculative tension beneath the surface of the formal gathering. But no one voiced his thoughts out loud; and Richard bore all looks with an equal indifference. He had risen, and perhaps he had fallen. But he was still a man.

The Rajah ignored him; Kedah made no effort to break away from the courtiers who formed a ring about his chair. Indeed, in all that evening Richard remembered only one exchange, and this was with Captain Sorba of the Palace Guard, whose duties took him to the dais. Sorba, an officer of limited intuition, less than expert in the niceties of palace intrigue, greeted him with deference, and remarked: 'What a pity that Captain Amin Sang could not be here in time to honour his grandfather's successor.'

'Is Amin Sang returning?' asked Richard, surprised enough to rouse himself from his studied unconcern.

'Yes, so I have heard. But, alas, he will come too late to enjoy our ceremony.' Captain Sorba sighed, a soldier's sigh of duty and regret. 'It is always the same – one misses so much when on garrison duty.'

Perhaps, thought Richard, Captain Sorba spoke truer than he knew; the whirling wheel of history had indeed moved on since Amin Sang had left the Sun Palace. It would be sad to meet his old friend with such a tale of woe, when their reunion should have brought only happiness. But in truth, there would be relief in meeting a friend of any sort.

He remained a short time after Sunara had withdrawn,

acknowledging greetings, exchanging a word with such chiefs as he knew, preserving his outward calm unaltered. He did not shrink from any contact; but, to the very end, no one addressed him with more than the customary phrases of salute, and no one spoke their thoughts or inquired his own.

There was one certainty, he thought, surveying the subdued throng of guests, and the ring of armed guards at their fringe; this thing was done. Colonel Kedah now stood next to the Rajah, in a position of paramount executive strength. There was no banquet to mark this elevation, no rejoicing, no horseplay with clowns nor boisterous drinking bouts. Not a man raised his voice in song or homage, not a dog barked. Within an hour, the Rajah had left the audience chamber, and Kedah with him.

But it was legal enough, for all that, and final.

V

'It is the people who deserve better,' said Richard, not for the first time on that night. He was in a dark mood, the darkest of his life in Makassang; though they sat in the soft luxury of their palace apartments, he could only brood on the danger and evil which was in the very air, even in this private corner of their world. 'They are such a happy people,' he said morosely, 'happy and loving – and now they have that butcher Kedah on their necks! You see how the lines are drawn? There is no one to protect them. God help them all, with Kedah at the head of power!'

'They must be set free,' said Sunara.

The Rajah's audience had ended at dusk; at midnight, Richard and Sunara were still talking, with an endless repetition, round and round the same subject. They had played with Adam, before he went to bed, and visited the sleeping Presatsang; they had dined privately, and then taken the slow, moonlit walk they often took, in the palace grounds below their rooms. But their walk was not the same as on other nights; no peace attended their steps; there were too many sentries posted, and shadows moving; too much of the watchful world was with them. Later they had begun to talk, in isolation and privacy; but by then the intrusion was of a different sort – the intrusion of a vast silence, an eerie holding of the breath by all within the palace, by the very coral stones themselves.

When their child cried briefly in a distant room, it was like a warning call from the innocent to the doomed.

Richard, sitting in a deep couch with Sunara at his side, returned again and again to this same thought – the sullen chaos into which he believed Makassang must fall, with the Rajah relapsed into his evil mood, and Colonel Kedah given a free hand in government.

'It is a monstrous prospect!' he declared passionately. 'If men cannot find happiness in this island, where under heaven can they find it? Yet we have as much chance of happiness now, as a man swimming in a school of sharks! Kedah will not rest till he has turned this island into a private kingdom – a private prison.'

'It is not Kedah,' said Sunara. She was as pale as before, but it was growing apparent that her spirit was not pale; late as was the hour, she was still alive with thought, and with the search for hope. 'I wish it were so, but it is not. Kedah, for all his villainy, is only the sword. It is my father who wields it.'

'Kedah makes a fine enough executioner himself – and a willing one also. In any case, between them they can turn this place into a slaughterhouse.'

'Then we must hurry,' she said. 'If Makassang is not to be ruined.'

'How, hurry?'

Sunara leant towards him. It was part of the aura of conspiracy that her voice should drop to a whisper; in their present situation, with all affairs in Makassang rising to a swift and murderous boil, intrigue and secrecy seemed inevitable. But it was still a shock to hear her murmur: 'My father must go. And Kedah with him.'

He was taken aback by the simple directive. 'What are you saying? How would they "go"? You might as well ask the lion tearing at his kill to "go"!'

But she was in a mood of insistence and determination, not to be baulked. 'Now that Kedah has the power, my father's rule will grow worse. It is happening already. The Da Costas were killed for no reason at all. Others have disappeared. The whole palace is full of spies and whispers. Did you know that the treasure vault has been barred, and put under guard? It is something unheard of – the vault has been left unwatched for two hundred years! And you saw how it was tonight, when we walked in the garden. The place is like a prison, like a tomb, and its walls will close in, until we are crushed. Must we wait for another planting of crosses on the Steps of Heaven? It will come – unless we act!'

He looked at her beside him on the couch, in mingled astonishment and doubt. 'I have never known you like this ... You must have been thinking as deeply as I have, though you said very little ... What is foremost in your mind, Sunara? What makes you say that your father must go?'

She was groping for the right answer. 'For me, it is the child, I think. Or the children together. No, it is us, Richard; the wellbeing of all our family. For you, perhaps it is the people ... But whatever drives us to try to withstand evil, I know that together we could make the future so much richer. Because we have the same feeling about power, the same pity ... If you were ruling in Makassang, it would be a happier place, and you would teach the people to make it happier still ... I love you, and the two children, and I love our island. So do you, as I know well. How can we stand by, and see it destroyed?'

'But you love your father also.'

'Oh yes! That is the crown of it. I love him too much to see him become so wicked in his old age. I remember him as a kind and generous man. He took pride in ruling without cruelty – you have often heard him say so. But now – now he rules by fear, and nothing else, and so he has chosen Kedah to make cruelty his chief instrument ... Why should this be, Richard? Why has he changed?'

'It is growing old, I suppose.'

'Are all old men monsters? Most men grow old with grace and kindness. Think of Amin Bulong – think of Mendel da Costa himself. He was greedy for money, perhaps, but he would not have killed and tortured for it, if he had had a whole army behind him! I tell you, there is some poison at work, and if it cannot be cured it will infect all of us, and we will wake up to find that we are as deep in cruelty and deceit as Kedah himself. That is, if we wake up at all!'

Looking at her, he said again: 'I have never known you like this.'

She intercepted the glance, and leant across to kiss him, becoming briefly a woman again, the loving Sunara with whom he had joined his life.

'I had it in mind,' she told him, almost shyly, 'to talk like a Western wife.'

'A Western wife!'

'Yes.' She smiled. 'I hoped that you would recognize it … Do they not take part in discussions, without shame, and even speak their opinions?'

'True.'

'I wished to be like that. But only for you, Richard. You do not mind?'

'I love you,' he answered, 'and I fear the future as much as you.'

'Then we must act,' she said again, 'and you must rule Makassang.'

At her words he rose, aware of discomfort, almost of irritation; she used these phrases, she propounded these panaceas for evil, without relating them at all to what was procurable … Round them, the palace continued its silence; beneath their open window, there came at intervals the firm tread of a sentry, and the ring of hardwood on stone as he grounded his spear; all else was a brooding stillness, a waiting for the next dreaded event.

Richard walked to the window, and looked out. He saw the beauty which was always there – the bearded silhouettes of palm trees, the dark slopes fading into darker nothingness, the moonlight on the sea far below. But now it all seemed menacingly hushed, a beauty muted by some force which might destroy it if it uttered a sound. Nearby, there was a faint scent of casuarina – that beautiful work of nature from whose milky sap clever men could distil their poisons … He turned back, and looked down at Sunara.

'What use is it to say that?' he asked. In his mood of tension and fear, he could not keep the irritation from his voice. 'Words will not make me Rajah … I can never rule Makassang. I have no power. I have no following. Kedah will make the laws now – and he will see to it that I play no part in government.'

'But you have a following,' she insisted. 'The people love you. When you walk in the bazaars, they press forward to catch your eye, to win a smile. You saw how the chiefs and the others looked at you during the audience tonight, when they heard the news. They hate Kedah! And they are coming to hate my father. But they love you.'

'Love, love,' he said bitterly, 'I cannot fight the Palace Guard with love. Who would help me? Where is my guard? The people are too afraid to do anything but submit and suffer. The first brave man to run to my side would be crucified – and the next, and the next! Who in his senses would buy such a passage to eternity?'

'Of course they are afraid, because they lack a leader.' She was gazing at him now with rapt eyes. 'But Richard, you can set them free, lead them to happiness. You were born to rule.'

He laughed. 'I was born to rule five hundred acres in Gloucestershire. Not to play the potentate, ten thousand miles from home.' His voice grew graver. 'This is not my country, Sunara. I am an English country squire, not an Eastern rajah. What is it to me, if Kedah turns Makassang into bloody ruin? These are not my people. Let them fight their own battles. You and I can leave tomorrow, if we will.'

'It is something to you,' she answered passionately, 'and they are your people, and we cannot leave tomorrow, nor any day until we die … Oh Richard, do not turn from them now. They need you desperately. You said yourself, "The people deserve better." When you said that, you were thinking of them, not of yourself.'

'I swear I did not mean to,' he answered caustically. 'This night air must affect the brain ...' Then he saw her deeply troubled look, and he went on: 'Forgive me, Sunara – I did not mean to scoff. God knows our troubles are nothing to scoff at. But when you say to me, "You must rule Makassang," I have to ask, "How?" And with murder and treachery as the certain reward, I have to ask, "Why?" as well. Why should I risk my neck, or worse, to win a country I do not want?'

She stood up; her small figure, divinely beautiful, had an appeal to more than the senses; in the midst of all their turmoil, it pulled at his heart as well. She came near to him, and said: 'How you can rule, must wait. We cannot make plans as we might snap our fingers. But why you should rule – that I can tell you. But not with my own words. Will you read something, Richard?'

'Read something?' he echoed, astonished.

'Yes.' She stood before him, slim and straight as a wand – his wife, and now his suppliant. 'I want you to read the journals of Andrew Farthing.'

He frowned. 'I had forgotten them ... You spoke of them long ago ... What have they to do with me – and tonight, especially?'

'You will see, if you read them. Will you read?'

'It is so late, Sunara.'

'It is later still, by another clock. Please read, for my sake, Richard.'

He shrugged. It seemed an absurd idea, at midnight in the Sun Palace; an idea rendered more absurd still by the pressing dangers and silences of the night. What could Andrew Farthing, an old Scottish minister long dead, mean to him at such a moment? He would be better off sitting with his back to the wall, nursing his pistols ... But Sunara still stood before him, her whole being strangely urgent, and presently he sighed in the face of this persuasion, and said: 'Very well. There will be little sleep for us, in any case. I will read.'

Already she had turned to a chest which stood in one corner, and had pulled aside the silken covering which veiled it. She bent, and lifted out some object wrapped in a cloth, and carried it to the table under the lamp. The bundle, unbound, proved to contain a pair of manuscript books, leather-covered, fastened by hasps with broad bronze hinges; and when she laid them down side by side, it could be seen that on the outside of each was printed, in faded Gothic script: Journal. A. Farthing.

'This will keep me busy till dawn,' Richard grumbled.

'He wrote a large hand,' she answered. 'It will not take you long.' She arranged the lamp so that its light fell on the first book, and turned a chair for him to sit down. 'I am hoping that when you begin, you will not wish to stop reading ... Will you have a glass of wine?'

'A bottle, rather ...' He sat down at the table, and opened the first book; the worn leather crackled, giving off a musty odour of age and scholarship. He read, in tall angular writing and pale Indian ink: 'MAKASSANG. January, the Year of Our Lord, 1817. By God's will I arrived safely – ' and then a sound distracted him, the first sound, save for the pacing of the sentry, which had been heard within the room for many hours. It was the sound of footfalls, ringing, heavy, approaching down the long passageway outside their apartment. The footsteps drew nearer, stamping and slurring on the marble floor; they were growing as loud as thunder in the still night. Then the curtains were thrust aside, with a forceful hand, and a voice said: 'Make way for the double-uncle!'

It was Amin Sang.

He could only stay a moment, he assured them, settling back in an armchair as though he would stay the night, at least; he must report his return to the Rajah, in accordance with the regulations ... Amin Sang was demonstrably in high spirits, delighted to be back among the blessings of civilization; he had still been armed, dusty, and dressed for the road when he made his lively entrance. Above all, as befitted a warrior returning from duty, he was already somewhat tipsy, and would have none of their gloom.

'I have ridden all day in this accursed heat,' he declared, with a flourish of his wineglass, when the first cheerful greetings were over, and Richard, unable to forget the present, began to talk of palace affairs. 'Spare me for a while, Tunku – at least give me time to swallow a small glass.'

'You have swallowed a small glass already,' said Sunara, with mock severity.

'I am on leave!' said Amin Sang. He drank, making no secret of his great contentment, and looked at Sunara with admiring eyes. 'Your Highness, you are more beautiful than ever, if a rough soldier straight from the jungle may pay you such a compliment.'

'He may,' said Sunara. She, like Richard, was finding it difficult to maintain a serious mood, with Amin Sang importing such lusty good humour into their surroundings. 'Have you just arrived, Captain?'

'This very moment, your Highness. I sprang straight from my horse, and into this room!' Amin Sang took another deep draught of wine. 'With a few moments' delay in the barracks cellar ... Imagine – they tried to challenge me, below. Me, a guard-captain! By heaven, wait until the Fifty of the Brave hear that!'

'The Fifty are somewhat scattered,' Richard told him. 'They are scarcely spoken of now.'

'So I have heard. There were six or seven of them sent to join the West Garrison, and grumbling about the duty. But no matter – we will bring them together again, and sing our songs all night.'

'We have had little singing lately,' said Sunara.

Amin Sang nodded. 'The palace seems gloomy, I will admit. Let it be my task to enliven it.'

For a short space, he did indeed enliven it, as far as Richard and Sunara were concerned, telling them such tales as garrison soldiers always told when they reached home – of the foolish blunders of other soldiers, of money won and lost at gaming, of unspeakable hardships connected with camp cooking, of arduous campaigns involving young women. To listen to him was a brief respite from the fears which pressed in upon them; knowing that it was in truth no more than a respite, they were at pains to enjoy it while they might. A cheerful hour passed, in laughter and drinking, with scarcely a thought beyond the lightest; presently Amin Sang tossed off the last of the wine, and stood up, and bowed to Sunara.

'My duty to you, Princess ...' He was unsteady, but not unduly so. He gave a swaying bow towards Richard also. 'Tunku ... Thank you for a fine homecoming ... Now I must report my arrival to his Highness.'

'It is late for that,' Richard advised him. 'Go to bed now, and report in the morning.'

'If there are still lights in the west wing, I will report,' said Amin Sang, who seemed at last to be recalling his military obligations. Ceremoniously he straightened his tunic and sword belt. 'Farewell!'

'Be careful,' said Sunara, smiling slightly. 'Remember, you were not in the highest favour with my father, when you left the palace.'

Amin Sang gestured. 'All is forgiven,' he declared magnanimously. 'I bring only sweetness and light.' He saluted, and was gone.

Sunara looked after him, listening to his footsteps receding down the corridor. She shook her head, as any woman must who contemplates the folly of the masculine world. Then she turned back to Richard.

'I am glad he is with us again ... Though he makes me feel as if I were a grandmother, at least ...' She touched Richard gently on the arm, restoring their privacy. 'Well, that is that. Now, will you read?'

VI

It was as she had forecast; once he started to read the journal of Andrew Farthing, he had not the least wish to cut short his study.

It was the simplest of stories, told without artistry; often, in fact, the writing was prolix and pompous, in the fashion of an earlier day. Yet it remained a most moving account of one man's effort to make something worthwhile out of a country and a task which slowly and inevitably defeated him – and this, after he had suffered an initial, crippling bereavement of another kind.

At the same time, the journal was no mournful chronicle of despair; it was most subtle in its ebb and flow, its alternation of joy and sadness; the large firm hand, unwavering to the end, set out a story which was less than firm in its course, less than predictable. It ranged over every human emotion, and every need of man, from his need of a full belly to his need for God; the tale was of triumph and defeat, yearning and rejection, the purest love turning to the purest hatred. Andrew Farthing, faithful man of God, had been a creature of deep feeling and wayward desires as well.

He had arrived in Makassang, in 1817, after 'a journey which put me in mind of the maritime ordeals of St Paul the blessed Apostle', with a heart full of hope and happiness, a burning thirst to build and then to serve the house of the Lord, 'Ten conversions this day!' was an early and ecstatic entry, firmly underlined. Against this, he had endured utter, heartbreaking misery when his wife died. He had regained hope and faith as he tackled the task alone; and he had come near to losing them both when that task proved beyond the strength of failing, enfeebled hands.

Richard Marriott read it at first with negligent interest, but soon with close attention; not a man alive could have failed to be enthralled by these leather-bound, bronze-clasped volumes in which Andrew Farthing had set down the thoughts, hopes, and fears of thirty-five crushing years. But crushing or not, he had shown admirable vitality and endurance; he had continued to labour mightily, in a vineyard which, at successive harvest times, returned him everything from a heady vintage to the bitter dregs of failure.

As Richard read further, his present world forgotten, the musty leaves entranced him with their zest for small triumphs, and shamed him with their Christian humility. The persuasive message of piety from the long-dead past put him in mind, constantly, of other echoes within his own life – of Sebastian Wickham charging him: 'Use your kingdom well', of his father counselling 'honour above interest, and duty above both'; even of the skull of the soldier of Sir Francis Drake, faithful unto death across the world's circumference.

The entries varied greatly in length. Sometimes they were long and prosy, as when he was describing the physical attributes of Makassang, or the 'misguided sense of worship' which impelled the Land-Dyaks to collect human heads as a kind of church ornament, rather than as evidence of martial valour. There were four pages, illustrated with skilful miniature watercolours, on the various species of wild orchid; and three setting out 'some observations on the custom of exacting talang-talong (bride-purchase between differing tribes)'.

By contrast, there were innumerable entries of the briefest kind, such as 'To Kutar', or 'A week at the Sun Palace', or 'Fasting'. Many times, the single word 'Ill' sufficed for several days. After the entry: 'Today I buried my dearest,' there was a whole month of silence.

But more and more, as Richard read on, the man's consuming love of Makassang began to shine through, and his plans for it assumed an air of continuous, possessive dedication. His eyes were forever lifted to the hills. Under the heading 'What Can Be Done', set down after some eight years in the territory, Andrew Farthing wrote:

'God's work in this island is enshrined in the two words, Instruction and Love. The people are backward, and must be taught, not only the Gospels, but the simplest forms of modern social intercourse. Though they are happy and generous by nature, they are constantly at the mercy of fanatics and tyrants of the most odious kind, and are often most cruelly used; Love must take the place of oppression and duplicity, and if it be Love armed and girded for combat, it is Love none the less ... The Rajah is, in the main, a benevolent man, but he is subject to violent extremes of temperament, no doubt the heritage of his father, Satsang the Second of callous memory; when baulked of his intent, he will still employ the sword, the thumbscrew, and the phial of poison, in preference to gentler methods of persuasion ... I shall not rest until Makassang, this undoubted jewel of the Java Seas, is a happy and united kingdom, whose public features are Modesty and Virtue, whose fabric is woven of Justice for All, and whose watch-word is Progress under God the Father.'

Such were the aims of Andrew Farthing, writing in his dusty and lonely mission house on the outskirts of Prahang. But his aims were not universally admired, nor ever more than modestly successful; more and more, as time went on, there were references to 'obstruction', 'double-dealing', 'betrayal of sworn promises', and 'setbacks engineered by those whose holy garb should, at the least, be a safeguard against such patent ill will'. His first church, half-built, was burned to the ground again; a school was emptied of children after it had been daubed 'with cryptic and perhaps indecent emblems'; converts on whom Andrew Farthing depended were presently found to be unavailable for further service in the cause of God. In a rare outburst, he once wrote:

'Behind all this malevolence is that insolent rascal, Selang Aro, the so-called High Priest of the Anapuri sect. When I reflect on the machinations of this wholly wicked man, I am sometimes tempted to forget my cloth, and to curse him for the arrant rogue he is. I am sure, though I cannot prove it, that he is directly behind the destruction of Katadi [a mission hall which had been pillaged and desecrated a few weeks earlier] and his manner towards me grows increasingly offensive and contemptuous. What the Lord Buddha, by whom he swears, would have thought of such conduct, passes my imagination; for the Buddha, though not the repository nor the agent of true faith, was certainly an apostle of gentleness and kindly dealing. Would that his consecrated servants were the same!

'Nor am I the only victim among his targets of ill will – indeed, I may be the least of them. It seems to me that Selang Aro entertains delusions of worldly grandeur also – this grandeur to encompass, in due time, the actual rule of Makassang, which his Anapuri sect enjoyed in days gone by. If that be so, then God help Makassang, when it comes under the dominion of this scheming mountebank and villain!'

It was the first intimation of failure, the first sign of the lengthening shadows; it was superseded, as often happened in Andrew Farthing's story, by happier recollections which briefly delighted the ageing missionary. One of these was the birth of Princess Sunara, 'a small and beautiful child, who, we may hope, will one day come to exert a softening influence on this ruthless dynasty'. He noted his regret that he could not baptize the new arrival, but later there were entries which showed that he was being allowed to play an increasing part in her education and upbringing. He went regularly to the palace, teaching her music, the classics, English literature, and 'such aspects of deportment as are within the province of a minister of the Church of Scotland'.

He noted, often, her 'bright spirit', her 'tenderness', her 'promise of great beauty'. Once, in a rare flash of happy satisfaction, he wrote: 'Today the dear child is twelve years old, and at her birthday party sang the air of "Loch Lomond", which I taught her, with exceptional grace and purity. She surprised and delighted all by her modest charm. Of all things done right or wrong in Makassang, perhaps I may be humbly proud that one flower, and that the rarest, has bloomed to such delicate perfection.'

Then, towards the close of the second journal, Andrew Farthing's account turned to the dark side again; the lengthening shadows began to obscure, altogether, the landscape which he loved. There were more examples of 'obstruction and malpractice'; he found that he was losing converts rather than gaining them; on one occasion, the Rajah had been 'angered by a book of Common Prayer found in the royal kitchen'. By contrast – and how many contrasts there were, in this chronicle of the tides of an exiled life – he wrote a sentence almost serene in its resignation: 'If, as it seems, I cannot teach the Gospel, at least I can teach.'

There followed, one by one, accounts of village schools opened, a small hospital and clinic set up; gradually there were fewer reflections upon religious and godly hopes, and more and more concerning pupils, patients, epidemics, the stemming of a bout of cholera which, he noted caustically, 'alarmed the monks of the Golden Pagoda to such an extent that religious differences were, for a time, forgotten'.

On one occasion, at a time of great crisis, he exclaimed: 'At last, a shipment of quinine!' as he had once written: 'Another convert to the Lord!'

But always, in this area as in any other, he wanted to do more; the nearer he drew to the end of his life, the more did his questing spirit shame all lesser dedication. Richard Marriott was reminded, once again, of Sebastian Wickham's final precept: Andrew Farthing also was striving to 'use his kingdom well', but he was sure that he had failed in his task. Indeed, sometimes he seemed convinced that he had done nothing whatsoever of merit, but had frittered away his life in the idlest of all pursuits – the pursuit of a dream. In spite of all his best endeavours, Makassang was still 'backward, heathenish, and poor', under 'a cruel despotism which heeds not the gentle Lamb of God, nor the avenging wrath of His Father'. In the face of such self-accusation – for he saw himself as the only undoubted culprit – all criticism from the lips of smaller men seemed sterile and impudent.

In the last years, the journal halted more and more; its entries grew scanty because of tiredness or ill health – 'Malaria, and dreadful pain', was the notation for his last Christmas Day on earth. It ceased altogether, on a foreboding half sentence – 'I am called to – ' on the evening that he was lured into the forest, and stabbed to death.

The last full page, written a month earlier, had borne witness to his mourning for what must be left undone, however long his life might be spared; its sadness revealed a heartbreaking sense of failure. But within the accents of despair, there was a dauntless message of hope; a message shining through undisguisedly, for all who might read thereafter:

'Someone – not I, because I am old and sick, and have taken the wrong road – but someone might well make an earthly paradise of Makassang. The task awaits the divinely appointed hands. But when they have accomplished this, they must give Makassang back to those to whom it rightly belongs, restoring the equity of the common people. [The style was stilted and formal to the end, yet fundamentally sincere and good-hearted, so that it transcended such limitations.] The white man's task in these islands, as I see it, is not to plunder, nor even to enjoy at leisure; but to teach, to serve, and then to liberate. Of such ministration is the true Kingdom of Heaven. I earnestly pray God that the right teacher and servant may be guided to this unhappy land.'

## VII

He had sighed deeply, and turned towards Sunara, who was watching his face under the lamplight. Andrew Farthing's story of the past was still with him, but it was bound up now with the present – part of the ferment of doubt, peril, and devilry which still infected all Makassang. He caught her eye at last, and smiled, and said: 'It needs no blinding flash to see why I was to read this. Sunara, it is all but irresistible.'

'He was a good man,' she answered. 'And so are you.'

'I – ' he began, but his answer was not to be known till long after. Once more, there was the sound of footsteps in the corridor; this time, they were light and fleeting, the patter of bare feet running, more urgent and alarming than any heavy tread. Richard stood up, as did Sunara, and faced the curtain which masked the doorway; his hand went down to grip the butt of his pistol. But this time it was a friend – his oldest friend of all. The figure who glided into the room like a moving shadow was the nurse, Manina.

She was distraught; even in the half-light, her wrinkled face worked uncontrollably, and her eyes darted from side to side as if seeking hidden enemies. The effort of running made her breath come short, but there was terror in this fast breathing also. When she advanced into the full light of the room, she was the very picture of ancient fear.

Sunara started forward, her hand to her breast. 'What has

happened?' she asked, on a note of anguish. 'Has someone harmed the child?'

Manina, breathless, shook her head. She was visibly trembling; her hands fluttered like birds in a net as she twisted the folds of her sarong, which had gone awry. But at last words came to her lips.

'Not the child, Highness ...' Her voice was cracking with pent-up fear. She turned to Richard, and sketched a curtsey. 'Tuan, they took your servant.'

Now it was Richard's turn to start forward. 'They took John Keston?'

Manina nodded, momentarily beyond speech again; then with a supreme effort she mastered herself. 'Yes, Tuan ... He was asleep in his bed, and soldiers came and carried him away ... They cursed him ... He was struck with a spearshaft when he tried to speak.'

'When was this?' asked Richard.

'Not five minutes ago.' Suddenly her head cocked to one side, in an urgent attempt to catch some sound, and she began to tremble more violently than ever. 'Tuan, I think one follows me.'

They all listened, with an equal alertness, but there seemed no sound of any kind within the palace. Sunara returned to her first fear. 'What of the children?' she demanded. 'Are they guarded?'

Manina nodded again. 'They are safe within the second room ... The girl Drusha lies across the threshold ... So was I lying myself, when I heard them take the Tuan's man ...' Suddenly she was listening again, almost sniffing the air for menacing sound. Then she said, in a frightened whisper: 'One follows me now.'

This time there could be no mistaking; their third visitor of the night was already drawing near, and this time he was a man, in whose firm and heavy tread a timorous ear might detect the very accents of doom. They listened to the footsteps growing louder, ringing on the marble floor, echoing among the lofty arches; there was a ring of metal also – a sword hilt, thought Richard swiftly, which caught on a buckle as the wearer moved. Once more his hand went down to his pistol; if this were a soldier, come on any errand save the most ordinary, he would have a soldier's answer, not a frightened old woman's ... The steps halted outside their apartment, and a heavy knock sounded on the doorpost. Richard called: 'Enter!' on a sharp note, and the curtains moved aside.

'Greetings to all,' said Colonel Kedah.

He was the very picture of military arrogance and pride; the contrast between this confident figure, and the atmosphere of doubt and fear which possessed the room, was shaming to anyone of the smallest spirit. Kedah strode forward into the room as a man of infinite authority, indisputably the new Commander-in-Chief and First Minister, without peer among such pigmies as he might meet on his official rounds. Richard found himself possessed with utter hatred as he looked at their latest visitor; in the tall figure, in the face set in its customary sneer, in the single menacing eye, was enshrined all that he loathed and despised in Makassang. He kept his hand prominently on the butt of his pistol, as he said: 'Kedah ... What brings you here?'

Kedah's glance, which had been moving from person to person with offensive deliberation, came round at last to Richard. The dislike on Richard's face was fully mirrored in his own, as he said: 'You were present at my investiture this evening?'

'You know I was.'

'Then you must know that I am to be addressed as Tunku, like yourself.'

'I wished to avoid confusion,' said Richard sarcastically.

'There can be none.' Kedah's eye began to rove round the room again, with the same leisurely insolence as before. 'You keep late hours,' he said at last. 'Or is it a matter of early rising? And armed also.'

'You are armed,' said Richard.

'I have military duties.' He was looking now at Manina, who crouched in the shadows, a mingled gleam of hatred and fear in her old eyes. 'As well as the duties of First Minister, of which you have now been reminded ... Certain movements were reported to me by the guard-commander. I came to see that all is safe.'

This was too much for Richard. 'I would not say that your presence here adds to our safety.'

Kedah shugged. 'If you are content – ' he said, and turned to go.

Richard would have given much to let him leave without further question. But with Keston in mortal danger at that very moment, he could not do so – and Kedah knew this perfectly well, and could thus afford to play his cat-and-mouse game to his heart's content. It remained only for Richard to pocket his pride, and say: 'The movement you heard was my servant, John Keston, being arrested. I must ask you where he is.'

Kedah turned again, with a thin smile of satisfaction. 'He is under guard.'

'Why?'

'He was found armed near the royal apartments.'

'I do not believe it!'

Kedah raised his eyebrows, in elaborate pantomime of a man confronted by the absurd. 'Whether you believe it or not, it is so. He had a cutlass in his hand, and he was loitering, for no good reason, in a passage in the west wing. He was immediately put under arrest.'

A new sound was suddenly heard in the room. It was Manina, from whose lips came that sharp hissing noise which was the universal expression of derision and disbelief among all Malays. As Kedah turned towards her, his face darkening with fury, she took a step forward, and croaked out: 'He was in his bed!'

'Silence!' shouted Kedah. 'You know nothing! Speak when you are spoken to! Old fool that you are – go back to your room!'

For the first time, Sunara entered the conversation. Her voice was freezing as she addressed Kedah.

'Do not give orders to my servants.'

There was such icy authority in her tone that Kedah paused, with a look of confusion. Then he took command of himself, and bowed slightly to Sunara, and said: 'I am sorry … She angered me with her lies …' A sudden oily gallantry came into his voice as he added, to their utter astonishment: 'You may be sure I would do nothing to offend you – my sister.'

Sunara's face, which had been cold enough, grew positively glacial as she stared back at him. She spoke in a low voice of absolute contempt: 'Do not address me in that disgusting manner.'

Kedah tried to rally beneath the lash of her look and tone. 'You know well enough, Princess, that I have been adopted as your father's son.'

'Yes ...' In the small figure there was the most steely pride Richard had ever seen. 'And I am more than ever happy to have been removed by marriage from such a connection.'

It was open warfare; the fact that her answer was less than accurate (for she had married another 'adopted son' herself) only pointed her overwhelming distaste. Richard, ashamed that Sunara should have been the one to give this lead, quickly jumped in to play his part.

'There are other ways in which you forget your place. You have no business to put John Keston under guard, without advising me.'

'I advise you now,' said Kedah.

'And I demand to see him.'

'He cannot be seen.'

'Why not?'

'He waits to be questioned.' Kedah, slowly regaining his self-confidence, faced Richard squarely. 'I must again remind you of this evening's ceremony. I have been given complete authority over the army, as over everything else in Makassang. Should I choose to arrest a man, and cage him, that is my affair, and no one else's.'

'If he comes to any harm,' Richard told him, 'I will hold you accountable. Remember that.'

'If he comes to any harm, he will have deserved it.'

Richard stepped forward, angry, his hand still on the pistol butt. 'Since you are so stubborn, I will appeal to the Rajah.'

Kedah, now fully composed, shrugged his shoulders. 'Please yourself. But I would not advise it. His Highness has been grossly disturbed once already this evening, and he will not be in the mood for another intrusion.'

'Keston did not disturb him – of that I am sure.'

'I was not speaking of your servant.' A sneer crossed Kedah's face. 'Not of that servant, at least.'

They waited for him to unwrap this mystery, but he made no attempt to do so. Once more, Richard was forced to seek the answer himself.

'You talk in riddles, as usual ... Who has disturbed him tonight?'

There was a long moment of silence. Then Kedah, instead of answering the question, put another himself.

'Was Amin Sang with you earlier?'

'Yes.' It was Sunara who answered, suddenly foreboding. 'Why do you wish to know?'

'I was asking myself who could have inspired him to his extraordinary behaviour.'

Richard, sick at heart, divined the odious theme of this play-acting, and cut it short. He would not pander to this monster's pleasure. 'Have you taken Amin Sang also?'

Kedah nodded. 'Yes.'

'This is lunatic! On what charge? Or was he also wandering the palace corridors with a cutlass in his hand, looking for victims?'

'His arrest is a graver matter altogether.' Kedah spoke with obvious relish. 'He threatened the person of the Rajah ... He was drunk, and he broke into the royal apartments... I find it necessary to ask what you know of this, and what part you played. When he was here, for example, did you ply him with wine?'

'Oh yes!' answered Richard, heavily sarcastic. What Kedah was saying was so ludicrous that he forgot his prudence, and his fear for his friend. 'Oh yes, certainly we plied him with wine! I myself laid him on his back, and poured a flagon down his throat, and then sent him off to insult his Highness!' He looked at Kedah with derisive contempt. 'What nonsense is this? Amin Sang would not insult the Rajah, if he lived to be a hundred years old.'

'He has little chance of that now,' said Kedah.

The words were carelessly uttered, but they struck home with a horrifying chill. Richard had the instant conviction that Kedah had used an exact phrase, with intent – that he had made up his mind that Amin Sang had not, in fact, very much longer to live. Indeed, there might be a worse construction even than that ... He asked, with a fear he could not keep from his voice: 'Where is Amin Sang? What have you done with him?'

Kedah was looking at him with a meaning smile. 'Ah – you are taking the matter seriously now? – it is no longer a joke? I think you are wise ...' His voice became matter-of-fact, a sing-song recital which was more terrifying than any display of anger. 'It is probable that Amin Sang bore some grudge against the Rajah, for sending him away from the palace. Whatever the reason, he tried to force his way into his Highness's apartment, long after midnight. He was drunk, and he was armed ... He made a disturbance, and he shouted for the so-called Fifty of the Brave ... He struggled when the Rajah ordered him arrested, and made an effort to come close to his Highness ... There is no doubt that the guard would have killed him out of hand, if his Highness had not intervened ... Amin Sang is now in chains, and so he will remain until he is brought to trial.'

There was but one more question to be asked, and Richard, steeling his shaken spirit, forced himself to put it: 'What will become of him?'

'I am new to the law,' answered Kedah, 'but I would say that there could be only one penalty.'

Silence fell on the room, complete and terrible. Manina had drawn a fold of her sarong over her head, and was rocking to and fro as she crouched in her corner, a classic figure of grief. Richard and Sunara had come close together, facing Colonel Kedah; it was the soldier's moment of triumph, and there was no single thing to be done save to accept the fact, and perhaps, on the morrow, to seek mercy wherever it might be found. But at this moment, on this fearful night, there was nothing more they could say.

Kedah, however, had not done with them. In the flickering lamplight his figure appeared to loom over them, enormous, not to be resisted; all weapons seemed to lie in his hand, all power pent in that single gleaming eye. When he spoke, he might have been Fate itself, pronouncing doom from a stronghold beyond mortal reach.

'Your Highness made some insulting reference to my adoption as a son.' The first words were to Sunara, but then his eye came round to Richard. 'You also have been pleased to hinder me, in any way you could. Perhaps you will now give some thought to what your situation is. You have not so many allies that you can throw out these challenges, these insults ... Your two Jewish traitors are no more. Your servant Keston is in disgrace. Amin Sang lies in the shadow of the death penalty. You are alone – you have never been more alone! ... So much for my first day as First Minister.' He drew himself up at last, ready to go, ready to leave the battlefield to its ghosts and its mourning. 'We will all see another day,' he went on, and the sing-song note had returned. 'But it will be my day, and all the days after it will be my days ... Remember, when you watch tomorrow's dawn, that men rise, as well as the sun, and that I' – he stabbed his thumb into his chest, with sudden brutal emphasis – 'have risen highest of all. There I will stay.'

At that, he turned on his heel and was gone from the room, with a click and scrape of his sword hilt; and then they were indeed alone.

VIII

It had been an awesome night; the little that remained of it passed like some fearful dream, moving past deadly hazards at a snail's pace. Kedah had left them in the deepest confusion and doubt; Sunara was distressed beyond measure by the happenings of these few fatal hours, and Richard was scarcely less moved. The murder of the Da Costas, so contemptuously brought about, had been a bitter blow; now trumped-up charges had removed yet more of their staunch friends, leaving bare a stage on which the two surviving characters listened in agony for the next blow to fall. For the remaining time of darkness, the heel of the night, they had to endure torments of indecision, of waning confidence, and of actual fear for their lives.

For now, where before a foreboding silence had reigned, there were too many sounds. There were sounds of feet, now slow, now swift; the precise feet of soldiers, the gliding feet of spies. There was the sound of shouting from the barracks, there was the sound of arms in the courtyard below; once there was a wailing, hideous cry, which sent them hot-foot to the children's room – to find both their dear ones wrapped in a sleep so innocent and calm that it shamed the whole adult world. But, for Richard and Sunara, there was never a moment of that night which loosed their tension or brought respite from their crushing cares.

It was when they were returning from the nursery, crossing a dark antechamber, walking hand in hand like their own children, that Richard said: 'I will demand an audience of your father this morning, and insist on seeing Amin Sang, and Keston too. It is monstrous that they should be spirited away like this! Kedah must have lost his senses.'

Sunara shook her head sadly. They were coming out of the dark room into the lamplight; her face, pale and spiritless, proclaimed all their defeated thoughts.

'Kedah is sane enough,' she said. 'Too sane for us ... He has his plans, and they are all coming true. He has made himself the greatest man in the island, after my father. But I cannot forget my father's part in all this. The cruelty and the harsh rule are his. They are his orders, which threw Amin Sang and your own servant into the dungeons.' She raised a weary hand to her forehead. 'That terrible cry ... I cannot put it from my mind ... How can we tell? – they may both be dead already.'

'If not they, then some other wretch ... Oh, this accursed country!' he burst out. 'It is becoming poisoned to the very roots.'

She asked suddenly: 'What keeps you here, Richard?'

He had sat down on one of the daybeds, and let his heavy head fall back on the cushions. The hollow void which was the window showed them that dawn was at hand; into its square of blackness there had crept a pale breath of light; a tree which had been a shadow now grew into substance; one star after another fled away.

'What keeps me here?' he repeated her question. 'Love keeps me here, I think. In fact, I know it. For me, it has always been love. Love of you, first. I used to think that I would not stay in Makassang, unless I loved you. It was true then, when I first thought it, but it is true no longer. Other loves have joined yours and mine. Love of the people here, of their nature. Love of what Andrew Farthing stood for – love of his love. I called it an accursed country, because it is becoming so. But it need not be accursed. That is the tragedy. I love it, and I mourn for what has been done to it, and I cannot desert it now, however hard we may be pressed and harassed.'

She had turned away, and was looking out towards the creeping dawn light. 'It will be an accursed country,' she said, very quietly, 'as long as my father lives.'

There was no need for her to say more; the fearful theme had been sounded; the music now echoed between them, acknowledged, loud to their ears and hearts; a bell sounding the knell of clear conscience.

As he took in her words, he had sat up. 'How can you say such a thing?' he asked, startled and shocked. 'You have never spoken such a thought before.'

She nodded agreement, regretful, resigned. 'It is an impious thought, the worst thought of my life. I have wrestled long with it, and it is still with me. To save these loves you spoke of – perhaps even to save our love – we must make up our minds to do a terrible thing.'

'Why do you say, "to save our love"?'

'It is simple. Because I am part of him, for as long as he lives. You will come to see the same poison in me, and you would never forget it. I will not have that! I will not lose your love, and you will not lose

Makassang. But to keep both, we must not shrink from the worst stroke of all.'

From far away, deep in the palace, a burst of raucous laughter rang out, more ominous than many other sounds of the night. The dawn was now at hand, the pale sky paler still; soon it would be day, with whatever horrors or ordeals that lay stored up for them. But Richard could not bring himself, even at such a moment when the balance of terror was weighted against them, to accept what she was saying.

'We cannot take his life, Sunara. Better for us to fail altogether … It would mean that we had become as wicked and brutal as he.'

She was insistent. 'I called it impiety. There could be no worse crime, for a son or a daughter. But it must be done! Why should we live in mortal danger, why should Makassang be brought to ruin, because my father in his last days has become a child of God?'

'A child of God?' he repeated. He had never heard the phrase before.

'It is our term for madness,' she explained to him. 'And I believe it is true – cruelty and fear and old age have turned his wits. When such a man is mad, and can destroy a whole kingdom, and take my life, and your life, and the children's lives, then an impious act is nothing! It becomes sanctified! It governs the survival of the innocent – and for that, my father must die, before we do!'

Richard was appalled still; and he knew what it must cost her, most dutiful and loving of daughters, to propose such a crime, and to defend it. He watched her, wordless. She was standing with her back to him, staring out of the window; the view from this small room was towards the Steps of Heaven, their terrible symbol of the past and the future. In a whirling instant, he knew that Sunara could be judged right; one only needed to turn the spectrum a little, and acknowledge that all action in Makassang had now reached an utterly degrading plane, and that there was left even to the most upright of men, only a choice of evils … To bring her comfort, to take his share of the burden, he said: 'It must be thought of … But I swear I will do it, Sunara, if we decide so.'

She did not answer; he thought she might not have heard. She was now staring fixedly out of the window, into the dawn light and the new world of today. Suddenly she said, in a very different voice: 'Richard! Please come here!'

He rose swiftly. 'What is it?'

'A most wonderful ship.'

He had feared instant anger; now his alertness relaxed into anticlimax. 'What is a ship to us, however wonderful?' he chided her gently. 'After what has been said, these last few minutes?'

'It is like no ship I have ever seen before. Come quickly, and look!'

Her voice was eager. But she did not yet know that what she saw, in the ghostly light at the foot of the Steps of Heaven, was the most remarkable ship-of-war on the waters of the globe.

§

3

It was not one ship, but three, Richard presently observed through the great telescope; as the daylight gained, two other shadows of grey emerged out of the mist as small paddlewheel vessels, possibly gunboats, anchored in attendance on the flagship. But they were only tiny fish in their giant shoal, dwarfed entirely by the iron bulk of Sunara's 'most wonderful ship', which rode to her cables in the full majesty of maritime power and prestige.

Richard gazed at her with avid eyes, shifting the telescope lenses constantly, dwelling with a sailor's critical care on a dozen aspects of her appearance. Since she was lying stern on to the Steps of Heaven, he saw first her name, which was HMS Warrior, emblazoned in great gilt letters on each quarter. She was a big ship, even by the modern standards of 1862; he judged her perhaps as much as nine thousand tons, and more than four hundred feet long, with a massive breadth of hull which must have been armour-plated. When she swung to her anchors, he counted nearly forty big guns, though he could not guess their calibre. As a strong man might say of his strength, it was doubtless enough.

But what struck his imagination most of all was the fact that she was rigged both for sail and steam; the combination of a long bowsprit and two funnels amidships proclaimed that she was one of the new brand of British warships, which were now transferring to steam power. Looking at this monumental example of what had hitherto been only vague rumour, he felt himself in the presence of history – and of professional doubt. She was the first steam-driven vessel he had ever seen.

Richard adjusted the lenses again, pulling back the focus so that, as the ship swung nearly broadside on, he could examine and enjoy her whole grey length. In spite of its immense power, it was a most beautiful hull, almost yacht-like in its long curved sweep up to the gilded 'warrior' figurehead; the towering spars dwarfed the funnels, the furled canvas gleamed like fresh paint. Indeed, she gleamed all over, stem to stern; the decks must have been holystoned daily, perhaps hourly – there was at that moment a watch of seamen, their trouser legs rolled to the knee, scrubbing and swabbing down the fore-deck, working like precise marionettes at their task. The brasswork, of which there was a lavish amount in every available space, shone like burnished gold wherever the sun caught its surface.

Aft, under a spotless canvas awning covering the quarter-deck, a congregation of officers, tremendous in gold braid, was assembling for some ceremony which he guessed to be the raising of colours at sunrise. Even as he looked, the ceremony approached its climax; there was a bugle call, audible across the water, followed by a concerted shrilling of bosuns' pipes; and slowly the white ensign was hoisted, while on the quarter-deck all stood motionless at the salute. The ensign, with the brave colours of the Royal Navy, completed a trio of noble flags which proclaimed the utmost in consequence –

the Union Jack at the bow, mark of a major warship, and the great St George's Cross at the mainmast, to tell the whole world that this paragon of ships carried an admiral in command.

The deck swabbing was completed; now the guns' crews were exercising the main armament, training and elevating the guns with a constant flickering of polished steel. Signal flags fluttered up to the yardarm, to be answered by smaller bunting from the two gunboats. Another bugle call rang out, and suddenly the decks were cleared, and HMS Warrior became herself again – serene, silent, spotless, ready for any trial of strength with any other ship afloat – or with any other nation.

Richard drew back from the telescope, envious and proud, conscious above all of sudden, enormous nostalgia. Here, he thought, were discipline, order, and command; all the things for which Makassang cried out, concentrated in a few hundred British sailors, a few thousand tons of tested steel. He came to his resolution, though it was a resolution already made for him by all the pressures of the past – his birth, his self-respect, his twin senses of benevolence and authority.

He had long hungered for some magic wand which would restore, not the trappings of rule, but a pattern of order on which decent, humble, and happy men could depend.

The time had come, having found it, to put it into action.

He had sent a messenger to the foot of the Steps of Heaven, ordering the state barge to be made ready, and to await his pleasure; he had called out a ceremonial guard of twelve men, under his own adjutant Paratang, a trusted man who was one of the Fifty. Now he dressed, very carefully, for his appointment with fate.

He was excited, and keyed up with the knowledge that this must be a great occasion; his movements were quick and nervous, and he talked without ceasing, on any subject that came into his mind. It was to Sunara that he talked – a silent Sunara who, helping him to dress, was much preoccupied with her own thoughts. In all, she spoke only two sentences during this girding on; once she murmured: 'It may be that I am to be saved from mortal sin,' and once she was constrained to say: 'Richard – stand still!'

For such an occasion, he could not very well wear his Dutch admiral's uniform; he was dealing now with people of consequence who took such matters seriously. He wore instead a longhi of royal purple, and a white tunic edged with gold thread; his turban was pure white silk, set with a ruby in the centre; his sandals were of ox hide, the straps inlaid with ivory emblems. He made two concessions, one to personal taste, and one to prudence; he wore his single gold earring, and he carried his pistols at his belt.

Finally, when all was ready, he gave swift thought to the selection of a present, without which no great visitor could be greeted; the thought recalled the days of long ago, when old Amin Bulong had first come on board the Lucinda D with the Rajah's gift of a magnificent ivory tusk. He summoned Durilla, his major-domo, and while he waited, he asked himself: What offering would be most welcome to a senior officer of the Royal Navy? Then he grinned, finding that he need waste little time in solving this particular puzzle. When Durilla appeared, bowing, Richard commanded: 'Bring me five thousand rix dollars, in hundred-dollar pieces, in a silk purse.'

Even Admirals of the Fleet were left, at the end, with no more than their half-pay pension.

When Durilla, who had gone on his errand without question, came back bearing the purse of money from Richard's private store, his curiosity overcame discretion. He inquired, with seeming servility: 'When may I expect the Tunku to return?'

'In due course,' answered Richard, whose mood, at long last, was one of unrelenting determination. Durilla, like every other servant in the Sun Palace, owed his place to the Rajah, and his loyalty was, at the best, divided. Anything said here, of any consequence, would be likely to reach other ears, even the highest, within the length of time it would take a man of unobtrusive gait to walk down one long corridor, and up another.

Durilla, a smoothly fat man who, as a companion and sometime friend of John Keston, had perhaps spent an uneasy night, was gently persistent. 'Be sure we will await you, Tunku. Is it to be a long journey?'

Richard, who was at that moment thrusting his primed and loaded pistols into his waist belt, looked up. With the die about to be cast, he felt that he owed it to his fortune to be frank. At certain crossroads, the time for action was also the time for truth.

'It is to be a short journey, Durilla,' he answered, with grim precision. 'I find that I lack friends in Makassang. I therefore go to seek some.'

With that, he kissed Sunara, called to Paratang and his escort, who were marshalled in the antechamber, and walked down the staircase and out into the palace grounds, towards the Steps of Heaven.

Though it was still scarcely full day, the whole of the Sun Palace was already in a ferment; the passageways and the rooms, big and small, were a-twitter with servants and hangers-on and even minor officers of state, receiving and exchanging the rumours which now ran thick and fast through every corner of the great building. The throng moved restlessly, talking and whispering without end; there was a constant surge to and fro, first to crowd to the windows to look at the ships below, then to gather in knots and exchange fantastic stories of what had been seen, and what fresh wonder might next come into view. An anthill disturbed by a giant foot could not have been thrown into a greater uproar, nor have seemed more ludicrous in its pigmy chaos.

The band of determined men surrounding Richard Marriott cleft through this chattering confusion like a knife through cheese; it hardly needed the bold show of arms, and the shouted words of command, for the throng to fall aside, to gape in wonder, and to be left behind like seawrack washed by the tide. Down the broad staircase they went, close-knit, unsmiling, intent; to Captain Paratang, a faithful friend, Richard had communicated his sense of urgent mission, and Paratang's own men had caught the breath of danger. When they passed through the great audience chamber, full of vague and fearful figures, they might have been hawks cutting their way through a flock of starlings.

But outside, on the lawn leading to the Steps of Heaven, there was a moment of high drama, which might have been a different matter altogether.

Here was drawn up a company of soldiers, greatly outnumbering Richard's bodyguard, under the command of Captain Sorba. Sorba's men had been staring to seaward, watching the ships, talking among themselves; they now turned to stare at Richard's advancing force. Their ranks were formed, their arms were ready; and they were stationed in an unbroken line across the head of the steps.

Paratang, at a sign from Richard, checked his men's advance. Then Richard stepped forward, confronting Captain Sorba with an easy confidence.

'I pass your guard, Captain,' he said formally.

Sorba was clearly taken aback. He looked long at Richard, then at his surrounding bodyguard; he turned slightly to look at his own men – a fatal moment of indecision which revealed the weak man in a position of uncertainty. Finally he swallowed, as if to find his tongue, and said, in another military phrase of equal formality: 'My guard stands fast.'

Richard raised his eyebrows. 'You did not hear me, Captain. I pass your guard.'

'I have my orders,' said Sorba, in great agitation. 'No one may pass here.'

'I will pass anywhere I please. If necessary I will fight to pass.'

'You are joking, Tunku.'

'Yes, I am joking.' Richard's tone was still careless, allowing a good-humoured end to this. 'Enjoy your laugh, and then let me pass.'

There was a silence of great uncertainty. Sorba looked again at his own men, and the sight could not have reassured him; already there was some broad byplay between Paratang's force and his own – the invaders making gestures of menace, the defenders falling back in exaggerated alarm. All of them were from the Royal Regiment, and all were thus comrades; it seemed clear that, if it came to a struggle, they would play at fighting also. Sorba, hand on sword hilt, did the best he could.

'My instructions are – ' he began.

Richard cut him short, with the simplest of all gestures – he drew both his pistols.

'My instructions to you,' he said, with the same easy confidence as before, 'are to stand aside. If you do not, I will kill you.'

Captain Sorba, most unfortunate of men, wavered. 'I am only obeying orders,' he said.

'Obey mine,' answered Richard.

At this point of crisis, Paratang also made his own simple contribution. He raised his sword arm, and shouted: 'Guard – advance!'

In a moment, without a drop of blood spilt or a bruise given, they were through.

Breathing more freely, descending the Steps of Heaven towards his destiny, Richard walked with his head high. The burnished breastplates of his guard were ranged on either side of him; his own figure was magnificent; the show was a brave one. But he delayed their advance to its slowest speed. Let them see him coming.

II

They had seen him coming. At the same moment as the royal barge left the foot of the steps, one of the gunboats, which must have hove short her cable, got underway smartly, and raced across the bay to meet them, her paddle wheels churning the shallow water to a pink cauldron of coral atoms. But it seemed a matter of honourable escort, not of precaution: the gunboat dipped her ensign as she met the barge – a salute which Richard, seated under his velvet canopy, gravely acknowledged – and then, after a boiling turn in her own length, settled down on a parallel course to accompany them to the flagship. The number of telescopes trained upon the barge was a flattering gauge of interest.

Close to, the Warrior was gigantic – a great looming bulk of grey like the side of an enormous building, towering above the royal barge as it edged alongside the lowered gangway. Richard prayed that his helmsman might make a good approach, and he was not disappointed: the shouted commands, the rolling beat of the drum, and a furious swirl of backing oars, put the barge into a position so exact and so motionless that he could step on to the ornamental ladder with scarcely an effort. As he set his foot on the lowest part of the roped platform, a waiting officer came to the salute, and inquired, with a certain swiftness: 'Sir, may I know your rank?'

'I am the Prince of Makassang,' answered Richard pleasantly.

'The ruling prince?'

'The son and heir of the ruling Rajah.'

The officer turned, with the same adroit swiftness, and made an unobtrusive gesture to someone above him on the maindeck. Then, as Richard Marriott began to climb the sloping stairway, with his guard following, the first of several gunshots boomed out, echoing across the bay, in the salute appropriate to the heir to a ruling house.

Richard stepped on to the quarter-deck, his hand raised to his turban in acknowledgement. A dozen bosuns' pipes shrilled; a line of junior officers equipped with telescopes sprang to attention; and he walked across a short space of deck towards another group of officers, this one a veritable sea of gold braid, frock coats, and ceremonial swords. From the midst of these, one small trim figure stepped forward, his hand outstretched, his arm heavy with an admiral's insignia of rank, and said heartily: 'Well met, Dick!'

It was his brother Miles.

Richard had been prepared for everything but this; for a moment he came within an ace of surrendering his carefully-guarded demeanour, and treating the occasion on a brotherly plane which would entail a lapse from dignity. But then he stiffened. In a cursory glance, he saw that Miles, though much improved physically, was now very much the admiral, and bore himself with all his old air of high-and-mighty consequence. A lifetime of remembered slights rose to choke a possible cordiality. Nor had he welcomed the salutation 'Dick', which had been far removed from his mood of high resolve. If Miles could be very much the admiral, he himself could be very much the Tunku of Makassang, prince of a country richer and greater than any ship ... He shook his brother's hand, with only the briefest of smiles, and sought for an appropriate answer. It came easily enough.

'Good day, Admiral,' he said, with some condescension. Then, conscious of a hundred staring eyes, an attendant frieze of gold lace, he went on: 'Thank you for your courteous welcome ... My title is the Tunku of Makassang ... Pray present your officers to me.'

It said much for Miles Marriott – indeed, it told much of the changes wrought by twelve years – that by no flicker of an eyelid did he betray any sense of the absurd; he went through Captain This, Commander That – with the gravest of politeness imaginable. The bowing, the saluting, the exchange of formal greetings occupied a full ten minutes, in the airless heat under the awning. Then it was Richard's turn, and Richard's pleasure, to play a gracious role in answer.

Leaving the last of the presentation line – a young lieutenant who stared goggle-eyed at him as if he were some unidentified character from Holy Writ – Richard signed to Captain Paratang, who in turn snapped his fingers at the soldier who bore the purse of rix dollars. Then Richard turned back to his brother Miles.

'My congratulations on a distinguished body of men, Admiral ... It is our custom here to welcome notable visitors with gifts, in token of our peaceful hospitality ... Pray accept this small offering.'

He handed the small offering, which weighed several pounds, to

Miles. Miles received the silken bag with a quizzical look. It might have contained anything; there was only one thing certain, and that was, that it was not empty. Every instinct of politeness demanded that he should not inquire what that 'anything' might be. But there was a limit to politeness, especially between brothers. Weighing the gift in his hands, he answered: 'I thank you, Tunku ... I accept your offering on behalf of Her Imperial Majesty, who reciprocates the compliment ... Perhaps you will understand my curiosity when I inquire the nature of your gift?'

'It is coinage of our realm,' said Richard, with especial delight. 'Five thousand rix dollars, to be exact. You would prefer to express it as one thousand English pounds. And though I heard you accept it on behalf of the Queen, it is in fact intended for yourself. It is our custom in Makassang to honour our visitors personally.'

Miles bowed slightly. 'I defer to your custom.'

'I was sure that you would do so,' said Richard.

'I think,' said Miles, with perceptible readiness, 'that the time has come to conduct you to my quarters below.'

In the cool of the admiral's day cabin, with its private sternwalk high over the water, the brothers shook hands again, with open emotion. They had not seen each other for twelve years; the memories of that parting at Marriott, though acknowledged to be hurtful, had faded with the years; now they had met, in extraordinary circumstances, and found that achievement and honour had wiped out much of the dross of the past, and had improved them. Miles, to his credit, was the first to pay this tribute. Having seen Richard comfortably settled with a cool glass of gin and water, he said with complete friendliness: 'It was good to see you step aboard, Dick. And by God, my small surprise did not shake you! You played that entrance magnificently!'

'You knew I was here?'

'Yes.' Miles gestured with his free hand. 'We have our agents. And you have fame in these parts, as you must know.' He grinned. 'Thank you for that purse of silver, Dick. It will not come amiss.'

'It was of no consequence.' Richard looked at his brother. 'I have changed much, Miles.'

Miles stared back at him. 'Do me the compliment of believing that I have changed also.'

It was true, as Richard swiftly realized; the prim and proper post-Captain, so sure that his candle burned bright and upright in a naughty world, had given place to a man of authority, who need strike no attitudes, nor stand on fancied dignity, to gain his place among men. Richard could even see that his first impression, out on the quarter-deck, had been mistaken, a relic of the unhappy past. Miles conducted himself like an admiral, not from conceit, but because it was necessary for him to play such a part to the world's satisfaction – as necessary as it was for the Tunku of Makassang to assume a bearing of gravity and consequence. They were both entitled to the great and small airs which marched with the rank they had won ... Richard, sipping his drink, found that he could at last meet and deal with his brother, without jealousy and without the poisoned rancours of the past.

'I believe you, Miles. Let us start afresh ... If you know of me, you know that I have married, that I have sons, that I have risen to some position in Makassang. If you have agents, you know what that position is worth today, and what could hang on your visit ... But we will talk of that later. Tell me of yourself, tell me of Marriott! How goes the house?'

'As well as can be expected,' answered Miles, 'with an absentee landlord who cannot oversee it. I have been much away on sea duty, these last few years, and the place as you know needs a constant eye. You would have made a far better squire than I.'

Richard could not forbear to answer: 'I had little chance of that.'

'I know it, Dick.' Miles was truly contrite. 'I played you false, I admit, and I have lived to regret it, in many ways.'

'Let us leave it in the past. It belongs there ... What of Sebastian Wickham?'

'The old man died, some ten years back.' Miles's eyes were briefly shadowed again. 'I saw to it that he did not want, though there is little merit in that. To my shame, I sent him away, and he could not stand the parting from Marriott. But there was no employment for him there, Dick – you must allow me that much credit. And Lucinda thought him too much of a friend to you – as may have been true. She did not want such a reminder.'

'You married Lucinda?'

'Within six months. But we have been parted now, for many years. She lives in London, where her chosen friends seem to be.'

'And children?'

'None.' Miles smiled at last, ready to assign this small tragedy to its appointed place. 'You may believe me, Dick, they were not the happiest years of my life.'

'I am sorry for that,' said Richard, and he meant it. 'But you have other things to comfort you. To be made admiral at thirty-three! And with a sea-command like this one. For the first time I am envious – I have never in my life seen a ship like the Warrior.'

'There is none in all the world!' Lured on by a matter of professional pride, Miles Marriott became boyish in his ardour. 'We call them broadside iron-clads, and this is the first one to be launched. She will do fifteen knots under her steampower, even though she is two-thirds armourplated, and we mount forty guns in all. Even my gunboats have an eight-inch gun apiece, and yet they only draw four feet. They are for close work inshore ... Oh, we have some fine new ships in the Navy – not before they were due! Mine is just the force for a business like this.'

'What business is that?'

There was a moment of hesitation before Miles answered; a small veil seemed to drop for a moment, coming between him and his mood of brotherly frankness; but after a second or so he replied readily enough: 'A business that will keep till later, Dick. But I meant, principally, showing the British flag, with all that it means. We find that the Warrior and her gunboats have a wonderfully calming effect ... I have been Commander-in-Chief on the China Station these past five years; the Warrior came out to show off her paces in the Indian Ocean and the China Seas, and to take me home again. But after Singapore I was diverted here, under sealed orders, with a certain mission.'

Richard smiled. 'Which will keep till later?'

'Till after lunch, at least. Come, let us join the wardroom, Dick. You can be the Tunku, and I can be the admiral, and we will see who is grandest.'

'Tunku or not,' said Richard, rising, 'it's good to hear some sailor's talk again.'

'Perhaps you should have worn your uniform,' answered Miles, straight-faced – and, at Richard's startled look, burst into a roar of laughter. 'I told you we had agents … Come, let's go to eat.'

Luncheon, in the best tradition of the Royal Navy afloat, was execrable – a great steaming stew of greasy pork chops, potatoes, dumplings, and carrots, followed by slabs of plumduff smothered with custard. It would have been difficult for the most talented of naval cooks to devise a meal more unsuitable to the tropics. Richard, toying with this mountainous repast, was amazed by the hearty appetite of those around him; from the highest to the lowest – and junior rank was no barrier to accomplishment – there was no one at the long wardroom table who, in a temperature approaching ninety degrees Fahrenheit, did not fall to with a will, demolishing heaped platters at a pace which would have made an elephant blench. Perhaps this was the actual 'stuff of greatness' by which the Royal Navy was reputed to be sustained.

But he enjoyed himself enormously. Seated on Miles's right hand, he had as neighbour a Post-Captain Templeton, the Warrior's commander under the admiral. Templeton was a most entertaining companion; he had recently voyaged round the world on an Admiralty charting survey, and there seemed no country, and no ocean, with which he was not familiar. It was fair to say that some of his garnered information was far removed from official hydrography.

But his account of the women of the Marquesas Islands, who, he swore, measured a man's social status by a most extraordinary yardstick, was broadly diverting. Richard was delighted to see that Miles could enjoy such anecdotes, and even cap them. A dozen years earlier, he would have quit the table with a sniff from a nose held unconscionably high in the air. While a moralist might deplore the change, a brother could only applaud it.

But afterwards, in Miles's day cabin again, the day began to go sour. Its decline set in sharply with the 'business' which Miles had mentioned earlier; a business which required the presence of a third party. This was a gentleman introduced by the admiral as 'Mr Possitter, my political officer'. Mr Possitter, who had not taken luncheon in the wardroom, could only be described as a snuffling weasel of a Civil Servant, pale as a slug, sharp as a ferret – in truth, thought Richard, there was no end to such rustic similes where Mr Possitter was concerned. But he was clearly a man of consequence, a Foreign Office under-secretary to whom even Admiral Marriott must listen, if not defer; and the business which had brought the Warrior and her escort of gunboats to Makassang was Mr Possitter's business, and no other.

Mr Possitter, who was dressed in a white silk suit which gave him a curious air of charade – his very nightshirt, one thought, must be cut from black broadcloth – Mr Possitter earned Richard's immediate dislike by addressing him as 'Marriott', in the Civil Service mode; when this had been corrected, with freezing dignity, his pronunciation of the title 'Tunku' was so elaborately formal that it could serve as an equal insult. But with this, Richard had to be content – and with much else besides.

Miles Marriott broached the new topic of his 'certain mission' warily enough; it was Mr Possitter, from what he deemed to be a position of strength, who produced chapter and verse for an astonishing proposal.

'I will be brief, Tunku,' he said, with the same sarcastic intonation as before. 'We have heard of your difficulties here, and your own position. The Satsang dynasty has never been strong, and even with the disposal of the Anapuri, in which you yourself played a major part, there seems no certainty as to who will eventually come to rule Makassang.' He paused, and sniffed, and put his spidery hands together; Richard could almost hear him now intoning: Paragraph Two. Sub-heading A. 'Makassang is far too valuable, in every sense of the word, to be left in this situation. Politics, as well as nature, abhors a vacuum.' He smiled a wintry smile, as if he had made a highly original joke – as he may indeed have believed. 'That being so, and bearing in mind certain Dutch ambitions in this area, Her Majesty's Government have decided to annex Makassang to the Crown as a dependency, and to confer the benefits of British rule – to use a loose term, of Pax Britannica – on this divided island. Peace and prosperity will follow in due course.'

Richard sat back, in utter amazement; the idea that Makassang could be taken over in this fashion, and all her troubles solved by a squeaky pen wielded in London, was truly astonishing. However much he had yearned for British stability and order, however much he needed allies to bring the blessing of peace, none of these things could ever be achieved by the help of such as Mr Possitter.

But because of the doubts he had brought with him on board the Warrior, and because he remained in desperate need of friends, he had to temporize.

'Makassang is a more complex country than you seem to think,' he began. 'Clearly you know something of the problems of this island, but you can know little of the people. They have divided loyalties at the best. A Sea-Dyak and a Land-Dyak, who have been at each other's throats for generations, could only combine to throw an interloper into the sea. Then they would turn upon each other again. They would never agree to alien rule, even backed up by warships and gunboats, without a prolonged period of discussion and persuasion, and probably a good deal of bloodshed as well.' He raised a finger to emphasize his words. 'They are not mere cyphers, Mr Possitter. They are people – proud people who revere their leaders and prize their freedom. They might never give their consent – or they might give it, and then turn treacherous and you would set a pattern of civil strife which might continue for fifty bloody years, and bring this country to ruin.'

'You must really give us more credit than that,' said Mr Possitter fussily. 'We would issue a proclamation! Setting out our objectives.'

'Our percentage of literacy, alas, is not high.'

'And of course we would hold talks.' Mr Possitter looked at Richard as if his objections were entirely frivolous. 'A series of round-table discussions, with minutes carefully recorded. We have had some experience in these matters, Tunku. And we are not without certain resources of a realistic kind. It is probable that one or both the gunboats would remain here, as long as might be deemed advisable. I propose to stay on myself, as acting Resident Commissioner, until a suitable appointment of a Governor is made.'

This was too much for Richard. 'Yourself and a gunboat? I did not realize the full impact of this. The Dyaks would have no chance!'

'Now, Dick,' interposed Miles Marriott, reprovingly. 'Hear him out. This is official policy, whether you approve it or not. And it is to be backed, without question, by the force that you see here.'

'It is official bunkum.' Richard was beginning to become angry. 'Makassang is not some ragamuffin kingdom that can be taken over by the stroke of a pen.' He looked at Mr Possitter; he felt that, if only to relieve his feelings, he could be scathing. 'My good man, do you know what the Land-Dyaks do to someone who tries to usurp the ruling power, and of whom they do not approve? They wear hoops of his gut strung round their necks until it shrivels to nothing ...' He was constrained to go further. 'You have gut to lose, Mr Possitter? Believe me, you will lose it tomorrow, if you try to put this absurd plan into action.'

Mr Possitter, who was not without spirit of a certain formal kind, drew himself up. 'I do not care for coarse expression,' he said. 'It is a mark of immaturity.' And after allowing this reproof to sink in, he went on: 'You say you are not a ragamuffin kingdom, Tunku, and in the interests of concord I will take your word for it. But we are not amateurs, either. Admiral Marriott has a force at his disposal here, entirely sufficient to deal with these Land-Dyaks of yours – and anyone else who may embark on a course of resistance. I repeat, anyone ... Our sole point is this: there is likely to be a vacuum of power in Makassang – '

'We can deal with that ourselves,' interrupted Richard, 'in our own good time. We can settle this, without becoming the creature of another country.'

'I wonder,' said Mr Possitter, with a keen glance. 'In fact, I take leave to doubt it. Our information is that from now on, a period of complete disorder is far more likely to supervene. Be that as it may, the fact remains that we cannot leave such a matter to chance. It would be deplorable, for example, if the Dutch took advantage of the confusion to annex one of the richest islands in the Java Sea. It would upset the local balance of power entirely.'

Richard's eyebrows went up. 'You confuse the issue. We are not interested in your petty wrangles with the Dutch, or with any other nation. Our balance of power lies within. I told you – we are people here, not pawns. You cannot annex us, and tuck us away in some Foreign Office pigeonhole, and expect us to remain there.'

The pursing of Mr Possitter's lips was in the best tradition of official rebuke. 'You are a people, if you allow me to be frank, living an exotic existence utterly out of touch with the modern world. A great deal might be made of Makassang, with some protecting power to guide her.' He had a sheet of notepaper on the desk in front of him, and he glanced at it unobtrusively. 'You have teak, silver, rubies, antimony, rubber, spices, and copra, some in great abundance. But they are scarcely developed at all – '

'Coffee,' said Richard suddenly.

'I beg your pardon?'

'We have coffee.'

Mr Possitter shook his head. 'No, no! The soil is quite unsuitable.

You have no coffee. It is not on the official list.'

'It is on my table, at this very moment.'

'Imported from Java, no doubt.'

'Grown on my own estate near Prahang, our capital ...' With an effort, Richard returned to serious matters. 'Mr Possitter, what you suggest is out of the question, however many proclamations you issue. The people of Makassang have a profound sense of dynasty. Some of it is admirable, some of it misguided and vicious. But it means one thing, one constant factor. They simply will not accept a ruler imposed on them from outside, a foreigner.'

'What about yourself?' inquired Mr Possitter shrewdly.

'I am in a special position. I have married into the dynasty. I have a son proclaimed as the Rajah Muda. I have lived here, and fought here, and I know their problems. I have a loyal following, as I can show you. But even so, as matters stand at the moment, my situation is one of the utmost difficulty.' He glanced at Mr Possitter, casually. 'However, I am open to argument. Are you suggesting that I should become Rajah, with your backing?'

Mr Possitter was silent for a moment, and Miles Marriott answered for him.

'We had it in mind, Dick, but the idea is not well-liked at home. We came to a similar arrangement with James Brooke at Sarawak –'

'A pestilent fellow!' interjected Mr Possitter.

'Now who is he?' asked Richard, who knew perfectly well. 'Is he a Malay?'

'Good gracious, no!' said Mr Possitter. 'He is an Englishman, ruling a mob of blackfellows.' The absurd term came out quite naturally. 'But we have had our troubles with Brooke, from the very beginning, and we do not wish to repeat the mistake.'

'What troubles are these?'

'To start with,' said Mr Possitter, 'he does not answer his letters.'

'It is not the worst sin in the world.'

'It is unforgivable,' said Mr Possitter.

The interview continued; now Richard scarcely attended to it, though he gave short answers when they were appropriate. The truth was, that he was in a worse state of indecision than ever. He had come on board the Warrior, with only the vaguest of ideas, but one of them had certainly been to solicit outside help in bringing order to Makassang. Now he was not at all sure. If order meant Admiral Sir Miles Marriott at his back, and a thousand armed blue-jackets to see fair play, well and good; if it meant Mr Possitter, with his proclamations, and tidy Foreign Office labels, and talk of 'blackfellows', and some nincompoop from the House of Lords installed as Governor, then it was another matter altogether.

The bulk of the people of Makassang would no more accept such a man, as the embodiment of rule from Whitehall in London, than they would accept rule by fanatic priests from the Shwe Dagon. The one was bloodthirsty and tyrannous, the other desiccated and absurd ... Suddenly he found that he had had more than enough of this political dialogue, for the time being, and he stood up, somewhat precipitately.

Mr Possitter, who had just embarked upon a dissertation on what he termed 'sound Christian instruction on a parochial basis' – one could imagine with what cries of joy the Anapuri would welcome this – Mr Possitter looked up, startled and offended.

'I was not aware that this interview was at an end,' he remarked with some tartness. 'Does this mean that you agree to our proposal, Tunku?'

'It does not,' answered Richard. His hands went to the pistols at his belt, and Mr Possitter followed them with a certain apprehension. 'But I am weary of talking – particularly such nonsense as this – and it is past my siesta hour. I will return to the palace.'

'But we have not covered half the ground,' objected Mr Possitter. His small figure positively bristled, behind a spectral mound of unopened files. 'What of the Rajah? How will he receive this suggestion? What arrangements are to be made about a proclamation? If armed sailors are landed, how will they be received? What is my own position? We cannot possibly break off – '

'You are dealing with me,' said Richard, going to the heart of the matter. 'Not the Rajah.' He turned to Miles, who was eyeing him with concealed amusement. 'Come to luncheon tomorrow,' he said. 'Bring Mr Possitter with you – we will give him some Makassang coffee to round off the meal. And you will have my answer then. Or some counter-proposal. There is nothing cut and dried in Makassang. Things change from day to day, from hour to hour. A wise man is not too proud to change with them.'

Miles nodded. 'You can guarantee us safe conduct?'

'Yes.'

'How can we be sure – ' began Mr Possitter.

Richard cut him short. 'I command enough blackfellows,' he said, with barbed emphasis, 'to see that my guests eat their luncheon in peace.'

When Mr Possitter was gone, a very monument of official disgust, Miles Marriott shook his head in mild reproof. 'You should bear easy on him, Dick. He is not such a bad fellow at heart.'

'I do not agree.' He looked at his brother straightly. 'Miles, his sort of rule will not do for Makassang. The people would never accept it.'

'But if it were anyone except Mr Possitter who had brought the glad tidings – ?'

'No. It is the pattern of the thing, not the man – though God knows the man is sufficiently tedious. We cannot be ruled by a stranger from London.'

'What, then?'

Richard Marriott made his greatest resolve of all. 'Myself as Rajah, with help from England. But not too much help, and not too long continued.'

Miles looked dubious. 'They will not like it at home.'

'They will not like it here, otherwise.'

'What about the present Rajah' – Miles grinned – 'your honoured father-in-law?'

'I have worse enemies than he,' declared Richard. 'But if I strike once, hard, I can defeat them all. Then we can make something of Makassang – we may even grow a crop of coffee, using seed from Whitehall.'

Miles looked at him. 'By God, I am not sure you need the Warrior at all!'

Richard smiled in answer. 'Believe me, I do. That is, unless something unforeseen takes place. And in any case, I am glad to see her here. And yourself especially.' He held out his hand in farewell. 'These are bitter times, Miles, as you must have guessed. A single chance can make or break me now and make or break Makassang. You may be sure that I am on the side of the angels – but I need an archangel's sword, as well.'

'At your service, Tunku,' said Miles Marriott.

Miles saw him to the foot of the ladder, with rare courtesy, and safely into his barge. While the pipes shrilled, and the guns boomed out across the bay, already cooled by the approach of evening, the two of them preserved the utmost decorum. But, when the last salute was given and returned, Admiral Marriott spoke a single sentence to the Tunku of Makassang. Leaning forward, he murmured: 'She grew very stout, Dick.'

Thus they parted, brothers again.

III

Until nightfall, and beyond, Richard Marriott did the hardest thing of all – he did nothing. Girding himself for an unknown future which could only bring severe ordeals, he waited, and watched, and nursed the strength which must inevitably be put to its sternest test, within a very short space of time.

Some of the omens encouraged him. When he had walked back through the Sun Palace, flanked by Captain Paratang and his bodyguard, all as determined as before, it was to a very different welcome. The officer who had the guard saluted him with tremendous

371

readiness, and allowed him unmolested passage; after that, it was smiles, smiles, all the way, from servants and courtiers and palace hangers-on, who vied with each other to bow low, and give way, and called out 'Tunku!' in an ecstasy of obeisance. Apparently he had drawn positive strength and virtue from his call on the Warrior. 'We heard the guns, Tunku,' murmured one of the chamberlains, in awe, as if the guns had been Richard's own.

Durilla, his major-domo, a nervous bundle of curiosity, had been equally obsequious. 'They say your servant Keston will return within a few hours, Tunku,' he had said, when he helped Richard to remove his formal clothes and put on more comfortable attire. 'It cannot be too early for me,' Richard had answered grimly – but he left it at that. He was not going to make any move, at this juncture. Let other people make their moves, and he would then judge his response. Above all, let there be a move from the highest quarter in the land, and he would treat it on its merits.

He had bathed, and rested, and played with the children in the nursery; when still no summons came from the Rajah, nor a message of any kind, he dined quietly with Sunara, and enjoyed her company as if this were an evening like any other evening. He could play this game of patience, with the best players in the world ... Sunara, gauging his mood, had been loving attention itself; with her own hands she had served their meal of gulls' eggs and cinnammon rice ('But make my portion small, for pity's sake,' he had pleaded, in groaning remembrance of the luncheon on board the Warrior), and afterwards had bathed his eyelids and rubbed his temples with sandalwood oil, to ease the stress of the day.

'My brother pays us a visit tomorrow,' he had told her at one point. 'He will eat with me at midday. There will be others – three or four. I would like him to be entertained to the best of our resources.'

Sunara smiled gently, divining what lay behind this. 'I will see that he has a welcome he will remember all his life,' she promised, stroking his brow. 'It is not everyone who has a prince for a host.'

'Perhaps the gold plate?'

'And the goblets from Ethiopia.'

How well she understood him, even to his childish urge to impress an elder brother ... For a short space, he surrendered to this loving care. It was all that he needed, in the lull that marked the eve of the struggle.

Before she withdrew, she asked: 'What now, Richard?'

'I wait,' he said.

'I am proud of you, Tuan,' she murmured, and kissed him, and was gone.

While he did wait, for a summons or a message, conscious all the time of the battle of wills which must be going on elsewhere, he had time to think more carefully of what the day had brought him, and what tomorrow might bring also. In his visit to the Warrior, he had been disappointed, but he had not been surprised; it was ridiculous, in cold thought, to suppose that a so-called prince of some 'ragamuffin kingdom' in the Far East could appear out of the jungle, go on board an English warship, and expect imperial support to confirm him in his rule. The Royal Navy, even in the person of his brother Miles, would have to think long and sober thoughts, before it gave any such aid.

But Mr Possitter was another matter. In assessing him, and his proposal, Richard had tried to be honest with himself; it might be, as Miles had suggested, that it was his bleak, graceless personality, not his actual plan, which had brought from Richard so quick a reaction. But in all fairness, he knew this was not so. Mr Possitter's scheme of rule from outside simply would not do for the people of Makassang; if they could rise and choke to death the Anapuri, their own sanctified priests, what would they do to a lord in a white suit from half across the world, proclaiming that the blessings of some unknown queen (a woman on a throne!) were now to be conferred on their island? Richard knew exactly what they would do, and the prospect was horrifying.

There had to be a transfer of power – so much had become

certain. But for very love of Makassang, it could not be to Mr Possitter. It could not be to Kedah. It could only be to himself.

Miles would help him, if he could show Miles that, of all the office-seekers, the men of ambition, he was the most promising, the most likely to succeed, the best-intentioned, the best.

A step sounded in the passageway, precise, brisk; a step on a certain errand. Richard did not stir, nor even make ready his arms. In spite of all, fortune's star shone brightly on him, at this strange moment. In his soul he knew that no one in the Sun Palace was going to kill him, tonight – and perhaps for many nights.

It was his major-domo, Durilla, who entered with a great air of importance.

'Tunku, his Highness summons you to audience,' he said, with a bow.

Richard, who had been reclining on a couch, smoking the last of a long cheroot, did not change his position. He looked at Durilla in silence before he answered: 'Who brought this summons?'

Durilla seemed startled. 'Tunku, I do not know ... It was given to me by another messenger ... I will inquire, if you wish.'

'Inquire,' said Richard.

Durilla returned within the course of a few minutes. 'Tunku, I have inquired. It seems it was brought by a soldier of Captain Sorba's guard.'

'A soldier?' repeated Richard incredulously, as if Durilla had said, a watersnake. 'Since when was the Tunku of Makassang summoned to audience by a soldier? Send for this soldier's commander.'

'Yes, Tunku,' said Durilla, unhappy. He was emboldened to add: 'Tunku, the Rajah waits.'

'I wait.' answered Richard. 'I will hear this summons from the lips of the guard-commander. Then I may come to believe it. But from no one else.'

There was a pause, a silence, a deal of whispering; then a longer pause, while Richard, following his star, reclined immovable on his couch, waiting for others to make their move. Presently there came a clink of arms and accoutrements, and Captain Sorba appeared, at a brisk gait which must have been dictated by pressing urgency.

'Tunku,' he said, saluting.

'You have a message?'

'The Rajah summons you to audience, Tunku.'

'What happened to this message, between the Rajah's lips and my ears?'

Captain Sorba, whose day had already been hard, swallowed. 'Tunku, I could not leave my post. I sent a soldier to bring it to you, as has been done before. I intended no lack of respect.'

'I hope not,' said Richard hardly, 'because I am in the same mood as this morning.' He added, almost as an after-thought: 'You had this message from the Rajah's own lips?'

Captain Sorba began to look apprehensive, as indeed he might. 'Not directly, Tunku.'

Richard waited, in silence. He would not go too far with this comedy, but he was in the mood to play it for what it was worth. 'Who gave it to you, then?' he asked, after a due interval.

'Tunku,' answered Captain Sorba, with extreme unwillingness, 'I had the message from Colonel – from the Tunku Kedah.'

'So ...' Richard nodded, as a reasonable man nods. 'We could hardly trouble the Commander-in-Chief to deliver it in person, could we?'

'No, Tunku,' said Sorba, thankfully.

'Yet I do not wholly believe this summons.'

'Tunku?'

'I will tell you why. I have not had the privilege of audience with the Rajah for several days now. On the last occasion on which I asked for it, he sent a message that he was indisposed. From that, I understood that I was in disfavour. I can scarcely believe my good fortune now.'

Panic peeped from Captain Sorba's eyes. 'Tunku, I know nothing of this ... I am not skilled in such things ... But I swear that this is a true summons to audience ... Tunku, the Rajah waits for you.'

'Yet I cannot believe it. I might have trouble passing the guard. This might be my day for such trouble.'

Sorba was in a sweat of anxiety. 'Tunku, I swear it!'

Richard shook his head. He felt strong now, and he made his resolve. 'There is only one thing which would make me believe this summons – '

'Sir, I cannot – '

'Be pleased to tell Colonel Kedah of my doubts. They spring from the worries and difficulties of the past few days, and of this morning ...' He spoke carefully, a man taking his last cast of soundings before voyaging into deep water. 'Tell Colonel Kedah, with my fraternal compliments, that I will not credit this summons, unless it is delivered to me by the voice of John Keston himself.'

He rose at that, dismissing Captain Sorba, refusing another word. He knew that he would get his way. And he knew that, in Makassang, he had now sat still long enough.


A strong man could afford to be affable; indeed, he need be nothing else.

'I am so sorry to have kept your Highness waiting,' said Richard, with the customary bow of greeting. 'My servant Keston was detained.'

The Rajah, seated before a table in one of the smaller council chambers, flanked by Colonel Kedah, stared back at him without speaking. He was furiously angry – so much was easy to see; his papery hands were shaking, his old face set in an expression of the most baleful kind. Kedah was another angry man, though more controlled; at this moment, the Rajah need give rein only to his feelings, while Kedah had to think and plan as well. It would be interesting to see how soon one of them, or both, lost his anger and grew afraid ... Finally the Rajah broke the silence, on a high note of impatience and complaint: 'What foolery is this? When I summon you to audience, I do not want excuses and messages sent in return! How dare you presume to make this delay?'

Richard allowed his eyebrows to rise a fraction. 'There was no foolery, and no presumption intended. When I heard of your Highness's summons, I could scarcely believe it, in the circumstances. I needed to verify the message, before I intruded on you. That was all that delayed me.'

'You try my patience, Tunku!'

'And after that,' said Richard, on the same careless note, 'I had to dress in a manner suitable for an audience. For that, I needed the help of John Keston.' His eyes turned to Colonel Kedah. 'His presence was most useful. But if I thank you for his release, that does not absolve from blame those responsible for his arrest.'

'I released him,' growled Kedah, 'because after examination he was found to be innocent.'

'A compliment, from such a great judge of innocence!'

'Enough, enough!' snapped the Rajah. 'I am not amused by these exchanges.' But he was examining Richard with more care, seeking to read his mind; if his own rage had not had its customary effect, there must be some potent reason which rendered it harmless. 'You have something to tell me, Tunku.'

'I? Nothing. I am here to listen to your Highness.'

'I warn you not to play with me.'

'I assure your Highness that I wait only to hear the purpose of this audience. But in fact, I have one question.'

'What is that?'

'May I have your Highness's permission to sit down? I have had an arduous day.'

'Be seated, then. What is your question?'

Richard, taking his seat in a comfortable chair, looked up in surprise. 'That was my question, your Highness. I wished to know if I might sit down.'

This was altogether too much for the Rajah. His voice became a menacing snarl. 'Tunku, I warn you for the last time! I will not be played with! And if you do not choose to speak, I will speak. But hear me well, and watch your answers! You went out to visit the ship without consulting me, or seeking my permission. Why?'

'For a very simple reason. Your Highness was not receiving me. When I asked for an audience earlier, I was told that you were indisposed.' He gestured towards Colonel Kedah. 'This man told me so. I believed him. If he was not telling the truth – '

Colonel Kedah, who had been silent and watchful, came to life. 'That was in the matter of the Da Costas. You know that well enough. This was a new matter. You should have asked for a new audience.'

Richard shook his head, as if in confusion. 'Who am I, to guess when the Rajah will receive me, and when he will not? I cannot gaze into crystal balls! If I have not the ear of his Highness – '

'Stop!' shouted the Rajah. 'You drive me mad with your stupid wrangling.' He turned again to Richard. 'We have laid this much bare – you went out to the ship, without my permission. You can have no business there, of any honest sort. The ship is foreign, unknown. Why did you go, and what did you do there?'

'Why should I not go?'

'Answer my question, Tunku! Why did you go out to the ship?'

'I was lonely,' said Richard.

'Do not talk like a child!'

Richard seized on the convenient word. 'Indeed, I felt like a child, a neglected child … Your Highness would not receive me. My servant had been spirited away, and my greatest friend in the island, Amin Sang, had been thrown into prison. I lacked companions … Who could blame me, for going out to seek allies?'

'Allies?' The Rajah's tone was sharp.

'Just so,' answered Richard. 'Allies.' Then he fell silent, content to let the moment rest upon this giant question mark.

There was a pause, a most understandable pause; the word 'allies' might have been innocent, but with the bright picture of the Warrior and her gunboats present in all their minds, it lost its innocence and became, as Richard had intended, ominous. The Rajah, now sunk in thought, drummed his fingers on the table, darting an occasional glance at Richard; Colonel Kedah, busy with his devious plans, must have been considering, and rejecting, a score of questions, some natural, some self-betraying, if his face were anything to go by. But finally it was he who spoke.

'Did you obtain these allies?' he asked.

Richard answered, as if he were discussing some minor subject: 'I found some friends, certainly.'

Kedah decided, as he thought, to pounce on this admission. 'Why should you wish to make friends, of such a kind? On board an English ship? What has an English ship to do with Makassang? Why should you need friends from an English ship? Why should you suppose that they would give you a hearing, in the first place?'

'Why, indeed?'

'Answer me, Tunku!'

'I am sorry,' said Richard abstractedly. 'I was thinking of another matter. As I told you, it has been a long day. What was your question?'

'You heard my question.' said Kedah, between clenched teeth. 'It concerned your need for friends. Why do you need friends from an English ship?'

'I no longer need friends,' said Richard.

'What are we to understand from that?'

'Is it so subtle? Presumably it means that I have found the friends I was looking for. But I can tell you – I need one more thing.'

'What is that?'

'It has been a long day,' said Richard. 'I need a glass of sangaree.'

In the sulphurous silence, the Rajah said suddenly: 'Send for it.'

'Your Highness – ' began Kedah.

'Send for it,' repeated the Rajah. 'And quickly.'

There were no servants waiting on them, and no bell to hand. Kedah rose, with black brows, and walked from the room in search of some attendance. Richard, smiling faintly, watched him go, and then said: 'Thank you, your Highness. My needs are greater than my courtesy, perhaps.'

The Rajah, staring at him, asked: 'Why do you provoke Kedah?'

'I do not like him. In fact, I would go further – I hate his very soul!'

'And you feel strong enough to show it?'

'I feel very strong.'

There was some loud shouting, on a note of anger, from far away; Kedah, having found a servant, was apparently less than satisfied with the man's despatch. But presently he returned, and sat down, thunder in his face. After a hard-breathing pause, he said: 'It is coming.'

'I beg your pardon?'

'Your cursed sangaree – it is coming.'

'You are most considerate.'

'Do not rely on it … And now, let us hear of these allies of yours.'

Richard held up his hand. 'First things first. You must allow me my refreshment.'

The moments ticked away; the silence, of Kedah at least, was positively murderous. Presently there were footsteps, unhurried, patient, and one of the palace wine butlers appeared, with a silver tray on which a tall glass of sangaree reposed. Trained in court etiquette, he bowed first to the Rajah, then precisely towards a spot midway between Richard and Kedah. Then he stood waiting.

'Hurry up!' said Kedah, almost shouting. 'Serve it, and leave us!'

The wine butler, an old man whose expression at the best was one of simple deference to the wishes of the great, began to tremble. The glass and the tray rattled perilously as he looked from one to the other.

'Serve it!' shouted Kedah, nearly beside himself.

'Tuan – ' whispered the old man, in anguish.

'It is mine,' said Richard. 'And thank you kindly.'

He took the glass, and, as the wine butler hurried fearfully from the room, raised it to his lips. The Rajah and Kedah watched him with terrible impatience. Finally Richard gave his verdict.

'A trifle sour, for my taste,' he said. 'But it will serve.'

'Do you expect me to fetch you another?' inquired Kedah viciously.

'Not for some ten minutes, at least.'

'Insolent dog!' shouted Kedah, provoked beyond his endurance. 'Take care how you answer me!'

'I am taking great care,' answered Richard. 'If I can make myself plainer, be sure I will do so.'

Kedah's single eye burned with fury; for a moment he looked as if he would start forward and run Richard through with his sword. Then the Rajah intervened.

'Why cannot you be friends?' he asked, querulously. 'I am tired of this wrangling, and we waste time instead of making progress.'

'Who could make progress,' demanded Kedah, 'with insolence such as this?'

'Be silent!' commanded the Rajah. 'It was you who provoked it.'

'Your Highness – ' began Kedah, astounded.

'Hold your tongue!' The old man turned to Richard. 'The time has come for truth,' he said, in a voice entirely changed. It was easy to divine that he had been thinking, and that his thoughts had been as swift as change itself. 'If you have secrets, you may tell them. If you have news for me, I will hear it. That is the purpose of this audience. But do not trifle any longer. You have enjoyed your play-acting. Now tell me of the ship.'

Richard set down his glass. For the first time, he felt ready to confront his enemies with the facts. It was true, as the Rajah had said, that he had enjoyed his play-acting; and true also that the moment of reality was at hand. For Kedah, he felt nothing save sworn hatred; but looking at the Rajah, he could almost feel pity for an old man whose star was waning. It was certain that he had brought it upon himself. But who could hold a grudge against cruelty which turned to fear, against strength which grew feeble? All one must do was to guard against surprise or treachery – and in that resolve, he felt as strong as he had ever been.

It was, on sober second thoughts, no occasion for pity, nor for the luxury of forgiveness. It was time to take a step into the inexorable future.

'I will be brief,' said Richard, and his tone was crisp and businesslike. 'I went out to visit the great ship, for reasons which must be clear to you. In any case, they are clear enough to me. I will not beg for friends in Makassang; I do not have to, I will find others – and I have found them today. The ship is called the Warrior; she comes from my country, as you have discovered; she is the greatest ship in the world – she is worth a whole navy in herself. There are two others in company, gunboats; altogether it is the strongest fleet in these seas, by far. I have seen the guns, as close as I am to your Highness; they are the most powerful afloat.' Richard paused, conscious that he was not in fact being brief, as he had promised, but somewhat garrulous; though judging by his hearers' expressions, his small touches of detail were not being wasted. 'I took the barge,' he concluded, 'and went on board.'

'How were you received?' asked the Rajah.

'How should I be received? Your Highness must have heard the saluting guns. I was received with honour. There was an added reason for this. The Warrior carries an English admiral. He is my brother.'

Kedah's face assumed its customary sneer. 'I am sure of it. All white men are brothers.'

Richard shook his head. 'Your bitterness is wasted – save it for your friends. I mean, he is in truth my brother – my father's son.'

After an astonished moment: 'Then you sent for him!' Kedah burst out. 'This was a trick! You knew the ships were coming to Makassang!'

'Not so,' said Richard. 'I was as surprised as you are now. The first I knew of it was when he stepped forward, and clasped my hand. I have no spies – how could I guess who commanded the ship?'

The Rajah, whose devious mind was playing freely with this fresh news, said: 'Whether you knew it or not, is no great matter. The fact is that your brother is here, with his fleet.' There was some alarm in the old man's voice, though not as much, thought Richard grimly, as there would be presently. 'Myself, I do not believe in such chance happenings ...' His old eyes, narrowing their glance, bored into Richard's face. 'You say that you did not know of his coming. But did he know that you were here?'

'Yes, your Highness.'

'And he came – to do what?'

It was the crucial question. Richard would have liked to have answered: He came to deliver me from such as you, and Kedah. But there were larger affairs at stake, a richer hand to be played; it was a moment when the plain truth was good enough to use.

'Your Highness, it is a greater matter than myself. He had heard that I was here, certainly. But his larger news was of Makassang itself. I will be plain. He had heard of the struggle with the Anapuri and the Land-Dyaks, which can always break out again. He had heard that the future of the rule was uncertain, that I was in disfavour, that this man' – he indicated Colonel Kedah – 'was plotting to seize power, either now or later.' And as Kedah sought to intervene: 'Be quiet,' said Richard carelessly. 'I have not finished ... I must tell you that my brother, with his ships, represents the Queen of England. England is afraid that, if the rule of Makassang is weak, some other nation – likely to be the Dutch – will take advantage of that, and seize the kingdom for its own profit.'

'So?' inquired the Rajah, though from his face he knew the answer.

'So he has come on a mission.' When the silence had stretched a long time, he said: 'His mission is to take this country for the Queen of England, and to choose some great man to rule it for her.'

The Rajah said, angrily: 'A great man rules here already.' After another long silence, Richard answered: 'But it is true that the rule is weakened.'

Kedah came out of his furious silence, as if a trap had been sprung, and he had jumped for his life. 'I am not plotting to seize power,' he said roughly. 'It is a lie! You are trying to slander me before his Highness!'

The time had come for this aspect of truth, also. 'You plotted to leave me standing alone,' Richard told him, with equal force, 'and then perhaps to kill me when I was friendless. You have divided the kingdom, and you hope to seize power out of it. You may succeed, for a day or a week. But you forget that there are other eyes watching. In the end, you will find that there is nothing to seize.'

'We must fight,' said the Rajah.

'We cannot,' answered Richard. 'This is not the Anapuri, with spears and knives. It is not the Dutch, with a few soldiers and settlers. It is the might of England, and a thousand men with modern arms.'

'They are determined?'

'They will not let Makassang fall to anyone but themselves.'

'We must still fight,' declared Kedah, echoing the Rajah's words.

'You fight,' said Richard contemptuously. 'You are the Commander-in-Chief.'

'You are afraid!'

'I am certainly afraid,' answered Richard, 'of eight-inch guns and armour-plated ships. If you are so brave, go ahead and fight! Sink them with your spears! I will hold your tunic while you do it.'

'Coward's talk!'

'If you had not been so quick to divide one man against his brother, Makassang would be stronger today, and no one would wish to seize it for themselves.'

Once again, the Rajah had been thinking his swift and devious thoughts; once again, he arrived at a swift answer, the answer of expedience.

'If we cannot fight, then we must talk, and delay.' He was speaking to Richard. 'Your brother, Tunku – he is not your enemy?'

'No.'

'He loves you?'

'Yes, your Highness. But he is a determined man, and he speaks and acts for England.'

'What is his intention, now?'

'He comes ashore tomorrow, to eat with me.'

'You must talk to him. Find out his plans. Even if England took this island for herself, I might still rule.'

'It is possible.'

'It has been done elsewhere.'

'Yes.'

'When does he come ashore?' asked Kedah.

'At noon.' Catching a certain expression in Kedah's eye, Richard continued forcefully: 'No, Kedah – there will be no treachery! He is not to be killed, or poisoned, or ambushed, or taken prisoner. If any harm befell him, this whole country would be put to fire and sword, within half a day. And there would be one man, above all other men, who would hang from the highest yardarm of the Warrior. Yourself! I have made sure of that.'

'Will you talk, on my behalf?' asked the Rajah. 'So that we may find agreement?'

'Yes, your Highness. I will do my best. But I have two conditions.'

'Name them.'

'My friend Amin Sang is still imprisoned.'

'He is freed.' The Rajah turned briefly to Colonel Kedah. 'See that this is done.'

'Your Highness – ' began Kedah, embarrassed for the first time.

'What is it?'

'It may not be possible to free him immediately.'

'You damned dog!' shouted Richard. 'Is he dead already?'

'No, he is not dead.'

The Rajah rounded on Kedah again, fiercely alert. 'What then? Speak! Was he tortured?'

'Your Highness, he was – questioned.'

'Fool!' shouted the Rajah. 'I said only to imprison him!'

'Your Highness, he threatened you with arms, when he was

drunk – '

'You say so … But if he dies – '

'He will not die,' said Richard, 'if he is well cared for. Is that not so?'

'Yes,' said Kedah.

'See to it,' said the Rajah. 'On your life …' He turned back to Richard. 'You had two wishes. One is the life of your friend. What is the other?'

'Safe conduct for my brother.'

'It is promised.'

'Your Highness, I must be certain of this. Otherwise, we are all ruined. I must have, at the very least, a guard of honour of two hundred men, chosen from the Royal Regiment by Captain Paratang himself.'

'Two hundred!' exclaimed Kedah. 'The Rajah himself does not have so many.'

'This is a stranger, as well as a great man,' answered Richard. 'Two hundred trusted men are not too many, when we think of what is at stake.'

'I agree.' The Rajah stood up, ending the audience; suddenly he was an old man, exhausted within a short space like other old men; bereft of strength, clinging to power at the will of strangers. 'See to it, Tunku,' he said to Richard. 'Talk to your brother – discover what is in his mind. He will not find me too stubborn … Nor too weak … After all, the dynasty of Satsang has loyal followers … My father was loved and feared …' He was wandering, and he knew it, and pulled himself up. 'The audience is ended,' he said formally, and went slowly from the room under a bowed back.

'I will walk with you,' said Kedah.

'I am armed,' replied Richard, 'and I have no hesitation in telling you so.'

'You mistake me,' said Kedah. 'I wished to escort you back to your apartments.'

'Exactly so,' said Richard. 'And I propose to arrive there in safety.'

They fell into step, in the long passageway, in the silence of the Sun Palace at midnight. Richard kept his hand on the butt of his pistol, and Kedah must have been aware of it; but no danger threatened from any side, no shadow moved where a shadow should have stood still. Together, two men bound by hatred and fear of treachery, they traversed the dark corridors of the night.

'One thing I do not understand,' said Kedah presently.

'What is that?'

'You said, the English would take possession of the island, and then choose some great man to rule it.'

'Yes,' said Richard.

'What great man is this to be?'

'I do not know.'

'Would it be a great man in Makassang, or a great man from England?'

'I do not know,' said Richard again.

Their footsteps echoed under the archways; the darkness rang with a small hollow dissonance. Kedah, as secret of thought as the night itself, pursued his questioning, his furtive search under the stones of the future.

'Then the ruler might still be the Rajah?'

'It is possible.'

'Or the greatest man in Makassang, after the Rajah?'

'It is possible.'

'Or your brother himself?'

'No. My brother has other duties.'

'Then, another great man from England?'

'It is possible,' said Richard, for the third time. 'But I do not know. All I know is that I want peace and order for this island, under a wise ruler, and that is what my brother wants also. Who gives it peace and order, is still to be decided.'

They had come to the end of a long colonnade; one passage led to Richard's stairway, the other to the barracks and Colonel Kedah's quarters. They stood still, eyeing each other in the dim light.

'So the chosen ruler,' Kedah persisted, 'might be the greatest man in Makassang. It might still be the Rajah.'

'Yes. You have spoken these words before.'

'Or his successor.'

'Yes.' In the eerie light, Richard felt a prickling sense of danger. It was the last of the night's hazards, and the greatest. 'I warn you, Kedah,' he said suddenly, 'I will shoot you now if I feel threatened.'

Kedah laughed, on a low mocking note. It was impossible to tell what was in his mind, save that it could not be well-disposed. 'You are nervous, Tunku?'

'I am prudent,' said Richard. 'If you choose this moment to try to become the greatest man in Makassang, I have a bullet waiting for you.'

'In that case,' said Kedah, 'I bid you good night.'

'The same,' said Richard. 'But I will watch you turn and walk away.'

IV

Behind each guest, three servants stood. There was a senior chamberlain who never moved, but, watching his appointed charge, snapped his fingers discreetly when a goblet or a plate needed replenishing; there was, for each, an under-butler who saw to the wine, and another who saw to the food. There were cooks bringing fresh dishes to the side tables, and other, smaller cooks who removed the food when it was no longer needed. There were punkah-slaves, and men with cool towels to wipe the brows of the guests. There were musicians who played on the pipes and drums, and Durilla, the major-domo, who oversaw the whole meal; and finally John Keston, resplendent in palace livery, who oversaw Durilla.

There was a fabulous service of gold plate, and the promised filigree goblets from Ethiopia. There was food in delicate abundance – rainbow fish in a transparent mould, a sucking pig which, from the fashion in which it melted upon the tongue, had died for this moment; turtles' eggs in a sauce of Spanish wine, avocados stuffed with wild rice and Amboina cloves; a salad of the tiny fronds of sea anemones; grapes from far-off Portugal, walnuts steeped in black vinegar, rivers of Javanese wine, golden ewers with scented water and poinsettia petals, for bathing the hands. As a final compliment to the English guests, there was an honest English Stilton cheese rescued from the ruined go-down of the Da Costa brothers ... Sunara had been as good as her word. It was a meal to remember.

'You keep some state, Dick!' declared Admiral Sir Miles Marriott, as he arrived at the top of the Steps of Heaven in the first of three gilded palankeens, accompanied by the two hundred-strong guard of honour, bravely decked in their burnished breastplates and scarlet Spahi pantaloons. From that moment forward, neither he, nor Mr Possitter, nor the admiral's flag-lieutenant, who completed the shore party, ever quite ceased to look as if they had been transplanted to fairyland.

In accordance with custom, Sunara did not eat with them. 'The Princess will join us after luncheon,' said Richard, in explanation. 'As one of the royal house, she should hear our discussion.' In the meantime, the only women present were the slave girls who danced briefly while the courses were being changed, drawing discreet side glances from Mr Possitter, and a more candid admiration from the flag-lieutenant, a personable young man who was of an age to give proper attention to this spectacle. As course succeeded course, a pervasive good humour ruled their meeting.

The talk was general, in vaguer form than that on board the Warrior, though still concerned with the affairs and prospects of Makassang. But it was clear that Miles Marriott had spoken to Mr Possitter, in precise terms and to some purpose; though the latter was not less prim and withdrawn, yet he seemed ready now to listen rather than to lecture, to discover what Richard Marriott had in mind for Makassang, even to hear evidence of his fitness to be a ruler. He sat on Richard's left hand, a small tidy skeleton at a lavish feast, and in the intervals of eating daintily, peeping sideways at the dancing girls, and appraising the table appointments which were unsurpassed in their richness, he assimilated the evidence for the disposition of one hundred thousand souls.

There was one point which Richard Marriott was eager to impress on his guests, even at this stage of their discussion; and that was, the unsuitability of a rigid 'foreign rule' for a country such as Makassang.

'I have seen it a thousand times,' he told them. 'In these waters, and in the Pacific islands as well. Europeans have a corrupting influence on simpler peoples. They may come with the best intentions, but they introduce unhealthy novelty, they change what should be left unchanged, they turn innocence into evil. It is a horrible thought that our most potent legacy, in many parts of the world, has been venereal disease ... I do not claim that we have an island paradise here, but I do say that if you clamp European rule on Makassang, and European customs, and that other European disease which is ingrained superiority, then the country will be utterly spoiled.'

'But all these countries must advance,' objected Miles. 'They cannot remain in a past century. If they do, they become a prey to something far worse than British rule, and that is, decay and eventual death.'

'They must advance at their own pace. Certainly we can help them, but if we hurry them – and it is usually done for selfish motives of profit – then we are likely to destroy all that is good.'

Mr Possitter, busy with birdlike appetite on a dish of shrimps which had come to a resplendent end in hot Madeira wine, looked up inquiringly.

'But you yourself are European,' he said, 'and you have had, as I believe, some influence in this country. Has that been harmful?'

'I hope not,' Richard replied. It was an important question, and he was at pains to answer it fairly. 'I have tried to learn from this country, as well as to teach. I have tried to promote the best of their customs, and to curb the worst, which are cruelty and corruption. I believe that my rule will – ' he smiled, ' – would be suited to Makassang, because it would be designed to nourish and help its people, not to turn them into dependants – and certainly not to promote the interests of white traders and rascals.'

Mr Possitter, sniffing the air for radicalism, frowned at this. 'You should not equate trade with evil,' he answered severely. 'Above all, you should not equate white penetration with rascality. You must be well aware that British colonial policy is generally benevolent.'

'I know that is its intention,' said Richard carefully. 'But – you must forgive me – it is easy to say one thing in London, and never to hear the echo of what you say, ten thousand miles away. Trade follows the flag, they tell us; but in too many cases, while the flag is proud and upright, the trade is licensed usury.' He looked at Mr Possitter, ready to argue, ready to smile. 'I know Makassang,' he said. 'I know what its people want and need – and the list is long. But I would rather it fell asleep for a thousand years, than that it made over quick progress under the British flag, and then woke up to find itself enslaved.'

One set of gold plates was borne away; the exquisite band of six slave girls danced a slow and sinuous measure to pipe and drum, as baskets of fruit were carried out from the kitchens. Mr Possitter, confronted at close quarters by a frieze of the most delicious bare bosoms imaginable, coughed behind his hand. But his solemn, official gaze never wavered. He was there, it seemed, to explore the customs of the country, be their detail never so elaborate.

Miles, catching Richard's eye, winked, and nodded discreetly towards this painstaking devotion. 'You are hospitality itself, Tunku,' he murmured. He leant across to his flag-lieutenant, a splendid young figure in full tropical rig with looped aiguillettes, who was also giving the entertainment his zealous attention. 'Well, Flags,' he said, 'what do you think of the resources of Makassang?'

'Sir,' said the flag-lieutenant, who had not lagged behind the company in accepting the ministrations of his wine butler,

'Portsmouth was never like this!'

'A rank heresy,' said Miles. 'But I subscribe to it ...' He leaned back again, till he could speak close to Richard's ear, and nodded towards Mr Possitter, who was still engrossed in his studies. 'You are making a really excellent impression,' he said.

'By proxy, I think,' said Richard. 'But a wise commander deploys his allies first.'

'These seem to be well enough deployed ... Dick, I think I could manage one single glass of wine more.'

Presently the magnificent meal came to an end, and after a short time Sunara joined them in another room. She was looking especially lovely, in pure white silk woven with gold thread; meeting her soft eyes as she came into the room, Richard thought, as on countless occasions before: Thank God I shall lie with her tonight. Neither time nor distraction could cool this loving ardour. The visitors' glances all showed unstinted admiration as they were presented. 'I never appreciated my brother's good fortune until this moment, Princess,' said Miles Marriott gallantly, bending over her hand. Even Mr Possitter, meeting for the first time royalty and beauty combined in this one exquisite form, was understood to make a complimentary reference to matchless pulchritude as he pronounced his spare phrases of greeting. As for the young flag-lieutenant, no words from his dropped jaw were needed to convey his rapt admiration. It was fair to say that Sunara, being a woman, greeted the handsome young man with a melting glance which would, on any other occasion, have sent him storming off to any quarter of the world, to do battle to the death on her behalf.

But her presence, strangely, did not affect the seriousness of this meeting; rather did it add to it, giving it an immediate quality of feeling not present before. Sunara had her own regal dignity, and she brought it to Richard's aid in a manner which could not have been bettered. After the first few moments, when they had sat down and begun to talk again of the future of Makassang, she held all their attention with a most moving account of what her father's senility had brought to his kingdom. For the first time, it seemed, both Miles Marriott and Mr Possitter might be sharing the same thought: that Richard and Sunara were fitted to rule.

Richard took up the tale, when Sunara had spoken of the Rajah's decline from benevolence to gross cruelty, and how it could only grow worse, as the tormenting suspicions of old age multiplied his enemies.

'It is best to be frank,' he said. 'This country, which I have come to love, has two foes, of a very different sort. First there are the plunderers and pirates, such as Black Harris, who come here to strip and to rob. Then there is his Highness, the present Rajah, whom we must call, with respect, a relic of the cruel past.' The memory of his own early morning visit to the bedside of Amin Sang, who, though now resting comfortably, had been brutally mistreated and would not walk for many months, rose up to give force to his words. Between them all, they must make a country where such bestial tyranny would be outlawed forever ... 'These are enemies who can be defeated. Black Harris, and adventurers like him, can be thrown back into the sea. A harsh ruler, such as the Rajah, or an unscrupulous usurper, such as Colonel Kedah, can be expelled from office. But there is a third enemy of Makassang, and that, I am afraid, is you.'

He was looking at his brother Miles as he spoke, but his eyes turned to meet Mr Possitter's. Without offence, the thought was clear.

'You are usurpers of another sort,' he went on. 'Supplanters from the modern world ... Of course you can take Makassang, with your Warrior and your gunboats, but you cannot hold it, except by this third kind of tyranny. You can fashion it into your own image – spoil it – destroy its true nature – and call it your own. But that is not holding it – that is raping it. I do believe,' he ended earnestly, 'that only I can properly hold Makassang.'

It said much for his persuasive eloquence that Mr Possitter, the true target of his words, did not scoff at his argument, or try to turn it to nothing. Instead he put his palms and fingers carefully together, as if to make his own words more precise, and asked: 'Why should it be you, rather than a man of goodwill from England? ... We have such men, Tunku ... Our pro-consuls are not fools, and they are certainly not knaves ... Why should it be you, rather than an Englishman of authority whose knowledge of the Western world is up-to-date, and whose link with it is more recent than your own?'

'I must answer that with another question,' said Richard. 'What is your real interest in Makassang?'

'To hold it under the Crown.'

'But for whose benefit?'

'For its own, and for ours, equally.'

'And also to play dog-in-the-manger with the Dutch?'

'Your choice of words – ' began Mr Possitter stiffly.

'Forgive me,' said Richard. 'I feel strongly, therefore I speak strongly ... But it is true, is it not, that your prime concern is to see that Makassang is not added to the empire of the Dutch East Indies?'

Mr Possitter might have given many evasive or delaying answers. Instead he replied, simply: 'Yes.'

'May I say that I share that interest,' said Richard. 'But for quite other reasons ... I do not want Makassang to become Dutch. I do not want it to become English. I do not want it to become Westernized at all. Why should it be? It is a happy island, and with planning and prudence it can become a prosperous one. But it must remain Makassang! Not Dutch Makassang, or British Makassang, but Makassang without a Western hyphen to its name ... I said before, you are strong enough to take possession of this island, and turn it into something else. But if you can share my love for it, and wish it to keep its own soul, then you should not take it. You should let me take it.' He sat back at last, near to exhaustion with the fervour of his plea. Then he added a last word: 'To make all secure, I would hold it under the British Crown, if you wish. But it must be I who holds it.'

The entrance of the Rajah was swift, and astonishing to all. At one moment they were alone in earnest conclave, at another their talk was shattered by an extraordinary irruption. The Rajah strode ahead through the portico, followed by Colonel Kedah; they burst into the room as if they had been waiting with explosive impatience for this moment alone. They were followed at a more laboured pace by two of the palace guards, bearing the body of a kitchen slave who, judging from the writhing contortion of his frame, was about to die an agonizing death. As they cast this horrible object down on the threshold, the Rajah pointed a finger at Richard Marriott, and said, with venomous fury: 'I heard your words, traitor! What is it that you must hold?'

V

He would hear everything, and he would not hear a word. He stormed and raged until he reached foaming incoherence, then – when Richard tried to answer – he commanded silence, and stared from one to another with frightful menace, daring anyone to speak. He had scarcely a look, and not a word, for the three strangers; his anger seemed reserved for Richard, and the world of plotters and enemies he swore were closing round him. His talk was wild, his manner wilder; Sunara gazed at him with frightened eyes, and Miles Marriott with a steady glance which said: If this is the Rajah of Makassang, then Makassang indeed needs a new Rajah. All the time that he talked and raved, the corpse, which had now writhed its last, lay sprawled between them, with twisted body and dreadful features – yet not remarked on, a grisly stranger upon a field of horror.

Finally, when the last of the silences had stretched to an unbearable length, the Rajah shouted suddenly: 'Answer me, Tunku!'

Richard, whose instinct had put him in a most watchful mood, spread his hands. 'Your Highness, what can I answer you? I am not an enemy of Makassang. I am not an enemy of yourself. Since I left you last night, I have done nothing save – '

'You have plotted!' shouted the Rajah. 'I have proof of it!'

'I have plotted nothing. I have talked to my brother, the admiral, as you commanded me.'

For the first time, the Rajah acknowledged the presence of these strangers – or of one of them. He looked at Miles Marriott, staring with hatred at the impressive figure, whose bearing was as remote and forceful as perhaps the Rajah might have wished his own to be. Then he said: 'This is your brother?'

'Yes, your Highness. May I have the honour to – '

'Enough,' said the Rajah, with extraordinary offensiveness. 'We have more important things to talk of.' He was working himself up to a fresh burst of fury, and Richard, who had come to recognize the ebb and flow of these transports, braced himself to meet it, wherever its vindictive course might lead. The Rajah's eyes, swivelling round in a horrible manner, came suddenly upon the contorted corpse he had brought with him, the despised baggage of violence. As soon as he saw it, he screamed out: 'Look on this man! Tell me if you dare who he is!'

By some mischance, his face at that moment was turned towards Mr Possitter, as well as to the body; and Mr Possitter, a near-sighted man, who was aware of a lack of decorum about the meeting, made worse by the fact that he had not been introduced, replied hesitantly: 'Possitter.'

The Rajah, interrupted in the full flow of his fury, started as if he had been struck, and shouted: 'What did you say? How dare you speak!'

Mr Possitter was not daunted. With thirty-five years of public service behind him, he had faced wrathful superiors before. He merely repeated, more firmly: 'Possitter. Foreign Office.'

It was a single moment of farce, and it melted swiftly away; for a word had been uttered sufficient to import fresh turmoil into what was already a fearsome brew.

'Foreign!' shouted the Rajah. 'We will come to foreign rule in a moment! Those who try to take power in Makassang do so at their own risk. We have had foreigners at our gates before, and where are they now? – rotting in the jungle, feeding the crabs on the seashore! Do not think that because you come with ships and – ' He broke off, since he was unable to hold a sequence of thought for more than a few moments; his mind must go where his eyes went, and once again his eyes went to the body lying on the marble floor. Pointing a quivering finger, he said: 'But it is not foreigners who have done this. It is one of my own!'

All this time, Colonel Kedah had been standing silent and withdrawn, examining the strangers, watching the Rajah, watching Richard himself, his declared enemy. At the Rajah's last words, he smiled grimly, and came forward a little into the room, and said: 'One of your own? In that case, we know who it must be.'

'Who are these "we" who know?' asked the Rajah, whose fury would admit no allies of any sort. 'I know who it must be, because I have proof.' His burning eyes went down to the sprawled corpse again; he addressed the general air, which he seemed to hate and despise also. 'You see this dead man? He is a kitchen slave. He tastes my food, before I eat it. Can you guess how he met his death?'

Silence fell; the ever-present question in all their minds had been answered: the truth – or the falsehood which now passed for truth – was more strange and more terrible than they could have imagined. All eyes turned towards the man on the floor; the reason for his racked body and starting eyeballs was now disgustingly clear.

But the Rajah would make it clearer still.

'He tastes my food!' he screamed, in double fury. 'Now he lies dead, of poison! He died in my place! ... And I know who it is! I have proof! It is not foreigners. One of my own sons plotted to kill me, and take my throne.' Suddenly he turned to the nearest of the two guards, and snatched from him his short throwing spear, a light weapon whose blade was sharpened to a razor's edge. Then he whirled again, and said: 'You – my two adopted sons! Stand forth! Stand there before me!'

Perhaps he had planned this macabre charade, perhaps his

tormented brain was fashioning it as the moments went by. But now he was dancing and mouthing with fury; flecks of foam from his lips spattered the floor; when he pointed to the spot where he wished Richard and Kedah to stand, his hand shook as if he were suffering an ague. Richard felt his scalp prickling as he stepped forward. He could not have disobeyed, any more than he could have denied fate itself; these were appointments which must be kept. But he knew that his whole life was sharpening towards its supreme crisis, and that it lay in the hands of this ancient maniac, who even now was raising his spear to throw it at his last enemy.

Kedah also stepped forward, but with less readiness; he had grown pale, and had lost his cold command. 'Your Highness – ' he began.

'Silence!' said the Rajah. 'Only I will speak, and only I will act.' He glared at the two men, his two adopted sons, standing before him like prisoners or penitents – and the others in the room looked at them also; Sunara with fear and dread in her eyes, Miles Marriott with sharp watchfulness, Mr Possitter with disbelief. The tall flag-lieutenant had put his hand on the hilt of his sword, but he seemed thunderstruck by what he was witnessing, as if he were too young for this scene of evil.

The Rajah drew back his spear; the light glittered wickedly along its edge. 'See my two sons,' he said, and his voice was suddenly calm and cold, and his hand no longer shook. 'My two dear and honoured sons ... One of them is innocent, one of them plotted to take my life today; if it had not been for the slave lying there, I would myself be dead. I know which son of mine plotted this' ... his voice, and indeed his whole body, were now coiled like a spring towards some shattering release – 'and that son will be dead before I lower my arm again. The innocent has nothing to fear, the guilty one dies.' Richard could feel Kedah, close beside him, beginning to tremble; the air was acrid with his fear. 'I know which one of you it is – I know which is the traitor who used poison today, the weapon of cowards, the weapon of lovesick women – and now my spear kills him – thus!'

It was with a shriek that the Rajah uttered the last word, and with a furious explosion of energy that he launched the spear. It was aimed – as Richard divined in the very last second – directly at the small space between Kedah and himself. He would have jumped aside, and then he thought: Not so – I am innocent – I stand fast ... As the spear whistled through the air, plucking at his very sleeve, and stuck quivering in an oak chest behind them, it was Kedah who dropped to the floor, like a puppet jerked by the giant hand of terror, to escape the execution he knew he had merited.

It was Kedah who grovelled in abject fear and shame at his uncovering; and Kedah who collected himself before anyone else could move, and who drew out the kris which was part of his ceremonial dress, and darted forward, and plunged its curled blade deep into the Rajah's breast. As Sunara screamed, blood spurted from the gross wound, and stained her father's white tunic, and then, as he fell inert, seeped out upon the marble floor on which his poor body collapsed.

Kedah turned, like a hunted animal; his course was run, his life at an end. His single eye darted frantically here and there, seeking his escape. He shouted, in fear and hatred: 'Keep your distance – let me be!' but he knew it could not be so. Miles Marriott and his flag-lieutenant had both drawn their swords; Richard, who had come unarmed, had retrieved the spear and now stood ready to use it. Let the dog choose his death, said Richard to himself, in the infinitesimal moment of time between thought and action; and then, while his victim wavered in hideous doubt, he took two steps forward, and stabbed the hapless hated man between his throat and his breastbone. Kedah's blood rose to choke out his life, before he could utter a word.

The Rajah, whose shrunken body was now cradled in Sunara's arms, was racing his dishonoured servant towards oblivion. 'I meant only to test you,' he said, looking up at Richard with waning eyes. 'Is the serpent dead?' He tried to turn his sight towards Kedah, but the effort was too much, and he fell back into his daughter's arms. Presently he rallied, and said to Richard: 'Bring your brother,' and when Miles, grave-faced, approached him, and bent to listen, the Rajah whispered: 'I give Makassang to my adopted son... The people love him, as they once loved me.'

Sunara wiped her father's brow; the end was near; the blood from his wound was ceasing to flow. 'I am called,' the Rajah said, almost pettishly. 'Who can be ready, at such notice? ... But remember my words ... Makassang is his.' And when he had said this, his body fell into dissolution, and he became obedient to death.

Sunara had been led away, weeping, with the flag-lieutenant in faithful attendance. The two guards had been dismissed; Captain Paratang, having ringed the royal gardens with his men, was busy on matters of security. At long last, peace was descending on the Sun Palace.

Miles Marriott, who had scarcely moved in the space of half an hour, looked at his brother.

'Do you truly want such a country as this, Dick?'

'More than ever.' Richard, exhausted and taut of nerve, was still firm in his answer. 'This is only the beginning ... More than ever, Makassang will need strong rule – and kindly rule too.'

'Then it is for you to provide it,' said Miles Marriott. He turned towards Mr Possitter, who had sat down, in prim disregard of all that had gone before, and was staring into space. 'What do you say, Mr Possitter? Shall we confirm Makassang in its new Rajah?'

Mr Possitter's air of disengagement was deceptive. 'It is not at all what we planned,' he said, disapprovingly. 'Nor should it take place so quickly. I will admit that such a compromise might be necessary, and acceptable. But I have grave doubts that events should move so precipitately...' He looked at Richard. 'In the first place, I would like to see your planned constitution set down on paper.'

So would I, thought Richard to himself; I am in the mood for comedy ... But he knew that he must not give such an answer. 'It needs no writing down,' he answered, with sober care. 'This country can be mine, and it can be yours at the same time. You should leave me to rule here. Since I need your strength, in the matter of arms, I will do so on behalf of the Queen. But understand, I am Rajah.'

'Done!' said his brother Miles, in the manner of a player making a wager.

Mr Possitter winced. 'It is not done at all,' he said, in extreme discontent. 'Do you realize what this entails? An entirely new presentation to the Prime Minister's office. An Order-in-Council for Her Majesty to approve ... It might even be necessary to confer a title ... Do you realize,' he burst out at last, 'that this business might involve us in at least two White Papers?'

At the same moment, Richard and Miles Marriott looked round about the room. Within their gaze, there was the same fearful frieze of figures; the dead slave with his body coiled in agony, Colonel Kedah lying in a pool of his shameful blood, the Rajah's small corpse covered by a silk shroud which could not disguise the dread lineaments of death. Even while Mr Possitter was speaking, Richard had been negligently wiping the blood from the spear he had used to kill the last traitor.

But at this self-same moment, he caught his brother's eye. He said: 'Two White Papers? – God bless my soul!' and they both dissolved into welcome, healing laughter.

VI

In the cool of the evening, in the muted beauty of the palace gardens, the Rajah of Makassang sat and talked with his Ranee, and watched their children play. Richard wore the white jewelled turban of his kingship; Sunara's pale green dress displayed no badge of rank – as ever, she could combine royalty and femininity in a perfect proportion.

The sun was nearly down, the air playing over the lawns and the poinsettias was light and scented; even the palace peacocks strutted about their arrogant business on a quieter note. Sunara's hand lay in Richard's, on the cushioned bench between them; sometimes they turned to each other, sometimes they looked down the Steps of Heaven, where Adam was hopping agilely from step to step, watched by his half-brother Presatsang who, as one who had still the greatest difficulty in walking on two legs, was lost in admiration of this feat.

'I am sure he will hurt himself,' said Sunara anxiously.

'If he does, he will not do so again,' said Richard, with a father's lack of feeling.

'Or he will fall, and hurt Presatsang.'

Richard smiled. 'Now that of course would be a different matter.'

A peacock shrilled, but mildly; the perfume of casuarina and flame-of-the-forest was subtly ravishing. For the two of them, it was a time of blessed tranquillity, after the fearful ordeals of the past; but for Richard, it was only a small respite from the cares of the present. After a year of rule, his life seemed more demanding than ever: always the Ivory Throne called him; even now, a deputation waited on his pleasure within the Sun Palace. Its pedestrian purpose, the provision of public bath houses for the sampan village near the old lighthouse, was a measure of Richard's preoccupation with things great and small.

He had done much in the past year, and there remained much to do; the cup of endeavour was never drained. The Council of Chiefs had been strengthened, and met on a fixed date each month. A survey for a light railway to the teak forests of the north was now being made. A modern hospital near the Shwe Dagon was already half built. The deep-water harbour would begin to take shape, as soon as a dredger and pile driver could come from Singapore. A jungle road along the east coast had advanced some twelve miles.

The beginnings seemed small, but they were, at the least, beginnings. As a moral counterpart of this, another sort of beginning had been made with the official abolition of slavery – in the face of outraged protest from parents who had children, particularly girls, for sale. There was talk of high-handed interference, even tyranny ... But Makassang must move with the times. Richard himself must be the only slave.

When he thought of these things, and particularly of the harbour and the new storage go-downs, shades of the Da Costa brothers rose to sadden him. Andrew Farthing and Sebastian Wickham seemed to peer over his shoulder, watching what he did, and how well. Even the skull cup of the soldier of Francis Drake was a reminder of a long, stern line of duty. But he could hope that these ghosts were benevolent. With a little here, a little there, he was beginning to use his kingdom well.

Sunara, turning suddenly, pressed his hand. 'Rest,' she said, as she often did. 'Enjoy. Refashion the whole world tomorrow.'

He answered the pressure of her hand, but he thought on. He ruled, but as a trustee for others; the link with England, though not burdensome, was close. He had to answer his letters ... A gunboat called now and then, watching the trade routes and the tides of Empire; the soldiers and sailors who made courtesy calls on the Sun Palace were good company, and were certainly well repaid for their trouble. Makassang was a stronger country now; the Dutch would not snatch it, nor would anyone else.

But just as he ruled as trustee for England, so did they all, perhaps, rule as trustee for the future – and the future was Makassang's. It was their task to bring the island forward, slowly yet certainly; taking care to break no customs which could not be replaced by better ones. Their prime blessing at this moment was peace – peace, and the end of cruelty. In this, he taught by his own example. Though he was stern to malefactors and usurers, yet his rule was benevolent; and his people seemed to answer it with the same quality. The fact was heartening, seeming to prove a cherished precept of Sunara's – that men were not fools, nor knaves; they were born with love, but sometimes lost it on the journey. If pressed, they would answer harshness with the vilest cruelty; yet it need not be – the example was the touchstone.

The two boys were coming up the steps now, towards their parents. Adam, sturdy of back, was carrying Presatsang; the small brown face peeped over the supporting shoulder, close to the white one. They were laughing.

Sunara called: 'Bedtime,' and laughter changed to wailing and protest. Manina appeared from nearby, prepared to stand no nonsense, and Sunara said: 'Take the Rajah Muda.' Presatsang was borne away, consoled by promises of a story after his bath. Adam, relieved of his burden, lingered for as long as he dared. He was growing into a solemn, watchful child, adoring his father, regarding his stepmother with critical affection. He and Presatsang were already allies against the tyrannies of the adult world.

When he had been kissed and despatched, Sunara was silent awhile. Then she said: 'Perhaps he is the Rajah Muda.'

Richard, awakening from a dream of public bath houses, asked what she meant.

'Perhaps Adam will rule.'

'It may be,' said Richard. It was a question he sometimes dwelt on, and then put aside for the far future. 'Time will show which of them is the worthier – and which the best for Makassang. I would not dictate my choice, nor, even for the sake of love, would you.'

'How do you know that?'

'I know you.'

She smiled, lovingly, brilliantly. 'I like to be known by you,' she said – and then blushed as he bent on her a glance which quite altered the meaning of her words. 'Richard!' she protested.

He raised his eyebrows. 'I said nothing. But now that I think of it ...'

It was time to go, and regretfully he rose, taking his leave. He would be with her later ... Walking back, his head bent, acknowledging Captain Paratang's salute as he passed the inner guard, he thought, very briefly, of the phrase he had used a moment earlier, when talking of the future ruler of Makassang: 'I would not dictate'.

He hoped that this could be made to come true, in everything else as well. Just as with the children, so with the people; one should give them direction, then stand aside and let them find the way. Above all other things, he wanted to make manifest the words of Lao-Tzu, as old Mendel da Costa had recalled them: that the secret of good government was to let men alone.

Ottawa – London – Barbados.
May 1960 – April 1961.

# Nicholas Monsarrat

## The Pillow Fight

Passion, conflict and infidelity are vividly depicted in this gripping tale of two people and their marriage. Set against the glittering background of glamorous high life in South Africa, New York and Barbados, an idealistic young writer tastes the corrupting fruits of success, while his beautiful, ambitious wife begins to doubt her former values. A complete reversal of their opposing beliefs forms the bedrock of unremitting conflict. Can their passion survive the coming storm …?

'Immensely readable … an eminently satisfying book'
*Irish Times*

'A professional who gives us our money's worth. The entertainment value is high'
*Daily Telegraph*

## Smith and Jones

Within the precarious conditions of the Cold War, diplomats Smith and Jones are not to be trusted. But although their files demonstrate evidence of numerous indiscretions and drunkenness, they have friends in high places who ensure that this doesn't count against them, and they are sent across the Iron Curtain.

However, when they defect, the threat of absolute treachery means that immediate and effective action has to be taken. At all costs and by whatever means, Smith and Jones must be silenced.

'An exciting and intriguing story'
*Daily Express*

'In this fast-moving Secret Service story Nicholas Monsarrat has brought off a neat tour de force with a moral'
*Yorkshire Post*

# Nicholas Monsarrat

## This is the Schoolroom

The turbulent Thirties, and all across Europe cry the discordant voices of hunger and death, most notably in Spain, where a civil war threatens to destroy the country.

Aspiring writer, Marcus Hendrycks, has toyed with life for twenty-one years. His illusions, developed within a safe, cloistered existence in Cambridge, are shattered forever when he joins the fight against the fascists and is exposed to a harsh reality. As the war takes hold, he discovers that life itself is the real schoolroom.

'… the quintessential novel of its time and an indictment of an age, stands today as a modern classic'
*Los Angeles Times*

## The Time Before This

On the icy slopes of the great ice-mountain of Bylot Island, set against the metallic blue of the Canadian Arctic sky, Shepherd has a vision of the world as it used to be, before the human race was weakened by stupidity and greed.

Peter Benton, the young journalist to whom Shepherd tells his story, is dramatically snapped out of his cosy cynicism and indolent denial of responsibility, to face a dreadful reality. He discovers that he can no longer take a back-seat in the rapid self-destruction of the world, and is forced to make a momentous decision.

'In his wry and timely novel Monsarrat unfolds a tremendous theme with gripping excitement' Edna O'Brien
*Daily Express*

# Nicholas Monsarrat

## The Tribe That Lost Its Head

Five hundred miles off the southwest coast of Africa lies the island of Pharamaul, a British Protectorate, governed from Whitehall through a handful of devoted British civilians. In the south of the island lies Port Victoria, dominated by the Governor's palatial mansion; in the north, a settlement of mud huts shelter a hundred thousand natives; and in dense jungle live the notorious Maula tribe, kept under surveillance by a solitary District Officer and his young wife. When Chief-designate, Dinamaula, returns from his studies in England with a spirited desire to speed the development of his people, political crisis erupts into a ferment of intrigue and violence.

'A splendidly exciting story'
*Sunday Times*

## Richer Than All His Tribe

The sequel to *The Tribe That Lost Its Head* is a compelling story which charts the steady drift of a young African nation towards bankruptcy, chaos and barbarism.

On the island of Pharamaul, a former British Protectorate, newly installed Prime Minister, Chief Dinamaula, celebrates Independence Day with his people, full of high hopes for the future.

But the heady euphoria fades and Dinamaula's ambitions and ideals start to buckle as his new found wealth corrupts him, leaving his nation to spiral towards hellish upheaval and tribal warfare.

'Not so much a novel, more a slab of dynamite'
*Sunday Mirror*

Made in the USA
Lexington, KY
20 June 2011